A Hole in the Earth

A Hole in the Earth

Robert Bausch

A HARVEST BOOK
HARCOURT, INC.
San Diego   New York   London

www.harcourt.com

Library of Congress Cataloging-in-Publication Data
Bausch, Robert.
A hole in the earth/Robert Bausch.
p.   cm.
ISBN 0-15-100529-X
ISBN 0-15-601184-0 (pbk.)
I. Title.
PS3552.A847 H65 2000
813′.54—dc21   99-046042

Designed by Lydia D'moch
Text set in Electra
Printed in the United States of America
First Harvest edition 2001
A C E G I K J H F D B

For David, a friend in all seasons, a hunting and fishing buddy, and best of all, my son; for my daughters—Suzi, Sara, and Julie—whose talent, sweetness, and beauty enthrall me every day; for Denny, as always, who is better at love than anyone I've ever known; and finally for Dad, who inspired it.

Although this is a work of fiction, certain elements of racetrack decorum and the gambler's vision of life have been suggested by my closest and best friend, Dennis Metter. We have won and lost many a race together and once, at the Washington, D.C., International, had only two dollars and a dime left between us with which to bet on the feature race of the day. (We lost.) Nonetheless, our long association has sustained me in many troubled times, and I thank him for his brilliant wit, his extraordinary generosity, and, above all, his true friendship for more than thirty years.

...A boy takes a lantern out to the garden:
he digs a potato, and pulling it free
he uncovers a deep hole in the ground,
the light of day pouring out.
Looking inside, he sees blue sky,
a river far below, a small cottage
                              in a clearing...

                    —Gregory Natt,
                    "A Hole in the Earth"

At the End

Of last summer I went underground to stay for a while. I didn't have any idea how long. Sometimes I thought I might be there to stay. You might say riding the subway was my job, although I didn't get paid for it. I am approaching middle age, and I was a fairly well-liked history teacher with the sort of responsibility that people respect, or at least pretend to—and I slept in a shelter at night. In several shelters, actually. But I was not truly homeless. I had a house, although I never went there. It was in a fairly manicured suburb called Prince William Forest, in Virginia. Not far from the nation's capital.

During the day, I stayed underground—in the biggest hole human beings ever dig, really. I rode the subway under the white monuments, the art museums, and government halls of Washington, D.C. I spent every waking hour underground, riding the red line, the blue line, the orange line. I rode from Alexandria, Virginia, to the metro center in town and then out to Landover, Maryland. I'd cross to the other side of the station and ride back into town and then I'd take the blue line all the way to the end. I didn't figure the cost. I had enough money to keep doing that until the end of the decade if I wanted to. Maybe until the end of the century.

At night I'd come out of the ground and look for a place to sleep. I didn't want to spend any of the money for a room. (Since I didn't know how long I would want to stay underground, it would have been foolish to spend my money too freely.) Still, I didn't want to sleep on a grate or in the lobby of a public building, either. So I'd look for a good shelter. In the best shelters you can take a bath, sleep on clean linen. Some even have a place to wash clothing. Such good, clean shelters are supposed to be hard to find, but there're two in Virginia—one in Fairfax and one in Arlington—and I also found one in Mount Pleasant, a Latino district in Washington. The shelter in Landover had a good place to take a shower but no Laundromat, and the sheets weren't always as crisp as I like them.

Of course, in an emergency I'd get a room in a motel or something. *If* I absolutely had no choice. But when I did get a room, I wouldn't use my real name. I'd pick some interesting name like Clark Grant, or Cary Gable. Anybody who might have been looking for me would not be able to find me.

I was lost for a while.

I was not running from the law, either, although that's not what the law thought. My disappointed, prominent father was a circuit court judge, and if I had seen him from a distance, I would have dodged him as if I was a convicted felon. I do not think of myself as innocent, but I was not a criminal when I went underground, if you define *criminal* as a person against whom charges have been filed.

Maybe I wasn't really running from anything. You can't escape memory, after all; and in spite of my incognito existence, I still had the memory of what I'd done following me everywhere I went. No, I wasn't running. I was just wearing a mask for a while. The world is full of hiding places, believe it or not, and you can do it for quite a long time without traveling a great distance. You don't have to *leave* home to leave home. I don't want to put too fine an edge on it, but I don't even think you could say I was actually hiding. I was just living away from everybody.

Away from my mother and father.

Away from Elizabeth. Sweet Elizabeth.

And Nicole, my once and future daughter.

I think all of this began with her. Not that it was her fault or anything. It's just that when she returned, things were already beginning to slip and her arrival sort of set in motion the chain of events that drove me underground.

Of course the Fates played a hand, as they always do.

You see, I am a father, too. More often than I wanted to be. Yet, that summer I was still worrying about what my father might be thinking of me. I was thirty-nine years old—headed for forty. Can you believe it? I don't know if it was a weakness in my father or me. All I ever learned from him was that I shouldn't cry.

Oh, and that I should do my duty. He was very serious about duty.

But sometimes, it's kind of hard to know what your duty is—and you feel like crying. You know?

My Daughter

Nicole, came home at the beginning of that summer. (All the rest of my life I will think of those months she was with me as "that summer.")

She arrived on a Tuesday, just after sunrise. She knocked on the door instead of ringing the bell, and when I saw her I didn't know who she was, although her face was very familiar.

I said, "Can I help you?"

She was pale looking, with long light blond hair and deep blue eyes. In spite of the bright new sun, the air was cold, and she was dressed only in a blue tank top, white shorts, and sandals. She had goose bumps on her arms and legs, and she stood in front of me, holding herself, shivering, her feet together, thin wisps of her hair blowing in the morning breeze. "Hello." She tilted her head and smirked. "It's me."

A young man was with her. He was Oriental, not very tall, and lean, with soft features and gleaming black tousled hair.

After a lengthy awkward pause, I recognized the high bones in Nicole's face, the way her eyes seemed to shimmer in the morning light. "Nicole?"

"It's me, Dad. God."

Like a fool, all I said was "You've lost a lot of weight."

"I'm Sam," the young man said.

"Sam?"

"Sam Foster, yes sir." No trace of an Oriental accent. He had clearly been born and raised in California. Yet when he smiled, his eyes

4

almost disappeared and his mouth sported a grill of faultless white teeth.

Another long moment of silence passed. Nicole stood there, incredibly reduced, shivering in the cold brightness, brushing her hair back with her hand, waiting for me to do something.

"What'd you do to your hair?" I said.

"I dyed it."

"You dyed your eyebrows, too?"

She frowned. "Can we come in?"

"Sure."

She flattened herself against the door frame to get by me, and I stepped back out of the way. I could see she felt awkward to touch me and to be honest, I didn't know what to do with my hands or what to say. It bothered me to look at her, because she was no longer a thirteen-year-old girl. She was a woman now, and she was slim and beautiful, and I had not seen any part of the transformation. I could not appraise her as I had so many other women in my life, including her mother, so I did not know where to let my eyes fall. And I now realize I should kick myself for not simply taking her in my arms. Why couldn't I have just held her for a minute and greeted her as any father would who has not seen his daughter in almost six years? Sam was saying "Great place, man. You got a great place here."

Nicole looked around the foyer, then wandered into the den. Sam followed her, and I discovered a sensation of having been intruded upon, as though these two were going to be very rude and I was going to have to endure it.

Nicole walked into the kitchen. "The house is smaller than I remember. Much smaller."

"I've got it pretty cluttered up," I said. "It's really good to see you here. I mean home. You're home." I was afraid she would mistake my shock for displeasure. I wanted her to feel welcome, although I didn't know what to do with her.

"You living with anybody now?" she said.

"No. I'm still by myself here."

She looked at me. "You don't resemble your picture anymore."

I'd forgotten how light blue her eyes were. They looked like ice. "I don't?"

"I miss the mustache."

"My girlfriend didn't like it."

"Your girlfriend?"

"Yes. I am seeing someone. Elizabeth."

"You don't look the same at all."

I had the feeling I should apologize.

"But then, I guess I don't look the same, either." She smiled, but I could see she would not like it if I mentioned her weight again.

"Your hair is pretty like that," I said.

"Thank you."

No one spoke for a bleak moment. Then I said, "I didn't know who you were at first."

"You must be getting ready to go to work," said Sam.

"No. My summer vacation has just begun in fact. I don't have any-place I have to be, right now."

Nicole said, "I want to see my room."

"You remember where it is?"

Sam said, "I'll go get our things."

I followed Sam out to a Jeep Wagoneer that was parked on the street.

"What is she doing here?" I said.

He looked at me briefly, then opened the back door of the car. He reached in and pulled out a large suitcase and set it in the grass by the curb. "I'll take that one." He leaned back in and pulled out a train case and a green plastic bag. "You take these."

"What's the deal?" I said. I took the bag and slung it over my shoul-der, then grabbed the case. "I don't understand."

"Hey, she wanted to visit home. That's what she told me. She said she wanted to see her father, man."

"Why didn't she call me? This kind of trip is usually best arranged by somebody."

"It was a spur-of-the-moment thing."

"But it takes three or four days to drive it."

"It took us three."

"That's a lot of hours."

"Sixty-two."

"She could have picked up a phone during that time, right?"

He slumped a bit. "It was a surprise, man." Then he shrugged. "I guess."

"Well, I'm sure surprised."

"This is our graduation trip." He smiled. "When you live at the beach, you got to go somewhere else when you graduate, you know?"

"So she graduated high school."

"An honor student. Straight As."

I started up the back steps of the house, and Sam struggled next to me with the big suitcase. I didn't want to seem like somebody's old man, but I wanted to know what he was doing here with my daughter. I caught him looking at me, and I said, "You an honor student, too?"

"Yes sir."

"And you ... you're—"

"I'm her friend."

I said nothing.

"We're very close," Sam said. He smiled reassuringly. "She's my best friend. I trust her completely."

"Well." I didn't know anyone I could say that about.

"I make her laugh."

"It would have been easier," I said, "if you guys had called before you came."

Sam put the suitcase down on the top step and took a deep breath. On the edge of laughter, he said, "Your daughter is very unpredictable." I thought he sounded a little bit like Kirk Douglas. He tucked his lower lip under the white teeth and squinted his eyes so that he looked—there's no other way to say this—like a Chinaman. Then he said, "So solly, so solly."

He wanted me to laugh. There was an awkward pause, then he picked up the suitcase and carried it into the house.

Nicole sat at the kitchen table, peeling an orange.

"Where'd you get that?" I asked her.

"I brought it with me."

Sam moved toward the stairs.

"Don't take them up there," Nicole said. "He's got my room packed to the gills with boxes of shit."

It was oddly disconcerting to be referred to as a *he*.

"Where can I put these?" Sam said.

"I don't know," I said. "I really don't know."

Sam looked at Nicole and she smiled. He jerked his head back to throw a black ribbon of hair off his forehead. "Well?"

"Just put them down for now," Nicole said.

He put the bags down and stood there. I was suddenly desperate for words. I wanted to say, "You're so tall now, Little One," but I was afraid she would not remember that I had always called her my Little One all those years ago when she *was* little. She didn't stay little for very long. The last time I saw her she weighed one hundred seventy pounds, and she did not wear it well. She was thirteen, sullen, and ineptly unhappy about me and everything else. Now she seemed self-possessed and aloof. Almost flippant about the distance between us. Her attitude humbled me, made me feel vaguely sordid and shabby.

"Why don't you both sit down?" Nicole said.

"I've got to use the bathroom," Sam said.

I went to the table, pulled back a chair, and sat down. I watched her pick at the orange for a time, then I said, "Well, look at you."

"Yes, look at me."

"You should have called, let me know you were coming."

She paid no attention to this, so I said, "It would have been a nice thing to look forward to."

There was a long pause. Presently I grew aware of my face, of a broad, awkward, fake smile planted there as though I were posing for a photograph.

"How's Catherine?" I asked.

"Mom? She bet me you would be living in a trailer."

I didn't say anything.

"She was sure you'd probably lost the house a long time ago betting on the horses."

"Well, she was wrong, wasn't she. Not the first time." I watched Sam come back in and sit down. "I still have the house."

"I'm thirsty," Sam said.

I said to Nicole, "Your mother sounds remarkably the same."

"She's happily married."

There was another silence. I didn't know what might be happening to the expression on my face, but I hated it that both of them were watching intently for it.

Sam laughed nervously. "You mind if I get some water?"

"Go ahead," I said. "Why would I mind?"

"We're thirsty but polite," Nicole said.

Sam ran the water in the sink, waiting for it to get cold. No one said anything for a long time. I started tapping my fingers on the table, not looking at anyone. Then I said, "So what's it been, six years?"

"What."

"Since I've—since we've been together?"

"Five years."

"Almost six years, though."

Sam filled a glass and turned the water off. Nicole studied the orange, worked the knife carefully. I watched her for a while, trying to think of something else to say. Sam came back to the table with his glass of water.

"So," I said, "you graduated from high school."

"Yes, I did."

"You're almost a grown-up, for Christ's sake." I couldn't believe it.

Sam gulped the water. You could hear it sloshing down his throat.

"What a surprise," I said.

Nicole smiled, folded back a sliver of orange peel, and placed her lips on the exposed pulp. Juice ran down by her mouth.

Sam put the empty glass on the table and gasped, "Man, I was thirsty. Thank you."

"You're welcome," I said. "You're both very welcome."

Soon after she finished her orange, Nicole announced she was tired and went into the living room to lie on the couch. I looked at Sam, wondering what I was supposed to do with him, and he smiled in a harried sort of way and said, "We been driving all night."

"You can stretch out in my room if you want."

He nodded.

"It's up the stairs, to your right. Why don't you just carry the bags up there? That's where you'll be staying."

He started to say something and stopped.

"If you need to take a shower or—"

"I think she expected you'd be very glad to see her," he whispered.

"Really."

"She dreamed about you—in the last year or so, she started dreaming about you, about coming here and starting over."

"Starting what over?"

"She calls this place 'home.'"

I didn't know what I was supposed to say to that.

He settled back in his chair and stretched. "Jesus, I'm tired."

"Go on upstairs."

"I'm so full of coffee, I don't think I can sleep."

I sat there for a while, staring at my hands.

"Nicole and I have known each other a long time."

"I'm glad to hear it," I said.

"Since she came to California."

"Right."

He crossed his arms and looked at me. I had the feeling he wanted me to offer him my room and bed again, so I did.

"In a minute," he said.

It may be he wanted to convince me by his attentiveness that his intentions were honorable where Nicole was concerned. He kept looking at me with a wary glint in his eye—as if he expected me to finally quiz him on their three-day trek across the country. When I asked him how the trip went, he seemed eager to discuss the sleeping arrangements.

"We had separate rooms all the way."

I'm sure he could sense the relief I felt to hear that. I didn't want to be a typical father, prying into the life of an adult child. To tell the truth, I didn't like thinking of her as an adult. It seemed perfectly natural to believe that I would never have to think of her that way. After all, we don't often think of adults as adults, right? They're just people. That's the way I wanted to think of Nicole. I was pretty sure I could do that since, for the past few years, I had striven not to think of her at all.

"We both got money for graduation," Sam said.

We are always tricked by time. The days seem like fixed things, and movement is only through the long seasons. We never realize how swiftly we are moving, all the time. Away from some things and toward others.

"We didn't think we'd ever graduate," Sam said.

There was another silence. He sat there looking at me, and it was very difficult deciding where I should let my eyes fall.

Finally I said, "It seems like Nicole was a baby only a few hours ago."

"You got any baby pictures?" he said.

"What?"

"Baby pictures. You know."

"Sure."

Perhaps looking through old family albums would get him in the right mood for sleeping. I really didn't know what to say to him, and I felt terribly awkward having him sitting there in my kitchen. He followed me into the den, and I retrieved all of my photo albums—seven fifty-page books—from under the end table, where I had kept them for a dozen years. I knocked the dust off the first one and stood there admiring it. Sam leaned over my shoulder.

"I've got pictures of her every year except the last five."

"Really."

"She sent me high school pictures over the years, but they don't count. I took all of these."

"That's a lot of pictures." He reached to take one of the books.

"Wait a minute. You have to look at them in order." I passed him the first one. "Let's go back in the kitchen and sit at the table. There's better light there."

Now I followed him. He was small, childlike in front of me, his thin, dark arms swinging back and forth as he walked. When we passed the living room, I saw Nicole curled up on the couch, facing the back cushions, her hair draped down over the edge of the seat, almost to the floor, and I was suddenly aware of a sense of failure, of having fallen short of her expectations.

I put the books on the kitchen table, and Sam sat down and adjusted himself in the chair as though he were settling in for a meal.

"This will probably bore you," I said.

He smiled, opening the first album. "I promise not to be bored."

It was easy to like his smile. It revealed a kind of willing innocence. There was something almost perfectly naive about him—he did not yet know the myriad ways in which the scaffolding of our lives can rot in the beam.

I could hear Nicole breathing in a deep sleep. I wished I had greeted her better. I knew she recognized how shocked I was to see her standing there on my porch, and it must have hurt her that I didn't know who she was at first.

"She was such a beautiful baby," Sam was saying.

It seemed as if only that morning she had been a tiny, almost weightless bundle, with hair so thin and fine it looked like currents of light. "Like I said, it went fast."

Sam looked at me.

"I was only a few years older than you are now when I took that picture," I said.

"Really."

"Makes me feel old."

He smiled, but he didn't look at me. He was studying the pictures.

When I was his age, the world was not only mine, but it was slow and warm and fine because I knew I would have year after year after bloody year of being young. Now I was almost forty—and in ten years. You see what I mean? When forty is just around the corner, you begin to realize that a year is nothing. A fifteen-minute break between one summer and the next. You start to think about how quick you got to forty. You start to realize that you've *been* young much longer than you're *going* to be young.

Nicole turned over and sighed. She was really asleep.

"If she wakes up and catches me looking at these," Sam said.

He wanted me to join him in a conspiratorial smile, but it wasn't in me. I couldn't even look him in the eye. He must have noticed my discomfort. He turned the page in the book, then he said sheepishly, "You *were* glad to see her, weren't you?"

"Of course."

"Anyway, we won't be in the way, I promise."

"I hope you'll stay at least a week."

He looked at me. "I think she was talking about staying through the summer."

"Oh," I said. "Good. I didn't know."

"Is that all right?"

"Of course."

He turned the page and studied the book for a while.

Then I said, "Both of you will be staying."

He nodded, still looking at the book.

The First Thing

I had wanted to do that summer was hit the track. I needed to supplement my teacher's income with a little successful wagering. The morning Nicole and Sam arrived, I'd planned on heading out around eleven or so toward Highland Park, a new racetrack in Maryland. I wanted to get there in time for the daily double.

When Nicole woke up from her nap it was already almost ten. At around nine Sam had finally gone up to my room to lie down, and I'd gone to get a racing form. I was sitting reading the form in the kitchen when Nicole came in, barely awake, her hair tousled, her eyes swollen, and her mouth stretched in a dry yawn.

"Where's Sam?"

I told her.

"So," she said, sitting down, "what'd you guys do all morning?"

"We looked at pictures of you."

She frowned. "Fat pictures?"

"No. I don't have any fat pictures—except the school pictures you sent me."

"I didn't send them to you."

"Whoever."

"Don't you have to go to work?"

"I don't teach in the summer."

"That's right. I forgot. Your summer vacation. So what do you do?"

"I work on other things."

She smirked. "Like what?"

"I have my real estate license."

"Really."

I didn't say anything. She was looking at me the way her mother always did—as if she was waiting impatiently for the truth to come out.

"You make a lot of money doing that?"

"Sometimes. I used to."

She yawned again and started looking around the kitchen. "I'm hungry."

I wanted to tell her I was really glad to see her, but I was afraid if I did that and then told her I was going to try to make the daily double, it would sound pretty fake. Still, the truth was, I didn't know what I was going to do with them for dinner, and Nicole was already making noises about lunch. I had had a few bad days at the track, and to tell the truth, I was nearly broke. You can't tell somebody—especially a child you love—"I'm so glad to see you, can you lend me a few bucks?" I felt terrible having to sit there in my own kitchen, hoping my daughter would not open the refrigerator.

Of course Nicole got up and opened the refrigerator. The light revealed a piece of Romano cheese wrapped in plastic, a carton of milk, a half a stick of butter, and a black banana. And that was it. In one of the door shelves, there was a bottle of beer, and a few bottles of salad dressing and mustard.

"I don't keep a lot of food in the house," I said.

"No shit." She closed the door.

"I eat out a lot."

"I guess I can eat another orange." She started toward the living room, where her bags were still piled on the floor.

"We can go out and get something," I said.

"What about Sam?"

I didn't want her to wake him, but I told her if she wanted to invite him along, go ahead.

"We can bring something back for him. Maybe we can all have lunch together."

I nodded, but I wasn't planning on lunch. I wanted to head right for the track. I realized if we only picked up a few things and didn't dawdle, I could still bring Nicole back to the house and make it to the track on time. I had already handicapped the first and second races.

Nicole stood in front of the mirror in the hall, brushing her hair. I watched her arms and the way she held her head as she worked the brush, and I felt momentarily finished—as if we were going out into some sort of final sun where death would take me and she would then inhabit all my earth. Don't get me wrong, it wasn't fear that gripped me, or anything like it. I think I may have experienced a weird variety of envy. She was just so young and lean and full of the kind of power only lots of time can give you. The future was so big in front of her, and it was all hers. Years and years of it that I would not have. She brushed her hair with the impassivity and assurance of a person who has not yet come to understand that she is mortal. I was helpless standing there in her space, waiting for her to be ready.

As we were heading out the door I mentioned that we would have to get what we were going to get fairly quickly. I was trying to manipulate her into hurrying, without giving up the reason, so when she looked at me—an innocent, quizzical smile on her face—I felt like a swindler trying to ferret the deed out of her hands. I held up the racing form and she turned and continued down the walk. To defend myself I said, "I'm just going for the fun of it."

She answered with her back to me and I wasn't sure what she said, so I reached out to take her arm. She stopped and turned to face me, and I bumped into her, then stepped back awkwardly.

I said, "Excuse me."

"Mom said I wouldn't be here twenty-four hours and you'd ask me for money."

"Well, I'm not asking you for money. I've got a hundred bucks in my pocket."

"She said you'd be off to the track, too."

I didn't know what I was supposed to say to that. I hated it when her mother was right about anything.

Nicole waited there in front of me, watching my face.

Finally I said, "You want me to wait until Thursday to go to the track?"

I was glad to see her laugh. "I don't want your money," I said. "I don't ever want it. I do just fine, thank you."

She shrugged, still smiling.

Then I said, "I *would* like to make the first race today, though."

"You're short of cash, aren't you?"

"Nothing I can't manage."

"What if I just buy your lunch today?" She turned and started down the walk, and I followed her.

It was almost ten-thirty and the race track was an hour away. I didn't want to go anywhere for lunch. I thought we'd go to the grocery store and get a few items for Nicole to eat, and then I'd be off to the track. "I don't feel like sitting down to lunch," I said. "I don't really have the time. But I'll let you pick up a few things at the store, and then I'm afraid I'm going to have to take off."

That seemed agreeable to her.

When we got to the store, she said, "What do we need?"

We were sitting in my two-year-old Hyundai, the late morning sun heating us through the windows, and she reached into her purse and started fingering what looked like a lot of cash.

I didn't want to watch her. I felt like a con man. "Look," I said, "you don't have to get the groceries. I'll write a check."

She handed me a hundred-dollar bill. "Will this be enough?"

I gave it back to her. It was sure a crisp bill, though, and I admit it occurred to me that I could make a lot more at the track if I was starting with two hundred instead of one hundred. "I don't need your money. I'll get the groceries."

"If you get the groceries and you won't go sit anywhere with me to eat, how can I buy your lunch?"

"You can buy my lunch some other time," I said. I reached over and touched her on the shoulder. "Really. I don't have a lot of time."

She smiled ruefully and I knew she was disappointed.

"I'm sorry, honey," I said, "but I've got to make the daily double." I withdrew my hand. It seemed the wrong thing to say to her, and I knew it. She got this look on her face—a slight shift of her eyes and a brief convulsion around the mouth—that told me she expected I'd say that. She looked exactly like her mother.

"Mom said I'd hear those very words—not just *daily double* but *I've got to make the daily double* before the end of the first day, and here we are."

"Your mom is such a prophetic person," I said.

She frowned.

"Meaning no disrespect," I said.

It was quiet for a while. Then I said, "If you want me not to go, I won't."

She said nothing.

"Really," I said. "It's up to you."

She reached for the door handle, still not looking at me.

"But there's a good chance on the first and second races. That's all. I think I've got it, and if I do, it'll be a tidy—"

She opened the door and got out.

I did the same. As I closed the door I saw her stand up on the other side, the cool breeze lifting her hair slightly off her shoulders. She was studying the lock on the door, and I said, "You don't have to hold the handle, just lock it and shut it."

She came around the back of the car and took my arm as we started into the store. "Tell the truth," she said. "You're still just as bad a gambler as you ever were, aren't you?"

I felt terrible, but I launched into this dissertation about how I was in the real estate business—I did have my license, and at one time I had been an agent. I told her how difficult it was sometimes closing deals and arranging settlements and collecting commissions. "It's the damnedest thing," I told her. "One month you're broke, and the next thing you know, the money's rolling in." Like her mother she listened, nodded her head, and counted up the ways in which I had avoided the subject.

We were in the frozen-food section of the grocery store when I finished, and she said, "So what time do you have to be at the track?"

I laughed, pretending to be charmed, but the truth was, I hated the way she reminded me of Catherine. I didn't want her to do anything that would make me think of her mother—and I especially didn't want her to nag me the way her mother always did. "I already handicapped the first two races this morning."

She gave me this disapproving stare, as if I'd wasted my morning.

"It's a lot of work, you know." I was telling the truth. Anyone who has studied a racing form—I mean really tried to handicap a race—knows what I'm talking about. It's incredibly hard work.

But Nicole didn't believe me. "Right," she said, almost sneering. "I'm sure it's a *ton* of work."

"It is."

"So what time do you have to be there?"

"No later than twelve twenty-five," I said. "Post time for the first race is twelve-thirty."

She seemed satisfied with that.

Before we left the grocery store that first day, we had a brief disagreement that blossomed into the same kind of argument we used to have when I was still flying out to see her. Like her mother, Nicole often thinks she has the truth. So if you take issue with her on anything she believes, either your thinking or your character is seriously flawed.

It started innocently enough. I noticed that Nicole insisted on buying only vegetables. "Don't you even want some cheese?" I asked.

"No." She was very blithe about it. "I don't eat animal products."

"What about Sam? What's he eat?"

"He's a vegetarian, too."

"Really."

"It's not healthy or natural to eat meat," she said.

"How'd you find that out?" We were strolling down the aisle, Nicole pushing the basket, and me walking alongside. We were just talking, not looking at each other.

"What do you mean?" she said.

"Who discovered eating meat is not natural?"

"It's just the truth."

"Well, it'll be a hell of a surprise to millions of meat eaters. Not to mention animals themselves. Surely you've noticed they eat meat pretty regularly."

"Very funny."

"Well, they do."

She was pushing the cart, looking rather peevish. "People just need to be educated about the damage meat does to their bodies."

"Right."

"It's true."

"You mean you *think* it's true."

"Human beings are not carnivores. They only think they are."

"They're not herbivores, either."

She didn't say anything.

"I presume you've heard of such a thing as an omnivore?"

"Jesus, you can be pompous." She made a face and said, "'I presume, I presume.'"

This really irritated me, but I let it go. It was quiet for a while. Nicole selected melons and cabbages and carrots. She was very good at finding the fresh, and the ripe and ready. When I was certain I could speak without sounding pompous, I said, "You know some animals eat both meat and vegetables."

She was ready for me. "People have been conditioned to eat meat. It's a primitive habit. That's all."

"I only *think* I like meat?"

"You may like it, but it's not natural that you do."

"According to whom?"

She stopped the cart and looked at me. I could see I was getting on her nerves and we were headed for familiar emotional ground. When she was in middle school she had to be forced to spend a few hours with me. We agreed on nothing of any importance, and the only good thing about me was that I was a long-distance father. I was a faithful visitor for most of her childhood, but it didn't take long to figure out what she wanted me to do once she started to notice boys: stay away.

"Look," she said now, holding on to the cart as though she were afraid I might try to jerk it out of her hands, "you live the way you want to; I'll live the way I want to."

"Fine. That's what I'm arguing for."

She started walking again.

I said, "You shouldn't say things like that about human beings as though you know what you're talking about."

"I know what I'm talking about."

"No, you don't."

"You know how I lost all that weight?"

"Not so loud."

"Do you?"

"Hunting carrots?"

"Eating vegetables. That's the right way to eat."

"For you, maybe. If I lost that much weight I'd vanish."

This hurt her and I immediately regretted saying it. She started pushing the cart faster, moving on ahead of me.

"Wait a minute," I said. "Don't get pissed off."

She denied it. "I just want to get finished here. I'm hungry."

"Wait up."

She stopped. "You're in a hurry, aren't you? Don't you have to *make* the daily double?"

"What are we arguing about?" I put my hand on her arm. Her skin felt soft and cool and brand-new. She looked at my hand and I removed it.

"We're arguing about animal rights," she said.

"'Animal rights.'"

"You think that it's OK to deprive—"

"Animal rights! For Christ's sake."

"You don't have to get abusive." She started to move away but I grabbed her arm again.

"Animals don't have rights."

"Yes, they do." She pulled away.

"They're mentioned in the constitution? The Bible? The Magna Carta? Where are these rights conferred?"

I had her there and she knew it. I pursued my advantage. "What do you mean when you say 'rights'?"

She got this cornered look on her face and I immediately felt as though I had beaten her with a stick. There was a long pause while she seemed to stare at the floor, and then she shrugged and said, "It's what I believe."

I felt really helpless. She seemed so suddenly dispirited and I knew there was nothing I could do or say that would reverse the tenor of our conversation. When I get angry, it shows.

"Come on," I said. "Let's not fight about this. It's silly."

"It's not silly."

"I mean it's silly to fight about it. You just got here. I don't care what you believe. Believe what you want."

She walked on in front of me, refusing to respond to anything I said. I tried to apologize, but I had offended her sense of decency, I guess. If she had not hurled her convictions at me like manhole covers, I might have found a better way to duck them. I hate people who get morally indignant if you don't live the way they do. That was the principal trouble Nicole's mother had. She judged everybody according to her own narrow standard, and because almost no one could live up to it, she was pretty pissed off most of the time.

Notice I didn't use the plural form of the word *standard*. Catherine had one standard. It would be difficult to find a single word to describe it accurately, but if there *were* a word, it would include the concepts of discipline, hard work, sensual deprivation, and cleanliness. If you weren't living up to these four things at one and the same time, all the time, you were what she called a tree sloth. She thought you were indolent if you weren't suffering in some way.

When Catherine left me, Nicole was barely six years old. Less than a year after the divorce was final, Catherine remarried and took Nicole to California. For the past ten years, if I wanted to see my daughter more than once a year, I had to visit her out there. I managed fairly well until she got into her teens. I'd fly out on Thanksgiving holidays and for a week or so in August. Every other Christmas, her mother put her on a plane and flew her out to see me for a week. Twice Nicole came for a week in the summer; but I thought it was better if she didn't have to travel all that way alone, so I usually went out there. Then, like I said, she got into her teens. Once that happened I didn't feel too welcome anymore—in fact, I felt like a damned nuisance. She had her friends, whose thoughts were much more important than me or her mother, or even her own health and welfare. What her friends thought, or might think, governed everything she did or said all day long. So it was pretty easy to let a year go by, and then another one, and pretty soon the time away from her piled up.

It is also true that the real estate market in Virginia collapsed, and since I was an independent agent and worked at it only during the summer, my business pretty well collapsed, too. Even if I had wanted to, I didn't have the money to fly out there. Nicole had not been in my house since she was thirteen. For all that time, whenever I thought of her—if I thought of her—I remembered a little girl who had long ceased to exist, having grown into an irritable and rather beefy teenager with great difficulty relating to a distant parent who could not afford to visit anymore.

Now, suddenly, here she was in the body of this new person: attractive and perhaps even sweet again, as though a vague memory had transformed and come to life.

In the checkout line at the grocery store two women stood behind us and chatted about the beautiful spring weather. They were both apparently in the dark about the eating habits of human beings. One of them looked at me, and I pointed to her basket and said, "Nice flank steak."

She smiled. "They're on special."

"Ah, but did that animal have a fair trial before it was unjustly butchered?"

You should have seen that woman's face. I had given her a mental hotfoot. You'd have thought I had just announced I was a Hare Krishna or a Seventh-Day Adventist and I had some good news for her.

I hoped that Nicole would start to laugh. Always before, when we had an argument, I could eventually tease her into laughter and we'd be all right again. But this time she turned from me and started arranging her vegetables on the conveyor belt.

"My daughter here is one of those vegetarians," I said. I couldn't help myself. I don't care if a person wants to abstain from eating meat, but I hate it when they suggest that I should, too, and if I don't I'm somehow immoral. "She's actually got me feeling pretty sorry for your flank steak."

Nicole looked at me, a wounded expression on her face. Then she seemed to remember something rueful. "If you want meat, go ahead and buy some, *Dad.*" She put special emphasis on the word *Dad.* I though her voice cracked a bit, and it saddened me.

"I'm just trying to make you laugh."

She didn't answer me.

"Come on. I'm only kidding you."

"No, you aren't."

Outside, as we put the groceries in the back seat, I said, "I'm sorry, honey. I really don't want to start arguing with you all over again."

She looked at me, then opened the door on her side.

"I said I was sorry. We wouldn't have these fights if you didn't feel it necessary to comment on my life."

"I wasn't commenting on your life."

"Well, that's how it felt."

She got in and closed the door.

We drove home in silence. When I pulled the car into the driveway, I said, "You shouldn't make me feel as though I don't know how to live my life. It feels impertinent to me. That's all."

"You do that to me all the time."

"Yes. But that's what I'm supposed to do. You really don't know yet."

She got this hurt expression on her face.

"People your age don't know yet. Not just you. Everybody your age needs to—"

She got out of the car, slammed the door, and walked into the house. I carried the groceries in myself and put them away. I had to hurry, because it was almost eleven-thirty.

Just before I left I found Nicole in the family room, flipping the pages in a magazine. I leaned over and kissed her on the cheek. "I'm going."

"Bye." She didn't look up.

"Wish me luck."

"Yeah, right."

I said I was sorry. I didn't know what the hell else I was supposed to do.

Nicole's First Day Home

Was probably a big deal to her, I know, I know. I should have stayed there with her and worked it out. All the way to the track I was kicking myself. I knew she might very well be gone when I got back, but I couldn't make myself turn around and give up the quest. I needed to parlay that hundred bucks into some usable cash. I had a mortgage due in ten days. Seven hundred dollars. Where was I going to get it? I had nothing in savings.

Highland Park is just across the Potomac, in southern Maryland. The place looks like an old-fashioned park, with white wood railings and a huge open grandstand with a high roof and small wood seats.

Oddly enough, when I got there I felt pretty good. That old hundred-dollar bill relieved a nagging sense of doom. It was a bright cool day—the kind of day when a horse barn smells wonderful and the breezes blow a horse's mane back in such a way you'd swear the animal was designed by a woman. On days like that, with the smell of horses in your nostrils, and money in your pocket, the world is perfect. I knew I had this problem with Nicole but I figured I'd get it solved somehow. The thought crossed my mind that I wouldn't have to if she really was angry enough to go back home. I'd just wait awhile and then make peace by long distance—call her, or write her a letter once she got over the truly stupid idea that animals are citizens.

I walked into the clubhouse at the track and realized I had been wise to handicap the first two races early. It was only ten minutes to post time for the first race. I bought a program and, just for the hell of it, glanced at the first race again.

You wouldn't believe the name of the three horse.

I don't want to tell you yet. First, you've got to know that I don't believe in pure chance where gambling is concerned. I never play roulette or blackjack or any of those other casino games where the odds are with the house. In horse racing, luck is a thing you take advantage of by carefully scrutinizing all the information you can gather and then selecting what you think is the absolute best choice after weighing all the intangibles. A horse is an athlete, with another athlete on his back. You have to examine the animal's past races, the weight he's carrying, the workouts in the last week or so, the speed rating of races he's won or lost, the class of horses he's been running against, what he's won this year and last year, how many starts he's had, when the last start was, how much money he's won, whether he goes to the front and tries to stay in position or lags behind and makes a move in the stretch, the distances he's had to run, whether or not he's got blinkers on, who his jockey is, whether or not the horse runs better in the mud or on the turf or on a fast track. All these considerations go into choosing a horse to bet on in any given race.

And yet, pure chance does exist.

You can be just right in all your thinking and the horse could fall down or the jockey could make a stupid mistake and take him too far outside or brush another animal and get disqualified because of a foul. Or another horse, whose record does not show it, could run the race of his life and leave your animal digging for third. Or your horse could decide not to run when he ought to. Once I picked a horse who went to the front out of the gate and took a ten-length lead by the quarter-mile pole. At the half mile I was patting my friends on the back and waving my ticket. I'd bet two hundred dollars on him to win. As he came around the turn into the stretch a good fifteen lengths in front, an airplane flew over the track. My horse went straight to the fence, jumped off the track, and kept on running.

That's pure chance.

So, sometimes you've got to play the odds while keeping chance in mind.

In the first race, the three horse was named Nicole's Lament.

What would you have done?

I don't know why I hadn't noticed that horse when I was handicapping the race that morning or why he wasn't in any of the betting combinations I had been considering. But I did something really crazy. I threw out King's Brew—the horse I really liked—and bet the daily double with Nicole's Lament. I then coupled him with all the horses in the second race. If Nicole's Lament won the first race, I would win the daily double no matter what. This sort of bet is called a back wheel. It has advantages, the most important of which is you don't have to consider anything about the other horses in the double. Since you've got them all in the bet, you don't have to go through the hard work of handicapping the second race.

Of course, it costs more. Most people bet two-dollar doubles. When you do that you get whatever the double price is, once. I bet the double five times—which meant if I won, I'd have two and a half times the daily-double price. Most people pick a horse in the first race and maybe one or two horses in the second race. For each double bet, you have to pay at least two dollars. There were eleven horses in the field for the second race. Since I was betting five-dollar doubles, I had to bet Nicole's Lament with eleven other horses in that second race at five dollars a shot. The bet cost me fifty-five dollars—more than half of all the money I had.

So, I prayed a bit, too.

I went outside and sat on a bench next to the grandstand. I was going to watch the race just sitting down, like a drunk. I hoped I could charm the Fates into letting me win, by pretending that I didn't care.

But I didn't have to do any of that. By the end of the race, I was standing next to the fence, screaming Nicole's name, and that beautiful horse crossed the wire a good half-length in front of King's Brew. I had my double.

I glanced over the daily-double figures on the board. The favorite in the second race was a horse called Fast Hilarious. If he won the second race it would pay sixty dollars for a two-dollar bet. For my five-dollar bet I'd collect a hundred and eighty dollars. Not bad, but not that good, either. The best price was a horse called Skinny Minny, who had never won a race. If that horse won, I'd collect well over three thousand dollars.

I knew better than to root for the long shot, but I hoped the favorite might get clipped. I can't tell you what a pleasure it is to watch a race where no matter what horse wins you've got it. I was rooting for all the horses in the race except the favorite, even though a small victory would have satisfied me. I watched the second race sitting high up in the grandstand, relaxing. I didn't even cheer.

I was again very lucky. A horse called Domino just nipped the favorite at the wire. I collected six hundred and forty dollars.

That was the beginning of my day. I was fairly careful handicapping each race after that, but I took a few more risks that I would normally, and I was willing to bet more money (oh, a lot more money) because, on this day, I had luck with me, too. I had the kind of luck the foul Fates give us every once in a while to seduce us into foolish hope and permanent belief. In the fifth race, a horse I had bet almost four hundred dollars on came in second. I didn't even get a chance to curse. He was placed first because the horse who won the race had bumped a horse in the stretch and was disqualified. You see what I'm talking about?

I walked out of that place with over four thousand dollars. Do you have any idea the kind of elation you have in your soul on a day like that? Another month taken care of: mortgage, electric, water, phone, car, and dinner for my daughter. I was still in business. And for the first time in weeks I felt happy about life.

For a while there, I was immortal. That's what pure chance coupled with careful handicapping can do for you. I was so happy, I forgot there was any other feeling.

I actually didn't mind going to see my girlfriend.

My Girlfriend

Elizabeth, is two years older than I am. She's tall, with black hair. High cheekbones seem to cradle her large dark eyes—eyes that glisten when she smiles. Very slight crow's-feet next to her eyes only make the light more fine in them. Her skin is dark and youthful. She is one of those women who grow more beautiful with age, who as young girls are a little too serene, a little too tall, a little too skinny to be noticed very much. Now she is positively regal.

The first time I saw her she was struggling with a lawn mower in a gully along the road in front of her house. I was driving by and saw her pulling on it. The mower was spitting dirt and stones out toward the street, and she'd gotten it caught somehow. She was wearing a white blouse, red shorts, and black running shoes. On first glance, I believed she was much older. I stopped to help because I felt sorry for her. I imagined she was cutting the grass for the first time. Maybe her husband had died, or perhaps he left her. But she fought the mower with such determination and scorn, I believed she must be taking her first assertive step toward recovery. When I got out of the car and approached her, she stopped, considered for a second, then decided to trust me. I reached for the handle, and she stepped back as though she had ordered me to take over. When she let go of the handle, the engine quit. I pulled the mower back out of the grass, where it had been caught in a small rut of gravel.

"Thank you," she said, wiping the sweat from her brow.

That's when I noticed that she was not so old after all.

"You want me to start it again?"

"I can do it." She took off her gloves and reached up to brush the hair from her forehead. I was still standing in the ditch.

"I wouldn't try this with the mower again. You need a Weed Eater."

"Thank you," she said again. She was definitely finished with me.

"My name's Henry Porter." I held out my hand.

She looked at it.

"Glad to be of help." I started back toward my car.

"It doesn't usually get stuck like that. I think I've got the height adjusted too low."

I stopped, encouraged. "You want me to look at it?"

"I can do it." She smiled. A breakthrough. I think women are more conscious of what their faces are doing than men are. I think they know when they are smiling, and they use expressions of wonder and awe on purpose. I think women bestow smiles when they want to give a person something of value. And finally, I think most men don't know this. So millions of smiles go to waste, and women spend a lot of time talking to themselves about how unobservant men are.

"You cut the grass often?" I asked. A really stupid question. I didn't know any other way to find out if her husband had just left her or if he had died or in what way she was being brave and if she didn't really need a kind of rescue. I wanted very badly to rescue her.

"This is not the first time." She could tell it was a stupid question, so the smile left her face. Now she seemed puzzled.

"I come by here often. I've never seen you doing it."

She smiled again. "I just moved in."

She offered me a cold drink and I accepted. In spite of my idiotic notions about why she was out there cutting the grass, I presently came to see that she was rescuing me. She went in the house and came out with two glasses of iced tea, and we sat on her front steps, talking and watching the traffic go by. I told her about my grass, she told me about hers. I told her what I did for a living.

"You're a teacher," she said.

"Yeah, why? Don't I look it?"

"I'm a teacher, too."

"Really."

"I teach English at the high school."

When I told her I taught middle school, she got this pained expression on her face. "It must be awful."

"Actually, it's quite fun."

She talked about the frustration and joy of teaching high school. I liked hearing her voice, and after a while, I knew if I asked her out she would go.

So, things just blossomed from that day.

For three years Elizabeth and I were inseparable. We spent the weekends together, sometimes Wednesday evenings. We'd have dinner together every Friday night. Either I'd cook or we'd go out to a restaurant. Sometimes she would stay with me at my house, but more often I would spend the night at her place.

It was very comfortable. Things just sort of settled and seemed to work exactly as both of us needed—or at least that was what I came to believe. I would not want to speculate as to whether I was led to believe that or I just found my way there on my own.

In any case, a few weeks before school let out that summer, almost suddenly—as though someone had told Elizabeth a terrible secret about me that made me repugnant to her delicate eyes—something in her attitude toward me dissolved. We were not the same together. The smallest sound—the clink of a fork on a plate as we were eating or the fragile clatter of a china cup on a saucer—seemed to bear emotional freight, as though the sound itself were an insulting development between us. She did not seem able to look at me directly, and always the weight of a thousand unspoken words pulled us down. I know I probably should have spoken some words of my own—words like "Is anything wrong?" or "What's troubling you, dear?" or even "What the fuck's up your ass?"—but I couldn't bring myself to open what I was sure would be a Pandora's box by doing so. I calculated that if she really wanted to get my understanding, she would ask for it.

As it was, when she did speak, it came to me like the first subtle step of a complicated strategy. We were riding in her car on the way home from a movie and she said, "Did you enjoy the show?" We'd just seen *Heartburn,* and I still had the song about the itsy-bitsy spider in my head.

"It was all right," I said.

"Just 'all right'?"

"I liked the music."

I'm sure I heard her let out this sound that was disapproving. A sort of combination *tsk* and *harumph,* given so slightly I might have missed it entirely if I hadn't been looking for it. I was convinced she was trying to orchestrate a fight about something.

"I always liked Carly Simon," I said.

She sighed, then she said, "Men."

"What about men?"

"Nothing." She stared out the window at the passing houses and road signs.

I waited. A long time passed. Then I said, "Did you like the movie?"

"It was all right," she said.

"Women," I said.

"Don't start now," she said, turning to me. I swear there were tears in her eyes.

"Are you upset about something?" I said.

"That movie upset me."

"The movie."

"Yes."

"Not me."

She said nothing.

"Because you're acting like I upset you somehow."

"Didn't anything in that movie bother you?"

"Of course," I said. "Absolutely."

"What? Tell me what."

I knew better than to do that. It was a challenge I couldn't possibly meet.

"What bothered you?" I asked.

She turned rather forcefully away. She had nothing to say the rest of the drive back to her place. But when we got there, she slid over on the seat and put her arms around my neck and kissed me. "I'm sorry," she said. "Forgive me?"

"Nothing to forgive," I said.

She kissed me again, then looked into my eyes. "How do you put up with me?"

"We put up with each other," I said.

She smiled, still looking into my eyes, then her face changed and she pulled gently away. It was as if she remembered something important. She was very quiet after that, but we made it through the rest of the evening rather pleasantly, I thought.

The next day she called me on the phone and apologized profusely for "last night."

"It's over," I said. "I enjoyed myself last night."

It was quiet for a while, then I thought I heard her crying. "Elizabeth?" I said. "You all right?"

"Yes, of course." Her voice was strong and I couldn't be sure she had been crying. "Why wouldn't I be all right?" she said.

I was beginning to think perhaps she wanted to encircle me somehow and get me to say something that would force the issue of marriage. So we had more and more days like that, and I worried through all the other days, afraid to talk to her and afraid not to. Marrying Elizabeth or losing her produced the same obscure sense of restlessness and anxiety; I found it impossible to concentrate or remain in one place without a gradually increasing presentiment of ruin.

It didn't help that summer was approaching like a funeral train and I had not saved a whole lot of money. I was a teacher on a nine-month contract. When my summer vacation began, so would a prolonged period without guaranteed income.

The summer before, I managed with credit cards. But those have a limit, and once you reach it, you realize your expenses during the year are almost impossible—and that keeps you from saving money for the next summer. As the last year of the eighties began, I was hitting the track more and more often just trying to keep my head above water. Sometimes I lost so much money I didn't have enough to pay all the bills for a month, and that would put me even more behind.

I tried not to think about what the future might hold, but every now and then I would be doing something simple, like tearing open a small packet of sugar for my coffee or wiping my glasses clean with a paper towel, and without warning I would think about my fate—about sudden and final disaster—and my hands would shake so bad I couldn't hold on to anything. At moments like that, whatever I looked at stopped me cold with nausea, as though I were living my last night on death row and all terrestrial things were a reminder that I would be executed in the morning. Summer was coming, and I was going to be cut loose.

You know, it occurs to me now, just now, that perhaps some part of my psyche already knew what was in store for me that summer when Nicole came home.

At any rate, the only time I felt safe was after a few small glasses of bourbon, because then I could escape into untroubled sleep. Sometimes I would come home in the early afternoon, go to bed without eating, and sleep until the next morning. This would give me a taste of brief, easeful death, and I would escape a whole night of bubbling fear.

What truly troubled me, though, was being awake. Having to pile up the hours each day, worrying about money, hoping Elizabeth would call, and praying she would not, feeling alone even when I was with her, because there was never anything to say.

Gradually I came to insist on seeing her only according to the pattern we had established, in the fear that if I did not have dinner with her on one Friday or if I missed one weekend, she would disappear out of my life altogether. I tried to convince myself that I did not mind being alone; that I might actually grow into permanent solitude with the sort of satisfaction usually reserved for the confirmed old bachelors one finds in the movies. But this was only spiritual survival—a small part of me wanting to emerge from my future intact and undamaged. Still, this gathering sense of doom clung to the back of my mind like a spiderweb.

Until the trouble started, the only thing I knew for certain was that I did not want anything to change between Elizabeth and me. She was a good, sexy lover who, for a time at least, seemed to want me, and now she was pulling away and I was walking around with my hands shaking.

I didn't know if I loved her. Since Catherine left me, I hadn't thought about love at all. I hate to say the word, and I think people overuse it so much that it has lost its radiance. It's now a very ordinary, common thing. Like lint. Or paper clips. Nevertheless, some days were awful because I realized I might not see Elizabeth.

And then again, sometimes I was terrified that I would see her.

A Woman Always Knows

What's happening on her face. It's a product of years and years of sitting in front of a makeup mirror. They get used to practicing expressions, and after a while, they come to know what it feels like to smile, squint, snicker, smirk, frown, scowl, glower, leer, and sneer. Thus, without fail and with unbelievably capable accuracy, they can encourage, console, repudiate, disapprove, tempt, solicit, beg, scorn, request, deny, disdain, or promise. If they don't feel like doing any of those things, they can seem to. Even if they feel like frowning, they can make themselves smile encouragingly. It has been said in many quarters that women are probably better at expressing their emotions than men are. They may be. But that is not the whole truth. They are also better (oh, much better) at expressing emotions they don't really feel. You see what sort of trouble this can lead to.

At any rate, you should have seen Elizabeth's face that night when I met her for dinner. I knew I was in for a very serious evening. If I pushed the hair on her forehead back about half a foot, she would have looked like queen Elizabeth right before she consigned Raleigh to the tower.

I hadn't even told her about Nicole yet.

"You look beautiful," I said.

She wasn't looking me in the eye. Always a bad sign with a woman. She sat down across from me and said, "You look happy."

"I do?"

"What's up, Henry?"

"I'm buying dinner."

"You always buy dinner."

"I'm buying it with cash tonight."

She didn't answer me.

"Is this going to be a somber evening?"

Again, she had nothing to say.

A waiter came to the table, handed us menus, and asked if we wanted cocktails.

"I'll have bourbon, straight, in a small glass," I said. I tried to catch Elizabeth's eye.

"I don't want anything," she said.

"Bring her a bourbon, too. I'll drink it if she doesn't want it."

The waiter seemed to snicker as he wrote on his pad, then he strode off.

"You are feeling good." Now Elizabeth looked at me.

"I have news," I said.

"So do I."

She sounded very serious. "You go first," I said.

"No. You."

It occurred to me that her news could not possibly top mine, so it might be uncharitable to go first. On the other hand, if I went after her, my news would dwarf whatever she had to say, and maybe that wouldn't be so kind, either. "It really is big news," I said.

"Well, tell me."

"My daughter's come home."

She blinked and then smiled. "Little One?"

"She's not so little. She's graduated from high school."

"Really." She studied the menu as she spoke. "The way you always talked about her, I thought she was just a child."

"She is."

Elizabeth shook her head slowly, amazed. "Has she come to stay?"

"She was thirteen the last time I saw her. She's grown now—or, she's older. Actually, she's shrunk down quite a bit."

"'Shrunk'?"

"At fifteen she could have been a linebacker at USC. Now I bet she doesn't weigh more than a hundred ten pounds or so."

"Good lord. She's not sick is she?"

"She's a vegetarian."

"Oh."

"She's even into animal rights."

"Oh." This was a larger *oh*.

We didn't say anything for a while. The waiter brought us the two bourbons and then took our order. When he had left the table, Elizabeth said, "So where is she?"

"Who?"

"Who do you think, Henry?"

"Oh. She's home."

"Why didn't she come along?"

"I came straight here from the track."

"Why didn't you call her, have her join us? I'd like to meet her."

"She's pissed at me right now."

"Really. And you looked so happy when you came in here."

"I really am, although..." I stopped, searching for the right word.

"What?"

"Nothing."

"What'd you do to her?"

"It was a minor thing. I just teased her a little about being a fanatic and real wrong where food is concerned. That's all."

"Well, I would like to meet her."

"I was more than a little worried about how I was going to afford having both of them here all summer."

"'Both of them'?"

"She came with a friend. A little Oriental guy. Pretty funny kid, actually."

"You *are* going to have a summer, aren't you?"

"I suppose."

"And have you had word from her mother?"

"Not on your life."

"You will."

Our food came and we ate quietly for a while. I had made a point of getting a New York strip, but Elizabeth had ordered the swordfish. After a while I said, "Am I going to have to guess your news?"

She put her fork down and picked up a napkin, but she didn't wipe her mouth with it; she sort of placed it up against her forehead and studied the table from behind it, almost as though it were a small tent she erected between herself and me. Then she put it down and said, "Oh, I don't know."

"You don't know what?"

"I don't know if I should tell you now."

I knew it. My news took the stuffing out of hers. I tried to be charitable about it. I told her I really wanted to know and even if it wasn't as exciting as my news, it was still news after all and might be just as exciting for her.

Her face changed. It kept changing. In the beginning it was sad and forlorn, then it shifted until it was almost an appeal, but at the same time, her eyes, the curvature of her eyebrows, and the angle of her head gradually seemed to reveal incredible forbearance and a sort of affirmation of her will to endure. Directly that expression merged into sorrowful resignation, as though she had just whimpered, "Do you see now what I have had to put up with?"

Then she said, "I'm pregnant."

I can't imagine what happened to my face. Thank god I didn't say anything. I think I looked at my fork. I know I stopped chewing.

"I wanted to tell you a long time ago," Elizabeth said. "It's been bothering me for weeks."

"So that's it," I said.

"That's what?"

"Nothing."

"What do you mean, 'so that's it'?"

"I knew something was bothering you." My face was burning. I wanted to put it someplace where she couldn't see it.

"I'm sorry."

"What are you sorry for?" Now I understood that she had been trying to prepare me for this news for quite some time. She may not have
been entirely conscious of it, but all along she had been trying to tell
me. In some ways, she had a whole hell of a lot to be sorry for.

But so did I. Already I began to feel how stupid and blind I was to
neglect the auguries of what must have been, for her, an intensifying
storm of fear and doubt. I let the silences expand instead of pursuing
their cause. I did not think *of* her as much as I thought about her.

She was looking at me and I didn't know what to say. I knew she was
expecting me to say something, and the longer I waited, the more terrible it was going to be once I did find words. I felt so sorry for her. She
gazed at the glass of water on the table in front of her, and in the weak
yellow candlelight, she looked almost tragic. She wore a blue dress with
a white collar, and her hair was pulled back into a single blue barrette.
With her head down I could see the candlelight flickering off the barrette, and for a moment I was reminded of a young novitiate kneeling
before an offertory candle, praying for absolution. There was something
pure about her, and also, I realized, something terribly fertile.

Then she said, "I'm sorry for letting this happen."

I didn't want to say something stupid and typically male like "It
sure complicates things, doesn't it?"

So I said, "Well, now we're in the big leagues."

"What?" She looked at me.

I could not stop stammering. "You're . . . you're . . . why, you're
pregnant."

"Yes."

"With . . . with a . . . a baby."

I was beginning to see scorn. "Of course with a baby. What'd you
think I meant, a baboon?"

I looked at my plate. The steak had taken on a brownish hue and
reminded me of rotting bark. "Man," I said.

She started fidgeting, picking up her knife and fork, putting them
back down, playing with her napkin.

The truth was, I didn't know what I was supposed to say. If I pretended to be happy—pretend is what I would have to do—she'd see right through it. And yet, I wasn't sure if you could call how I felt *un*happy. The question of one's happiness seemed silly to me.

"I want you to know," she said, "I have no expectations—"

"Don't," I interrupted her. "Don't say anything like that."

"Let me finish."

"I don't want to hear it. You're—"

"You shouldn't think—"

I reached over the table, took her hand, and stopped her. "We're going to have a baby."

She looked at me, her eyes glittering in the light. I was pretty sure I'd said the right thing.

"Oh, Henry."

"Now don't start crying," I said.

"I didn't want this to happen."

"I understand."

"I really didn't." She wiped under her eyes with the napkin.

I wished she would just stop talking and give me time to think. I wasn't sure what I felt or what I would do. It was important to say all the right things, but I needed time to think, too. I tried to tell her. I patted her hand and stammered, "Honey, I think... I think... we should..." I could not think of another word. There she was, tears in her eyes, looking like the purest rendering of the spirit that informs and animates all women, and in truth I just wanted to shut her up and get her away from there. I sat back and wiped my mouth with the napkin, stalling for time. Suddenly I had this image of myself all relaxed in a quiet chair, under a seventy-five-watt lamp, reading a book, smoking a pipe. I was alone. I had no problems. None. It was all dark around the light and I was intensely comfortable with my book and my pipe and the light.

I am not a peaceful man. I have never much liked sitting under a lamp reading, and I don't smoke a pipe. My father smoked a pipe. I couldn't stand to be in the same room with him when he did. The

image was, I now see, probably the first intimations of renewed fatherhood as my terrified psyche pictured it.

"I'm going to have this baby," Elizabeth said.

"Of course you are."

"I want to do it right."

"Oh, sure."

There was a brief silence. Then she said, "Whatever you decide."

I went back to my steak. She watched me struggling to cut a piece
of fat from around the edge. I felt as though I were cutting up her pet
squirrel or something, the way she looked at me. "I've been a new father before," I said.

"I know."

"I've been through all this before."

"Right."

"I mean that in a positive way."

"It sounds like it."

"Don't let's be ironic, OK?"

"I'm not being ironic."

If I could have made myself remember the early joy with Nicole—
if some part of memory had given back even one of those perfect days
when my life was consumed with just touching Nicole's little pink
hands, kissing her cool, soft cheek—I might have said just the right
thing. But Elizabeth didn't expect that from me. I came to see that she
was waiting for me to ruin everything. No memory could break
through the profound sorrow and hot humiliation of being judged less
than worthy in such circumstances. My steak was cold but I kept eating, trying to fight back anger and resentment. Oddly enough, her expectations were producing the worst possible reaction in me, so she
would shortly get what she expected.

"What do you want me to do?" I asked.

"Nothing."

"What would you like me to do?"

She didn't answer me.

"Go ahead, say it."

Still no answer.

"I know. Let's be happy about this? How about that?"

"Please, please, please don't be sarcastic." Now she was weeping openly. People in the restaurant were beginning to take notice.

"I'm not being sarcastic. For Christ's sake."

She placed her napkin over her plate and got up to leave.

At that moment, I might have convinced myself that I hated her. "Sit down."

"I've got to go." She was wiping her eyes, but tears kept streaming down her cheeks.

"Sit down. What is this? Why are you behaving like this?"

"Don't," she said. "I can't stand this."

"We'll be happy," I told her, "if you'll just stop. Give me some time to process this . . . this . . ." I reached out my hand and she came around to me, and I got up and kissed her wet cheeks. Everyone was watching us, and I held her there while she sobbed into the crook of my shoulder. I patted her back, then reached up to stroke her head and in so doing, I knocked the barrette onto the floor.

"Oh," she said, leaning down to pick it up. Her hair fell down around her shoulders. She had some difficulty grasping the barrette, and I looked at the crown of her head and she was suddenly just a person there, a person, and I loved her again. I felt as though I had pushed her down. No one was eating their food anymore. I almost shrugged my shoulders at all of them, as though I were in a little comedy. I wanted to tell them all to mind their own goddamn business, but Elizabeth finally stood up, wiping her eyes now with the back of her hand. I didn't know where to touch her. She seemed fragile, wounded, ready to crumble to dust. I wish now that she had had somebody better than me to love her.

And you know what? I was already beginning to worry about what I was going to tell my father.

News of a New Baby
in Our Family

Might have been viewed as a positive event if one chose to look at it properly: that is, with a late-twentieth-century cast of mind. The problem was, my father looked at the world with the same sort of liberal understanding as, say, Tomás de Torquemada. Next to my old man, Mother Teresa looked like the Boston Strangler.

Not that his attitude had anything to do with my reaction to Elizabeth's news. I mention it only because I had planned to take Nicole to my father's house in Baltimore for a visit, so my parents could see her all grown up, and the irony seemed almost too powerful to believe: I was bringing them their long lost granddaughter—they had seen her only three times in the ten years since she'd gone to California—and, at the same time, I was bringing news of a kind of reprieve. They would have another grandchild to coddle and spoil and watch grow.

Makes you feel like there is a God after all, doesn't it?

Not that I believe overmuch in God. It's a nice idea: a grand, big, venerable senior citizen with a white beard, watching over us. But it isn't really a very convincing one. I think the reason God works in such mysterious ways is because we've misunderstood what really drives the world. I think it's more reasonable to believe the world is governed, if it's governed at all, by a group the Greeks called the Fates. I don't think the Fates are women, though, and there're more than three of them. I think there're probably six or seven. Like God, they look to be well past middle age, or close to it. Unlike God, these guys don't get petulant, childish, and pretty well pissed off if you don't regularly take time to praise and adore them. They'd rather you didn't pay any attention to them at all. (They hate it when people say "Knock on wood," much less actually knock on wood.) They probably sit around some sort of office. I bet they wear brown shoes, ties loosened at their necks, suspenders, slouch hats. I can see old coffee cups on the desk, papers everywhere. They are probably overweight, and for sure they don't give a damn about secondhand smoke. Chomping on those cigars, they observe everything we do and say. They laugh deeply and coughingly, like old reporters around a news desk. The small facts of your life come in over a ticker.

They like irony. That's why you can't miss a traffic light when you need to and why women with straight hair fight with curlers and permanents, and those with curly hair spend a fourth of their income making it straight. That's why a man who hates shaving always has dense facial hair, and the one who wants to grow a full beard needs a fortnight to produce a small patch of soft down on his chin. That's why suffering takes forever and pleasure is over before you know it.

And that's why you never say never.

Surely you can see that if the earth really is constrained and managed by Fates as I have described them, then virtually everything that happens makes sense. We don't need to be speculating about the Lord and his frightening will. It's not a mystery anymore. It's just mischief. Nothing more subtle or malevolent than your average prank. Except when it turns toward evil—when it elevates our suffering to the level of cancer or warfare or holocaust. Those things happen when the Fates have done with us. When we're not fun anymore. If you keep the Fates laughing—that is, if you maintain your innocence and hope—they'll keep you breathing. Maybe.

That ought to keep a bounce in your walk and prolong your efforts, eh? Maybe?

My father, even after a dozen years, was still getting used to the idea that I was divorced. I was pretty sure he disapproved of Elizabeth as well, although he was usually very cordial with her. So I didn't think

I'd have to interpret his facial expression to figure out his response to the idea.

I grew up in Baltimore and my parents still lived there. It was only an hour or so distant from my house, so I could drive over there pretty frequently, if I wanted to. The problem was, to get to their house, I had to pass by the racetrack; so sometimes an intended visit with them turned into an extended visit to the horses. Thus, many of my visits had to be unplanned so they would not be expecting me.

Aside from my divorce, it had been extremely difficult for both of my parents to adjust to the idea that one of their granddaughters was a vague rumor they occasionally got a card from. They blamed me for this distance, so whenever I did go to Baltimore, they were never very glad to see me.

I should take that back. They were glad to see me, but they were never too happy about having me around for very long, because it only reminded them of how old they were getting and how rotten I had turned out (in their eyes). I felt compelled to visit my parents because I knew that at their age, the time was drawing nigh when I would not be able to visit them aboveground, and I did love them after all.

My father is a good man. Maybe a great man. He had been a lawyer and then a highly regarded judge for the U.S. District Court. When he retired, it made the *Washington Post*. He went on to work without pay as a judge for the Howard County, Maryland, Orphan's Court.

My mother is a fine mother. She was a homemaker in the traditional sense of that word. I'm not talking about cooking, doing dishes, washing clothes, dusting furniture, and vacuuming rugs—although she did all those things. I'm talking about being the strong ligament that holds our family together. All the other children turned out fine. They are all happily married; they all produced cute, cuddly, loud, unruly children. My sister Pauline is a podiatrist, and after her came Theresa, a heart doctor. Theresa is the only one who lives far away—she maintains her practice in Cincinnati. My oldest brother, Phil, became a successful lawyer, and Robert manages a very large grocery store chain in which he owns considerable stock. My father is a proud man, who enjoys reciting the names of all his grandchildren—or almost all of them. It irked me that sometimes at family gatherings, he'd forget Nicole.

"Oh, yes," he'd say. "The one in California who I never see."

I am the youngest in our immediate family, and I came late, so naturally most of the intensity of parenthood had pretty much worn out by the time I came along. What I got was the halfhearted impatience and rootless discipline of very tired parents, and the stale ineffectual guidance of older brothers and sisters, who had more important things to do.

I got ordered around a lot, but I didn't get much practical instruction. That's what I would repeat to my father whenever I sensed that he was about to make the unfavorable comparison between me and my more successful, hardworking, productive siblings.

Still, whenever I was going to see my father, I imagined myself a grown and accepted son—another man—speaking pleasantly with him. He'd be smoking his pipe and we'd grunt disapproval of the young people all around us.

It was so easy to talk to my father when I imagined our conversations, because in my imagination, I had never failed him and I could imagine that I remembered what it felt like to have him regard me with pride. Although, to tell the truth, I couldn't isolate very many times in my life when I was certain that he was proud of me. Probably when I was very young I got to loll awhile in glory, but any satisfaction I may have gained from my father's pride was ruined by another little trick of the Fates: Childhood triumphs have no lasting effect, and they are usually marred by the obvious fact that good parents are supposed to be proud of their children, even when those children have achieved nothing more difficult than climbing down out of a high chair.

When I Was a Kid

My whole family used to go swimming at a rock quarry in Maryland called Sylvan Dell. I should say it *used* to be a rock quarry. It had filled with water from an underground spring, which created a very large swimming area—you could probably put two or three public swimming pools in it. The water was dark, clean, unchlorinated, and deep. Great stone cliffs surrounded it, and you could swing from a rope that was tied to a thick branch in a tall spectacular oak that leaned out over the edge of the quarry, then let yourself fall fifteen feet or so to the water. At the far end away from the rope nestled under more oaks and arching willows was a sort of clubhouse, with a patio that extended to the edge of the water, at the shallowest side of the quarry. A crude diving board jutted out over the water there. That end of the quarry was called the Diving Range, but the board was not any higher than the ones at public swimming pools. The water was only fourteen feet deep at that end, so it was less cold than the deeper waters farther out. I'd jump off the end of that board and swim to the left across the deep water to a rock wall with steps carved out of it, and I'd climb up the cliff and stand in line to get to the rope. When it was my turn I'd swing out as high as I could, then drop to the cold water below and swim back across to the diving board and get in line there for another jump. I never stopped, even for lunch. Sometimes I'd be in midair at one end of the quarry or the other when my mother would call out to me that it was time to go home.

I thought I was pretty much of a daredevil. Fifteen feet. Across from the rope and much higher up was a cliff we called Daredevil's Roost. It was really just a stone that jutted out over the deepest part of the quarry. Even from the top branches of the oak where the rope was suspended you had to look up to see the cliff across the way. It towered over everything. My father said, "You just fall from the sky when you leap off that thing." And yet, all day long there would be a line of people over there—mostly young men—who put on a loud blustery show for everybody as they leaped off the edge. I'd watch the distant small pale bodies dropping down and down like single kernels of grain into the black water below. They seemed to stab the water when they hit—as though they were breaking through a hard surface—and for the longest time I could not get up enough nerve to go over there and look down, much less jump off.

My brother Phil, however, jumped off Daredevil's Roost several times. Each time he did, it was a production. He would prance over there as though he were being escorted by mounted, ironclad horsemen with lances and banners and plumed helmets. He kept his head at such an angle, I was certain a flourish of horns and trumpets echoed in his ears. My sisters would squeal with excitement and alarm. Mother would refuse to look, although she'd tell everybody she met who had ever been to or heard of Sylvan Dell, "My eldest son jumped off that high cliff there many times."

The reaction I couldn't stand, though, was my father's. He would drop everything and labor like a scholar to find a place among the rocks where he could see it all, the entire descent. Once, he watched it from the water. He was like a publicity man, gathering people to watch. And Phil would hesitate, taking deep breaths, preparing for the fall as though it might kill him. From my vantage point near the rope swing, he looked a little bit like a tiny Christ, waiting for the guys with the hammer and nails.

God, I hated him then.

I know. It wasn't real hate. I was simply feeling a childish sort of envy, but Phil made such a big deal of it, and you couldn't convince him that two thousand people had jumped from the same spot that summer, and probably two thousand more would do it before the summer was over. On some days, he had to wait in line for an hour just to get a chance. And the whole time, my father would be gathering himself in a comfortable spot among the piled rocks near the cliff. I'd watch him getting settled, and increase my swimming speed in the hope that he'd notice what I was doing. It took much greater endurance to swim the length of that quarry forty or fifty times than to just fall from a rock.

Then, one cool August day near the end of the summer—I believe this was around the time of my ninth birthday—after one of Phil's jumps, my other brother, Robert, announced he was going to try it. He was not yet seventeen. My mother vetoed it at first, but Father looked at her as though she were crazy and said, "Why not?" I was watching Robert's face and when my father gave his approval, all the color went out of it. He hadn't expected that.

But my father's approval was spoken with such pride, I blurted out, "Go ahead, Robert. If you do it, I'll do it, too."

"You're not going off any cliff today," Mother said to me.

I think I really was disappointed, although my memory of this event is clouded by the fact that it has since become more or less emblematic of much more than a simple leap into deep water from a height that could kill me. It is just possible that the prospect of pleasing my father with something of myself, with some act I performed, was so intoxicating that my mind was stripped of all other considerations. At any rate I seem to remember trying so hard to convey the extremity of my displeasure that it began to feel as though I was acting. I admit that it is entirely possible, if not probable, that I was.

My father looked at me—or, I should say, he sized me up. His eyes went from my feet to my face and back again. "How old are you?"

He knew that. "I'm nine, sir."

He seemed vaguely annoyed, as if I'd asked him a stupid question while he was trying to concentrate, although he was only sitting on a picnic bench, with his hand in a bag of potato chips.

"You think you're ready for that jump, Robert?" he asked, turning back to his chips.

"I'm ready. I think so."

"You climb up there, you can't climb down. The only way down is off the cliff and into the water." This was a family rule of my father's. You didn't get up on a diving board, or any other place where people lined up to follow you, and then change your mind. Once you were there, you were going to do it, whatever it was. The first time I swung from the rope, I hung on for ten minutes—until the rope had stopped swinging entirely—before I finally let go. To his credit, my father didn't stand at the edge yelling at me like other parents I had seen. He waited there at the edge, shaking his head back and forth, watching me dangle until I let go. Then he smiled down at me, waved to show he was pleased, and went on down to the clubhouse to get some tobacco for his pipe.

"I think I'm ready," Robert said.

"Me, too," I said. I am certain, now, that back then I had become certain, that they would never let me jump off that cliff. So I could insist I wanted to do it and get a kind of credit for bravery without having to be particularly brave. I could also be honest about it, since at some level I very much wanted to be *able* to make the jump.

Phil said, "Let the Little Shaver do it. It'll shame everybody here."

He always called me the Little Shaver. I looked at him walking back to us, drying himself with a blue towel. He'd made the leap twice that day. A hero returning for the second time is less dramatic and interesting, so we didn't notice his return until he said, "Let the Little Shaver do it."

"Yeah," I said, "let me."

Robert was strangely silent.

Mother said, "You're too young. Your bones would break into a million pieces."

"No, they wouldn't. I jump from the rope."

"The cliff is a much longer fall than that," Phil said. "The rope is a child's sliding board compared to that cliff. It's two hundred feet." He plopped down on the bench next to Father.

"It's not two hundred feet," Dad said. Again he seemed annoyed. "Who told you it was two hundred feet?"

"Well, it's pretty high."

"It's about half that."

Robert walked over and sat down next to Phil.

I was standing in front of them, feeling really small. I wanted to be as big as they were and sit with them and be like them. "I can do it," I said. "I've done it before." I don't know where the words came from or why I said that, but immediately I regretted it. They all seemed to stop moving at once. The words of my lie hung there in space, almost as if a string of lights adorned them, and like a true fool, I repeated them. "I've done it before." Phil and Robert started taunting me about being a liar. They spoke in unison, telling me I was a little liar, and I said I wasn't, and then my father came to my rescue. He put his hand up and quieted them. "Wait a minute, wait a minute." Then he turned to me and leaned forward a bit. I noticed a small piece of potato chip lodged in the place where his lips came together.

"You've jumped off the cliff before?"

"Twice," I said. I figured that would lend more credence to my story, although it wasn't as important to me that they believe me as it was that my father not find out I was lying. It didn't matter anymore what I had said, only that he believe it.

"Once, the last time we were here." I knew I could at least claim it, because they all left me to my own devices there, and many times, as I said, I'd swim back and forth between the swing and the diving board all day without anybody paying any attention to it at all. It would have been easy for me to swim in the other direction off the diving board and climb out of the water over by the high cliff. There was no way they could prove that I was lying as long as I didn't admit it.

Or, at least, I didn't think there was.

"Well," Father said, "let's just cross over there and watch you do it again."

I don't remember the long walk around the ridge of the quarry or the climb up the steep rock wall. I'm sure I must have been as conscious as anyone ever is whose bluff has been called, but whenever I think about this particular event my memory always shifts forward rather suddenly to the first long minutes of standing on the edge of that cliff looking down. I could see tiny points of glistening light on the surface of the black water, which was so far below me I felt my legs empty out, as though the bones suddenly dissolved. Phil and Robert were there, along with my father, and across the way, standing by the oak, which looked quite small in the distance, my mother and sisters watched. In my memory now, they appear to be praying, although I'm certain there was no way I could have known that. From that distance they were so small, I couldn't tell for sure that they were even watching me. Perhaps I hoped they were praying, or they told me long after the event that they had been doing so. At any rate there I was, at the precipice. It was my turn. I had walked out there in the firm belief that I would just leap off and not think about it. It was important to me not to hesitate; I knew if I did, it would be obvious that I had never made this leap in my life. But once I got to the edge, as I said, I looked down. I seemed to awaken there, looking down, as a matter of fact.

It was windy. My feet were bloodless and I could not move.

"Well," Father said.

I took a deep breath, tried to stand the way Phil always did.

"He's never done this before," Robert said.

"It's never easy," said Phil.

I turned to them. "Why don't you try it, Robert?"

"After you."

Two burly men came up and stood behind Robert. They dripped water and had their arms crossed against the cool breezes. One of them was shivering.

"Go ahead, son," Father said.

I looked down again. The water was so far away I could see the entire array and sweep of patterns the currents of air created on its sparkling surface.

At the far end, by the diving board, I saw a man approach the end of the board. He was standing exactly as I was, only from this distance he looked like a frayed particle of white rice.

"I should have brought a towel," one of the men behind me said.

"Go on," Father said. "Jump."

I turned to him. And that was one of those moments, a very brief span of time as he looked at me, that I felt his pride. I mean it. I was truly conscious of it as though it burned in him and gave off heat. In the same instant, I knew I'd be a perfect disappointment to him if I didn't make this leap. He would know that I lied, that I was not brave, and that I was envious of Phil.

"I'm thinking of diving," I said.

"No, don't do that."

"Why not?"

"You might hit the water wrong and break your neck."

"Hey, Henry," Phil said, "keep your legs together."

"I always keep my legs together."

"You'll smash your balls if you don't."

With those words the Fates let me know I could never make that jump. I discovered at that moment—and for all time—that I was absolutely terrified of heights.

"There're people waiting, son."

I looked for the man on the diving board, hoping he would still be there and I could time my leap with his—when he went, no matter what, I would—but he was gone.

"I'm starting to dry off," one of the men said.

"Hey kid, shit or get off the pot," said the other.

"I'll go," Phil said. He stepped up next to me and gently took my arm.

"Come on Shaver, it's just too far down."

"It is not," I tried to pull away from him but he wouldn't let go.

"Come on."

Father glanced back down the path toward the stone ladder.

"I can do it."

"Well do it, then."

Just then a hawk flew overhead. I heard the rush of its wings, and the swiftly moving whistle of air took my breath away. Quite without warning, I began to cry.

"Come on, Shaver," Phil said. He pulled my arm and I followed without a struggle, defeated.

"Wait a minute," Dad said. "You know the rule."

"You're not going to make him," said Phil.

"It's the rule."

I stopped, a few feet down the path. Phil let go of my arm. I was too upset to even think about going back up to the edge.

"Go on, get back up there," Dad said evenly.

"I can't."

There was a long silence. My voice seemed to echo in my ears and I realized that I sounded like a little girl.

Dad looked down briefly, then he said, "You want to come down?"

"Yes." I was still crying. I couldn't stop it, although I wanted to so badly that even now when I remember it, I am humiliated and ashamed.

"You know the rule."

"Yes."

"What is it?"

"I have to."

"Say it."

"I got up there, so I have to jump."

The two men behind Robert edged forward and the one who was shivering asked my father if he minded too much if they went ahead.

"In a minute," he said impatiently.

"I'm going," the other one said. He walked past me and stood at the edge for a brief moment, then threw himself off.

"Go ahead," Dad said to the other one.

He went off, too, screaming and clamorous.

Now we were alone up there. Just me and Father and my two brothers. And the clouds. At that time in my life, I might have believed God was lurking nearby. We seemed so close to heaven. Phil stood next to me, his hands on his hips. Robert pawed the ground with his foot, trying to avoid eye contact with my father, who was now directly in front of me, kneeling down to look in my eyes.

"You lied, didn't you, Henry?"

I would have told him anything, even the truth, to avoid jumping off that cliff. "Yes," I said.

"You've never made this jump, have you?"

"No."

My father stood up and shook his head. I'll never forget the sound of his voice that day, coming to me in the quiet breezes at the top of that cliff and in the midst of my shame. "A good man will sometimes lie for a good reason. You want to be the sort who lies for no reason at all?"

"I didn't mean to lie," I said.

"You can't lie by accident, son."

I didn't know what to say.

It was quiet for a long time, then Robert stepped past me toward the cliff. "I'm not afraid," he said.

There was a moment when, though he was still looking at me, my father seemed distracted and Phil leaned over and touched him on the shoulder as if to say, "Look, he's actually going to do it." Then I saw Robert's hands go up, as if he were begging the sky, and Phil said, "Wait." But he was gone. He disappeared instantly. Phil leaned over the edge, and father got to his feet and walked up to the precipice.

"He did it," Phil said.

Dad made this noise in his throat—a brief sound of amazement he often gave forth when he discovered the world could still surprise him.

"See you down there," Phil said. He raised his arms into that crucified position and moved to step off, but Dad grabbed his arm. "Wait a minute. Is he all right?"

They were both looking over the edge now, and I felt a sudden pale tremor of fear that something had happened to Robert.

It seemed like many minutes passed. Then Phil pointed. "There, see? He's swimming toward the other side."

"Look at the little son of a bitch," Dad said with obvious pleasure.

"He's fine," Phil said.

Watching them, I realized this would have been the scene if I had jumped: My father would have been referring to me when he said, "Look at the little son of a bitch."

"I'm off," Phil said. He turned slightly and gave a silly wave, then leaped over the edge.

Dad watched him fall. Then he came back toward me. "Come on." He passed me, and I started to follow, but he stopped and looked at me. He leaned down and in a quiet, calm voice, he said, "When you lie to me, you truly hurt me, son."

"I'm sorry."

"You're not a liar, are you?"

"No sir. I'm not." I wiped my nose with the back of my hand.

"A true liar can't help himself, I guess." He put his hand on my head. "If you're not a liar, then you really must try from now on to be truthful. You don't want people thinking you're a liar, do you?"

"No, sir."

He withdrew his hand.

I started to cry harder, but I worked to control it. "I will tell the truth from now on," I said. "I just couldn't jump. I was too nervous—"

"You don't have to jump. You have to make an effort to tell the truth."

"Oh, I do. I will."

"You must insist on being truthful. And you must *never* lie for no reason."

"I had a reason. Honest."

"Oh?" He tilted his head.

"I wanted you to let me jump off the cliff."

He brushed the hair out of my eyes, and though he was frowning, his eyes seemed to be on the verge of laughter. He stood up. "Just remember that when people catch you in a lie, it's usually a long time before they ever believe you again."

As we made our way back down the path, I found myself talking to him, chattering as though I'd been gone for a long time. I was so excited with relief, rescue from panic, and recovery from tears, that I couldn't stop. I was the only one who talked. Dad walked in front of me until he came to the steps, then he climbed down the side of the quarry one step at a time, watching his feet as though he was not certain they would do what he expected. He never once looked at me. I told him how I sometimes spent the whole day jumping off the board and the rope, swimming as fast as I could between them. I told him I could swim the fifty yards or so to the board and back again, faster than anyone I knew. I said I was sorry I didn't tell him the truth, and I'd never lie to him again. I told him he could always count on getting the truth out of me from now on. "When I'm Robert's age, I'll jump," I said. "I know I will. I promise I will."

He never answered me, or if he did, I can't remember anything he may have said. In my memory of it, he walked silently in front of me, smiling enigmatically whenever he looked my way. It's possible he just listened to me. The only thing I know for certain is that he was not proud of me.

Of course, by the time I was Robert's age, Phil was long married, Robert was a freshman in college, and we didn't go to Sylvan Dell anymore.

The Day After

Nicole came back, I got up early, dressed quickly, and then folded the mattress back into the sleeper sofa. Sam was upstairs in my room and Nicole was sleeping on the couch in the den. I opened the curtains in the den and stood by the couch for a moment, looking at her. She snored slightly, her hair strewn across the pillow. I could smell her perfume—a vague suggestion of lilacs. I noticed her bare feet outside the blanket. Once, not so long ago, I could hold both her feet in my hand. She would come to me at night, her small white feet moist from a bath, her hair wet and fragrant, and she'd curl up in my lap and say, "Warm my toes, Daddy." Now her toes were painted red and there were calluses on her heels. I took a corner of the blanket and covered them, then I went upstairs to her old room.

I was astonished to see how ruined everything was. Through the years I had just stopped going in there, except to throw another box or two on the heap. The work it would take to clear it out and make it a room again was daunting, but I went ahead and got started. I carried all the boxes and magazines and old newspapers down to the basement. Then I dusted what furniture was left in the room: a dresser and two end tables, a single bed with four tall white posts. I vacuumed the rug, brushed all the cobwebs out of the corners, washed the windows, and cleaned out the closet. I washed new linens for the bed but realized I'd have to replace the mattress. It was so bowed to the ground and softened by years of supporting the deadweight of books and magazines in boxes, I was fairly certain if Nicole even sat on it, it would break. Still, in no time at all, the room was spotless, although it was kind of bare and cold looking. I decided I would go that very day and get her a new bed and maybe a matching nightstand or two. Something to make the room look lived-in again, and like it was all a part of my home.

When I thought Nicole had had enough rest, I went back to the den and began to clean up in there. She did not stir while I picked up and stacked newspapers, dusted the lamps and furniture. When I turned on the vacuum cleaner, which sounded like an airliner passing through the room, she turned herself almost petulantly and faced the back of the couch. I could not tell if she was sleeping or only pretending to. It seemed to me she was pissed off because I was making so much noise. I wondered how long a person could sleep before they were officially wasting life.

I did not want her help, but part of me was disappointed that she did not make the offer, anyway. I turned off the vacuum cleaner when I was finished and put it back in the closet. Then I crossed the room and stood by the couch, watching Nicole.

"Time to wake up," I said.

She groaned, not opening her eyes.

I wasn't sure if I wanted her to wake up. I knew it was impossible to fix up her room before she saw what I'd done already, but that's what I wanted. I was going to get her a new bed, new blankets, and a comforter. Maybe a lamp to set by her bed, in case she wanted to read before she went to sleep. All these things were germinating in my mind as I watched her stirring into wakefulness. I wished I had not disturbed her sleep.

She opened her eyes, trying to shield them from the light with the back of her hand. "What are you doing?" she asked, frowning against the light but trying to see me clearly.

"Nothing," I said.

"What time is it?"

"It's late," I said. "Almost noon."

She closed her eyes and turned her face back to the cushions of the couch. I waited there for a while, until it was clear she was not going to get up, then I went into the kitchen and made myself a cup of coffee. The house seemed to pause, after all my work. It was almost eleven-thirty.

As I sipped my coffee, I remembered Elizabeth and suddenly felt slightly feverish. What was I going to do? It seemed like she was way down at the end of some sort of road and I was at the beginning of it, and she was beckoning to me, entreating me to follow her. She was just so far ahead of me, wanting to be finally formed, finished, and ready to start a family. I didn't like the idea of not being new anymore. Does that make any sense? I still felt—well, there's no other way to say this, and maybe when I do, you'll understand more clearly—I felt *embryonic*. As though we were still—even after all of our time together—at the beginning of something, with all of its possibilities, all of them. Not just the one possibility.

I got up and poured the rest of my coffee in the sink. I didn't want to feed the terrible sense of apprehension that seemed to be simmering on the horizon. I concentrated on washing the cup, and put Elizabeth out of my mind.

Sam came down the stairs, running his hands through his hair and yawning. "What time is it?"

With some incredulity I said, "Five minutes to twelve." I looked out the kitchen window, hoping my tone of voice did not betray any sort of antipathy—even though I simply cannot approve of anyone sleeping until half the day has burned away. I know, not everybody is an early riser, and how long a person sleeps in the day is not usually a gauge of either ambition or talent. I am always nonetheless appalled whenever I'm confronted with a person who sleeps until noon. To soften things, I said, "You must have been really tired."

He sat down at the table. "Nicky get up yet?"

"No."

"Got any coffee?"

"Sure." I got it off the stove and poured him a cup. When I handed it to him, he smiled.

"Good morning," he said.

I smiled but said nothing.

"I could sleep the rest of the day," he said.

"Whenever I'm tempted to sleep most of any day," I said, "I try to remember that sleep is an easy, mostly kind sort of temporary death. I don't like the idea of being dead, so I don't make it a practice to sleep for most of the day."

"Sleep is rest for me."

"Yeah, well."

"No, really. I don't see it as death. It's rest."

"I was just remarking on the similarity between being unconscious, and being—"

"Yeah," he said. "I know. But sleep isn't like being dead for me. I always know when I'm doing it."

I sat back down and looked out the window. A long silence ensued, then I said, "You call her Nicky?"

"Sometimes." He yawned again. "She hates it."

"I used to call her Nicky."

Sam's eyes were not yet accustomed to the light. "What's it like out there?"

"Sunny. In the sixties."

He said he was glad to have some California weather.

"Can I use the Wagoneer today?" I said. "I'm going to be picking up some things for Nicole."

"What things?"

"A new bed. Stuff for her room."

"Want me to go with you?"

"If you'd like. I won't be gone long."

He went into the den and picked up his jacket.

Nicole turned over and faced him. "What's going on?"

He leaned down and patted her brow with his hand, gently pushing her hair back. "Go back to sleep," he whispered.

She smiled.

"We'll be right back," he said.

"Where are you going?"

"With your dad."

She struggled against the cushions but managed to sit up, still not fully awake. "I'm going to town," she said. "You want me to wait for you?"

Sam looked at me, and I shrugged. Then he turned back to her. "I don't know how long we're going to be."

"Well, I'm going exploring, is that OK with you?"

"Sure, but—"

"But what?"

"We're taking the Wagoneer."

She looked at me. "What?" As she said this, I tossed her my car keys. Sam intercepted them. He saved her from getting hit with them, because she had not moved a muscle. She was still staring blankly at me.

"Sorry," I said. "I thought you were looking."

She shook her head. Sam put the keys down on the table.

"Take my Hyundai," I said to her.

Her hair was tossed pretty badly, and I think she was embarrassed for me to see her like that. She forced a smile, then fell back on the couch and covered her head with the blanket.

"Want me to bring you back some ham or beef jerky or maybe a little jar of pickled pig's feet?"

I heard her mumble, "Very funny," under the covers.

Sam and I went to Sears, and I bought a double-bed frame, a mattress and box spring, sheets and a pillow, and two nightstands that matched the bed. I bought several blankets and a soft down comforter. Sam said he would go get the car and meet me at the loading dock so we could pick up the box spring, the nightstands, and the frame.

While I was waiting in line, I noticed a woman standing in front of me, wearing a dark blue dress with a white collar and black pumps. She was carrying in her arms several brightly colored baby clothes on tiny hangers. She was probably three or four years younger than me, and very attractive in a ruined sort of way. A slightly worn and tired expression on her face made her oddly alluring, as if her beauty had hardened suddenly from a prolonged period of anguish. Her hair smelled like roses. She turned and looked at me, and I asked if she thought I had se-lected appealing colors. She smiled and nodded her approval. It made me feel good. I liked her eyes, the smooth skin by her mouth.

I studied the baby things she was holding: a little pink dress with white lace around the sleeves and collar, a tiny pair of pajamas with matching booties so small I don't think they would have covered my thumb, a yellow blanket, and a pair of tiny black shoes. Nicole used to wear shoes like that and pretend to be Dorothy in Oz, clicking her heels to go back home. I could almost hear her innocent lost voice. I re-membered how it felt to hold Nicole on my hip or hoist her up on my shoulders, and then it hit me that maybe it wasn't such a bad thing that Elizabeth was pregnant. As a matter of fact, I was suddenly very happy about it. I can't explain this, but I actually wished Elizabeth were there so I could tell her how I felt—so I could proffer this joy as though it were a gift to her in some way. Also, it was such a pleasure to think of my circumstances without anxiety. It would have been fitting if a musi-cal score had been playing in the background. I believed I had crossed a threshold, and I wanted everybody to know about it.

I must have emitted some sort of sound, because the woman with the baby clothes turned and smiled.

"My daughter just came home," I said. I was feeling absolutely ter-rific. "She's been gone a long time."

The woman said, "She'll like those."

"Thank you." I thought I might tell this woman everything. She had a lovely soft voice and an open face, and her eyes looked back at me. I wanted her to know how wonderful I felt and that in an odd way she was responsible for it. I wished there was some way to return the favor, so I tried to strike up a conversation. "It's a wonderful day, isn't it?"

"Yes, it is."

"My wife—" I stopped, realizing what I had said. "My wife is pregnant."

"Oh, congratulations."

"You might say we're starting all over again."

"That's wonderful."

It was quiet for a while, but she was still looking at me. I said, "Are you shopping for your little girls?"

She held up the little dress. "This is for my granddaughter."

I was sincerely and properly shocked. "Your granddaughter."

"My *third* granddaughter."

All I could think to say was "God."

"Pardon?"

"I didn't think you were *that* old."

"I'm not. How old do I look?"

"I didn't mean that the way it sounded." But that was not true and I could see she knew it. There was no way I was going to try to guess her age.

She was looking off now, thinking, perhaps remembering something pleasant. Then she said, "It all goes so fast."

I nodded.

"It seems like only an hour ago I was buying clothes like this for my son. Now here I am shopping for one of his children."

"I can't believe you're a grandmother," I said.

"Sometimes I wish I wasn't." She looked at me again. "But not very often. I wasn't ready for it. It all happened so fast. All those years of raising children, it never hits you how quickly it's over and you're done with it."

I said nothing.

"Still, I don't often miss being a young mother, though sometimes I'd like to be young again."

I didn't know what to say.

"Not that I'd change a thing," she went on. "Having my children was the most wonderful experience of my life."

"Yes," I said. "Isn't it."

"Nothing, ever—no other activity or endeavor, no other success or triumph, absolutely nothing in life—is better or more deeply fulfilling than having children. All other experiences pale in comparison. In fact, all other experiences are cheap and shallow compared to it."

I nodded. I couldn't very well tell her that my experience with children had pretty much ended when my daughter was six years old. But I knew what she was talking about. Sometimes, when Nicole was little and I held her in my arms, I felt as though I was in a kind of paradise — as if this was all I'd ever need of Eden. And no experience of love is more bittersweet or more profound.

"I feel so sorry for those poor souls who have never had a child and who throw their love at a dog or cat. They can never understand what love really means."

I didn't know how to keep talking to her. I was still so embarrassed to find out she was a grandmother. She wouldn't have believed me if I said she looked like a young mother. She didn't look or act like any grandmother I'd ever seen. Both of my grandmothers were fat and dressed like late nineteenth-century immigrants: hair pinned up, dresses long and plain, black shoes with flat heels, and nylon stockings bunched at the knees. Both had puffy spotted hands and round faces. When they wore makeup, it looked like somebody had written all over a tetherball.

"Having grandchildren is almost as rewarding," she said. "In some ways, it's even more so, because you don't have so much of the responsibility for them."

"Yes," I said.

"Do you have grandchildren?" she asked. She was serious.

"I'm not even forty yet," I said.

"Well, guess what. I had my first grandchild when I was thirty-six. I'm only forty-one now."

"Really." My heart sank. She was Elizabeth's age. She was a grandmother. I *could* be a grandfather. I was not interested in this woman in any sort of sexual way, but do you see what was going on there? How could we relate — strange man to strange woman — if she was going to see herself as a grandmother, and if she saw me as a potential grandfather? What earthly good was her attractiveness if she was wrapped in such a matronly roll?

She smiled and turned back toward the counter, and I realized that our brief conversation had suppressed my mood. I felt as though a door had been slammed in my face, and I knew the Fates had placed her there to rob me of any hint of joy about my predicament. I watched her paying for all her items, now chatting with the clerk about her grand-children, and she seemed to grow older before my eyes.

Nicole wasn't home when Sam and I returned with the new bed, so we carried it up to her room to put it together. I was glad she wasn't home, because I wanted to have everything set up and surprise her. As I worked, Sam watched me. He was strangely silent, and I realized he was not so much a comedian when Nicole wasn't there to laugh at him. While I bolted the headboard to the frame, I caught him gazing at me as though he were waiting for me to say something.

"What is it?" I said.

"What's what?"

"Why are you looking at me like that?"

He smiled. "I don't know. You're suddenly in a big hurry."

"I want to get this done before she comes home."

I knelt on the carpet, turning a bolt with a small wrench, and Sam sat across from me with his legs crossed Indian-style, watching. "You don't think she's just going to move back in with you, do you?" he asked.

"No, I don't." I stopped and looked at him, feeling suddenly that the question was impertinent. "I really don't. But I want her to have her own room as long as she's here."

He nodded.

"This *is* her home, after all. Even if she doesn't live here."

My response took him aback, I think. He blinked, then for a brief moment his dark eyes seemed to register sadness. "Of course," he said.

Suddenly I felt sorry for him. "Look," I said. "I know I don't have any right—I just want to know. Are you and Nicole—do you have some sort of claim on her?"

"What do you mean?"

"I mean are you . . . involved."

"I'm involved, all right." He was not very good at subtle irony.

"Is she your girlfriend? Your—"

"Oh. No."

"No?"

"No. I'm just her friend."

"But that's not the way you want it."

He lowered his head, on the verge of a smile but still kind of sad looking. "She's keeping her options open."

I stopped working and stared at him. I didn't like the way he said that. It sounded almost contemptuous.

"Those aren't her words," he said. "She doesn't know."

"Doesn't know what?"

"How I feel."

"Why don't you tell her?"

"I've tried. It's harder than you think."

"I know it's hard. I'm not naive about it. I've had a bit of experience, remember."

"Not with Nicole."

"Are you afraid of her?"

"I'm afraid of what she'll say." He looked at me as if I ought to have understood that.

I did understand it, but I asked the question because I wanted to see if he did. After a short silence, I said, "You're both pretty young yet."

"Yes, I've heard that," he said.

"Someday—someday real soon—you'll say it to somebody."

He frowned. I'm sure he didn't have a clue what I was talking about. I wondered at that moment what my father would say to me when I told him about Elizabeth. One thing he could not say—for certain—was that Elizabeth and I were "both pretty young." And yet, my anxiousness over the whole thing, how I felt about telling him, made me feel like a teenager. So I was feeling pretty young again, myself.

"When are you old enough?" Sam wanted to know.

I started laughing. I could see he was pleased that he was a comedian again, even if by accident, but he had no idea what was so funny. "Maybe you're never old enough," I said.

I worked for a while longer, then he said, "I don't have any expectations. Maybe that's what being too young means." His voice was soft, almost a whisper.

He wasn't a bad kid. I think I was beginning to understand him. I remembered myself at that age—just starting in the world, believing I would be a good man worth knowing if I could just figure out how to dramatize my positive emotions and keep all the other ones to myself, believing romance would come to me exactly as it had come to every character I'd ever seen in the movies or read about in a book, and it would be perfect.

Sam didn't know what love was. No, not at all. But of course, he believed—as everyone else does, as I sometimes do in my more foolish moments—that he knew all about it.

"How long have you known Nicole?" I asked.

"I told you. All my life."

"Well, that's not really that long is it?"

"Not yet."

I looked at him. He was not smiling. "She's had plenty of boyfriends. I've watched them come and go. I think I'm the only person she really trusts, though."

I didn't say anything.

"And you, of course."

"Nah, I don't think she trusts me very much."

He said nothing, which seemed to be a sort of agreement with what I'd said. His silence saddened me.

"I had to hear about every one of them," he said.

"What?"

"All her boyfriends."

"That must have been tough," I said.

He smiled now. "She trusts me," he said again, ruefully.

Believe It or Not

A few days later I took Elizabeth and Nicole to Baltimore to visit my parents. Sam came with us. He kept imitating different actors as we drove along, and I tried to pretend it wasn't annoying. Elizabeth and Nicole were instant allies. They laughed hysterically at everything Sam said, and talked so easily to each other, I began to feel like an intruder. I don't know why it bothered me the way it did, except I was pretty well left out of the laughter and conversation. I felt as if I were the longtime and familiar chauffeur of a close, happy family. It made me sad and even a little envious, although I don't know if I could say who I envied. I guess when you're feeling left out, you never really know who to blame. Perhaps it was my fault. I know I was more than a little perplexed by how much fun the three of them were having while I drove.

My day with Nicole had not started out very well. She was quiet, almost pridefully distant, all morning, and I figured she was probably still smarting over our argument of a few days before. She had been in bed when I got home that first night—a circumstance for which I was very grateful. I didn't really want to deal with her, to be honest. Also, she might have noticed that I was worried, and I would have had to lie to her about Elizabeth. Some deranged part of my psyche actually believed the problem didn't exist as long as I didn't tell anyone about it.

I think Nicole may have been further peeved by what I made for breakfast the morning we went to Baltimore. She ate a few carrots and drank a glass of water, but I made myself a couple of eggs and some bacon. The whole house smelled absolutely wonderful. Then, while I was eating, I tempted Sam with a strip of the bacon.

I hadn't meant to. He happened to mention that when he used to be a meat eater he'd loved bacon.

"You probably still love it, then," I said.

"No."

"Oh, of course you do. You just don't eat it anymore."

Nicole, who was sitting across from me, munching on her carrots, said, "He doesn't like it anymore."

"You mean he doesn't eat it anymore."

"No. I mean—"

"I suppose I'd still like it if I ate it now," Sam said. He stood by the sink with a glass of orange juice in his hand.

"You'd love it. You said you used to love it."

Nicole snapped a carrot in her mouth.

"I don't want to argue about this," I said. "I'm sorry. I just wanted to point out that when you make an intellectual decision not to eat something you love, you don't just stop loving it. That's all."

She didn't answer me.

"Here, Sam. Let's see if I'm right." I held out the strip of bacon. "Just eat one or two."

"Will you stop it," Nicole said. She was completely exasperated.

Sam held up his hand.

"It's a small test," I said.

"You're just being obnoxious," said Nicole.

"If I remember, you used to love bacon, too."

"Now I hate it." There was a pause, and I'm certain she wanted to say "I hate you, too," but she thought better of it.

I spent the rest of the morning trying to be friendly. I could see that she was too serious to be teased very much, and I was fighting the gradual realization that she was sometimes not a very likable young woman. I didn't put this into words, but if I had thought about it at all I'm certain I would have come to fear that Nicole was becoming the sort of person I couldn't stand to be alone with for more than five minutes:

committed to a single idea, passionate about being passionate about that one idea, utterly humorless in all circumstances where the idea might come up, unwilling to believe there has ever been any other idea, and absolutely blind as to how she is being perceived. Know what I mean? Such people are basically impatient, unkind, and dictatorial. They dislike people who don't agree with them. And yet, they don't really want to change anybody's mind. They want to offend you until you are shamed into changing your behavior. They don't care what you think, only what you do. And the best of them are unable to distinguish between influence and insolence. The worst of them can't tell the difference between kindness and cruelty. They are the kind of people who will kill you for your own good.

So for most of the drive to Baltimore, Sam talked in the backseat—a running commentary on the scenery and the traffic from an assortment of Hollywood stars and recent politicians—and I tried to find something to say or do that would cancel the awkwardness between Nicole and me and allow me to break into the general camaraderie.

I really did want to be closer to her. I did not want to dislike her. I loved her too much.

As we were entering the city, I took advantage of an opening between Sam's rendition of Robert De Niro and Dustin Hoffman and said, "I can't wait until Mom and Dad see you, Nicole. They won't believe it."

I had turned around as I was driving, and she looked at me with this pained expression and said, "Watch the road."

I realized I had once again pointed out how fat she had been.

"They'll be very proud of how much weight you've lost," I said into the rearview mirror.

"The last time I saw Granddad, he wanted to bet me that I weighed more than he did."

"Good lord," Elizabeth said.

I said nothing.

From the back, W. C. Fields said, "Ah yes. Every pound was beautiful, though. She's all sweet loveliness."

Nicole scowled at him. "Knock it off."

"OK." He shrugged and stared out the window. I felt sorry for him.

"You've got to give them a chance," I said to Nicole.

"I will."

Elizabeth said, "Don't worry, honey. They don't like me very much, either."

"That's not true," I said.

"It's not?"

"They don't approve of us. They don't approve of me."

Now Nicole said, "Good lord."

Elizabeth laughed, then put her arm up on the seat and turned herself to face Nicole. "We'll stick together, OK?"

I was afraid she would announce that she was pregnant. I almost said something to her, but then Sam started talking like Jimmy Stewart and they were both laughing again.

When it quieted down, I tried to catch Elizabeth's eye, but she was looking out the window at the passing town houses and white marble steps. After a while I said, "Are you nervous?"

"A little bit." She didn't look at me, but something in her demeanor softened. It was as though she had recognized a source of anxiety and knew she would be able to master it with my help.

"You don't plan on making any announcements, do you?"

"What?" She looked at me, and I realized I had upset her. She knew what I'd said.

"Well, you know. I'd like to be the one to tell them." I spoke quietly, so Nicole and Sam wouldn't hear me.

"I swear, Henry. Sometimes—"

"What?"

"Nothing." Her eyes lost some of their fire and I felt like putting my arm around her, but she was leaning away from me, against the car door, so she could see Nicole and Sam in the backseat.

Beaver Cleaver said, "Gee, how much farther is it to this place, Mr. Porter?"

"We're almost there."

74

Nicole was smiling, watching the road, her head tilted slightly forward. Jesus, she looked like her mother. It was difficult to look at her. She seemed to remember something, then she said, "Are Granny and Granddad still so religious?"

"Not so's you'd notice."

"Really."

"They still have a few of the pictures and all, but they don't talk about it to me anymore."

She looked relieved. "I remember they had a picture of Jesus in the hallway, and when you walked by it, the eyes would follow you across the room."

"You're kidding," Sam said.

Elizabeth laughed. "They were really *sad* eyes, too."

I said, "It was one of those holograms, or whatever you call them. The eyeballs had three positions so, when you passed in front of the picture, they seemed to move and follow you."

"It was eerie," Nicole said.

"I just thought it was tacky," Elizabeth said.

"Jesus not only saves, he scans," Gregory Peck said.

I pretended to laugh. Nicole and Elizabeth really did think it was funny.

"They've taken that picture down," I said.

"Thank god," Nicole said.

"They don't talk too much about religion anymore," Elizabeth said, "but they still quietly judge people. They're very good at doing that."

I thought of her pregnancy and had a sudden blast of fear. Not so much because I feared the judgment of my parents, which I knew would not be very pleasant, but because the idea of being a new father again, at my age, set my head spinning like a globe. I didn't think I could do it. I didn't know if I wanted to. At some level, I knew I had to get out of it, somehow. Without leaving Elizabeth in the lurch.

You see what sort of predicament I was in? I wanted Elizabeth to have her baby, but I didn't really want her to have *my* baby. I wanted her to stay with me, but I didn't want her to stay with me if she was going to have a baby. The more I thought about these things, the more terrified I became.

At a stoplight I looked at my face in the rearview mirror. Since the age of fifteen I've had thick brown eyebrows and blue eyes, like Nicole's. The dark brows always make me look a little sad, I think. But fear never really registers. (When I played football in high school, people thought I was fearless. Only *I* knew I ran so fast because I was afraid of broken bones.) I've always thought my forehead is a little too high, but my nose and mouth are long enough that it doesn't look as though my features have dropped to the bottom of my face. Most of my life people have said I look a little like Andrew Jackson—except my hair is dark and I don't scowl so much.

Looking at myself then in the mirror, I managed to think of high school and those other days, and I got ahold of myself. I was presently very glad that Elizabeth was there. Time seemed less constricted because she was there, laughing and apparently happy. It consoled and calmed me when I remembered that I would have perhaps several days before it would be necessary to do anything about her condition. Right then, I didn't have to tell Nicole or my parents or anyone. I could go on as if I didn't know yet. These little facts sustained me as we pulled into my father's perfectly black driveway.

Even at my age, I was a little nervous around my father. The earliest memories of him included the black judicial robe he wore every day on the bench. He towered over me like God's boss. And he'd judged me enough times when I was a kid that perhaps a small portion of my fear had to do with what I might try to do to him if I ever lost *my* temper.

Still, he was my father. A tall gray powerful man. He could take a bottle cap between his thumb and forefinger and fold it in half. At sixty-nine, he could still do this. He'd grab my hand and squeeze it until the bones touched. He had a terrific sense of himself—a grand adult vision of the world as his own province.

He was very happy to see Nicole. "My, my, look at you."

Nicole had gotten out of the car and approached him like a young princess. My old man seemed to study her while he held to my hand.

"Why, she's a young woman now. And so thin."

"That's right."

"Quite beautiful."

Nicole lowered her head, almost as though she were about to curtsy. Then Dad saw Sam and Elizabeth. "Who's this?"

"Sam's my friend," said Nicole.

"Hello, Judge Porter," Elizabeth said.

"Yes, Elizabeth. How are you?"

Sam offered his hand, and Dad let go of me and took it. "Glad to meet you."

"Ouch," Sam said. "Ouch. Ouch."

Dad let go. "Come on in the house."

Sam looked at me as though I were responsible. He held his hand out lamely and shook his fingers to get the blood back. I could tell by the look on his face that he wished he'd stayed home.

Mother was unbelievably happy to see Nicole. She escorted her into the living room and showed her pictures of all her cousins and aunts and uncles.

The house smelled wonderful.

"What's cooking?" I said.

"Oh, you'll see," Mother said.

"Is it lamb?"

She smiled, happy I guessed it. My mother made the best leg of lamb in the Milky Way. It would have altered the course of history if it had been offered to Napoleon at Elba. He would never have left the place. I turned to Nicole, expecting to see excitement on her face—she loved my mother's roast lamb when she was a little girl—but her somber expression reminded me of her political affiliation.

"Oh, I forgot."

"What's the matter?" Mother said.

"Nicole eschews meat," I said. I put special emphasis on the word *eschews*.

"What?"

"She doesn't eat meat," Elizabeth said curtly.

Dad looked at me as if I'd announced that Nicole wanted to piss in the potato salad.

"She's a vegetarian," I said.

"Certainly she can eat my leg of lamb," Mother said.

"No," I told her, "I don't think so. She'd eat a leg of carrot, though."

My mother is a delightful, strong, sometimes irritating woman. She doesn't listen very well—although we've had plenty of doctors tell us that her hearing is quite normal. She is extremely stubborn—the sort of person who will continue to try to light the candle with the wet matches until she's struck every match in the package. She once told me that she could never vote for Jimmy Carter, because he had a southern accent. "I won't vote for a man who says 'Lard' when he means 'Lord.'" She couldn't believe Nicole would say no to her leg of lamb. "Honey, don't you remember how delicious lamb can be? You used to love it."

"I'm sorry, Grandma," Nicole said. "I know it's probably wonderful."

Mother turned to me and said, "Does the poor thing belong to some religious group that won't let her eat meat?"

Nicole and I both said, "No."

"Certainly she doesn't choose—"

"She chooses," I said, with finality.

Nicole looked at me.

"Well, whatever you say." Mother seemed slightly befuddled. Then she said, "I can't imagine a person wanting only leaves and roots to eat." Nicole went over to her and kissed her on the cheek. It was a sweet thing to do. My father was smiling and I felt pretty good, myself.

"It's so good to see you," Mother said.

"The lamb smells wonderful," Elizabeth said.

We sat around and chatted for a while. After Nicole had seen pictures of the whole family, my mother disappeared into the kitchen and came back with a plate of carrots, cauliflower, and mushrooms. In the middle, surrounded by all the vegetables, were a few pieces of rolled up ham.

"The ham's for you," she said to me.

I watched Nicole eating the mushrooms. She wanted to be pleasant, but I think the ham was starting to look good to her.

My father insisted that she call him Doug instead of Granddad. I felt sort of embarrassed for Elizabeth. He had always let her call him Judge Porter, and apparently that wasn't going to change.

Just before dinner my mother asked Nicole how her mother was.

"She's as happy as ever," Nicole said. "She's going to celebrate her tenth wedding anniversary this summer."

There was an unbearable silence. As far as my mother and father were concerned, I was still married to Catherine; I would always be married to Catherine until one of us died. This was what the priest had said when we were married, and that was that. As you may know, Catholics don't approve of change, and they are especially unhappy if you change your spouse. My father looked at me and said, "Well, after all this time, I guess she's entitled to celebrate."

I said, "She really is. She could make ten years seem like twenty."

Elizabeth smirked. It was the beginning of a laugh that she quickly suppressed when she saw the look on my father's face.

"I hope she'll remain happy," the old man said.

"I second that," I said. "Fervently."

"I'm happy for her," Mother said.

"She got tired of him throwing money away," Dad said to Elizabeth. There was a smile on his face, but he was serious.

"That's right," I said. "I just kept throwing money away. After a while, I started burning it. Did you know it makes green smoke?"

"Let's talk about something else," my mother said.

Nicole sat on the arm of a chair next to my father. She swung her leg and observed the conversation as if she were enjoying it. "I think if your mother wants to be happy," Dad said to Nicole, "she deserves it."

"I think so, too," I said. "I think she deserves whatever happens to her."

Elizabeth squeezed my arm. I don't know if she was trying not to laugh or if she was telling me to stop.

"She's happy," Nicole said. "And that makes me happy."

"That's what it's all about," I said. "Getting happy. I'm happy she's happy. I'm happy that you're happy that she's happy. I hope that she's happy that I'm happy that you're happy that she's happy." My father's expression did not change, but he lowered his head a bit, still watching me, so that his brows (I inherited my thick brows from him) seemed to sink over the tops of his eyes.

I said to him, "Are you happy that I'm happy that she's happy that her mother's happy?"

He studied my face for a moment, then he said to Nicole, "Did you go to mass this morning?"

She looked at me.

I turned to Elizabeth. "Are you happy that I'm happy that my father's happy that Nicole's happy that her mother's happy?"

"Henry," Mother said, half scornfully. She was definitely amused.

"Sam," I said, "are you happy that Elizabeth's happy that—"

"Dad," Nicole said.

"He doesn't know when to quit," Mother said.

"I'll feel much better after I've had a beer or two," I said.

"I don't have any beer," Dad said.

"Whiskey, then. Whatever."

"Are you upset, dear?" Suddenly Mother was very concerned.

"Of course not."

I saw my father look away, as though he was getting bored and ready to go into some other room.

"You seem so ... so ... unsettled at the moment."

"I'm not at all. I wish I could go to Catherine's anniversary party. I couldn't go to the wedding because I'm allergic to rice."

I really was tempted to tell them about Elizabeth. I wanted to announce her pregnancy and our wedding plans all at once, right at that moment. I would have if I'd thought I was actually going to get married again. The problem was, I didn't know what I was going to do about

Elizabeth and I didn't want to think about it, either. But now it seemed that I was being cornered into thinking about it.

I've gone over all this a million times since that day, and I still don't understand why hearing my mother and father talk about Catherine's happiness disturbed me so much. It wasn't something in their attitude. My mother tried very hard not to show her contempt for Catherine, and Dad made a modest effort not to show his contempt for me. I am certain it wasn't because I still loved Catherine. Except to nod my head and wave from a distance of at least thirty yards—that's how far it was from the street in front of her house to the front door—I hadn't seen Catherine for more than ten years. I did not care about her. It didn't make me happy or sad that she was having a good life.

Maybe I just hated the feeling that circumstances were beginning to gang up on me, as though the whole world would stop if I didn't do something. As though the Fates were watching me, waiting for me to decide what to do so they could get their cigar-stained fingers in and screw everything up.

I never liked that kind of stress.

Monday

I stopped at a floristry and ordered one dozen long-stemmed roses for Elizabeth. I had been sitting in my car at a traffic light, on my way back from Highland Park, and I had been thinking about how things had gone at Dad's. As I was scanning the stores surrounding the intersection, I noticed a man coming out of the shop with a handful of white flowers. He looked cheerful, sure of what he wanted.

It hit me how good it would feel to be cheerful again.

When I pulled into the parking lot in front of the florist's shop, I saw another young man coming out of the store, carrying a bouquet of yellow roses. He reached into his pocket for his car keys and looked up just as I was getting out of my car.

"Spring's the time for blossoms," he said. He had dark perfectly manicured hair. He settled himself in the front seat of his car, a movement that reminded me of youth and effortless motion. I stepped past his open door, nodding when he looked at me.

"My mom," the man said. "Her birthday."

"I'm going to get some for my girlfriend."

The young man's face changed. His eyes seemed to drift down momentarily, as if he were noticing something about my shoes, then he smiled and started his car. "Have a nice day."

I waved, suddenly aware of how foolish I sounded talking about a girlfriend at my age. I wanted to tell him I'd gotten her pregnant and I was trying to figure out what to tell my mother and father.

The florist was a short heavyset woman with tightly curled brown hair, cut short, and brown horn-rimmed glasses. When she had boxed my roses, she asked me what I wanted to say on the card.

"I don't know," I told her. "What do you recommend?"

"Well, what's the occasion?"

"No occasion. Just—" I stopped. She waited there, a pen in her puffed fingers.

"What if I just say 'with love' and sign my name?"

She started to write, but she didn't look pleased.

"No, good, huh."

"If that's what you want to say."

"How about this: 'I really think we can work things out'?"

She shrugged.

"'I'm sorry about my reaction to the news. I thought you were on the pill'?"

Now, she frowned.

"Just kidding," I said.

"What do you want me to say on the card?"

"Well, I just don't know."

She waited there impatiently.

"Just let me have the card and I'll write something on it."

She handed it to me. I wrote, "Looking forward to our future. We'll work things out. Love, Henry."

She looked at the card, then at me.

"I'm going to try," I said. "I really am going to try."

"You want me to write *that* on the card?"

"No. I'm just—I was just thinking out loud."

When I got home I found Nicole in the kitchen, cutting up broccoli. She had just sliced an onion, so her eyes were red and watery. She looked up briefly when I walked in, then went on with the knife as I stood by the counter watching her, wondering what sort of expression my face must have registered when I first saw her there making herself so at home.

She pointed to the box of roses. "Who are those for?"

"The flowers?" I put them on the table. "They're for Elizabeth."

"Are they roses?"

"Red roses. Where's Sam?"

"He's gone to the store for me."

"What are you up to?"

"I'm fixing dinner."

"You are?"

"If you don't mind."

"That depends." I had this vision of myself eating sawdust and bark.

"Don't worry. Sam went to get some fish for you." She was not wearing a lot of makeup, and her hair, which was freshly washed, appeared silky and delicate. She was wearing the tank top and shorts again, with thin leather sandals. Her skin was smooth, and her hands seemed new and perfect, the nails white, unpainted now and naturally curved. She concentrated on what she was doing, her hands working the knife, and as I watched her, I realized with unexpected pride how really beautiful she was. She would not be a movie star—her nose was a little too long for that, and there was a slight downturn of her lower lip when she smiled, which made her whole face seem slightly out of balance. But her eyes were large and an uncommon shade of luminous blue, surrounded by dark lashes and perfectly shaped, thinly defined brows. She did not need to use makeup at all, although, with the light color of her eyes and hair, and the thin outline of her brows, she looked almost preternatural without it.

I took off my sports jacket. "What are you and Sam going to eat?"

"You'll see."

I threw my jacket over the back of a chair and walked across to her. She did not stop what she was doing.

"So you know how to cook?"

"A few things."

I put my hand on her shoulder and immediately regretted it. She seemed to stiffen. She was small-boned, soft, and her cool smooth skin embarrassed me. After an awkward pause, I withdrew my hand. "I remember when you used to pretend to cook for me."

She didn't say anything. I watched her for a moment, then I said, "It wasn't so long ago." I went to the bar in the living room and mixed myself a martini, then I came back into the kitchen and sat down. Nicole finished with the broccoli and started rinsing lettuce at the sink.

"I don't suppose you want a drink," I said. With the water running she could not hear me. While I watched her I tried to imagine what we might talk about. I felt this obligation to say something, anything. My day at the track had been average, so I didn't want to talk about that.

I should probably have told her about Elizabeth, but I just couldn't make myself do it. I didn't even want to think about it. Anyway, I was hoping that she already knew—that somehow Elizabeth had already told her.

When she was finished with the lettuce and had turned the water off, I said again, "Have a drink?"

She looked at me. "Sure."

In a way I was disappointed. "What do you want?"

"What is that?" She pointed to my glass.

"It's a martini."

"What's in it?"

"Vermouth and gin."

"What's vermouth?"

"You really don't know what vermouth is?"

"I've heard of a martini, and I've heard of gin. I've never heard of vermouth." She took a towel from the counter and wiped her hands.

"It's a kind of wine." I got up and went to the bar. "Come here. I'll show you how to make one."

She followed me into the living room, but she didn't go to the bar. She sat down on the couch. "I'm tired."

While I was fixing the martini, I said, "What'd you do today?"

"I read Saturday's newspaper."

"Oh?"

"That's right."

I said nothing.

"What are the red roses for?"

"Elizabeth."

"No, what's the occasion?"

"No occasion."

"I like her."

"I must have mentioned Elizabeth before. I've been going with her for several years."

"We haven't really talked for several years."

I had nothing to say to that. I handed her the drink. "There you go. It should have an olive or two in it, but this will have to do."

She sipped it, made a face. "It's awful."

"Some things you've got to acquire a taste for."

She took another sip, closed her eyes and seemed to cringe. I drank mine down, then held up the empty glass. "You're not supposed to drink it quite so fast."

"I don't know how you can stand it." Her eyes were still watery from having sliced the onions, but now the gin seemed to increase her discomfort. "I really don't think I will acquire a taste for this stuff." She smiled, looking at me directly for the first time since I had walked in, and for a brief moment of silence I could not look away from her. I was worried that she might think I was on the verge of saying something important, so I was desperate to say words that mattered to her. Like an idiot I said, "You're very pretty."

She averted her eyes.

I set my glass down on the table. The late evening sun glanced off the rim of the glass and gleamed on the wall across from me. She was not looking at me, and I was conscious of her quiet breathing. I could not think of what I should say to her.

Finally she said, "Can I see the pictures you showed Sam the other day?"

"Sure." I felt relieved, and rose from the couch too quickly. "They're just in here." I moved toward the den. She came after me, still carrying the martini.

"So, are you and Elizabeth . . ." She didn't finish the sentence.

I stopped and looked at her. "I might end up marrying her."

"No kidding."

"It's possible."

"She's a very nice lady."

"You two seemed to get along," I said.

"I can't imagine what it will be like to have so many parents."

I didn't say anything.

"Especially after having only two for so long." She blinked, as though she had not expected to say that.

I thought it best not to acknowledge it. I said, "You're not getting drunk are you?"

"Of course not." She started to take another taste of her martini but I reached over and gently took the glass away from her.

"You don't have to acquire a taste for it tonight." For a second I was embarrassed, and I really didn't like where the conversation was taking us. I took a long sip, watching Nicole over the rim of the glass. Then I said, "After a while there, it didn't seem like you wanted me around."

A long silence ensued. Then she said, "I'm going to tell you something Mom said I shouldn't tell you."

"Why?"

"I don't know why. Just now, I feel like doing it."

"Well," I said, gulping the rest of her martini, "should I sit down for this?"

"I have seventeen hundred dollars."

She peered into my eyes. I heard a car pass by outside, thought briefly of Catherine. In spite of all the years since she had left me, I could still recall the numberless times I would hear a car door slam or someone stepping onto my front porch and how the image of her returning, as on any normal day, would flash across my memory.

Nicole put her head down.

"What's the matter?" I said.

"I just wanted to tell you."

"Tell me what?"

She looked up, meeting my gaze again. "I have seventeen hundred dollars."

"That's what you were not supposed to tell me?"

"Yes."

I started to laugh, then turned from her, beginning to realize what Catherine still believed about me. "Jesus Christ," I said.

"What?" She reached for my arm as I moved away.

"Nothing." Then I stopped and turned back to her. "Thank you for telling me."

"It's in cash. If you need a little money, just ask me."

"I don't need any more of your money. I won't ever need it." I reached into my pocket and took out my wallet.

"You don't have to give me anything."

"Yes, I do." I gave her a thousand. "Now you have twenty-seven hundred bucks."

"I can't take this." She tried to give it back, but I took her hand in both of mine and folded it around the money.

"I want you to have it. It's your graduation present. Use it this summer." There was a long pause while she looked at my hands, then I let go of her and went and got the photo albums and set them on the coffee table. "Here. Come on and look at these now. These are the ones with you and your mother in them."

She put the money in her pocket and sat down. I thought she looked as though she might begin to cry. She took one of the albums, placed it in her lap, and opened it. I went around to the lamp next to her and turned it on. She seemed to open the first book with reverence. Her hands brushed lightly over the first page, as though she wanted to caress the glossy photos there of her mother and father standing in a green yard, holding a pink infant between them, and smiling innocently at the camera.

Later That Night

I got up the courage to take the flowers over to Elizabeth's. They were still pretty fresh, but I opened the box and sprayed them lightly with water before I left the house. They smelled wonderful.

Outside, the air was moist, and it looked like it might rain. Clouds kept blocking the sun, but there was not much wind and it was very pleasant riding in the car with the windows down.

Elizabeth had just gotten home from a long meeting at work and she seemed embarrassed to see me, but she smiled when I put the box of roses in her hands.

"What are you doing here?" she said.

I followed her into the house, watched her as she arranged the flowers in a tall blue vase. She set them on the dining room table, then stood back to look at them. She was wearing a gray suit, black high heels, a white blouse with a black loosely knotted tie. You would never have known she was pregnant.

"You really are perfectly beautiful," I said.

She glanced at me and then back to the flowers. We stood there for a long time, not saying anything. She seemed determined not to look at me until I said something, and I had no idea what to say. I had told her she was beautiful, which was definitely true. She had nothing to say to that. I didn't think it would be appropriate to say she smelled real good, even though that was also true. Her perfume nearly intoxicated me, and it sent the idea of sex right to the foreground of my mind. I remembered all the times I'd brushed my lips against the smooth fragrant skin of her breasts, and this quickened all my senses. But I was not a complete idiot. I knew that the worst thing I could do at that moment was to try to seduce her. I needed to get her to seduce me. If I could. I started sending out powerful thought signals, *willing* her to suggest that we sit down and have a drink, relax a bit before deciding on what to have for dinner.

She looked at me again, and like a parrot I said, "You really are perfectly beautiful."

"You said that, Henry."

I looked at the floor.

"Where's Nicole?"

"She's home. I left her home."

'Have you had dinner yet?"

This perked me up, so I lied. "No. I thought we might relax for a while, maybe have a drink or two before we eat."

"Whatever you say." She didn't seem very enthusiastic. In fact, a casual observer might have described her as fairly listless.

"Are you all right?"

"I'm fine, Henry. I'm so fine I can't stand it."

"I wanted to talk to you."

Now she seemed less enervated. "Go ahead."

"Let's have a drink first."

We went into the living room, and I fixed us both a whiskey and water. I didn't have a plan. How could I, being the victim of several overwhelming aspirations and purposes? In spite of a truly powerful desire to continue our relationship, I was aware of an equally powerful need to get her to see the foolishness of her pregnancy. This seeming clarity was counterbalanced by my wish to please her—even if it meant proposing marriage—and an equally capable longing to have one more chance at fatherhood. Are you beginning to see my problem? I wanted with equal passion contradictory things. This thoroughly paralyzed me at the very moment when calm decisiveness was absolutely required. Can you imagine how speechless you might be in circumstances like that?

We sipped our drinks for a while, both of us thinking. I proposed a toast, but the only thing I could think to say was, "To the future."

She gave me a wry smile.

"To our future," I corrected myself.

After another silence, she said, "Henry, what are you afraid of?"

"What am I afraid of?"

"Yes."

"What do you mean?"

"What part don't you understand?"

"The part about being afraid of something."

"Look, let's be honest, OK? Tell my what you're afraid of. Can't you do that?"

I said, "I'm afraid of cancer. Stroke. Heart disease. Dying in a fire. Drowning. Getting stabbed. I don't want anybody to shoot my balls off—"

"Stop it."

"I'm sorry. I was only answering the question."

"That's not what I meant."

I knew it wasn't what she meant, but I resented her question. Women always assume a man doesn't want to get married and start a family because he's afraid of something. It's got nothing to do with fear. It has to do with logic.

Of all the irrational things human beings engage in—war, terrorism, lynching, rioting, mass-marketing, politics, religion, advertising— only marriage is bereft of a winnable goal and is therefore completely irrational. According to the statistics, five out of ten marriages end in divorce and seven out of ten are unhappy or dysfunctional. If you went in for a biopsy and the doctor told you, "Don't worry, seven out of ten of these are malignant," would you be greeting this news with unfettered optimism? I'd be in a panic if he said seven out of ten are *not* malignant. And yet, people get engaged and married with sincere expectations of an earth-altering permanent arrangement. The marriage "vow" is really only a temporary understanding. It should read like this:

Do you, Henry, promise to love, honor, and cherish Elizabeth— as long as she doesn't change into some other person you can't stand and as long as she's still fairly attractive or until you change into some other person she can't stand, and as long as you're fairly civilized, or should it go that long, until one of you gets bored, or until old age, nursing homes or hospices or death do you part?

The trouble is, you see, when people get married they see themselves as being the way they are forever, when it's just not how the world works. Elizabeth looked like a cross between Demi Moore and Angelica Huston. But someday she's going to look like a cross between Menachem Begin and a basset hound. What would happen to her personality when she couldn't bear to look in a mirror anymore? You don't have to trouble yourself with how I would look by then. My eyes were already beginning to sag. I might end up looking like a blowfish. And in any case, I would have begun the long twilight battle most men have to wage with mucous membranes, sinuses, and their prostate glands. Would Elizabeth and I love one another then? Would we be passionate lovers then?

I know. I know. Love is not about how a person looks. I've heard that and it's probably true, or it ought to be. But sex *is* about how a person looks. That's probably one of the major reasons people do it in the dark.

So Elizabeth wanted me to propose marriage. I knew she wanted me to do that, and I knew she knew I knew it. We sat there sipping whiskey and water, waiting for something to change. A storm would have been nice. Or a ringing phone. If the Fates had been in a kind mood, something would have happened.

Finally I said, "I've given this a lot of thought."

She looked at me.

"I want to be completely honest here."

"I think I know what you're going to say."

"You do?"

She bowed her head, staring into her drink.

"I can't talk to you without making you sad," I said. I don't know why her predictions made me so angry, except that they put a hell of a lot of pressure on me to be unpredictable, which seemed vaguely manipulative. No, I take that back. Not *vaguely* manipulative. *Precisely* manipulative—part of that skill women develop looking into makeup mirrors three hours a day.

"I'm going to write it all down," I said.

"What?"

"I can't talk to you about this. I have to write it down and let you read it."

"Is it that bad?"

"No. To tell you the truth, I don't know. I really don't."

She put her drink on the coffee table. "You don't have to write it down, Henry."

I swirled the ice in my drink.

"This isn't happening to you," she said.

"It is, too, happening to me. It's just that I'm taken by surprise."

She started to get up, but I grabbed her arm. "You want this to go badly, don't you?" I said.

This startled her.

"You want this. You're orchestrating it."

"How can you say that?"

"I'm not talking about the baby. I'm talking about what's happening to us right now. You've upset yourself and now you're trying to upset me."

She pulled her arm free and stood up. "I'm not upset. I just don't know what you want me to do."

"I thought we were going to dinner."

"I don't feel like it now." She went into the kitchen, and I followed her. She poured the rest of her drink in the sink. "I shouldn't be drinking."

"Why not?"

"I've read it may be bad for the baby."

"The baby," I said, suddenly conscious of that third presence—the incipient soul that waited inside my girlfriend for the light. It was almost as if an inanimate object like a curtain or an ashtray had interrupted our conversation; had spoken words we failed to understand. "The baby," I said again.

She looked at me, and for a brief moment I thought she was going to laugh. "This ... situation ... is not as bad as you think, Henry."

"I don't know what to think."

"I'm not unhappy."

"Neither am I."

I went to her and took her into my arms. She seemed so much more grown-up and self-possessed now that she was pregnant. I was afraid I couldn't joke with her anymore; even laughter seemed irreverent. I did not remember feeling that way when Catherine was pregnant with Nicole.

Elizabeth stepped back and leaned against the kitchen counter, watching my eyes.

"I'm not going anywhere," I said. "I'm not going to pressure you into anything."

She really focused on me when I said that. Her eyes looked positively black. "What do you mean by that?"

"I'm trying to say the right thing here," I said, "but it's not working out."

"You don't have to 'say the right thing.'"

"Of course I do. If I don't you'll ..." I was smart enough not to finish the thought.

"If you don't I'll what?"

"Nothing."

"What? What were you going to say?"

"Let's just go eat."

"Tell me."

"I wouldn't try to get you to do anything."

"Anything like what?"

"You know."

"No, I don't. Tell me."

"An abortion."

Her face changed to stone. "I'm not going to do that."

"I know. I know."

"I can't believe you'd suggest such a thing."

"I *didn't* suggest it."

The shocked look on my face must have convinced her, but I'm sure I noticed a slight convulsion by the corner of her mouth. I couldn't tell if she was trying not to cry or laugh. She said, "Why are we talking about it, then?"

"We're not talking about it."

"Well, you brought it up."

"No, I didn't. Honestly, hon." When I called her hon she softened a bit. But she did not change her expression.

She stood there staring at me for a moment, then she said, "If you don't mind, I really am too tired to go anywhere tonight."

"You want me to order out?"

"I think I'm just going to go to bed. Do you mind?"

"No." I could tell she wanted me to leave. As I turned to go, she reached and took hold of my arm.

"Good-bye, Henry," she whispered.

"Good-bye?"

She blinked, smiling softly. "Good night."

"I'm going to write it all down. Everything."

"You do that, dear." She kissed me on the cheek.

I locked the door on my way out. I figured that really was the least I could do.

That Weekend

I decided to get away from the pressures of the moment and take in some fresh air. Nicole, Sam, and I went to the night races at Charles Town, a little place in West Virginia, right across the state line. It's only about ninety miles or so from my house. The track is called Shenandoah Downs. It's a cheap run-down sort of place, with mostly low-grade animals and a fairly small turnout each night. In fact, you could bet a hundred dollars on a three-to-one shot and the odds might shift to even money just from your bet. Still, it was a track and it was horse racing.

I promised Nicole she could get french fries or a pizza or some other meatless entrée at the track, and she seemed happy to come along. I think she wanted to see me gambling, just to know what it was like. Or maybe she figured she owed me for setting her up so nicely in her old room. I had just about remodeled it by the time I was finished. Sam said it looked like a room you'd see in a magazine. When Nicole first saw how I'd fixed it up, she cried. She tried to hide it, but I saw the tears. She hugged me around the neck and said, "Thank you, Dad."

"No trouble at all," I said. "Welcome home."

She didn't deny that she cried, but she seemed supremely embarrassed whenever Sam mentioned it. He said something about it on the way to the track and I thought she might reach out and pinch his ear if he didn't shut up. I swear, only a woman can scold so thoroughly with a look. Sam bowed his head and apologized without saying anything — a skill most men develop because of the wordless scorn of women. In the end I was glad she showed her displeasure, because during the entire drive to West Virginia, Sam didn't imitate a single celebrity.

When we walked past the paddock at Charles Town, I was momentarily transported by the odor of horses, sweat, manure, and hay. The wild grass that grew in the infield and around the white fence posts was freshly cut and dark green. Just walking along the fence of the track made me feel young and full of hope and belief.

I bought a program and a racing form for each of us, and then we took seats out of the late-setting sun in the grandstand, away from the crowd. At every track, the grandstand smells of popcorn and cigar smoke mixed with the faint odors of Old Spice, beer, and whiskey. You don't want to spend an hour at a racetrack if you can't stand the smell of tobacco—especially cigars. I tried to study my form while Nicole harried me with questions. Sam had been to a track before, so he knew what he was doing. I wanted to be patient with Nicole and teach her, but it was nearing post time for the first race and I wanted to handicap the daily double.

"What are all those numbers?" Nicole said, pointing across the track at the tote board.

"Those are the odds," Sam said.

"They're up there on the TV screen, too," I said, without looking up from my racing form.

"Tell me how to read it."

I explained it to her. She listened, still watching the lights on the board across the track. I pointed out that the numbers by one horse were four to one. That meant the horse paid four to one on a two-dollar bet. "See," I said, "if you bet two dollars on a four-to-one shot and he wins, you'll get back eight, plus the two you bet."

"That sounds easy enough."

"It's not," Sam said.

"It can be," I said. "As long as you know what you're doing and you read the form carefully."

Nicole looked at me. "That newspaper tells you who will win?"

"Well, sort of."

After a while, Sam announced he was going to bet on the four horse. I thought it was a bad choice and I told him so.

"Why?" Nicole asked.

I placed the racing form across my lap and hers and showed her how to read past performances. I pointed out that while the four horse was an attractive bet at four to one, he had never done very well against the three, a front-running chestnut named Top Brandy, who was favored in the race.

"So Top Brandy is going to win?"

"Top Brandy is the favorite, but I don't think he's going to win."

"Why not?" Nicole and Sam spoke at the same time.

"Foolish Pleasure."

Sam looked at his program, and Nicole watched over his shoulder. "The five horse?" Sam said.

"Right. Bet on him."

"Why?"

"Now you can both learn something," I said. Sam was on my right, and Nicole on my left, and I had the racing form spread out half on my lap and half on Nicole's. "Look at this," I said, pointing to the line on Foolish Pleasure. "He's been racing at Laurel and Highland Park, in Maryland—both much better tracks than this one—and he's been racing against higher-class animals." I pointed to the past performances. Sam leaned in so he could see. We were all studying the form, and we must have looked like we were working together to solve a complex equation. "Foolish Pleasure's last two races have been twenty-five-thousand-dollar stakes races."

"What's a stakes race?" Nicole said.

"It's a damn sight higher-class race than we got here."

"I see what you mean," Sam said.

I watched Nicole study the form. She was really getting into it. I could see the mystery of the racing form was giving way and she was beginning to discover the joy of figuring things out for herself. It becomes, in its own way, like a complicated puzzle that you know you can solve if you're patient enough and have enough time. She was enjoying herself, even if it seemed like too much to remember.

"See," I said to her, "this is a sixty-five-hundred-dollar claiming race. That means these nags are for sale at that price for anybody who wants to claim them. It's also what they call a maiden race, which means none of these horses has ever won a race. But the five horse, Foolish Pleasure, he's been in very high-class races, with some high-class animals."

"He's never run a step," Sam said. "Never finished in the money."

"You can't just look at that," I said. "He held his own in the last race. Came in fourth in a class field."

"Still he's never been in the money."

"A horse is an athlete," I said. "This one has been up against much tougher competition in the past and held his own. It's sort of like putting a pitcher like Nolan Ryan in a Little League game. You'd have to bet on Ryan, right?"

Sam just looked at me.

"Bet this animal. The five. You'll make some money."

"You going to play him in the double?" Sam asked.

"Sure. I'm putting him with the eight horse in the second race."

Sam stared at his form. Nicole moved over next to him and was now looking over his shoulder. I felt oddly detached—as if I were observing a young couple I did not know. They *were* a young couple, although it was clear Nicole did not know it yet. I couldn't believe what good friends they were. Sam behaved in front of her as naturally as a man who has been happily married to the same woman for fifty years. It was also clear that she trusted him—far more than she'd ever trust me or any other person. And yet, I knew by the way she took him for granted that she might not ever love him. It seems like there's a tension women need—perhaps fed by ambition or power or steadfast determination or character or maybe pride or even the very real potential for utter failure and disaster—some taut pressure that is difficult and frightening in a man that women unconsciously want and search for. I don't think many of them like a fellow to be completely relaxed in their company.

"I don't know about Foolish Pleasure," Sam said.

"Well, you don't have to do what I do." I got up, turned to Nicole and handed her my wallet. "Keep this. And no matter what I say, don't give it to me."

Her face changed, but she took the wallet. "Are you serious?"

"Never more serious," I said.

Sam reached into his pocket.

"I'm not holding your wallet, too," she said.

He laughed. "I'm just getting some betting money."

I realized I'd forgotten to take the money I needed out of my wallet, so I reached to take it back but Nicole held it away from me. "No," she said.

"I need the money I was going to bet with," I said.

She put it behind her back. "Sorry."

I laughed. "After I have the money I need, that's when I want this to start."

"Did you give this to me and tell me not to give it back to you?"

Sam laughed.

"Yes," I said. "But —"

"Sorry," she said.

I tried to grab it out of her hands but she resisted. I had my arms around her, and we were both laughing.

"Come on," I said. "I'm going to miss the daily double."

"You said not to give it back to you under any circumstances."

"I don't want you to give it back to me. Just give me the money I was going to bet with."

Sam poked me in the shoulder. "Looks like I'm the only one going to be betting this race." He laughed again.

"It's not funny," I said.

Nicole opened the wallet, holding it out away from me, and withdrew a hundred-dollar bill. "Is this what you were going to bet with?"

"I need two of those," I said.

She gave them to me. "That's it," she said, holding up one finger like a teacher. "There will be no more money where that came from. The wallet is mine until we get home." The smile on her face was so playful and beautiful, I just wanted to hold her and laugh with her.

"You're really something," I said.

"Flattery will get you nowhere."

"Take a twenty out of there for yourself," I told her. "In case you want to bet."

"I won't bet." She was serious.

"Go ahead. Put two dollars on Foolish Pleasure."

"At eight to one?"

It pleased me that she could already speak the language. "You'll clean up."

"Where do I go?"

"I'll make the bet for you," Sam said.

I left them and made my way to the fifty-dollar window. The quick banter and easy laughter with Sam and Nicole made me feel as though I had triumphed over something dreadful — as if I had somehow overcome a terrible illness.

And here I was at the track, getting ready to bet on a horse.

I had a strong sensation of beginnings — of potential and possibility. It was not only the thrill of gambling that drew me to the horses. I loved everything about it: the sky over the paddock, white clouds that adorned the sun and made shadows across the grass; windblown pennants on top of the grandstand; the white fence around the green infield; and the brown dirt of the track. I wanted Nicole to see and understand, as her mother never could, the loveliness of racing; the swift, pounding hooves of the most beautiful animals in the world, coursing by like one powerful, striving beast. The whole experience thrills you, redeems you. As long as you are there — cheering for a horse you have bet on or concentrating on the form or carefully studying the horses as they parade by — you do not know about the rest of the world or any of its troubles. No one exists outside the cigar odor of that grandstand and the anticipation of the next race.

At the window I put fifty dollars on Foolish Pleasure to win, then I bet the double: Foolish Pleasure coupled with the eight horse in the second race, Little Bold Johnny. I bet the double ten times, which cost me forty dollars. As I was leaving the window, it occurred to me that Top Brandy really might win the race. Or if he didn't, he might run second. The horse was favored in the race, going off at even money. I went back to the window and bet another forty dollars on Foolish Pleasure and Top Brandy in what is called an exacta box. If either horse came in first and the other second, I would collect. A "box" cost four dollars, so I had the bet ten times. Then I realized that should Top Brandy win the first race, it would kill me in the double. So I bet Top Brandy in a double with Little Bold Johnny. I had that bet five times, which cost me another twenty dollars. I didn't think any other horse would be close to those two, so I felt safe. When I walked away from the window, I had bet one hundred and fifty dollars on the race. If things went as I hoped, I would collect the daily double ten times and the exacta ten times. If not, I might pull some money out of the race, anyway, with the other combinations. What I could not afford was for either Foolish Pleasure or Top Brandy not to win.

When I got back to the seats, Nicole was sitting there alone.

"You didn't bet?"

"Sam's making the bet for me."

There was a pause. The loudspeaker announced two minutes to post time in the first race.

"Who'd you bet on?" I asked.

"This one." She held up the form and pointed to Top Brandy.

I shook my head. It bothered me that she'd decided to pick her own horse. I felt as though she were ignoring my advice on purpose, to make a point. "It's your money," I said.

"No, it isn't. It's yours." She laughed again. A sweet high music I always loved. When the sound of it died away, the echo in my memory reminded me suddenly of all the birdless mornings when I had missed the sound of her voice. Presently I was conscious of this grown child again, this little girl I'd loved, who'd grown into a woman secretly, away from me, and I suppressed a powerful urge to tell her how much I wished I could prevent the passage of any more time. I wondered what she would say if I told her that sometimes all I wanted was to make the world retreat back to her sixth year so I could once again have a chance to say no to losing her.

She said, "I wish I had binoculars."

"You can watch the race on television," I said. I longed to feel tenderness for her. In a sad way, I almost hoped she would win her bet. It was as though she were in a school play and I wanted to spare her the humiliation of forgetting her lines.

"I hope you win," I said, and I meant it.

"You do?"

"It could cost me if you win and my horse isn't in there somewhere. But yes, I do. I hope you win." I looked at her but she met my glance only briefly. Then she looked beyond me.

"There's Sam."

I watched the horses being led to the starting gate. Sam came back and sat down. He handed Nicole a ticket and put several in his shirt pocket.

"What'd you bet?" I asked him.

"An exacta with the one and three."

"That's it?"

He winced. "No. I bet both of them straight up, too."

"What's that mean?" Nicole asked.

"I bet each of them to win. Five bucks on the one and five bucks on the three."

I said, "Well, only one of us can win here."

"Nicole's got the three. Ten bucks."

I looked at Nicole. "You bet half your money on the first race?"

"Well, I didn't just want to bet two dollars."

"That's inherited," I said.

Sam laughed.

I sat back and put my arm up over the back of Nicole's chair. "Yep," I said. "It definitely runs in the family."

Stable boys pushed the horses into the starting gate.

"Here we go," I said.

From the loudspeaker a voice said, "It is now post time."

A bell rang, the gate flew open, and the announcer said, "And they're off!"

The race was one mile, and for the first half a mile Foolish Pleasure was dead last. He had almost fallen down coming out of the starting gate. Top Brandy went to the front and took a big lead.

"I can't see a thing," Nicole said. "They look like a bunch of ants."

"See that ant way out in front?" I said.

"I see him."

"That's *your* ant."

That got her attention. Suddenly she was cheering with everybody else. Just after the half-mile pole, Foolish Pleasure began to move. It looked like the other horses were pulling back, the way he flew past them. If you had taken my pulse at that moment, I bet you'd have thought I was running in the race. You just can't imagine how it feels to watch something like that: a horse you've selected and believed would win, coming from way back in the pack, heading for the lead. Down the stretch toward the finish line, Foolish Pleasure passed Top Brandy.

I heard Sam say, "Goddamn it."

Top Brandy strived to regain the lead. His jockey started whipping him but the horse had nothing left. The six horse came up behind him, trailing by about a half a length, but Top Brandy dug in and stubbornly refused to yield; he was absolutely heroic. Coming toward the finish line, as they passed in front of the grandstand, it was Foolish Pleasure by four lengths and Top Brandy in second, barely holding on against the six horse.

"Stay that way," I screamed, leaping to my feet. "Five three, five three. Stay that way! Stay that way! Stay that way!"

Foolish Pleasure crossed the finish line first, and following behind, several lengths back, was Top Brandy.

"Goddamn," I shouted. I turned to Nicole and grabbed her arms. "I got it. I got the whole damned shooting match."

She jumped up and down, clapping her hands. She looked like a cheerleader, her hair bouncing on her shoulders. I'll never forget how the late sunlight reflected in her eyes.

I could not contain myself. "I got the winner, I got the five-three exacta, and I'm alive in the double with an eight-to-one shot. Man am I hot."

"Nicole's got a winner, too," Sam said.

"She does?"

"I do?"

He held up the ticket. "You bet Top Brandy to place."

I put my arm around her. "A smart bet, honey." I squeezed her, clapping my hand on her shoulder. At that moment I was so proud and happy, I could not have remembered anything wrong with the world.

"What's that mean?" Nicole was saying. "How did I win?" She squirmed from under my arm and turned to Sam. "What did I win?"

"You asked me before I went down there if there was some way you could bet that a horse would finish second. I figured that's what you wanted me to do, so I played it safe and bet your horse to place."

"That's what a 'place' bet is," I said. "It was a pretty smart thing to do."

"So how much did you win?" Sam asked me.

"I don't know, but it's plenty." The truth was I *did* know. My fifty-dollar bet on the five to win would pay me close to four hundred dollars. I had bet a four-dollar exacta ten times, with Foolish Pleasure the winner and Top Brandy in second, which, as the numbers flashed on the tote board announced, would pay two hundred and ten dollars for each bet. That meant, for the first race, I had risked one hundred and fifty bucks and I would collect over twenty-four hundred when I went to cash in my tickets. Also, I had won half of the daily double. If Little Bold Johnny won the second race I would collect another six hundred and fifty dollars. The Fates were really asleep.

"Let's go get some fried chicken," I said. "Then we'll cash in our tickets."

"I don't have anything to cash in," Sam said.

"And I don't want fried chicken," Nicole said.

Sam handed Nicole her ticket, then snapped open the racing form and leaned back in his seat. "I'm going to handicap the second race."

"Bet on the eight," I said. "Little Bold Johnny."

Nicole and I went downstairs to a food-service counter in the enclosed area under the grandstand. Across from us, high above the doors, a bank of televisions replayed the first race. To the left, an old man in a checkered coat and a brown fedora studied his racing form. Next to him a young woman in spiked heels, jeans, and a black vest over a fluffy white blouse leaned against the counter and smoked a long cigarette. When the replay was over she cursed the TV, then she slung her purse over her shoulder and walked almost defiantly toward the grandstand entrance.

"You can always tell who's winning and who's losing at the track," I said, trying to be funny.

Nicole had a sick look on her face.

"What's the matter?"

"They were whipping those horses near the end there."

"Of course."

"I didn't notice that when I was cheering—"

"It doesn't hurt them. It just stings a little. Makes them run faster." I turned away from the expression on her face, hoping to impede her rising emotions about the horse's pain by refusing to acknowledge them. It was a natural and automatic reaction; I didn't want her to sully my triumph with any mawkish displays of sympathy for a dumb animal that weighs fourteen hundred pounds and has a brain the size of a lemon.

There was a long silence while I refused to look at her. Then she touched my arm and said, "This is fun."

I was happy to realize that the moment had passed. She was not going to ruin everything with a principled stance on animal suffering. I wanted to kiss her, but I just put my arm around her shoulder and smiled. "I'm glad you're enjoying yourself," I said.

Paramutual tickets, cigarette butts, paper cups, and crushed cigars littered the white tile floor. Above the wide double doors of the entrance to the grandstand was a large lighted tote board with the odds posted for the next race. The odds on Little Bold Johnny were three to one.

I watched the board, wanting to consecrate each second of this experience. Not only winning so perfectly in the first race but doing it in front of Nicole. This was what I had dreamed of when she was only a toddler—that I would one day have the good fortune to show her the infinite joy of wagering and getting it right.

I ordered fried chicken and fries, and Nicole said she only wanted a ginger ale.

"It's a shame you can't have the chicken," I said. "That's a daily-double tradition among my betting friends."

She frowned.

"I know. I know. But it's a tradition."

When the chicken came I took a few french fries out of the basket and handed them to her. "Cooked in vegetable oil."

"So, why is this a tradition?"

"It's just what we do. When I'm alive in the double, I go get some fried chicken and eat it. For good luck."

We ate quietly for a while. The track announcer began calling out names of the horses in the second race. Through the double doors that led back out to the grandstand I could see dark evening clouds shifting and growing on a red horizon. It would be raining before the night was over.

"I love to hear you talk about luck," Nicole said. "I think I always loved it. I remember when I was very little you used to tell me stories about Lady Luck."

"Winning that race wasn't luck."

"Well, it was partially. You—didn't you—"

"No," I said. "That was called handicapping. I picked the right horses in the right combinations because I read the form and made the right decisions."

"Isn't luck involved in that?"

"Sometimes. The only real luck you have at the track is bad luck. You can pick the right horse; he can win and then have an objection lodged against him for bumping another horse or for some other interference, and the judges could take him down. Then you don't win a thing. Or your horse could be coming down the stretch and break a leg or throw his jockey. All sorts of things can happen. You read the form to eliminate guesswork, pure chance. If it was just luck, you'd flip a coin and bet."

She didn't say anything. She ate another french fry, then wiped her mouth with a napkin.

"I make the right decisions, I'm in the money," I said. "Sometimes I make the wrong decisions and I lose. Luck rarely has anything to do with it."

"Well, you said you were eating that chicken for luck."

I smiled. "That's just an expression."

"Whatever you say."

I hated it when she sounded like her mother, giving up by agreeing with me. Nevertheless, I clung to the residue of my good feelings for her, and I was very careful not to let on that it bothered me.

I said, "It's just something my old track buddies and I started. I don't know. We used to feel like we could spend money on some food if we were alive in the double. We were halfway to a winning day, and spending some of our betting money on food was a way of showing confidence."

She took another french fry out of my basket and ate it, staring at the television screen overhead.

"You going to bet the second race?" I asked her.

"Sure." I could see she was remembering the excitement of the first race, and then she realized she could collect her winnings and bet again. "When is the next race?" she wanted to know. "I can't wait to handicap it."

This made me laugh and she laughed with me.

"What's so funny?" she asked.

"Maybe you inherited more of my genes than you know." Just then I wanted very much to be close to her. I tried to charm her, thinking I might win her friendship, at least. I made her laugh about her organic need to gamble, and there was a moment there while we were both laughing when she leaned toward me, almost as though she were going to rest her head on my chest, and I opened my arms to welcome her. But she smiled and settled herself back against the counter, and I let my arms drop to my sides. I figured if I reached for her then, it would only embarrass her. To anyone who might have been watching us, I had only appeared to give a sort of benediction to our mirth, a gesture any friend might make to another.

I talked Nicole into betting on Little Bold Johnny—ten dollars to win—and although the horse was never really challenged, she screamed throughout the race. The odds were four to one so she got back the ten dollars she had bet and forty dollars more. I was so elated, I laughed out loud when I saw the look of wonder on her face as she counted the money.

"Now you've got a little more money to bet with."

Sam won some money on Little Bold Johnny, too. "I think I'm going with your judgment from now on," he said.

I picked the exacta in the third race, won another two hundred and twenty bucks, while Nicole and Sam each won twenty-two dollars. I was beginning to think that the Fates were so busy screwing with my personal life, they were completely unaware of what was going on with the horses. Sometimes, even when you're making the wrong decisions, luck leaves you alone and you get everything you want. But I was making the *right* decisions and luck was *with* me.

I didn't see how I could lose.

Then, in the sixth race, a horse called Shoefly fell down. I had bet five hundred bucks on him to win, so I was pretty upset about it. I didn't pay much attention to Nicole's reaction to what followed, but I should have.

You see, thoroughbreds have incredibly spindly legs—they're bred that way for speed—and they're never really off the ground when they run. At no time, even at top speed, do all of a horse's hooves leave the ground. One hoof is always solidly planted on the track. So, they don't just trip very often. Something has to make them fall, and it's usually a broken leg.

Now, it's unfortunate but true that horses don't often lie down. If they do lie down for any extended period of time, fluid collects in their lungs and they get pneumonia and die. They carry too much weight to stand on a broken leg, so you can't set it and wait for it to heal—you have to "dispose" of any horse with a broken leg. That's just the way it is. It doesn't matter if the animal is worth millions of dollars, as some of them are. Every racing fan remembers the tragic match race where the great filly Ruffian broke her leg. Ruffian was one of the most extraordinary race horses in history. Her lines in the racing form showed nothing but ones. She won every race wire to wire. First place out of the gate, first place at each of the quarter poles, first place at the finish line. All ones! She never lost a race until she fell down.

When a horse breaks a leg on the track, they put him out of his misery right away. A crew goes out to the animal and erects a tent over it, so what they do is out of sight. I'm pretty sure the vet gives an injection to kill it. Once they put that tent up, you never see the horse again. They take it away with the tent.

I explained all that to Nicole during the long delay in which they took care of Shoefly. I mentioned that it was a pretty good example of the luck I had been talking about earlier.

The way she looked at me made me ashamed. You would have thought I'd slapped her. She had definitely developed her mother's capacity to punish me with a look. "You mean they're killing that horse right now?" she said.

"Of course. So he doesn't suffer."

"And you're complaining about *your* luck?"

"Yes. I had five hundred bucks on him."

"What about the horse?"

"Horses don't have luck."

"Why not?"

"For Christ's sake. You have to have wishes and dreams to have luck." I think my tone shocked her. She looked at Sam, then back at the tent on the track, then at her hands. I could see she was resisting her anger, which was another of her mother's traits. She could simmer for hours.

"I'm sorry," I said. "It's just the truth. It's the way the world is. There's a reason animals don't keep calendars and celebrate birthdays."

Sam was quiet and, to his credit, pretended to be reading the form.

It rained very hard on our way back home. I was relaxed, almost sleepy. In spite of the brief setback in the sixth race, I had had what gamblers call a monster day. I won close to four thousand. I would have had over fifty-five hundred, but I got careless and a little greedy in the last race and put fifteen hundred dollars into it. I was showing off a bit, perhaps, but I picked the wrong combinations.

At any rate, I had the second-best day I've ever had at the track. (You know about the first-best day. It had been just the week before.) I had a pocketful of money, and in spite of herself, Nicole had a good time, I think. She didn't say anything more about what happened in the sixth race; and although she was quiet on the ride back home, I didn't think it was a particularly sullen silence. I think she was just sort of entranced by the rain and the sound of the windshield wipers. When I asked her if she had had a good time, she smiled at me, and I reached over and patted her shoulder.

I was very happy. You might even say, jubilant.

It Got Really Hot

And steamy all the rest of that week and into the next. Each day, the temperature reached eighty degrees by seven in the morning, and before noon it pushed toward a hundred. I stayed in the house mostly. I didn't even want to go to the track. I spent most of my time writing my thoughts down for Elizabeth, as I'd told her I would. In the back of my mind I hoped writing everything down would help me decide what the hell I should do. If not, at least she would know how I felt—even *I* might know how I felt—and then whatever followed from that, we'd have to see.

I still had not told Nicole that Elizabeth was pregnant, and as far as I knew, Elizabeth had not said anything to her, either. I had requested that she leave that to me—so I assumed my request was being honored. Although, you never really know with a woman. It was, I knew, entirely possible that Nicole knew everything. She and Elizabeth had gone shopping and had a few lunches together. But Nicole never said anything to me about it, and I was happy with that.

Nicole and Sam came and went as though they were tenants in my house. We all complained about the heat and thanked God for air-conditioning.

I would have said that, except for the heat, the days were fairly pleasant. Still, Nicole would do things that made me wonder if anyone had ever said no to her or if she'd ever said no to herself. She was so utterly willful and determined to have everything she wanted, *when* she wanted it, I found myself disapproving of her a lot. This saddened me, especially since she began to joke with me as if we were beginning to be new friends. It was very difficult at times to look upon her and feel the sort of affection I wanted to feel. It's hard to explain. Sometimes I'd stare at her and wish for some residue of the tenderness I had felt for her when she was a little girl dancing for me, whirling in a pink dress, her curls bouncing. But all I could muster was mild satisfaction that she had probably turned out all right. I would find myself looking at a picture of her when she was a child, and longing to hold her again, thinking of all the captured memory, and she would be sitting in the next room reading a magazine. You understand, of course, that I loved her. It was just that I could not muster the feeling of tenderness, which all those years ago had always robbed me of speech.

She was a young woman now and I didn't know how to be with her.

One night near the end of that steaming week, she woke up and came downstairs, looking for something to drink. I was up late, sitting at the kitchen table, working on my letter to Elizabeth, and I covered the papers in front of me when Nicole walked past me. I tried to be discreet, but I knew she was curious about what I was doing.

I asked her what the matter was.

"You got any orange juice?" She leaned over and looked in the refrigerator. She was wearing only a halter top and very short shorts, and I did not like having to look away from her so that I would not see the very clear structure of her ass.

"Why don't you wear a robe?"

"Sorry." She may have looked at me. I folded up the papers in front of me and put them in my shirt pocket.

"What are you doing?"

"I was writing a letter."

"I want some orange juice."

"There isn't any."

She left the room, and I assumed she went to put her robe on. But when she came back down, she was wearing a pair of Levi's cut-off shorts, a white blouse, and sandals.

"So who are you writing to?" she said.

"You don't have to get dressed."

"I'm going out."

"Where are you going at this hour?" I felt like a disgruntled father when I said that. The reason I felt that way was because I am her father and I *was* disgruntled because she was going out so late. It was almost three in the morning.

"I want some orange juice."

"So you're going to get it now?"

"Sure."

"It's the middle of the night."

"So what? There's got to be an all-night store around here some-where."

"You're going to go looking for an all-night store?"

She looked at me as though she wasn't sure if I was serious. Knowing as I did that she would not brook even the slightest criticism from me, I tried to smirk so she'd assume I was only half serious. But I wanted her to know that I *was* half serious.

"I didn't do that when I was a chain-smoker and ran out of cigarettes in the middle of the night," I said. "Even an addiction couldn't make me waste the gasoline to satisfy it."

"I'll walk, if you want me to."

"Why is it necessary for you to go at all?"

"It's not necessary. I just want to."

"So you just go? No matter what time it is or where you are?"

"What's wrong with that?"

"Well, it's irrational, isn't it."

"Why?"

"You can't always have everything you want."

"I know that. But I can have orange juice. It's easy. All I have to do is go out and get it."

"It just seems abnormal. You decide you want something and then you just go get it, no matter the time or place. You give in to the slightest whim, to the most insignificant wish, and try to instantly satisfy it."

"Why is that such a big deal?"

"It's unnatural. It's hedonistic. It's un-American."

She smiled. "You can't really think of a good reason, can you?"

"For one thing, at this hour it's dangerous."

She rolled her eyes.

"I'm serious now. You think all the young women who are raped and murdered in this city get that way because they believed it was dangerous? And you won't end up that way because you believe it isn't?"

"What?" She was very emphatic, and I understood that she didn't know what I was getting at.

"You will admit that the dangers are there?"

"Yes. But that's true at any time of the day or night. Rapists and murderers don't only roam the streets at three o'clock in the morning."

"So you maintain that there's no good reason for a person to be genuinely shocked by a crime 'committed in broad daylight'?"

"Dad." She looked at me as though I were speaking nonsense.

"You think women who get raped or murdered believed it could happen to them? You think they expected that was in their schedule?"

"No. Of course not."

"But you don't have to worry because it can't happen to you, right?"

"I refuse to live in fear."

"It's not called fear. It's called common sense."

"And you're talking to me about common sense?" She laughed.

I liked her laugh, but nonetheless it pissed me off. She looked like her mother and she argued like her mother and she was just as completely illogical as her mother.

"Suit yourself," I said. "It's your life." I got up and retrieved a spare house key for her.

"Thank you," she said curtly. "I'll be right back."

"Take the car. It's safer."

"Whatever you say."

She was gone for over an hour. I had just started to worry and curse myself for not telling her where she could find the nearest convenience store—a 7-Eleven only five blocks east of my house—when she came back in with her orange juice. She was angry because it wasn't fresh squeezed.

I told her I was surprised she didn't decide to drive to Florida, pick her own oranges, and squeeze them herself. "Or maybe to save time, you could have broken into a grocery store."

"Very funny." She sat down and sipped her juice. After a while, she said, "Want some?"

I stood up, stretched, and arched my back. I was so tired every bone hurt. "I'm going back to couch."

"What?"

"I can't say I'm going back to bed. I sleep on the couch."

"You don't have to."

"I don't mind it. Really."

"Sam can sleep down here and you can have your room back."

"No. I was just joking."

I thought she looked a bit disappointed, so I sat back down. "I shouldn't drink orange juice now. It will give me indigestion and keep me awake for the rest of the night."

It was quiet for a while.

She took a long drink of the juice. Then she said, "I don't want you to be angry or think I'm not grateful, but I didn't feel like I could keep that money you gave me. I knew you wouldn't take it back. So I donated it."

I'm glad I wasn't drinking orange juice, because if I had been I would have sprayed it all over the room. She must have noticed the way my eyes swelled up and my mouth opened. I couldn't believe it. A thousand bucks. It was almost half of all she had.

"I gave it to the Hopewood shelter. The man I gave it to was so thankful, he almost cried."

"You gave away a thousand bucks?"

"Are you angry?"

"I'm shocked."

"I don't know why; it was for a good cause."

"A thousand bucks. I wanted *you* to have that money."

"I know. And I did have it. For a while. Then I donated it. That's simply what I did with it."

"You didn't have it long enough for that."

"What?"

"You should have had it longer. It wasn't yours long enough for you to do that." I tried not to reproach her, but I really was fighting back an odd sort of anger. I can't explain it, except to say that now I think I know how a man might feel who has earned the Congressional Medal of Honor and who, in a moment of sincere love and generosity, gives it to his daughter and she turns around and gives it to a draft dodger. Not that I think there is anything wrong with a shelter or with people who live in one. It's just that she gave away my winnings—I was as proud of my day at the track as any war hero is of a medal—and I had given her the money to show her I am trustworthy and capable and generally all right. She gave it away. She gave it to a place where there are no gamblers of any kind. People who stay in shelters have given up. There's no fight left in them. They are not willing to gamble on a sales job or a janitor's work or washing dishes or robbing a convenience store. I believed I would try all of those things before I'd live in a shelter. I would, in other words, as the song says, "go down gambling." That's what I thought at the time, anyway.

"I'm sorry if you're upset," she said. "I did what I wanted with the money, and I thought when you gave it to me—"

"Why did you think I'd be upset? Tell me that."

"Because…" She considered it for a moment, then she shrugged her shoulders. "Because."

"That's the beginning of a sentence. Because…" I gestured for her to continue.

"I don't know. I just knew you would be."

"Well, think about it. You can't just know a person will react a certain way unless you are aware of some component in your behavior that would provoke it."

She finished the orange juice and set the glass down in front of her. "I don't know, Dad."

I shook my head. "I'm sorry. I don't know what else I can do." I got up and went to my coat, reached into the breast pocket and pulled out my billfold. I took another thousand dollars and put it on the table in front of her. "Here. I want you to use this for yourself."

"Dad," she said, pushing it away, "I don't want your money."

"Keep it," I said. "Put it toward college. Buy some clothes. Get a new stereo or something. I want you to have it."

Her hands shook as she folded the money and held it firmly in her lap. She studied me as I went to the sink and got a glass of water.

"I'm sorry," she said. "I didn't think it would hurt you."

I gulped the water, then put the glass in the sink.

As I was passing her to go back to the couch, she grabbed my hand. "You don't have to give me money, Dad. I love you, anyway."

"I know that," I said, indignant.

There was a pause and then she said, "I do."

I took my hand away. "That money is for you, do you hear?"

She nodded, properly scolded.

"I don't want you to spend it on Sam or your mother or me or the homeless or the Pueblo Indians or the whales or the visually impaired or the disabled veterans or the league of animal voters. You got it?"

"Thank you," she said softly.

"And by the way," I said lamely, "you're a wonderful daughter. I'm very proud of you." My voice cracked. I was remembering her little girl's smile, the flash of her bright eyes when she was so small and new and unspoiled by time and divorce and distance, and I thought my heart might break.

She smiled, running her hands nervously through her hair.

"You're a wonderful daughter," I said again.

She put her hand down, still smiling. "Thank you."

I left her there and went into the living room. I knew I wouldn't sleep. I was so full of remorse for handing her a broken childhood; for looking at her the last few days almost without affection. I wanted to kick myself for not saying "I love you" back to her. I couldn't understand what had happened to us. For so long I had lived every day just to hear her voice.

I wished she were a little girl again, just for an evening. So I could maybe hold her in my arms, feel her tiny fingers in my hands. So I could read her a story and smell her hair; her moist baby skin. So I could kiss her again.

What I Wrote
to Elizabeth Was

First, I am going to be brutally honest.

No doubt you will be reading this in a calm state, without tears or other displays of emotion that might take place if I were in your presence. I'm sorry if you are insulted by that, but I'm afraid that is how I felt the other night—as though the tears were automatic and part of a strategy of some sort. I'm not saying that is how you were behaving—or even if you were intending that behavior—only that the tears made me feel that way and I think this made it impossible to say what I wanted to say.

I am trying to be as truthful as I can here, but you must understand there are many things I just don't know, even about myself, and much of what I say will be in the nature of speculation.

I do know that I do not want our relationship to end; I care about you and what happens to you, and I am hoping you care about me in a similar way. If that's not love, I don't know what else to call it. I have friends I care about and for whom I wish only the best, but I do not think my life would be changed disastrously if any of them decided to move to Seattle. My life would be altered in ways I don't even want to contemplate if you and I stop seeing each other. So I must love you. I think it's sad to have to say these things so inductively, but as I said, I am trying to be as truthful as I can be.

If I'm sure of my love right now, I am not sure of very much else. That's the unfortunate truth. I don't believe I'd be a good father, nor do I think I'd be a very happy father. I had a child once—she's now returned to me. I lost her long ago, and the fact that she has returned is more troubling to me than pleasing. I am glad to have her here, but everything she does reminds me of the years I have lost with her. She is so different from me as an adult—we have almost nothing in common, and there's not much we can say to each other. Sometimes when we do talk she says things that only anger me because I sense her mother's attitude toward me in every syllable. Also, she is a devout member of the lunatic fringe in what she believes about life, and I can't stop ridiculing her for such nonsense. There is less tension between us now than there was when she weighed a hundred seventy-five pounds and treated me as though I were covered with compost, but I still don't know how to feel about her. I don't know how to be around her. I sense that I am more an adversary she has to contend with than a confidant who provides guidance. I know it is my duty to love her and try to provide for her in whatever ways fathers do with grown children, but I don't really know anything about that. I don't want to be like my own father. As you know, he has never provided for me in any appreciable way that I know of, except to disapprove of me and what I have become under his very nose, as he might crudely put it. All I ever learned from him is that I don't measure up. I know he probably loves me, but he doesn't like me very much. The last time I saw him, it was to introduce him—or reintroduce him—to Nicole. You remember that day. The reason I was so quiet on the ride up there, while you and Nicole and Sam were laughing and having a high old time, is I was so worried about what his reaction would be to her. I hoped he would be glad to see her, and I would somehow sense approval.

Don't think that I believe it is normal for any man my age to want or need approval from his father. Sometimes even I can't believe how awkward I am in his presence, or how difficult it is to talk to him about anything that matters to me. There is so much I would never say to him. But you see, I've never had his approval or acceptance, or even very much of the ordinary praise parents bestow on their children automatically. It always seemed I was just not good enough for him. I was simply his "last child"—spoken of with relief and a glimmer of exhaustion.

So I have come to need his acceptance, at least. Let him see me as a *fellow. I'd take that. He is easier on his friends than he is on me. When we took Nicole to see him, I wished I could tell him about you, about the baby, but I was dealing with his reaction to Nicole. At one point we were in the kitchen mixing drinks. You and Nicole were in the garden with Mother, and I had a chance to talk to him about things. It did not cross my mind to tell him about you, but he asked me how you were. He does things like that. He could have just as easily asked you, but he waits until you're outside and then he says, "How's Elizabeth doing, anyway?" And I know he's really trying to find out if we have plans for marriage; if we intend to give up "living in sin," which is, I'm sure, what he thinks we are doing.*

You have to understand that he has never really accepted you. It's not that he doesn't like you. He just will not allow you into the family because for him that would be a kind of betrayal of the person who he still feels is my wife. He welcomed her into the family—got along better with her than he ever did with me—and he will not have her outside the family simply because she has divorced me.

This is what I still can't get over. She divorced me, and yet he blames me for it. Get this, now. He still corresponds with her. He sends her birthday cards and Christmas cards and every now and then articles from the newspapers. You want to know how I know this? Because he's always telling me about it.

So we were in the kitchen that day making drinks, and I told him Nicole was going to stay for the summer.

He looked at me and shook his head.

I asked him what was wrong, and he said, "Nothing."

I said, "Why did you shake your head like that?" And do you know what he said? He wanted to know if Nicole's mother knew she would be staying with me that long.

I told him I had no idea, but I could tell he was thinking I'd be bad for my own daughter. I wanted to knock him down.

But I love him. He's my father, and in spite of the trouble between us, I can't change how I feel about him. If I didn't love him, I might not be so angry at him, and I might not require that he approve of me a little bit.

He ought to trust me. I can't believe he still expects that I will make the same decisions in life that he would make and if I don't, I've failed, or worse, he's failed in some way. Several times he has said, "Where did I go wrong?" As if what's happened to me in all the years since I've left home has been completely unimportant. Everything I have become is because of some lapse in his parental skill thirty years ago.

I can see your face as you read this. I know you're thinking I'm a case of arrested development and I should just ignore my father and his wishes and demands—but I've done that. I've lived the kind of life I want, in spite of his moral indignation. I truly have.

I hate to hurt him, though. I don't often confront him about the differences between us, because I can't stand to hurt him. I know nothing I say will change his mind about me or my life. Nothing he says will change anything about the way I choose to live. So it's very easy not to talk about anything important with him.

You want to know what all this has to do with you?

I don't just want to be truthful here. I want to be accurate, too. What I'm about to say is all mixed up in my mind—playing on everything I feel and do. I am not willing to confront my father about you yet. I might get to be soon. I don't know. What I have to do is tell him we are getting married. I think I can do that and leave out the part about the baby. He will like you better for it, and perhaps he'd even welcome you into the family, eventually. Marriage would probably guarantee that. If he knew about the baby now, he would say that you were shacking up with me—and if you'll shack up with me, you'll shack up with anybody. He would mean that. Remember, his parents were born in the nineteenth century. He was raised a strict Catholic. He lived through the depression and World War II by praying and working hard and digging the deepest foxholes. He attributes events to God's pleasure or wrath. He thinks the trouble with the world today is there's not enough hardship and discipline. He believes I am the way I am because he had mellowed over the years raising the other children—my successful brothers and sisters all agree with this assessment—and he was not hard enough on me. If he makes up his mind that you're a "tramp"—well, maybe you know what I'm going to say. How would either of us ever be welcome in the family?

I know I should be able to tell my whole family to fuck off. If they don't accept who I am, then they can all catch the next terrorist flight to Lebanon, for all I care. I should be able to do that, but who really can? It's my family, after all. If my father were rich and I stood to inherit a fortune, nobody would have any trouble accepting the fact that I ought to somehow please him, keep his love, seek his approval. But I don't care about money. I care about love.

Don't you?

Could you tell your whole family to take a hike? Would you want to? Of course, if I had to choose between you and my family I would certainly choose you. You are part of my adult life—the largest part of it. As I said, I would not want to live without you.

What I want to do is avoid having to make such a choice. I want to try to have you and my family.

So I'm back to marriage. We have to get married first, then I can tell my father about the baby.

This is where all the wires get crossed and several short circuits take place. After the experience of my first marriage, I didn't think I would ever again be able to marry. You already know how I feel about marriage. But perhaps you need to know a bit of why I feel that way. This may sound irrational, but it isn't. It's logical.

I was married once. Once I took that vow to love and cherish and honor and all the rest of that shit until death do we part. That vow comes from the idea that love is eternal. A lasting thing.

But it isn't, as you and I both know. It may be the most transient thing on earth. More transient than hate—which requires so much energy it eventually wears out and turns to a kind of burned-out forgiveness. Most people feel more charitable toward a person they used to hate than one they used to love.

And I did love my wife. I believed Catherine was the woman for me, and I'm a one-woman man, and our lives were going to be filled with children and traditions and remembered holidays and piles of photographs. She would be my partner and friend and lover and wife through all the long years and changes and sweet routines; we would build a whole life together. Living one life, really.

But she couldn't take the gambling. She started in on me early and never let up. In a way, it was almost as if she was taking up where my father left off. And I tried to please her. It didn't seem so difficult a thing to do at first. I merely had to give up a thing I loved to do because she was threatened by it. We did have times when there was simply no money, and I pulled a few things that she disapproved of. I've told you the stories. Using her credit card to get cash advances, paying bills a little late so I'd have the money to gamble with. I wrote a few bad checks at the grocery store. All of these things were minor embarrassments to me, but Catherine was humiliated.

Once she was standing in the line at the grocery store and she saw a sheet of paper on the cash register that said, "Absolutely no checks, Henry or Catherine Porter." She had to leave her groceries and run out of the store. When she got outside, the mechanic in the gas station right next to the store recognized the car. He had done some repair work on it the week before, and the check I gave him bounced. He chased her down the street, hollering for her to stop the car. Anybody watching must have thought she'd just robbed the grocery store and the gas station.

I thought these things were funny. I've always, as you know, had a running battle with creditors, but everybody gets paid eventually. I've never run afoul of the law. It wasn't like I was committing crimes. I remember one time Catherine and I didn't have enough money to pay all our bills, so we put them in a hat and picked them out one at a time until all but one hundred dollars of our paychecks were gone. We kept the hundred dollars to buy food. Later that month, some weasel from the gas company called to complain about the fact that we'd paid the bill so late. I told him about our little trick with the hat, and then I said if he bothered me again he was going to be out of the raffle.

Catherine laughed so hard at that. I felt like a hero.

And yet, she left me in anger. It was a mean divorce. She acted as though she hated me. The whole eruption came as a complete surprise to me. It really did. In the beginning of our marriage, I had stopped gambling on the horses for a long time, but when we had some money, I didn't see what was wrong with it. Some men spend a fortune every year on camera equipment, or baseball cards. I went to the track. Since I wasn't putting us in any real jeopardy, I didn't see what the problem was. So I refused to quit completely. I told her it was just a part of who and what I am, and it enthralls and excites me, and as long as I didn't risk the house or our personal welfare, I was going to continue with my hobby. I told her life's a gamble, for Christ's sake.

I never dreamed it would ever come to such a case that she'd actually walk out on me. And I truly hated her for taking Nicole and then telling her all her life that I had had a choice between my family and playing the horses and I chose the horses.

The truth is, my gambling never, ever, harmed her or the child. I live the same way today. Sometimes you've said to me, "You can't keep expecting to pay your bills that way," and I can hear Catherine's voice. Don't get angry because I've made that comparison—I know you don't have the same attitude as she does, and I'm not accusing you of that.

But do you see? What would be the purpose of getting married? I'd be your husband because circumstances beyond your control and mine have made me a father again. This happened without your consent or mine. I'm not accusing you of anything—but you have had time to consent to it and I haven't. I am just expected to affirm or deny without much thought at all. That is the unfortunate truth.

Also, believe it or not, I'm still wrestling with the idea that if I become a father again, when the child is Nicole's age, I will be almost sixty. I'll be in my late fifties trying to adjust to a teenager. I will face the specter of death every day, and what sort of father will I be then? Maybe the Fates are at work here, but the whole idea seems foolish to me. I already have a grown child.

But I want to make it absolutely clear that I am not saying I don't want you to have your baby. Or even that I don't want to get married again. I know you think I am contradicting myself, but I'm really not. And it's not really that I'm afraid of anything. Not truly. Still, the idea of marriage does scare me. Having another child at my age scares me. I have to do both, I can't do one or the other. (I wouldn't dream of asking you to abort this pregnancy, and even if I did, I know you wouldn't do it.) My problem is I don't know what I want. I have to figure it out. But apparently you think I should know and if I don't, then that's some sort of sign that I don't love you, or that I want to break off our relationship. You keep expecting the worst from me, and I respond, perversely, by giving it to you.

So here I am with all this uncertainty and you staring at me as if I've just asked you to blow up an orphanage. I haven't asked you for anything, and if you think about it objectively—even a little bit—you might come to the inescapable conclusion that you are inadvertently asking me for a whole hell of a lot.

You need to give me some time, even though I know I have to decide pretty soon, anyway. I'm finding it difficult to think about this rationally right now because my first thought is usually a forlorn wish that this hadn't happened—that our lives were as before. I don't blame you for reacting the way you have, but I hope you'll understand that I am forced into a decision here, constricted by time and circumstance, and I have not been consulted about any of it. I have had this decision thrust on me at a time when I am just beginning to confront some painful memories of my earlier, failed life.

When I lost Catherine and Nicole, a large part of me died. I have unconsciously pursued and maintained that death for many years. Meeting you and getting to know you was a kind of revival, but I had no idea the extent of my sleep, until this happened. I feel as though I'm about to get born again, knowing all I know about the ways in which life disappoints and shackles us all.

You must forgive me if I hesitate a bit before I allow myself to be hauled back into the world.

Everything I've said so far is simply what I think. But I also love you, and naturally I want to please you. That is how I feel. Somewhere between what I think and how I feel is my whole future. I'm going to do the right thing, I promise. I don't think it is unreasonable to ask that you give me a little time to think about everything. You should also think about what the right thing might be—for yourself as well as for me. You need to think about us—not just yourself—in this. I will do the same. I'm sure it will work out, honey.

Love,
HENRY

The Heat Wave

Went on into the next week and the one after that. It didn't seem as if it would ever end. On Monday of the third week, I couldn't put things off any longer, so I called Elizabeth and made arrangements to meet her for lunch. I told her I had written everything down and I wanted to get my feelings out in the open. There was a long pause, and I immediately regretted referring to my feelings as though they were wild game. She was restrained and fairly cold, but I chalked that up to her phone manner and a natural sort of early-morning tartness that would wear away by the time she'd had some coffee. I didn't think she was holding anything against me, although I was certainly aware of her awareness of my awareness of her awareness of the problem between us.

You want to know how I felt about meeting her for lunch? There have been men in foxholes who were more calm.

I resolved to be brave. I am always brave by not allowing myself to contemplate a single millisecond of the future beyond the pathological moment where the source of my fear resides. I would hand her the letter. After that, I didn't have a clue. By that I don't mean I didn't care—only that I was not going to consider what might happen next. I was going to go through with it no matter what.

In spite of my resolve I sat around most of that morning thinking about all the things that could go wrong once the Fates woke up. The first indication that an alarm had probably gone off in heaven was when my father called around eleven to invite me to a big family gathering to welcome Nicole "back into the fold."

I've already introduced you to my father, but I haven't really done him justice.

Like most of his contemporaries, my father fought in World War II. When a veteran of that war says he "fought," he usually means much more than most of us can possibly comprehend. My old man was in the first wave at Normandy, and he "saw action" (a variety of understatement that is most peculiar and even less meaningful than "fought") in Belgium's Ardennes forest and, later, in Germany itself.

"The Germans were great soldiers," he used to say. He would think for a moment, puffing on his pipe. Then he would mutter, "But they were the first industrialized and civilized nation on earth genuinely devoted to iniquity."

He was not a career military man, although something of the simplified approach to living—the regimen and the lack of emotional or spiritual awareness that is so typical of military life—may have appealed to him.

When war broke out in Korea, he was young enough to enlist again and go to Asia to fight. He "saw action" there, too.

During World War II he was wounded three times. He got hit in the foot in France, was nursed back to health at an aid station and sent back "into action." He lost the little finger on his left hand—the hand he does not crease bottle caps with—in the Ardennes. A few weeks later, at a little town called Eindhoven, near the Ruhr river, he was wounded all the way up his left arm. A shell fragment glanced off the bone in his wrist and traveled just under the skin up to his elbow, where it lodged in the socket and caused his whole arm to swell to the size of a football. I think that was the wound he was most proud of. He got a buddy to take a picture of it.

He never did get a "million-dollar wound"—the one that would send him home. In some ways, I wish he had—I would like to know if he would have willingly retreated from the war. Maybe they would have ordered him to go home. He went to fight the Germans when he was twenty-four years old—just out of university. When he went to Korea, he had to talk them into it.

In Korea he was very fortunate: his feet got frostbitten and he suffered terribly from dysentery and pneumonia, but he didn't get wounded.

My father was and is a hero. I say that without irony, and I mean it simply and sincerely. I know I could not have done what he did. The first time anybody shoots at me, I surrender. I'd feel bad about it and hate myself in the morning, but at least I'd have that morning, and I'd be looking forward to it.

My father tells me that I am a member of the "white-flag generation." "You've all surrendered," he says. He thinks I'm somehow hurt and challenged by that accusation; that I will rise to defend my youthful tribe. I won't do it, though. I tell him, "You're right." This little surrender really sets him off. But how can I live up to what he has done? How can any of us?

His generation went to war when they had to, and together they saved the world from its greatest and most resolute evil. War was their duty. Some of them—even guys who, like my father, didn't have to—went to war again only five years later to "nip the thing in the bud" when evil seemed on the verge of breaking into the light again in Korea.

My generation—the one born shortly after the last great war with Germany—went to war, too. Most of us went reluctantly. Unwillingly. Noisily. Many would even say badly.

"We saved the world," my father used to say to me. "What are you going to do?"

Now I'm at the age where he thinks he has the answer to that question. According to my father, our generation gave the world: Ronald Reagan, the National Organization for Women, political correctness, a significant and intractable drug problem that won't go away, video games, music TV, game shows, Prince, Madonna, porn video, action movies, sports celebrities, miniseries, the sound bite, computer-generated mail, toxic waste, Geraldo Rivera, and AIDS.

That's it.

Although, as he points out, at least we are all pretty damn physically fit. We all *look* pretty good.

It doesn't help that, for the most part, I agree with my father when he rails against these things. I hate most of them myself. I agree they are insidiously foul, if not downright evil. I agree that the decline of our culture is not only real but unbelievably steep; that this country is, as he says so often, "an international disgrace." But none of it is my fault. I don't think I should be blamed for what's happened since Rosemary Clooney stopped making hit records. But, you see, although my war included terrible suffering and death and, especially, savagery, I didn't witness any of it. I went to Vietnam and served twelve months at a hotel in Saigon. Nobody shot at me. I collected camera equipment and the best recipes for basmati rice in the Western world. I was in charge of communications for the military police in the city and cannot remember if I ever heard shelling—though I must have because I was there during the Tet Offensive. None of my buddies got killed. None of them got wounded.

My father saw his friends blown into segments, their bodies so cleanly divided and quickly killed, there was hardly any blood. "You have not seen anything like it," he said to me once. "A man's brain when it's blown out and stretched looks like a skinned squirrel. If you shatter a man into pieces fast enough, only a little blood leaks out. The rest of it stays in there to keep the piece warm and make it steam in the cold."

For my father, you are not truly grown-up if you have not suffered as he has. I think that's one of the reasons he liked Catherine so much: She believed in suffering, too. Neither he nor I could tell you in what ways she suffered, besides the obvious fact that she was married to me, but something in her demeanor—the way she seemed to face the world and grit her teeth and prepare for disaster—appealed to my father. Maybe he could see courage and fortitude in her determined and willful belief in a loving God. She was never much of an evangelist at home, but when my father engaged her in religious conversation, the two of them could go on for hours. I used to dread Thanksgiving dinners because I knew he'd say grace and then he and Catherine would start talking about how much we all had to be thankful for—even if I'd lost a couple hundred at the track the day before and we were putting the car payment off for a month or two until I could get some of it back. Before I could finish my cranberry sauce, they'd be discussing the value of faith and giving thanks. They even seemed thankful for our suffering. That's the part I didn't get.

My mother thinks I just haven't "found the way, yet." She has faith that I will be redeemed; that I will find my own "special kind of suffering," and it will save me.

I love both of them, I can tell you. But I think my special kind of suffering is having to listen to either one of them for five minutes. And that was just what I was going to have to do the following Saturday, so I greeted my father's invitation with the same enthusiasm as, say, a colonoscopy. The big gathering was to be at my brother Phil's house, in Arlington—I was happy about this because Arlington is a hell of a lot closer to Prince William Forest than Baltimore, Maryland—even though it had been a long time since I'd seen my brother Phil and I knew I'd get ribbed about how derelict I'd been not giving him a call. Phil never calls me, of course, because—according to him—I never call him. That's how families stay fragmented until somebody dies and they can get together at the funeral and talk about how they should stay in touch.

I was not at all happy about having to bring Nicole to Phil's place and put her on display for everyone to see, but I didn't know how to tell him that. All I said was, "I'm looking forward to it."

"Hold on a minute," Dad said. "Your mother wants to talk with you."

Mother came on and said, "Wait until everybody sees how much weight Nicole's lost."

"I hope they don't embarrass her, Mom."

"I've lost weight before. Believe me, she likes it when they notice."

"I don't think she does anymore."

"Sure she does."

"Listen," I said. "I'm bringing Elizabeth."

There was a silence. Then she said, "Elizabeth?"

"Yes."

"Elizabeth who?"

"Simmons. You know her, Mother."

"Oh, of course. Bring whoever you want, dear."

"Thank you."

"You might tell her it's just the family."

"We've got news," I said.

"News?"

"Oh, and what about Sam?"

"Nicole's little Japanese friend?"

I didn't answer her. She knew who I was talking about.

"I'll strangle you if you don't," she said finally. "I think he is so amusing. And he doesn't even have an accent."

"He was born in this country."

"And he sounds just like an everyday American."

"Well, he *is* an American every day."

"Of course he is. I'm serving pork spareribs. Phil's going to put them on the grill. I'll also have sautéed red onions and rosemary potatoes."

This news compensated for more suffering than I'd care to admit.

"Is Nicole still a vegetarian?" she asked.

"I'm afraid so."

"Well, I'm having a pasta dish and a fruit salad for her."

"That's very sweet, Mom."

"Don't make a thing of it at the party."

"What do you mean?"

"Don't mention it to anybody, about what she eats."

"Oh, I won't."

"And can Elizabeth eat meat?"

"You know she can, Mother."

"Did you say you have news?"

"Yes, I did."

She waited.

"I'll tell you when we get there," I said.

"You're not going to make me wait the whole week are you?"

"It's not that big a deal, Mother."

"Then why are you calling it news?"

"OK. Let's call it something else. We have information. How's that?"

"Whatever you say, dear."

"Don't be upset, now."

"I'm not upset."

We chatted a bit about the hot weather, then just before she hung up, she said, "Inform Elizabeth that we will be dressed informally and shorts will be fine."

"Absolutely," I said.

If it weren't for the food she was planning I might have fabricated some excuse to get out of it. I just knew it was not going to be a terrific time, with my father shaking everybody's hands until the bones touched, and the rest of my successful family looking at me and my meager group as though we had kidnapped the Lindbergh baby.

The Great American Food Court

Where I went to meet Elizabeth, is a huge plant-infested room, in which the air is usually maintained at sixty-five degrees with an ambient relative humidity of 30 percent. High above all the plants, white ceiling fans whir in slow concert tumbling the cold air.

I had driven over in my car, the interior of which had reached at least three hundred degrees in the afternoon heat. The air conditioner had not even begun to cool it down by the time I'd reached the restaurant, so I was close to medium rare and dripping when I got out of the car.

Elizabeth greeted me at the front door. I took out my letter and waved it at her. "I've got it all written down here."

She smiled in a plundered sort of way and said, "I've got something to tell you, Henry, but I'd like to wait until we're sitting down."

"Fine."

"In fact," she said, as she opened the door, "I'd like to have a glass of ginger ale or 7UP first."

"Sounds important," I said.

We had to hike our way through a forest of ficus trees, dumb cane, corn plants, and date palms. I felt like a figure in a Rousseau painting. Since my shirt was wet, I was also freezing, so it was difficult to stop shivering.

When we were well situated in our little jungle corner of the restaurant and the waitress had brought us our drinks, I once again took out my letter. I didn't push it toward her, thank god. I placed it next to me like a napkin and waited for her to say what she had to say.

"I'm sorry you went through all that trouble," she said, pointing to the letter.

"What trouble? I told you I'd have it all written down for you—to clarify things, both for you and for myself." The shivering made me feel as though I were trying to speak normally in the middle of a roller-coaster ride.

Elizabeth looked serene, as though she had already had the baby. "Are you cold?"

"I'm freezing."

She didn't know what to say. She was wearing a white short-sleeved blouse and a blue skirt. Her skin looked dry and warm. She was the picture of comfort. My shirt clung to my back and froze. I felt as though I were in the grip of a giant icy clam.

The waitress came and took our order—I asked for hot chili and Elizabeth ordered a tuna salad. We didn't say much until the food came. She talked about the heat and the plants that overhung our table, and I said I wished I had brought a parka with me.

She laughed and that relaxed me a bit. "Here," I said, finally, holding out the letter. "Read what I've written and then we'll talk."

"I don't want to read it, Henry."

"Why not?"

She bowed her head, forked her tuna salad a bit, then said, "I've been behaving terribly toward you in all of this. I've had a lot of time to think, and when I finally considered something other than my own feelings, I realized I'd been pretty selfish."

"No."

"Let me finish." She took a sip of her soda, looking off toward the front windows. "When you took so long for this, I thought you were just trying to let me know you were going to go away. I believed you were . . . you were just going to be gone."

"I'm sorry. I really have been think—"

"Please," she said, looking right at me now, "listen to me. I never considered your feelings. I assumed you'd be negative, but I never realized that you had every reason to respond the way you did."

"I wasn't aware that I had responded yet."

She smiled, looking into my eyes with a kind of tenderness I hadn't seen in a long time. "You responded, honey."

"No, this is the response." I held up the letter. I really wanted her to read it. I'd taken so long to write it. "I want you to read it."

"You don't understand. I don't need to. You're completely out of the picture on this."

"I can't be out of the picture, unless you're breaking up with me."

"You shouldn't call it 'breaking up.'"

I didn't think she would say something like that. I thought using a phrase like "breaking up" might cause her to reach out, as I wanted her to, and take the letter. I had hoped after she read it, she would agree to give me more time, let me decide in a week, or two weeks. At the outside I might get a month before I had to do anything. A month would be ideal, but I would have settled for two weeks. Anything to keep me from having to make any sort of permanent decision right then.

"Look," she said tenderly, "we've had a wonderful time. The last few years, we've both been..."

I wanted to keep her from talking. I knew what was coming.

She was not looking at me. She toyed with her napkin while she said, "We've both gotten what we wanted out of this relationship. But we were never—we never had what you would call a permanent arrangement."

"We were going together. You were my steady girlfriend..." I hated how silly those words sounded.

"I'm forty-one. Women my age don't go steady."

"You know what I mean."

"Honey. I really don't want this to be bitter. I want it to be lovely and sweet." She looked at me. I could see she meant it. She was going to leave me out of it.

"Don't do this," I said. My heart felt like a stuttering sack.

"I'm not doing anything, honey. Something is just happening to both of us. What we had has just run its course."

"It hasn't run my course."

"I'm going to have this baby. I'm going to dedicate my . . . my days to the child from now on. I'm happy. I really am."

"I thought you said you loved me." It was difficult to steady my voice.

"I do love you. That's why I'm setting you free of this."

"Maybe I don't want to be free of it."

"Isn't that what your letter says?" She reached for it.

I folded it and put it back in my shirt pocket. "I'll tell you what the letter says. You want to know what the letter says?"

"You don't have to be angry."

"I'm not angry."

"I don't want this to end badly."

"I don't want it to end at all, goddamn it."

I was loud and this made her sit back and look around her.

"You want to know what the letter says?"

She held out her hand.

"The letter says that I want to marry you. That's what it says."

She let her hand fall to the table and looked into my eyes. I was afraid she could tell I was lying, but then she smiled. "You don't really mean that, darling."

"Of course I mean it. You think I'd lie about something like that? I want to get married as soon as possible."

She reached across and took my hand. There were tears now brimming in her eyes. "You don't have to do this."

"I know I don't. I want to. I've always wanted to."

"Let me see the letter."

"You don't need to see it now. I just told you what was in it."

"It would mean a lot to me. It's not often that a woman gets a proposal all written out."

"It's not very polished." I took it out of my pocket, pretended to look it over. She reached for it and I held it against my chest. "I want to fix it up a bit. If you're going to make a big deal out of it."

"I just want to see it."

"There's a poem in it. It's embarrassing."

"Come on." She reached for it.

"I think I need to rewrite it one more time. OK? I want it to be perfect."

She frowned.

"You haven't answered the question," I said.

"Why couldn't you just ask me? Why did you feel you had to write it down?"

"I said I was going to write how I felt down, and that's what I did." I patted the pocket where I'd placed it. There was no way she was ever going to see it now. "Well?" I said.

"'Well' what?"

"You going to marry me?"

She seemed to shrink a little, and she turned her head to the side a bit—sort of like a puppy when it hears an odd sound. "This is what you really want?"

"More than anything," I lied.

She came around to my side of the table and kissed me on the lips. Then she sat down again. I didn't know what might be happening to the expression on my face, but she looked truly happy.

I realized I was going to be a husband and father again.

I was about as elated over this development as a person who decides to switch permanently to a sugar substitute. But what was I to do? She had truly decided that it was best for me and for her if she went off on her own to have the baby. She thought she was doing me a favor.

Hell, maybe she would have been. More likely she would have been doing *herself* a favor.

But some sinew in my heart simply could not stand the thought of losing her.

On the way home, it hit me that I'd have to tell my mother and father about my good news. Nicole would have to know. All of them would probably have to know eventually that Elizabeth was pregnant. It would seem to them that I was coerced by her condition into getting married. It would seem that way because that's exactly how it was.

To tell you the truth, I hated the idea of telling anybody about it. I wished Elizabeth and I were already married and settled into the kind of life we'd been living all along. I wished she wasn't pregnant and I wasn't going to have another child who might be taken away from me. I wished I had more control over my own goddamn life.

Still, I also knew my parents would be very excited about another wedding and god-knows-what sort of family shindigs they'd cook up to prepare for the big event. That is, if my father didn't want to fly to Rome and ask the pope for special dispensation so that my first marriage could be annulled.

That might take some time.

Before We Parted
That Afternoon

I invited Elizabeth to Nicole's re-debut. I explained that it was all my mother's idea, brought on by a secret desire to have her entire family around her all at once. I explained that my mother would not be very solicitous or welcoming and that she would probably see Elizabeth as an intruder, but that she would be polite—especially if I announced our engagement.

"That word seems so bizarre to me," Elizabeth said.

"What word?"

"*Engagement.*"

"Oh."

"I've never been engaged before."

"Why not? I can't believe a woman who looks—a woman like you hasn't been pursued all her life."

"I've been pursued," she said ruefully. "In fact, I've been hounded. I've just never been engaged. Never wished to be engaged."

I wanted to believe that she had no desire to be engaged until she met me, but I knew that wasn't true. She never wanted to be engaged, until she got pregnant. That was the truth.

There was a brief silence, then she tilted her head a bit and looked into my eyes.

"What?"

"We should set a date."

"A date?"

She frowned.

"Oh. How about July?"

She liked that idea. "Is that soon enough?"

"Why not?"

"The baby will be showing a bit by then. It's due in November."

"We'll get married very early in July."

"Aren't you worried about what your parents will say?"

"I don't care what my parents say."

"You're sure."

"Fuck 'em," I said. Right then I really didn't care. That was always my problem, though. As soon as I saw my father looking at me as though I'd just molested the Virgin Mary, I'd care a whole lot.

I kissed my intended before I left the restaurant. She touched my cheek with her hand. Everything had been settled, so we were both a little subdued and delightfully calm, like people who have just recovered from a powerful sickness.

Thus, I arrived home that evening a snared man.

Nicole greeted me at the door with the news that she was going to the beach in the morning with Sam. "It's soooo hot," she said.

"Which beach?" I walked past her into the kitchen.

She followed me. "Ocean City."

I got a glass out of the cupboard and filled it with ice. "That's a long drive for one day."

"We're staying until Sunday."

"Sunday. There's a big party for you on Saturday."

"What big party?"

I told her all about it. She was not pleased, but she said, "I can be back for it."

"The whole thing's for you."

"I know it is, but I wish she wouldn't—"

"She's going to have all your aunts and uncles there if she can—your little cousins."

She shrugged. "I'll come back on Friday."

"Just remember the party is for you." I went into the living room and mixed myself a martini. I couldn't imagine how I was going to tell her the news, but I wanted to say something before she and Sam went off somewhere in search of wind and surf and tan people their age.

"Well," Nicole said, "I've got some packing to do."

She started upstairs but caught me looking at her. I needed to ask her if she and Sam were going to stay in separate rooms, and I think she must have been aware of that somehow. She clearly didn't want to broach the subject unless I did, but I'm certain she read my look and knew what I was thinking. Finally I said, "Where are you going to stay?"

She was happy to tell me that they had reserved two rooms in the Voyager Beach Motel.

"Have a good time," I said. She turned back to the stairs but I said, "By the way," and stopped her again. "Want to go to a wedding?"

"What?"

"I'm inviting you to a wedding."

"When?"

"First week in July."

"Who's getting married?"

"I am."

She came back down the steps and approached me.

"I thought you'd like to know." I don't know why I was so embarrassed, but I couldn't look at her. She came right up to me and stood so close I thought she was going to whisper something in my ear. I stood there, stirring my drink.

"That's wonderful," she said.

"Yes."

She reached up and touched my shoulder, then she kissed me on the cheek. "I'm happy for you, Dad."

It didn't sound like she meant it. "I'd like you to be there," I said.

"Sure."

She took her hand away and stood there for a moment while I sipped my drink. Then she said, "I'm really happy for Elizabeth, too. I knew this was what she wanted."

144

"She told you that?"

"Sure."

"Did she tell you anything else?"

"Now, now," she said. "That's not fair."

"What else did she say?"

She frowned. "Nothing Dad. OK?"

"She's going to the party on Saturday."

"Oh, good."

"You're not disappointed?"

"About what?"

"Well. You're going to have two sets of parents."

"No, I'm not. I'm grown. My childhood is—" She paused, considering. "My childhood ended when I graduated from high school. Besides, I like Elizabeth."

"I didn't mean to imply that you're a child."

"I've got one mother and one father. They're going to be married to different people. I hope Elizabeth and I will always be friends. I'm already—I get along with Pop just fine."

"'Pop'? You call Mitch Pop?"

"Yeah." She seemed vaguely embarrassed.

"Pop?"

"He's my stepfather. I'm not going to call him 'Step-Pop.'"

"You could call him Mitch."

"I call him that, too, sometimes."

"Yeah, well. He's been a good father to you, I guess."

"Yes. He has."

"I'm glad."

"They're talking about having another wedding for their anniversary in August. So I might be attending two weddings this summer."

I knew from this when Nicole's visit would end. In an odd sort of way it was terribly disappointing. I realized I didn't want to know when Nicole was leaving. I preferred the incredible length of an indefinite period, in spite of the increasing turmoil in my life.

"I really do like Elizabeth," Nicole said. I could see she meant it, and I almost reached out and took her in my arms. Just then I wanted to hold her and tell her about the baby, but she turned and sauntered out of the room. I watched her skip up the stairs in that youthful, purposeful way of hers—as though she owned the wooden planks under her and the banister she held to and me.

I was still fairly moist from the ride home in the car, so I went up to my room and changed into dry clothes. While getting dressed, it hit me that Nicole was going to the beach with Sam and she'd be gone for three days. I would be alone in the house. I was now engaged to Elizabeth and I could have her with me in the house tomorrow night, and the next night, too. It would be a change of venue, a new setting for our changed circumstances. We would be alone—with wine and candlelight. Elizabeth was happy now. She would be at ease with me for at least the next few days. It had been so long since we had made love without anguish of some kind.

And then, just like that, the Fates gave me an image of Nicole and Sam, alone in a motel room, in darkness like ours, with candles and wine. I almost shook my head to rid my mind of any trace of the picture. It irritated me that my mind wandered down into that realm so automatically. I didn't understand why Nicole's sleeping arrangements mattered so goddamn much. Like she said, she's grown. I reasoned that perhaps my anxious regard had something to do with the simple biological fact that I was her father and I loved her as a father does: I worried about pain and harm. Naturally I did not want her to be used the way I had used women when I was a young man. I knew better than she did what most men are interested in where women are concerned. I had never been able to trust myself around the so-called fair sex, so it wasn't likely that I'd be able to trust any man (outside her immediate family) with my daughter. Not even Sam. Thus my interest in her virtue was much more nobly inspired than the average man's desire to exclusive access to the sexual wares of his wife. This is not to say that a man's wish to have a faithful wife is particularly shameful. I understand completely why a man would want to count on his wife's virtue, and I don't think it has very much to do with possessiveness. Or at least it isn't possessiveness by itself. I may be alone in this, but I really believe that what most men cannot endure about infidelity in a wife is the simple and unbearable idea of divided or shared intimacy—an unknown measure of secrecy and tenderness is dissipated and lost forever. It is not so much a betrayal as a violation—the circle of privacy between a man and his wife is broken, and the breach is usually almost impossible to mend. So it is worth fighting for and defending.

I think it is also true that intimacy means more to women than it does to men because women spend much less time lying about it. Or at least they don't imitate and manufacture it for the benefit of other purposes as men so often do. Men get used to a kind of intimacy—the kind that engenders further and further incursions into sexual activity—but true intimacy is possible only with their wives, if at all. I admit, for some men, intimacy with anyone is as impossible as finding a carton of eggs labeled "small." I am also ready to admit that what I have just said about men and women and infidelity might be construed to mean that I accept or even approve of the old double standard: A man can engage in extramarital sex because he is not emotionally involved, while a woman cannot because she is. Perhaps there is some truth to that statement after all, though I would not dare insist on the point. If I were to turn the point around a bit, however, and insist on it in a different way—if I were to suggest that women have much more tolerance and are more forgiving than men and therefore do not rush to the divorce lawyer at the first sign of infidelity, while men are just the opposite and rarely leave room for even the slightest sexual misconduct on the part of their wives—perhaps I would not have to insist on the point.

At any rate, I didn't want to be worried about Nicole's sexual behavior, whether it was nobly inspired or not. For one thing, I kind of liked Sam. He was irritating sometimes, but he was talented and seemed genuinely interested in Nicole's well-being. He was her friend, and probably a good friend at that. What could it matter if they occasionally took off their clothes and engaged in a bit of trifling, private, friendly, noncommittal screwing. It might feel good for both of them. They probably understood better than any generation of people in history the consequences of doing it without taking precautions. Now that sex was lethal, they would surely be more aware of the dangers. At any rate, they understood that if they got themselves into a fix like mine, it was a small matter to clear up. A brief trip to a clinic, and presto, problem solved. Back to the brief and friendly screw.

Really, why not? Why can't men and women fuck with each other any time, any place? Sex between friends is probably a whole lot better and less fraught with pain and anger and sadness and rage than it ever is between lovers.

So why did it really piss me off that Nicole might be having sex with Sam? Or with anyone?

A therapist would have a ball with me, wouldn't he? I knew it was both illogical—and real wrong—that I even considered the issue. What Nicole did with her private life, with the great treasure of her intimacy, was her business. She was smart enough not to believe that men want the same thing as women, so she would probably not be used badly. If she was used, it was her life and her pain.

I resolved not to ever think about it again—and to do my best not to show that I was thinking about it when I did.

Summer School

Was keeping Elizabeth very busy—she had "thousands of papers to grade"—so she couldn't come over until Thursday. She said, "Wear your black robe."

"I will."

"Wear it for dinner. And I'll put on something thin and silky."

"Great." I gulped. Just hearing her talk about it excited me.

On Wednesday I put all my winnings in the bank and paid all my bills—even the ones that didn't have to be paid yet. I cleared my desk drawer. I wrote out mortgage checks for the next two months and placed each one in the proper envelope and stamped it. I would only have to reach in my top drawer, withdraw the next month's check when it was due, and drop it in the mailbox.

I paid the car payment.

I still had two thousand or so in the bank and a hundred or so in my pocket.

Maybe I was kind of happy, who knows? Nervous, but happy. I knew I'd probably never have another great day at the track, but I still had some money and the summer was pretty much paid for. I only needed a few hundred or so to keep myself in food. And Elizabeth would have money.

I didn't want to go out of the house. The humidity was so high, you had to be outdoors only for a few seconds and you could feel your skin beginning to sag from the bone. I spent most of my time in the den, relaxing in air-conditioned comfort. I wanted to go to the track, but I didn't.

On Thursday morning Nicole called to tell me they were having a "spectacular time," and they'd met some people who were "absolutely awesome."

"'Awesome'?" I said.

She said nothing.

"You met some people who are awesome?"

"Yes."

"What's awesome about them?"

"What do you mean? They're fun. They're exciting and funny and—"

"The Grand Canyon is awesome. The Pyramids are awesome."

"OK," she said.

"No, seriously, people can't be awesome."

"OK, Dad. I don't want to argue."

"Maybe Lincoln was awesome. Martin Luther King. People like that."

She sighed.

"I'm just kidding you." I wished she had a sense of humor.

"I'll definitely be home Friday night."

"How late?" I really wanted to know.

"Sometime Friday night."

"Can't you give me some idea?"

"I don't know. We're leaving after dark. So, what—eleven or so?"

"Don't be too late."

"What's too late?"

"I don't want you to wake me out of a sound sleep."

"OK." She sighed again.

"You don't have to sound vexed."

"I'm not *vexed*." She mocked me.

"I didn't say you were vexed. I said you *sounded* vexed."

"We'll be home early Friday night."

"Whatever you say."

"Whatever *you* say."

"If that's the way you want to look at it."

"Is eleven-thirty or so OK?"

"So now it's eleven-thirty?"

"Bye, Dad. I love you."

"Bye," I said, but she'd already broken the connection.

I realized that sometimes she made me feel like my father. I wanted to tell her that it was only common courtesy to tell a person that you are coming—she had arrived that summer without warning, remember—and that it was also mannerly and thoughtful to give an estimated time of arrival.

I should have cleaned up the place a bit before Elizabeth arrived. Maybe if I had, things would have gone a little differently. Instead I laid around the house all day, and just before she got there I cooked her a flank steak with sauteed mushrooms, baked potato, and fresh asparagus. I made a point to clean up the mess in the kitchen, but I overlooked the rest of the house, including my bedroom, which is where I wanted us to end up an hour or so after dinner.

We ate by candlelight and I don't really remember much of what we talked about, except that we were once again at ease with each other, and I know we were as happy as human beings ever get. At least I was. I think I was even happy about being married again.

I remember one thing we discussed near the end of dinner that had the potential to disrupt our passionate plans, but we both handled it nicely. Elizabeth broached the subject of her name. I hadn't even thought about it one way or the other but she wanted to know if she should keep it.

"If you want."

"I think I should."

"Go ahead. What about the baby, though?"

"She'll be Porter-Simmons." Elizabeth was certain she was going to have a girl. A woman does not know these things, but all of them believe they do.

"Porter-Simmons," I said.

"That has a nice ring to it, don't you think?"

"Yeah." I wasn't convinced and she sensed it.

"You don't think so?"

I had finished my steak (when I'm expecting to get frisky in the bedroom, I eat pretty fast) and I was sitting back, playing with my napkin. I didn't want to talk about anything truly serious right then. I wanted to drink a small glass of bourbon and water and then wander upstairs.

"Does it bother you that I want to keep my name?"

"No. It's just…"

"Just what?" She put down her fork.

"Well, what if we do have a girl? Her name will be Porter-Simmons. Then she grows up and she wants to marry. Maybe the person she marries is named Hanson. Then her name will be Porter-Simmons-Hanson."

"If she wants."

"That's if she doesn't meet somebody who already has a hyphenated name. What if she marries somebody named Watkins-Hanson? Then her name would be Porter-Simmons-Watkins-Hanson."

Elizabeth considered this information.

"Then," I went on, "what if she has a daughter? We're just talking about one generation here—our granddaughter. If she marries a man from a similar family—let's say she marries some guy named Whelan-Phillips-Johnston-Wellingham—are you beginning to see what's developing in just a few short years?"

"What does any of this have to do with us?"

"You don't see how crazy that is, keeping names and hyphenating them all over the place?"

"You are serious, aren't you?"

"We're going to need phone books the size of New Mexico."

"I'm keeping my name," she said, laughing. "No matter how irrational you get."

"I think I'm being quite rational." I was. You know I was. Elizabeth knew I was. But I didn't want to get into an argument over something so silly. If she wanted to keep her name — her father's name — fine. Later generations will have the technology to record and keep track of people whose names are longer than the trans-Siberian railway. "If you want to keep your name, I'll give up mine. I'll be Mr. Simmons from now on if you want."

"Henry, does it matter to you that much?"

"Of course not," I said. "I'm only kidding."

Later we went upstairs. I was still wearing my robe and nothing else, she was still wearing her silky gown. We embraced for a long and sensual kiss on the bed, and then I began to caress her arms, her neck, her shoulders. I teased her a bit. She was pretty excited to tell you the truth. I had all her molecules vibrating, and then I got up and announced that I was going to take a quick shower.

That was my mistake. I had always loved to emerge from a hot shower, naked and moist, and fall on the bed next to her, breathing as if there wasn't enough air in the world. We were always like first lovers at times like that — new and young and passionate. She knew that, and she knew, too, how to take advantage of it. The gown would be gone and she would be lying there in the most alluring and provocative way. When I rose from the bed and announced my intentions, she smiled wickedly and said she would sip her wine and wait for me. It was always so exciting to know that she wanted me; that her passion would be even more intense from the wait.

I was in the shower for only a few minutes, but it was long enough for her to find the shirt I had worn that day I took her to lunch; long enough for her to pick the shirt up and discover what was folded up in the pocket; long enough for her to take it out, sit down, and read what it said.

When I came out of the bathroom, she was sitting on the edge of the bed, still fully dressed, holding my letter in her hands.

"What's the matter?" I felt like a little boy discovering shame.

She had tears in her eyes.

I stood there for a long time, staring at her, feeling absolutely foolish.

"Put something on," she said in a weak voice.

I was too embarrassed to move, and I had nothing to say. My mind was as empty as the Grand Canyon.

She folded the letter and put it down next to her. I picked up my robe and lamely put it on.

"Well shit," I said. "I wish you hadn't read that."

"But I have."

I moved toward her. "Don't," she said, getting up. She moved over to a window that looked out into the backyard. She raised the shade and stared out at a pale half moon that dangled over the trees.

I wrapped the robe tightly around me and tied it at the waist. "I'm sorry," I said. "I wrote that a long time ago. Everything's changed now."

"You're trapped, Henry. And I've trapped you."

"No."

"Everything's wrong, isn't it? Everything."

"Stop crying," I said. "I hate it when you cry."

"I'm not crying." She sobbed.

"It's sure a fair imitation."

"I need to think." She shook her head—as though she were casting something out of her hair. "I need to think."

"Look, forget the letter. I've asked you to marry me, and you've said you will."

"What you say in this letter is right. I am asking a lot of you."

"That's an initial reaction."

"I've trapped you, Henry. Isn't that how you feel?"

I couldn't look at her, and I couldn't find words to say.

"I'm so sorry," she whispered.

There was a long silence. Then she came back across the room and sat down next to me, a look of durable resolve on her face. "Listen, Henry. Just listen to me." She wiped her eyes with her hands, a languid gesture that broke my heart. She was thinking only of me, of what I had been through, and I didn't want her to do that.

"I shouldn't blackmail you into marrying me," she said.

"You didn't blackmail me."

She picked the letter up again. "Sometimes you're the sweetest, most generous, person—but then you...you—"

"So marry me for Christ's sake."

"Listen to you."

"Well, do we have to make it such a...such a—"

"What?"

"I don't know. Such a problem. Everybody gets married."

"Henry, this is wrong. You must believe that I didn't know I would get pregnant, and I didn't know how I would feel if I did..."

I reached for her but she took my hands and placed them in my lap. "You don't know what you want. I do. I took advantage of that, and I took advantage of you. If we got married now, it would be a terrible mistake."

"All marriages are a terrible mistake. So what?"

Something changed in her face. It was as though she registered a sharp pain behind her eyes.

"I didn't mean that."

"Yes, you did, honey." She reached up and with the tips of her fingers touched the side of my face. "Nothing is ever as we think, is it? That's why we have hope," she whispered.

"What do you mean by that?" I said.

She forced this loving smile—it was almost pity—then she rose from the bed and walked out of the room. I followed her downstairs where she got her purse and fished in it for her car keys. She was not crying anymore and there was such purpose in her movements, I was certain she was going to leave without saying another word. Still, all I could do was watch her. I knew it would be utterly senseless to beg her not to leave.

"Take some time," she said at the door.

"What do you mean 'that's why we have hope'?"

"Take all the time you need. This is just what you wanted, isn't it? Take all the time you need... Think about what you want, and then maybe..."

"I don't need any more time."

She smiled. "Everything just feels wrong now, Henry."

"It does not."

"I tried to tell you this in the restaurant," she said. "I'm all right about this. I don't need you."

"I know you don't." There was something else I wanted to say. I was so upset that she was leaving I couldn't get my mind to work. She stepped out and quietly closed the door. Then I said, "Maybe I need you, did you ever think of that?"

But I waited too long to say it. I don't think she heard me.

Some Philosopher

Said, "I think, therefore I am." He didn't finish the sentence. He should have said, "I think, therefore I am wretched."

Another woman had left me. It hit me that I'd lost two women, for opposite reasons. Catherine because I was a gambler, and Elizabeth because I was not willing to gamble. That was the story of my life in a nutshell. Maybe it is the story of every male's life: No matter what you do, you can't win where women are concerned.

The hot weather broke like a fever during the night and a cold front passed through. A violent display of lightning, thunder, and rain woke me early, before full daylight, and I got dressed and went out on my back porch to watch the morning come. The wind was constant and furious. Most of the small maples in my backyard were stooped toward the white grass, and gales of rain lashed everything, sweeping along the ground like a machine.

I was possessed by a cold and desolate sense of doom. I guess such turns in the weather can only intensify what we are already feeling. I was unhappy, so naturally the dark clouds reminded me of some of the sad facts I would just as soon not be thinking about. I was alone again. Elizabeth would probably not come back to me. This idea produced an aching mixture of anger and sorrow, and it made me think once again of the speed of my life. Years and years had passed so swiftly, thousands of days heaped one on the other, until decades had begun to accumulate.

I would be getting old soon, and all of my future would shrink, until even a single evening's passing would become a thing to dread.

We are such temporary witnesses to everything.

And yet, there's something about a violent storm that suggests the eternal, steady, measured power of the ocean. You don't have to be far from the sea to forget its majesty, but a rainstorm—with enough wind and water and thunder—can seem like the ocean coming back to haunt you. Like an old fright or, if you're in the mood for it, a new pleasure. I tried to focus on the image of the sea; the ebb and flow of waves on the shore. I hoped the metaphor would begin to work its magic on me and I'd begin to see my life coming back like the tide.

I watched the telephone most of Friday night, but it didn't ring once. I made up my mind I was not going to call Elizabeth again. I had called her at work three times during the day, and each time was told she was "not available" and asked "would you like to leave a message?" Right. What sort of message could I leave? I just said, "Have her call me when she has the chance."

I wanted to call her again, but I mustered a certain amount of pride—I'd say, on a scale of one to ten, my pride was at about .0000000000001 percent. But it was enough to cancel my vigil by the telephone. Besides, I didn't want to become a stalker. Ironically, when I gave up the wait, I was proud of myself.

I went to the sofa bed early, before ten. At a little after midnight, Nicole came home. I was still not asleep. I heard her test the door to see if it was open before she knocked. "I forgot my key." She had been drinking, but she was polite and fairly quiet, so I didn't see the point of remarking on it. Sam was absolutely plastered. He kept trying to imitate Gregory Peck in a loud debate with George Bush and Ronald Reagan, but the result was a slurred, barely intelligible series of broken sentences that were not funny.

"Why don't you put him to bed?" I said to Nicole.

"He's all right."

We were in the kitchen. I was standing by the sink and Nicole was at the table, leaning over Sam, trying to get him to sip some coffee. Her skin was darker, and her blond hair seemed to glow in the light. Sam, too, was tanned and healthy looking, although he could barely sit upright.

"Come on," she was saying to him. "Take a little more."

"Don't feel so good."

"If he gets sick in here, he's going to clean it up," I said.

"I won't get sick. I'm too sick to get sick. I jus' want to sleep."

"Take him upstairs," I said. "He can sleep it off."

He tried to rise from the table. Nicole had ahold of his arm. She looked at me, expecting help, but I didn't want to touch him. "You need help?" I said, lamely.

Sam sank back down in the chair. "He's not that heavy if he'd just get up," Nicole said.

"How'd he get so drunk?"

"He drank a lot of beer while we were sitting in traffic."

"He was driving?"

"At first. Then I took over."

"A good thing," I said.

"The rain," Nicole said. "God, people are stupid in the rain."

She tried to lift him out of the chair again. This time I grabbed his other arm and helped her walk him up the stairs. We threw him on the bed in my room. Nicole took off his shoes, then pulled the covers out from under him.

"It's OK," he said. "Don't bother about me."

"Be quiet," Nicole said.

"I'm quite all right, sir."

She pulled his socks off.

"Mind your manners," he murmured, "or I will chastise you severely." He was already snoring when she covered him with the blanket and tucked it under his chin. She stood there for a moment, regarding him. I motioned for her to come on, but she leaned down and smoothed the black hair off his forehead.

Something had happened between them; something important. Perhaps I was just reacting to the fresh sense of rearrangement going on in my own life, but I thought there was a kind of receptive peace about Nicole's demeanor that suggested some issue between the two of them had been settled. She seemed to care for him in a completely different way.

I said, "Good night," and went back downstairs. I turned the lights off and settled back into the sofa bed. I was going to stretch out on my back and try not to think about anything until I went to sleep, but Nicole came back down and walked by me into the kitchen. I waited for a while, to see if she'd come out to talk to me, but she didn't even turn the kitchen light back on. When I finally got up and went in there, she was sitting at the table in the dark, sipping the rest of Sam's coffee.

"You all right?" I asked.

"Sure."

"Why are you sitting here in the dark?"

"I don't know."

"What's the matter?" I sat down across from her.

"I'm just finishing Sam's coffee."

In the darkness I could barely make out her shape, but I think she was sitting there with her head down. It was quiet for a while and then I said, "Do you remember the first time you ever got drunk?"

"Sure. I was at a beach party."

"No, You were with me." I saw her move a bit. I got up and turned the light on.

"Jesus." She shielded her eyes with her hand.

"I'm sorry. You want me to turn it off?"

"Yes." She acted as though the light was painful.

"I like to look at you when I talk."

"Put the back porch light on."

That was a good idea. I had a bug light on the back porch, though, so when I turned the kitchen light off again and put the porch light on, we were both bathed in weak yellow light and Nicole looked jaundiced and ill.

"You look absolutely sickly in this light," I said.

She made a slight whimpering sound and I couldn't be sure if she was suppressing laughter or tears.

I went over to her and put my hand on her shoulder.

"Today was a terrible day," she said.

I got her a Kleenex and she wiped her face with it. Then she settled herself in front of the cup, her delicate hands wrapped around it as though she needed it for warmth. "So tell me about the first time I got drunk."

"Are you crying?"

"No."

"You sound like you were crying."

"I'm just tired."

"What happened today?"

"Nothing. I don't want to talk about it."

"You can tell me."

She didn't say anything. I watched her sip the coffee, and after a while I got up and poured myself a cup. I knew I'd never get to sleep that night, anyway. "Look," I said, as I sat back down, "I had a real shitty day, too. I'll tell you mine, if you tell my yours."

I couldn't see her eyes real clearly in the light, but I think she looked at me with a mixture of pity and exasperation.

"Does it have to do with Sam?" I asked.

"No. Not really." She wiped her nose, then sat forward recovering her composure. I could see she'd made up her mind not to tell me anything.

"I'll go first," I said.

"Dad."

"Elizabeth broke up with me today." My throat felt hot, and I almost didn't get that last word out. Suddenly, when I knew what I was about to tell her, I didn't want to talk either.

Nicole leaned toward me, reached out her hand, but she didn't say anything right away. There was this terrible awkward silence. I felt like a fool. She was looking at me, waiting there for me to finish, and I couldn't help this sensation that I was not telling her anything she didn't already know.

"Did you know about this?" I said.

"Of course not. How would I know?"

"Maybe she mentioned it to you."

"We didn't talk much about you," she said. "Honest."

"Well," I said, "I don't think she'll be going with us tomorrow."

"What happened?"

I went ahead and told her about the letter and my fears about getting married again. When I mentioned that Elizabeth was pregnant, Nicole sat upright.

"You didn't tell me she was pregnant."

"I haven't told anybody."

She laughed briefly.

"What's so funny?"

"Nothing."

"Why'd you laugh like that?"

"I wasn't laughing. I just—it seems odd to think I'm going to have a little brother or sister."

"So Elizabeth didn't tell you about it."

"No. I wish she had."

I didn't have anything to say in response to that. I sipped my coffee, feeling as though I were pouring hours of wakefulness down my throat. After a long time, Nicole said, "So you're going to have a baby."

"I'm not. Elizabeth is."

"She hasn't really broken up with you."

"Sort of. She said she wants to think."

There was no response. We sat there for a while in silence, then I said, "Why do I get the feeling you don't like the idea of a little brother or sister?"

"I don't know; he'll be here with you, and I'll be so far away."

"Oh."

"I'll miss a lot, I guess. It seems wrong to me. My family's so spread out. I have to get used to the idea."

"So do I."

"Do you want to have another child?"

"I don't know," I said. "Sometimes I do. I remember what it was like to hold you when you were little—your mother and I used to fight over who would get to carry you—and that makes the idea of a new child kind of pleasant..."

"I called Mom today."

I had nothing to say to that.

"I don't know why, but I missed her terribly. I think I'm nervous about meeting all the aunts and uncles."

"Don't worry," I said. "I'll be there with you."

"I would have been more comfortable if Elizabeth were going to be there."

I had no response to that. I was certain she didn't mean it the way it sounded. After another long silence, Nicole said, "Why did you and Mom split up?"

"I already told you she couldn't take the gambling anymore."

"It can't be just that. Nobody decides to break up over something that simple."

"How do you know?"

"I just know."

"You think you know. Sometimes that feels like actually knowing, but it isn't, really."

"I can't believe Mom would break up our family over a few extra dollars you lost at the racetrack." Her voice had risen a bit.

"It was a lot more than a few extra dollars, but I couldn't believe it, either."

"Were you unfaithful to her?"

"What kind of question is that to ask your father?"

"So you were."

"Of course not. She knows it. If she told you otherwise—"

"She didn't tell me anything."

I said nothing.

"Neither one of you has told me anything." Now the yellow light made her look a little bit like a guard in a prison camp. Her eyes flashed as though she were wary of movements in the dark.

I tried to soften my voice. "There are two kinds of people in the world—really, only two kinds: those who think most people are basically rotten, and who expect the worst from them in most circumstances, and those who think most people are probably pretty decent if you'll let them be. The ones who think people are rotten make all the rules, I'm sorry to say. Your mother was one kind of person, and I was the other. It was between her and me. It had nothing to do with you."

"Still, I want to know."

"Why? What difference does it make?"

She lifted her brows in a slight shrug.

"Don't take this the wrong way, but you're asking questions you have no right to ask. It's none of your business. All you need to know is that none of it was your fault."

She smirked as though she'd heard that a hundred times.

I finished my coffee. Put the cup down with a clanking sound on the table. Nicole gazed out the window at the bugs that danced around the yellow light.

"Let's not argue," I said.

"Do you believe in marriage, Dad?"

"What do you think?"

"I just want to know."

"Are you thinking of marrying?"

"I'm—I don't know what I'm going to do. I want to go to school. I was just wondering how you feel about it."

"I don't know how I feel about it. I know what I think, though."

She studied my face, sipping the last of her coffee.

"You take an oath when you marry a person," I said. "You swear to live the rest of your life with them whether you want to or not. When you first get married, you truly long to be with each other. I don't understand why anybody would think it necessary to take an oath to continue doing something you want to do very much. The oath is for when you don't want to do it anymore. Everybody's forgotten that."

"Did you forget it?"

"Your mother did."

She looked at her hands. In the yellow light her hair looked like a kind of frozen fire. "So you think people shouldn't ever get divorced?"

"I think they shouldn't ever get married. Either that, or we should change the oath."

She turned and gazed out the window for a moment, then she turned back to me. I thought she was about to say something, but she only tried to force a smile.

"What?" I asked.

"Nothing."

"I'm just telling you the truth. Marriage is a foolish thing to place any faith in. It takes only one person to break up a marriage, and two people to keep one together. The odds don't favor it."

"You and your odds."

"That's your mother talking."

She shook her head.

"Probability governs everything in life that isn't in the past," I said. "Whether you like it or not, probability involves considering the odds."

"It's just the way you think about everything."

"That's right. Because I'm alive, and life's a gamble. People who don't think so, never take any chances and they lead shitty lives."

"And *your* life's not shitty. Right." She was surprised to have said that, and I could see she immediately regretted it.

"Well." I didn't know what to say to her. I felt injured, even though I should not have been surprised that she accurately perceived the exact condition of my life. She was looking at me with a mixture of tenderness and consternation, and I was suddenly afraid she would try to tell me that she didn't really mean what she said. It was quiet for a long time.

I realized that she had directed our conversation so far away from what was wrong with her, it would take a major breach of conversational logic for me to bring it up. I was just about to launch into it, anyway, when the Fates intervened with another sortie. The phone rang and scared the living hell out of me. It was an unfamiliar male voice asking for somebody named "Nick."

"There's no Nick here," I said.

"She gave me this number."

"It's for me," Nicole said.

"You want Nicole?" I said.

"Yeah, Nicole."

I wanted to say, "Who the hell do you think you are calling here at this hour," but I only said, "Sure, she's right here."

I gave the receiver to her and sat down. I don't understand why I didn't react right away, unless some part of me was secretly hoping Nicole would let him have it. She seemed happy to hear his voice.

"Chad," she said, "what's the matter?"

She listened for a bit, then she laughed. "That was my father."

Another pause. "No. I can't."

I watched Nicole's face, and by degrees I came to see that something definitely *had* happened between her and Sam. It was Chad.

"I've got to go to a family thing, with my father."

I was picturing Chad. I would have bet the house that he was tan, probably dark or blond hair, square jawed, with deep-set ocean blue eyes and perfectly defined muscles in his arms and legs. I figured he would probably be slim, not too tall, and from the sound of his voice, he was certain to have a brain the size of a peppercorn.

"Maybe Sunday," Nicole said, her voice now coy and slightly breathless.

"No. I don't know what he's going to do."

Nicole looked at me, and I thought I noticed moisture in her eyes. But it could have been a trick of the yellow light. I got up and went to the sink.

"Right now he's passed out," said Nicole. "He'll understand. It's not like he's my boyfriend or anything."

Poor Sam. I knew all at once what was up and why Sam was so drunk. He had to watch Chad and Nicole all weekend, pretending to be her friend through it all. Cruelty is often dished out with such tenderness in the curious drama between men and women, it is no wonder so many of the love songs in human history have to do with pain and loss.

Nicole whispered good-bye and hung up the phone. I said, "Who's Chad?"

"Some guy I met at the beach."

"Let me guess. Is he tall, dark hair, nice muscles?"

"He's cute. He's not tall."

"Dark hair?"

"Why?"

"I just want to know."

"Yes. He's got dark hair."

"Poor Sam."

"What do you mean by that?"

"Surely you know how he feels about you."

She got up and put her cup in the sink. Standing next to me in the shadows I couldn't tell if she was angry or sad or what.

"Imagine how he must feel," I said.

"He has no right to feel that way."

"We're not talking about rights. One does not consult a lawyer about feelings."

"He knows we're not..." She stopped, staring down into the sink. She seemed to shudder slightly. "I just wish he'd go home."

"Jesus Christ."

She looked at me.

"You meet some guy, and in only three days you want Sam out of your life?"

"He's never been in my life that way. He's always been my friend, and he knows that. And incidentally, this is none of *your* business."

"I've got your friend, or whatever he is, sleeping in my bed upstairs."

I had gotten a little too loud. I went on more softly. "You're about to lavish your heart's intimacy in some sort of romance with a 'cute' person you've known for all of three days, while Sam pines away here with me? Is that it? What am I going to do with him Sunday if you're out with Chad?"

"Forget it."

"I can't forget it."

She moved toward the door.

"Wait a minute," I said.

"Just leave me alone."

"What are you going to do about this?" I followed her into the living room and grabbed her arm. She turned to me briefly. In the moonlit room her face looked like a vision of her mother glaring back at me the way she always did, with hurt and anger and defiance and pride and almost perfect disdain. Someone who did not know her would have thought she was trying to suppress a smile, but I felt as though I had stricken her. "For Christ's sake," I said. No other words came to me.

"I'm going to bed." She pulled her arm free. "Good night, Dad." She stood there for a second, as if to see if I'd grab her again, then she turned and went up to her room.

I leaned on the banister at the bottom of the stairs and watched the light from her room illuminate the hallway momentarily. Then she closed the door and it was dark again.

The disappearance of the light in the hallway struck me like a sudden dull presentiment of ruin, and I remembered that Elizabeth had left me; that I was alone again; that I had to go to my brother's house in the morning and be with my whole family; that Nicole would be there with Sam, both of them tottering on the brink of emotional trauma; that I was stuck with my hateful past, and unhappy with all the possibilities of my future.

If I could have fallen asleep, I would have been happy to stay that way.

The Ride

To my brother's place in Arlington the next morning was awkward and mostly silent. Nicole set her teeth and insisted on ignoring me, and I didn't see the point of trying to force a conversation. She and Sam did not try to disguise the fact that something was going on between them, but I didn't want him to know I was aware of it. I couldn't think of what to say to him. He looked so diminished in the back seat. He was no longer interested in showing his talent as an impressionist, and I think his head might have hurt as much as mine did. Besides, every time I tried to think of something to say, I'd suddenly have this vision of Elizabeth holding a baby in her arms and waving to me from a great distance. Then my heart would sink, and the silence didn't seem so bad.

My mother and father were already at Phil's house. Mother greeted me at the door, wearing a baggy pair of white Bermuda shorts and a light blue sleeveless blouse. Her arms were pale and thick. My father was sitting in the den, smoking his pipe. I could see he had been reading the newspaper. When Nicole went in to him, he said, "Welcome," and stood to greet her.

Phil wore an apron that looked like a Washington Redskins uniform, with the number 10 on the front. He was no longer the slim, athletic, darkly handsome lad who leaped from the great heights at Sylvan Dell, but he still called me Shaver. Now he had grown paunchy and he was beginning to lose his hair. He was always rattling ice in a glass with a touch of scotch in the bottom of it. Sometimes I found it hard to be in the same room with him for longer than fifteen minutes or so because he was a very successful lawyer and he believed I was always just on the outskirts of the criminal element of society.

"Come on in," Phil said. "I'm about to light the grill and put the ribs on."

"We're having ribs?" Sam seemed short of breath.

"Some of us are," I said.

Nicole looked at me briefly.

"Don't worry," Mother said to me, "I've made a delicious eggplant for Nicky."

Nicole's expression changed.

"You don't like eggplant?" I said.

She was not happy that I pointed this out.

"Nonsense," Mother said. "Everybody likes eggplant."

My father sat down, shaking his head. "Not everybody, dear."

"The way I've prepared this, you won't even recognize what it is."

"I'll try it," Nicole said.

My father said, "I don't much like eggplant." Then he noticed Sam leaning against the doorjamb. "Well, young man. Are you going to come in?"

Phil moved over and put his arm around Sam. "What's the password?"

Sam said, "Sick."

"What?"

"Sick."

"Sick?"

"I don't feel so good." Sam's eyes rolled back and he fell into Phil's arms.

Phil screamed, "Look out!" and dropped him on the floor. Sam's eyes were wide open. He landed hard on both elbows. Phil said, "I think he's going to be sick."

I didn't see what my father's reaction was, but I heard Nicole say, "Help him for Christ's sake." Somebody else said, "Oh my." There was so much commotion I didn't know what to look at. I saw Sam pick himself up and stagger out onto the front porch, my mother and Nicole following him. Mother dragged him back into the house and took him down the hall to the bathroom. When things got past the immediate shock, I glanced over at my father, who sat in his chair, shaking his head.

I went out onto the back porch and sat down in a lawn chair back there. Phil's wife, Darlene, came out.

"I'm sorry," I said.

"Is he all right?"

"I guess."

"What a terrible thing to happen. The poor kid is probably so embarrassed he won't be able to look any of us in the face."

"I shouldn't have brought him here."

"He looked so pale." She smiled. Her eyes were always kind. I really did feel better just looking at her. When Phil first married Darlene she was a dainty sort of delicate compilation of fine white skin and small bones. But over the years she put on weight in all the wrong places, especially in her face, so that now she looked a little beset and imprisoned—as though her body had somehow collected too much fluid and it might burst any minute through the puffed skin around her eyes.

"I hope it isn't something serious," she said, clearly worried.

"It's not dangerous. He's just hung over. He drank so much yesterday he passed out. I shouldn't have brought him here. It was a terribly stupid thing to do."

"It isn't anyone's fault, really."

Phil came out. "Well things sure took a turn, didn't they?"

Darlene laughed. "I think we can wait awhile to start the coals."

"Is he all right?" I asked.

"I don't know. He's in the bathroom."

"Your mother is with him," Darlene said.

Phil looked at me and gestured toward the inside of the house with his head. "The old man says the kid was drunk."

"He's not drunk," I said. "Not now. He was drunk last night."

"Nicky told Dad he was drunk."

I shook my head.

Darlene said, "Are they..." Then she waited.

"No, they aren't," I said. "But he wants them to be. That's why he was drunk."

"Kids today," Phil said.

"Kids any day," I said. "Nobody young knows a thing about how to be old, so of course old people disapprove of them."

"And they don't have any respect for older people," said Phil.

"Right," I said.

"We're not old people," Darlene said.

"I didn't say 'old people,'" Phil said.

"Old people, older people—what's the difference?"

"Well," I told her, "we're not young anymore, that's for sure. And in any case, we're different. We have to let those who are young *be* young, without hounding them about it."

Phil seemed to grow a bit taller. "I haven't hounded anybody. I merely remarked on weird behavior of kids these days—a remark that was provoked, remember, by the fact that your young friend lost consciousness on my den floor before he said hello to anybody."

"Which was a perfectly stupid thing to do. I'm agreeing with you."

"It didn't sound like it."

"Well, I am. Everything you've said is exactly right."

"What is it with you today, Shaver? You look like you want to murder a family, and yet you seem to be possessed by this sort of virulent fairness."

"What?"

"Don't be so agreeable."

Darlene gave a short laugh. "Leave it to Phil to insist on being disagreeable."

"I'm insisting that he be himself and stop pretending."

"I am being myself," I said. "And by the way, *you* dropped the poor kid on the den floor."

"That's the Shaver I know."

"I'm sorry to say this," I added, "but I think it was pretty rotten of you not to hold on to him, or at least break his fall. It looked like you threw him down."

Phil smiled and looked at Darlene. "Is *he* drunk, too?" He pointed at me.

"Sam was drunk last night. He's sober now," I said.

"He doesn't look sober now."

Several minutes later Nicole came out. Her eyes were red, and I thought she might have been crying.

"What's the matter with you?" I asked.

"Nothing."

"Is Sam all right?"

She gave me a sour look. "Granddad was very unhappy that I said 'Jesus Christ.'"

"It's all right," Phil said, putting his arm around her. "No harm done."

Darlene rose and took Nicole's hands. "Can I get you something dear?"

Nicole shook her head, looking at me. "I had no idea Sam was that sick."

"Well," I said.

There was a long silence. I could feel Phil and Darlene looking at me, but I kept my eyes on Nicole. "Is he still sick?" I said.

"I don't know. Grandma took him to the clinic."

"You're kidding."

Phil went back into the house. Nicole sat down next to me and Darlene stood there in front of us for a moment, then she went into the house, too.

"My mother," I said.

"She was nice to him," Nicole said.

"I'm sorry about all this."

She didn't say anything. I felt her eyes on me, and I wondered if she was as embarrassed as I was. I didn't want to go back into the house for anything. I could just see my father, shaking his head, looking at me as if I had launched a turd into the salad.

"I wish we hadn't come here," Nicole said. "I don't know these people."

"'These people'? They're your family for Christ's sake."

"They're *your* family."

Now I looked at her. "They're *our* family."

She turned away, her hands resting in her lap.

"This whole thing is for you. Try to remember that."

No reaction.

"We shouldn't have brought him along," I said. "If he knew he was so sick, he shouldn't have..."

She looked at me.

"He should have told us."

A little later there was a clamor in the house. Darlene came back out. "Robert and Dianne are here with all the kids."

"Well," I said, "where's Phil?"

"He's talking to Dad."

"You want me to light the grill?"

"Pauline's not here yet. Maybe we should wait awhile."

We waited a long time. Robert and Phil started telling stories, then my father got going. We were all nervously waiting for my mother to return with Sam so we could get past what had happened. If I were Sam I would have kidnapped my mother and driven to Seattle before I'd let her take me back to the scene of the crime. But he did come back, sheepishly, his head sort of dangling on his shoulders, his hair combed, and more color in his face, but he was not the old Sam.

Late in the afternoon I went back out and stood with Phil while he started the coals.

"How do you think Dad looks?" he asked.

"What do you mean?"

"You think he looks normal?"

"Of course."

"He's getting old."

I didn't have anything to say to that. I sat down in one of the lawn chairs.

Darlene came out. "Pauline's here."

"It's about time," Phil said. He went in to say hello. Darlene stood by the door frame, looking out into the yard. I couldn't think of anything to say to her. I could hear Pauline's children caterwauling in the house.

After a long silence, Darlene stepped out of the door frame and sat down in front of me. Now I had to look at her. For an awkward second I saw her conquered eyes and I didn't know what to do about my face. I didn't know what expression she might have seen there.

"What's wrong, Henry?"

"What?"

"You look so unhappy."

"I'm fine." I sat up in the chair. "I haven't had a lot of sleep. Why's everybody asking me what's wrong?"

"Where's Elizabeth?"

I sat back. "She couldn't make it."

Darlene leaned over and peered back into the house as though she were checking to see if the coast was clear. Then she said, "Are you and Elizabeth having some difficulty?"

"Not particularly."

"It's none of my business, I know. But I can understand—I would understand, I think."

I didn't think she would understand. She was a woman. No matter what she might say to me, she would not understand.

Nicole came through the door with Pauline and pointed at me. "Here he is."

"Henry," Pauline said. I stood up and she hugged me. Darlene got up and put her arms around both of us. We hugged each other briefly, and Nicole sort of fidgeted in her chair.

"Your daughter is so beautiful," Pauline said, turning to her. "She looks like an actress."

Nicole blushed.

"She does," Darlene said. "She looks a little bit like Sondra Locke."

Nicole said, "Who's Sandra Locke?"

"Maybe a little bit of Meg Ryan mixed in," said Pauline. "And of course she really looks so much like her mother."

Nicole smiled.

"How is your mom?" Pauline asked.

"She's fine."

"And Mitch?"

I saw Darlene look at me.

Nicole said, "They're celebrating their tenth anniversary."

"That's wonderful," Pauline said.

"And now Dad," she gestured toward me, "it looks like he's getting married again."

There followed a stunned silence, in which Nicole blushed and then awkwardly said, "If he can work things out. He and Elizabeth are—"

"Nicole," I interrupted her, "enough already."

Pauline's expression was so bright eyed and pleased you'd have thought she'd won the lottery. "You're getting married again?"

Darlene squealed. It was a sound she should never make in public. "Why didn't you tell anyone?"

Pauline hugged me again. "That's so wonderful."

I didn't know what to say. I looked at Nicole, absolutely terrified that she was about to gild the lily by announcing that Elizabeth was pregnant, but when I caught her eye, I could see that she was aware of what she had done. She raised her brows and tilted her head a bit as a way of letting me know that she wasn't thinking and she was sorry.

Then my father came out. "What's everybody so happy about?"

"You'll never guess," Darlene said.

Pauline put her arm around his shoulder. "Does he know?"

"Nobody knows," I said.

"Shaver's getting married again," Pauline told him.

"Really." Dad looked at me. "When?"

"Soon."

"This is definite?" Darlene said.

"We haven't decided on a date, but sometime this summer."

My father walked over and looked at the coals burning in the grill.

Pauline said, "I'm going to tell Mother." She went back into the house, and Darlene and Nicole followed her. I sat back down in the chair.

It was suddenly very quiet. I watched the back of my father's head as he stared out into the yard. I was trying to think of something to say to him, but then he said, "So, I guess it will be a civil ceremony?"

"We haven't talked about that."

He leaned over and seemed to study something in the hot coals.

"Who knows. Maybe it won't happen, anyway," I said.

He looked at me. "It won't happen?"

"We were planning it. But something's come up."

"What?"

He was waiting there, and I knew that if I told him Elizabeth was pregnant and had decided to have the baby without me, I'd be adding another pound on the bad side of the scale of weights and measures he had used to judge my character. I wanted to tell him everything, because I couldn't stand the idea that he would die one day soon and I would never know him and he would never know me. If that happened I didn't see how we were any different from a pair of dogs.

"I guess she's having second thoughts."

"Well," he said, "you can't blame her. She's been shacking up with you this long."

I shook my head.

He looked at me. "It's just that faithfulness is not a prerequisite for merely living with a person."

"Apparently it's not a prerequisite for marriage, either."

He let out a short laugh. "You're right about that."

"Yeah."

"Maybe she has other interests."

"You don't like her very much, do you?"

"Oh, of course I do. Whatever gave you that idea?"

"Well, you don't approve of her—"

"Why does she need my approval?"

"She doesn't."

"Then what are we talking about?" His eyes were bright and alert, on the verge of a smile. I never knew anyone whose mind was so quietly visible in his expressions. He was being patient with me, and kind. Still, I sensed a judgment going on—his Catholic sense of justice was always just behind his demeanor, like an assassin behind a curtain.

"I guess we're talking about your tone of voice when you use phrases like 'shacking up.'"

He had no response to this. He looked out into the yard, and for a moment, I felt sorry for him. Phil was right. He seemed much older now and on the verge of brittle, helpless existence.

I said, "Look, Dad. I haven't led the kind of life you expected me to. I know that."

He shook his head and got this expression on his face, as if to say, "What's new?"

He wasn't ready for it. I could see he was intent on preserving his fun, enjoying his children and his grandchildren, all of whom loved him beyond reason. This great bear of a man, a soldier, a judge, with graying reddish hair and freckled arms and steady blue eyes. He'd done everything he said he was going to do. He didn't have the slightest notion of what it was like to try to say the right thing or to avoid a person's eyes in the hope that he would not have to confront secret weaknesses or woe.

I couldn't stand the idea that he was ashamed of me already and he didn't even know the worst of it.

"I didn't mean to be a disappointment," I told him.

"Son, you're not a disappointment."

"I'm not?"

"Of course not."

It was quiet for a minute, and I almost believed him, but then he said, "Aren't you disappointed in yourself? Aren't you the least bit unhappy about how your life has—"

"But I don't think about things like that."

"Yeah, well."

"I don't. I know how you feel about it, but I don't. I've never been one of those people who always gets what he wants. As a matter of fact, I sort of expect *not* to get what I want. I think that's safer."

He shook his head. "You've led a privileged, happy, safe life. You've been unbelievably lucky."

"I know."

"Look at it, son. Do you want me to point it out?"

I knew where he was heading. He'd always presented the differences between me and my brothers and sisters reluctantly, ticking off the successes and college degrees and professional achievements on each liver-spotted gnarled finger. It was his way of passing judgment without actually pronouncing any sort of sentence.

"You have talent. You're smart. You could have done so much more, son. That's all. And you know it, don't you?"

"I've done what I wanted."

"You never wanted anything else?"

"No. What do you think I should have wanted?"

He slowly shook his head. "You should have wanted to use your talents fully. You should have wanted more out of life than adolescence — living alone and spending your days at the racetrack."

"What do you care, as long as I'm happy?"

"Are you happy?" He looked at me.

"Well, yes. I am." It wasn't a very convincing yes.

"The evidence is against you," he said, a wry smile on his face. He seemed to want to smooth things over a bit. "It's your life, son. Not mine. I'm not disappointed in you. It's not my place to have the sort of expectations that would engender disappointment one way or the other."

"So, you had no expectations where I was concerned."

He frowned. "Don't turn my words like that. You know what I mean. I had no expectations where *any* of my children were concerned. *They* had their own expectations."

I didn't know what to say to him. You see what I was dealing with? Now *I* was at fault because I had no expectations of myself. But he wasn't disappointed in me. No.

He moved back toward the door. "Whatever's going on between you and Elizabeth, you better not get your mother all excited for no reason."

"I haven't told her anything. Pauline's taking care of that."

He shook his head. "You'll never change, will you."

"What?"

He turned to leave and I stood up and said, "Tell me what you mean."

"Son," he said, putting up his hand, "just make sure your mother doesn't get excited over nothing."

"I'll try," I said.

He tried to smile, but he was shaking his head as he went back in the house.

I know I should have simply denied the whole thing. All I had to do was laugh when Nicole first brought it up and tell everybody flatly that it wasn't true. But you see, when I told Nicole about it, it *was* true. Once I was cornered with all those pleased smiles and happy faces I was doomed.

The rest of the afternoon I kept thinking about Elizabeth and where she might be and what she might be thinking. I figured there was one hell of a lot to overcome before anybody threw any rice on me.

More Than a Few Days

Went by. Clearly Elizabeth was not going to call. I got off the couch Wednesday morning determined to settle things once and for all. I didn't care if she came to think of me as a stalker, I couldn't let the whole thing just die. I had to talk to her. Everybody in the family knew I'd asked her to marry me. I decided to simply go to the school and try to catch her between classes. But just as I was getting ready to leave, Chad showed up.

I've got to give you a brief picture of this guy. He's the new male. He wears jewelry. He wears it where women have traditionally worn it, and in places they've never dreamed of. He has a small gold ring in his right nostril, and his left eyebrow. Jewels sparkle in the lobes of his ears, and several earrings curl up the outside edge of each ear.

The average woman would kill for his hair. He has a tattoo on his right forearm. It's a picture of a pair of lips, open slightly, a red tongue sticking out. Underneath the lips it says *phht!*

He does not yet wear eye makeup or high-heeled shoes, but how can that be far behind? Women, after all, are now wearing combat boots, brogans, and wing tips. They've started cutting their hair short as men did in the early fifties, even though many of them have not noticed yet that their ears are incredibly prominent and unsightly.

Chad's arrival on the scene was a major turning point in that disastrous summer, and it was a thing I set into motion.

When I opened the door, he said, "Hullo."

I said, "Yes?"

"Nicky here, man?"

"I don't think she and Sam are up yet," I said, purposely putting Nicole and Sam together in Chad's little mind. "They don't usually get out of bed before late afternoon."

He looked at his feet. He was one of those guys who imitates the California lingo. You know the type. They say "dyodd" for *dad* and "dyewd" at the end of most of their utterances. Words like *important* and *really* are pronounced "amportant" and "rilly." They think people should know what they're "all about, man." They've never read a book or a newspaper, and they think Karl Marx is a "bitchin" clothing manufacturer. They think "hangin' out" is doing something. They sit around and drink beer and watch music videos and consider the problems of getting a really good soul kiss. They have real short conversations like this:

"You hangin' out tonight?"

"Ya."

"Cooall."

You'd rather spend ten years undergoing daily rectal exams than spend an hour with one of these guys.

"Did she know you were coming?" I asked. Just then the door in the hall upstairs opened and Nicole emerged. She was wearing her white shorts and the halter top I first saw her in. She sauntered down the steps.

"Hullo," Chad said again.

"Well, she's up after all. And before noon."

"This is Chad," she said to me. Then turning to him she waved her arm at me and said, "My father."

"Hey, dyewd."

"Come on in," said Nicole. "I have to get some juice."

"How you doing," I said.

Chad shrugged, waiting for me to move.

I stepped back and he went past me. He smelled like petroleum jelly. He followed her down the hall toward the kitchen. She went on in, but he stopped just as he got to the opening between the foyer and the kitchen.

Nicole poked her head back out and looked at me. Then she took his arm and said, "Come on."

I waved.

He disappeared around the corner, and I heard them whispering and then laughing. I went in the living room to the bar and poured myself a small glass of whiskey. There, by the bar, the morning light through the windows should have been positively uplifting but it only made me think of lost time. I thought the whiskey might taste warm and smooth. Instead it made my teeth feel brittle.

I finished my drink anyway, then went back into the kitchen. I hadn't had breakfast yet, so it's just possible that the whiskey was working in me a little bit.

That's probably why I ended up doing what I did.

Nicole sat at the table, drinking a glass of orange juice, and Chad had hiked himself up on the counter, leaning forward so that his triceps puffed just right. I noticed him looking at them while Nicole announced that she and Chad were going with some of his friends to a studio to hear a band recording a few songs.

"You have friends in the music business?" I said to him.

"Not rilly."

I could barely hear him. He didn't smile. He looked neither sullen nor happy. His face was a blank tablet with dull blue eyes.

I waited for him to go on. He wouldn't look at me.

"Well," Nicole said, putting down her glass, "shall we go?"

"What should I tell Sam?" I said.

She turned to me. "He knows where I'm going. He said he doesn't want to go."

"What's he going to do? I'm not going to be here today."

"I don't know, why don't you ask him. He's got a car. He can go wherever he wants."

"What if he comes back before we do? Is he just going to sit outside until one of us gets here?"

Nicole sighed.

Chad jumped off the counter. "Give him yer key, hey," he said to her. "We'll prob'ly be pretty late. The studio's in Baltimore."

"Baltimore," I said. "That's a long way to go to hear people who aren't *rilly* in the music business."

Chad smirked, chewing his gum. He stood there holding one arm across his chest, just slightly twitching his thumbs. He was all suppressed energy and potential movement—like a lizard on a bare rock.

"I'll leave him my key," Nicole said. She ran back upstairs.

There was a long silence. Finally I said, "So what do you do?"

Now he looked at me. "What?"

"What do you do?"

"I'm a student, prob'ly."

"Probably?"

"In the fall."

"Where at?"

"Right now I'm clueless, man."

"So, you just graduated, too?"

"No, I been out a couple years."

I didn't say anything.

"I'm prob'ly going to major in business administration or something like that."

"So you can go into business."

"Yeah." He smiled briefly, averting his eyes.

I couldn't take my eyes off the ring in his nose. How did he keep the damn thing clean? I wondered how he could blow his nose when it was necessary? Didn't he care what might happen to him in circumstances when he really did want his nose clean and working perfectly? I said, "What kind of business you want to get into?"

"I don't know. Maybe politics."

"Yeah. That's not really a business, though."

"I'm not just interested in making money. I want to help the world, sort of." He smiled, a crooked morose turn of his mouth. "Do something for people, man. That's where it's at."

"Still, it'd be nice to make money while you're doing it."

"Royatt." He leaned back, gave me the thumbs up sign. His smile turned into a sort of grimace. He looked as though he was struggling against an oncoming high-risk fart.

There was a long pause. We heard muffled voices upstairs. Chad didn't like the silence, so he started snapping his fingers.

"That's a tough life," I said.

"What?"

"Politics."

"I think somebody has to get in and straighten everything out."

"Yeah," I said. "It's a mess."

"Everything, man."

"Right."

"You know I rilly mean it."

"I know you do."

"I think the black people and Hispanics have caused more trouble as a group, and they're the ones the government is in favor of, rilly."

"Rilly," I said.

"Fer sure. They got all these . . . all these royatts, man. Yew know? And then they murder and do drugs and kill innocent bystanders, man. It's mostly those two races doing it all. And yew know, the Democrats ruined this country for white people, man."

I didn't say anything. There was another awkward silence, then Chad said, "I think somebody has to defend the rights of white people, yew know? I mean there are people in favor of Hispanics and Blacks and Jews and"—he glanced up the stairs, as though to point with his eyes—"and even chinks."

"'Chinks,'" I said. "Rilly?" I pretended I couldn't believe it.

"Somebody should help the white people, man."

"I thought the Republicans were doing that."

"Right. That's why I'm a Republican, man."

I'm not a fatalist or anything, but I was beginning to think that Chad might be the wave of the future. Only it wouldn't be a "wave" really. I think it might be more of a gesture, and an obscene one at that.

It never occurred to him that I might have a slightly different view of things than he did.

"Speaking of trouble," I said, leaning toward him, speaking secretively. "Has Nicole told you yet that she tested positive?"

That grabbed his little mind. "Huh?"

"Has she been frank with you about her—about her problem?"

"What problem?" He'd lost something of the edge in his California drawl.

"Whatever you do, don't mention it to her. It would kill her if she knew I told you."

"Told me what, man?"

"She might even get violent."

"Whoa." He looked up the stairs where Nicole had gone.

"She's a grown-up and I respect that. I wouldn't want to interfere. She makes her own decisions, just as I'm sure you do. Don't get me wrong."

He had nothing to say.

"Just take precautions, you know what I'm telling you?"

He turned to me, still frowning. You'd have thought there was not enough light to see me clearly.

"I'm sorry I had to tell you," I said. "She just won't accept it, even though she knows she might infect someone else if she isn't careful."

"Whoa, man."

"Remember what I said. Don't say anything to her. There's no telling what she might do. She's from California, you know. She's checked out on all sorts of weapons."

"Jesus Christ, man."

"Shhhh. Here she comes."

Nicole came back down the stairs. "Let's go."

She brushed past me, turned back, and kissed me on the cheek. "Bye."

"You'll be here for dinner?"

"I don't know. I'll call you."

Chad followed her down the hall.

"Glad I met you, Chad."

"Yeah." He slouched a bit more, flexing his arms slightly, then he oozed out the door.

I figured I'd fixed his little wagon.

I went back in the living room and poured myself another whiskey. This time it tasted pretty good. You might disapprove of what I told Chad, but if you were standing near enough to breathe his oxygen, if he was waiting in *your* living room, to take *your* daughter to Baltimore, you'd have done the same thing or something similar. You just have to take care of your children whenever they demonstrate the sort of personal taste and judgment you'd expect to find in a housefly or a tick.

I heard Sam moving around upstairs. I didn't want to talk to him, so I gulped the whiskey, then headed for the door.

He came out of my room, all dressed, his hair combed.

I felt like he had caught me at something. I was standing by the door, my hand on the knob. I said, "Good morning."

"Hi." He seemed engrossed in some thought. Then he said, "Where are you going?"

"What?"

"You going somewhere?"

I shrugged, "I have to get some things."

We stood there awkwardly facing each other. He wanted to avoid me as much as I wanted to avoid him.

"So," I said. "You got a key, then?"

"What do you think I should have done?"

"What?"

"Should I have gone with them?"

"Did she ask you to go?"

"She seemed surprised that I wasn't going."

"Did she ask you?"

He seemed to slump a bit.

"You expect her to guess how you feel? Talk to her for Christ's sake."

He shrugged.

"She doesn't have to deal with you about this if you don't tell her. She'll just keep pretending it's OK the way it is. Don't you see that?"

"I'm afraid I'll ruin it. I'll lose her—" He caught himself. "I'm afraid I'll lose her friendship."

"You don't have to push her. It's not something that has to be decided right this instant. But you've got to let her know you're in the game. Anyway, it's not really friendship you're talking about, is it."

"I guess not."

"Is she really interested in this … this Chad fellow?"

"I can't stand him. He's a fake."

"Is she …"

Something seemed to dawn on him. "She's just enjoying her new body."

I didn't like the sound of that, and it must have showed. He hastened to explain: "She's thin now, and pretty. For the first time in her life she's attractive to lots of guys, and she's enjoying that. She isn't serious about him, either. She told me that."

"She did?"

"She said she doesn't want to get serious now with anyone. She just wants to—you know. Date."

"Yeah. Date. And that's not serious."

"No. It really isn't. She thinks he's weird. She had fun with him at the beach though, and she wants to hang out with him. That's why she went with him today."

"To hang out."

"Yeah."

"What the fuck does that mean?" I was still standing there holding onto the door handle. He was still on the landing, looking down at me. "What does 'hang out' mean, exactly?"'

He seemed puzzled. "You know."

Against my will I suddenly felt pretty fatherly. "No, I don't know. It sounds like a terrific waste of time."

He smiled, halfheartedly.

There was a long tense silence, and then I remembered that I was about to go out and corner Elizabeth.

"I got to be going," I said. "You gonna hang out here?"

He was a smart kid. The stricken smile on his face told me I'd hit home. "Yeah, I'm going to 'hang out' here. So long, Mr. Porter."

"You're a lot better man than Chad," I said. "Give her time."

"Yeah."

"I mean that," I said. "You are a better man."

He bowed his head modestly. Then he smiled. "Yeah," he said again.

I really did feel bad leaving him there all by himself.

At Potomac High School

An older, faultlessly clean woman told me Elizabeth wasn't there. "Her summer classes are in the main administration building," she added, eyeing me over the rims of her glasses. She stood at a counter with a lot of papers stacked in front of her. She was clearly busy. Her eyes, glaring at me above the lenses, looked like a pair of pearl onions hovering over two small cut-glass bowls. She smelled like chalk.

"And where is the administration building?"

"It's in Manassas." She blinked slowly, still assessing what I might be up to.

I didn't want to go all the way to Manassas. "When will she be back here?"

"Not till this fall."

I was frustrated and it showed. "How come her classes are down there?"

"The building's air-conditioned."

"Oh."

She stacked some papers in front of her.

"Do you know what Elizabeth's hours are?"

"Is there something I can help you with?"

"No."

"If it's about a student or—"

"No, it isn't. It's about our baby."

The skin on her forehead shifted back, so that the entire graying

190

mane of hair on the top of her head looked as though it might slip off. She gazed now through the lenses at a chart of some kind on the counter in front of her. "I can't really say what her hours are," she said. "The school day begins at 9:00 A.M. and ends at 3:30 P.M."

"She must eat lunch."

"I didn't know she was"—her eyes rolled a bit, the lids half closed—"in the family way." It cost her a lot to say that.

"She hasn't told anyone yet."

There was a long pause while she decided whether to believe me or not. Then it hit me that I had probably let some sort of cat out of a bag. After all, this was Virginia—one of the most medieval states in the Milky Way. Elizabeth was a teacher, a molder of young minds. The old woman had a very serious look on her face. I felt as though I had just told her that Elizabeth was humping the Mormon Tabernacle Choir.

"We're getting married," I said.

In a rather haughty tone she said, "I hope you'll be very happy."

I asked her for directions to the administration building, and she reluctantly gave them to me. Then she told me I should definitely not interrupt Elizabeth's classes.

"Her office is on the sixth floor," the old woman said. "You should go there."

"I'll just wait in her office."

I turned to leave, and she went back to her papers. You could tell it had been a very, very long time since she had been very happy about anything.

The whiskey I'd drunk that morning hadn't helped me much. I was too nervous. It was about ten-thirty when I left the school, and I had plenty of time to catch Elizabeth before lunch, so I went to the store and picked up a six-pack of cold beer and a bag of pretzels. I didn't want to sit in my car and drink, so I took two of the cans and pocketed them, and then went to a small park near the high school. I sat down on a flat bench in the shade and opened one of the beers and the bag of pretzels. There was no one under the canopy of trees but me. In the distance, I could see the sun gleaming off passing cars and storefront signs. It was already getting hot. Lazy currents of air could barely stir a single leaf. I held the cold can of beer against my forehead to cool off.

Here in the shade the ground was dry and bare. The bench had been carved up pretty good with hearts and arrows, the names of couples like Suzi and David, and Betty and Skip. I ate the whole bag of pretzels, thinking about what was expected of me. It occurred to me that marriage would be a wonderful thing if all you had to do was carve your names in the wood on a park bench or the bark of a tree and that was it. If you stayed married until the bark grew back or the bench got painted. If you didn't have to tell everybody in your whole family and all your friends so they would all be there to watch you embarking on what the odds say will be a failed enterprise. If you didn't have to pretend you were certain about what you would want when you were a decade or more older.

A squirrel came down the side of the tree next to the bench and looked at me. I had no pretzels left, and I didn't think he'd drink the rest of my beer. His eyes were small and wary. When I popped the top of the second beer, he dashed back up the tree. He didn't know beer is a pretty good thing as long as you don't overdo it. I figured maybe I was a little like that squirrel. I'd been married once before, and it ended up so bad, I was a little skittish about it. Certainly I could get Elizabeth to see that. If I could convince her I really wanted to get married. How could she hold my initial panic against me? I was willing to give that squirrel a sip of my beer if he came down out of the tree and let me know he wanted one.

I didn't have any trouble finding the administration building. I took the elevator up to the sixth floor and searched for Elizabeth's office. I walked down a long hall to a pair of double glass doors. Before I went in, I realized I probably smelled of beer, so I took a left down another longer hall, looking for a men's room. I figured I'd drink a lot of water, wash my face, try to look a little less disheveled. The hall was fairly dark, with bright floors; and a pair of windows at the end of it reflected light along the tiles like the moon on water at night. I couldn't see very well. I imagined I'd get halfway down the hall and see a silhouette coming toward me, and I'd wonder if it was Elizabeth. We'd approach each other until I would see that it was her, and she'd recognize me, and it would be one of those truly romantic moments that couples tend to remember when everything is gone out of their love and they don't have much to say anymore. But no one came out. The hall was bare, and I suddenly realized the beer had finished with me and I was going to have to find a bathroom pretty quickly.

At the end of the hall was a ladies' room. All the way down at the other end of the hallway, in the other direction from the double doors, was probably the men's room. You can see what was going on there, can't you? It didn't matter which way I turned at those double doors. Left or right. Whichever way I went, the men's room was going to be in the other direction.

I was just ill-tempered enough to say the hell with it. I went into the ladies' room.

Elizabeth was standing at the sink, washing her hands. I scared the living daylights out of her.

"Jesus Christ," she said. "You can't come in here."

I didn't know what to say. I had to take a piss too bad.

"What are you doing here?" she said.

"I wanted to talk to you." I hurried past her into one of the stalls and took care of business. When I came out she was standing there, her hands on her hips.

"Maybe we should go back to your office."

She shook her head, half amused. "You're the only person I know who would just come walking in here. How did you know where I was?"

"I didn't. I just had to go."

"You are simply crazy," she said. She was exasperated, not charmed.

I went to the door and held it open. She leaned her head out and checked that the hall was empty, then she signaled to me and I followed her out.

"I have a class to get back to."

"When's lunch?"

"I can't have lunch with you today."

"Why?"

She didn't want to tell me. "I just can't."

"We have to talk."

We went around the corner by the double doors and stopped at the elevator.

I pointed to the double doors across the hall. "Is your office in there?"

"Yes, but you can't wait, Henry. I'm just not ready to talk yet. I've been doing a lot of thinking."

I couldn't get her to look me in the eye. That, and the fact that she had been thinking, was always a bad sign.

We waited there by the elevator, and gradually I realized she was not going to talk to me. Not unless I forced the issue.

"It scares me that you've been thinking," I said.

"Heaven forbid I should think."

"No. Look, I have to say this to you." I was in a hurry to say everything to her, and she noticed it. She met my gaze briefly, but I thought I read pity in her eyes and it made me feel foolish as I talked. "I love you. I want to marry you. I think we'll have a wonderful life. I've told my whole family we're getting married, and they're all very excited."

She seemed to recall something when I said this, and then she looked away again — as though she was searching for something on the floor or behind me.

"What's the matter?" I said.

The elevator door opened. She turned back to me briefly, then moved into the elevator. I followed her. The doors closed. She was staring at the floor. The elevator started down. In between the second and first floors, I pried the inner doors open and the elevator stopped.

"I don't care about anything else now," I said. "We have to talk."

She looked frightened. "What'd you do?"

"I stopped the elevator."

"But how?"

"You just force the doors open. It almost always works if you can get them to open."

"Well, you close them right now."

I pushed a few buttons. "We're stuck now. See? We may as well have a conversation."

"Close the doors."

"I can't." I pretended to try. "See? We really are stuck."

"What about my class? I can't just let them—"

"You're stuck on an elevator for Christ's sake. Nobody can fault you for that."

I pushed the alarm button. We heard a bell ringing somewhere. It seemed perfectly natural to look at her and smile reassuringly. "I can't think of anybody else I'd rather be stuck in an elevator with."

"This isn't funny."

"I'm not trying to be funny."

She said nothing.

"Well?" I said.

She was not looking at me again. "I don't have anything to say."

"I love you. I want to marry you."

Nothing.

"I mean it. I really mean it. I really really really mean it."

"Henry," she turned to me. She looked so sad, it momentarily startled me.

I believed this was the most romantic, the most unorthodox, the most incredibly creative way to propose to a person.

Then she said, "I know you want to be wonderful, but..."

"But what?"

"But I just—I just..." She shook her head. "I'm not going to talk to you about this now. I want you to get the goddamned elevator going again."

"You needn't get angry. I'm just trying to—"

"You just have to have everything your way, don't you?"

"This is a proposal."

She turned away and started pushing buttons herself.

"I thought you wanted to get married," I said.

No answer. She kept pushing buttons. The alarm bell stopped, then came back on again. She hit the door CLOSE button, and the elevator jerked violently.

"Be careful," I said.

She looked at me, and I noticed her eyes were getting kind of teary. "Henry, please do something."

"Are you scared?" I reached for her, but she batted my hand away.

"I'm getting really angry." Now she was starting to cry.

"Come on," I said. "Just say you'll marry me."

"This is not a proposal. It's an abduction. That's what it is."

"It is not. I'm proposing to you. You know I won't hurt you."

"You are holding me here against my will." Her voice shook but I couldn't tell if she was angry or afraid.

"Come on, Liz. For Christ's sake. I just wanted to talk."

"OK," she said, dropping her arms. She got control of herself. "Talk."

There was an awkward silence, then I said, "I already said what I have to say. I want to marry you."

"I *don't* want to marry you."

"Come on, you're just pissed off because I stopped the elevator. I'm serious here." I reached for her but she backed away.

"I'm serious as well," she said coldly. "I said what I meant."

"I don't believe you."

"I will not marry you, Henry. Not now, not ever."

"Why?"

She shook her head. "Henry." She drew my name out into a long sigh.

"No, why? You wanted to before. What happened?"

"I've had time to think."

"And?"

There was a long pause. The alarm clanged inside my head, but she seemed to calm down a bit. I could see that she really was thinking. "I've come to see that everything about us is wrong, that's all."

"Why?"

"Do we have to go over all this?"

"Yes. I think I deserve that."

"You know, you give the impression that you're a complete person, that you're an adult. But you're not all there, are you?"

"What's that supposed to mean?"

"Not that you're not smart or . . . or sane. It's just that you're not all there. A part of you is always reserved, held back to comment on everything and everyone. It's almost as if you were outside yourself watching your life, calculating the odds."

"So it's the gambling. That's it."

She got this really pained look on her face. "You just don't get it, do you?"

"I guess I don't."

"You're always watching for what your true self might want. And when you can't figure it out, you stall."

"I think about things, like anybody else. Like you."

"No. You're always holding something back, Henry, because you can't figure out what you want soon enough, and you always know what you should want. So there's a gap there. A huge place missing from your soul that you have to fill in by pretending."

"If you're trying to get me angry, it's not going to work."

She almost laughed. "You really don't know yourself at all, do you?"

I couldn't stand the way she was looking at me now. "I'm just who I am," I said. "That's all."

"You're so sad, Henry."

I pushed the alarm button again trying to shut it off. "This thing is driving me nuts."

She shook her head.

"I'm not sad. You're sad," I said, still pushing on the alarm button. The elevator jerked again.

"Goddamn it." She glared at me, so I stopped. "Just leave it alone. Somebody will send help."

"I'm sorry," I said.

I didn't know what to do with my hands. She stood there looking at me. Then I said, "We were engaged. You said you'd marry me."

"I finally realized what our relationship meant to you, Henry. Even if you never realize it. You would rather lie to me than tell me your real feelings. You actually have to take time to figure out what your real feelings are. Most of the time you're just acting. I won't marry you, Henry, because, whether you know it or not, you don't want to get married. You don't even want me to have this baby."

These words rattled all the nerves in my heart. "Jesus Christ," I said.

Now she gazed into my eyes with a kind of awed pity. I don't know how long we stood there like that.

"I'm sorry, Henry," she whispered. "I truly didn't realize it until all this happened. It would just be a big mistake."

I had nothing to say to her. There was a long pause while we began to fidget. We were like strangers, and we had this situation.

"I've got to get back to my class." She looked at her watch. She actually looked at her goddamned watch. "Oh, I don't know, Henry. I'm so sorry." She was starting to cry.

"I have to find some place to sit down," I said.

"Isn't there some way you can close the doors again?" She pushed on them herself.

I tried to force the doors to close but they wouldn't budge. "If we hadn't touched the alarm, I could probably close them," I said.

"You set off the alarm." She started to pace.

"I know. I'm sorry."

Goddamn. *Estrangement* is an accurate word. I was too embarrassed and ashamed to be where she could see me. It really was getting hot in there. I felt stupid and completely helpless. Oddly enough, I wanted to help her. I wanted to get the doors closed and the elevator moving again to rescue her from me and to get myself out of her loveless sight. My desire to help her was almost spiteful. And yet, the more she paced there, the more I realized I really did love her. In fact I was never so certain of anything else in my life. It hit me with tremendous force that now I was going to lose her and our child and any chance I ever had of once again having a family I could call my own. Of course, the Fates made absolutely sure that I never realized how much I wanted these things until the precise moment at which I knew for certain I would not have them.

I just couldn't stand there anymore without doing something. The ceiling did not look promising. For one thing, I couldn't climb up there without something to stand on, and it was covered by a grill of some kind that looked pretty well permanent. I couldn't even be sure if there was a door up there, and I didn't want to waste energy trying. The only thing I could think of was trying to force the doors all the way open. So I pushed on them and you know what? They opened.

The elevator shook.

"Whoa," Elizabeth said.

The doors stayed open. I could see the opening for the first floor below us. It was about six feet. If I lay on my stomach and reached straight out I could get my hands in between the opening on the outer doors there.

"I think I can open the outer doors, but I don't know what good it would do."

"See if you can do it," Elizabeth said. "Maybe we can jump down."

"I don't think that would be wise."

"Do it, but be careful."

"Right," I said, looking at her with what I hoped was an expression of wry irony.

I guess I felt like a hero. On some level I must have believed that if I rescued her, she'd take me back. I wasn't thinking at all about how we got into such a predicament to begin with. I tried to separate the outer doors with all my might, but they were clamped tight. I sat up to catch my breath. "Damn, that's a hard position to get any leverage."

"Why doesn't somebody come?"

"That alarm bell is loud, somebody will be here soon." I looked into her eyes and saw hope there. She wanted to act as though we were never lovers, as though this was a problem we found ourselves in as friendly strangers. It made her sort of happy and relieved, now that everything was definitely settled. I could see she wanted to remain friends. But then again, the only person who could help her was me. "I'll give it another shot," I said.

"Don't hurt yourself."

I scrunched myself closer to the opening. I could see to the bottom of the shaft, where slivers of light leaked in under each door. It was eerie, like a wide coffin. With all my might I pushed on the doors, and this time they came open, first slowly, then completely.

"I did it." I was so proud of myself, I actually thanked the Fates.

"What do we do now?"

"Well, we'll call for help."

Now we were both lying on the floor of the elevator hollering for help. We could see the tile floor in the hallway and back toward several office doors. A woman came down the hall and looked up at us.

"Stuck, huh?"

"No," I said. "Just before we were ready to step off, the building went down."

Another voice came from up the hall. "Is that what the alarm is about?"

"That's it," the woman said. Then she turned back to us. "Somebody will be right here. We can't get it to work, so we've called maintenance. They said they'd send over a repairman."

"Great," I said.

Elizabeth looked at the woman and shook her head.

"In the meantime," the woman said, "could you turn off that alarm?"

"I don't know how to," I said.

Elizabeth stood up and started pushing buttons furiously.

"Pull the alarm button out," the woman said.

Elizabeth pulled on it and the alarm stopped.

"Thank you," the woman said. She had lipstick on her teeth and deep lines around wide scornful eyes. The impression she gave was of a woman who had spent most of her life alone, taking care of a small yapping dog.

Elizabeth said, "I have a class waiting for me in room 121. Could you send someone down there for me?"

"What's the room?"

"One twenty-one."

"OK." The woman clacked off in her heels.

"Do you know her?" I asked.

"No."

Suddenly Elizabeth was laughing. Then I was laughing. We were quite a pair, lying on our stomachs with tears in our eyes, howling.

The woman came back and asked us if we wanted something to eat.

It was getting near noon.

Elizabeth said, "I've got to get out of here."

Other people wandered into the hall now, maintaining their distance. We had been asked several times if we needed anything.

Elizabeth said, "I think there's enough room for me to swing my legs out and drop down to the floor."

"You think we can do it?"

"Sure. It's not that big a leap."

"Don't try it. You might fall."

"You have to go through a pretty thin slot to fall."

"Don't do it," I said.

"I have a class to get to, and I'm going."

"Seriously, I don't want you to try that. They'll get help and—"

"I'm going," she said. "Are you going to help me?"

I studied the opening. It did look possible to slip down and jump a short distance to the floor below. The only thing that bothered me was the gaping black hole of the elevator shaft. If we didn't land right, we could fall back into it—and I didn't know how far we'd fall.

Elizabeth turned over and got into a seated position on the edge.

"Wait a minute," I said.

She looked at me.

"I'll go first." I turned over on my stomach and dangled my legs down, then I pushed myself off and landed on the floor below. It was no more difficult than jumping down from a bunk bed. Everybody clapped.

"You were right," I said. "It was easy."

Now Elizabeth scooted out and dangled her legs. She was in a terribly awkward position and she started to laugh again. To steady her I reached up and put my hands on her outer thighs, and she laughed even harder.

"Pardon my hands," I said. She had a great laugh. I was laughing, too, listening to it. She was facing me, though, and very determined.

She was still laughing, trying to get control of it. I said, "After what we've shared, we should get married." This really got to her. She laughed so loud and so easily, even now I can't really decide if she was only laughing or if she might have been crying a little, too.

She looked right into my eyes, and for a fraction of a second there, I had the feeling that we were in love again. "Don't," she said. "I can't get my breath." Even the people around us had started to laugh.

"Come on, now," I said. "Swing down, I've got you."

Just as I said that, she let go.

I didn't expect to have her weight in my hands. I grabbed for her. She had taken off her shoes and her bare feet in the nylon stockings hit the edge of the floor and she slid from my arms and down so fast I felt as though I had tried to catch a spirit.

Elizabeth

Fell down to the basement floor. It was about thirty-five feet, and she didn't scream or make a sound. When she hit the floor below, I heard her shocked bones echo in the shaft.

What happened next is a complete blur to me. Probably there was a lot of noise. I remember pushing people away from me, and I must have been shouting Elizabeth's name. Everybody kept trying to pull me away from the shaft and I heard all these voices telling me to calm down. Everything was completely dreamlike, and then I remember how suddenly quiet it was.

People were hushed all around me, and I was lying on the floor trying to see down into the darkness of the shaft. I just knew she had to be all right. She didn't fall that far. I might have been saying that out loud, "She didn't fall that far. She has to be all right. Elizabeth. Elizabeth." Even now I can't remember much of anything else but the sudden silence.

This is the part that I can't get out of my mind: At the bottom of that shaft, lying there shocked and frightened, Elizabeth must have lost consciousness for a while and then awakened in the darkness and wondered where she was. She could probably see the light and shadows above her, and for some reason she started calling out in a weak voice, "Is anybody up there?"

At first I couldn't hear what she was saying. I called her name.

Then she said it again. "Is anybody up there?"

I started crying. I hadn't wept since Catherine took Nicole to California, but there I was lying on that floor staring down into the darkness, listening to Elizabeth gasping for air. She kept saying, "Is anybody up there?"

I wanted to tell her: There's somebody up there all right.

I Watched the Ambulance

Take Elizabeth away. I wanted to go with her, but the rescue team closed the doors so fast, I didn't have the nerve to ask them to open them again. I stood there wondering what to do.

A pudgy fatherly county policeman named Puckett came over to me and gently put his arm over my shoulders. He wanted to know if I was all right. He had been waiting there by the entrance to the building when they carried Elizabeth out and placed her in the ambulance. She didn't look good when they brought her out. The side of her face was all bruised and bleeding and swollen, and her left arm was folded funny across her breast. Two paramedics shoved the stretcher back into the darkness of the ambulance, and then one of them gently moved me out of the way. The last thing I saw was Elizabeth's shocked and sorrowful eyes. She was just staring into space. I couldn't even tell if she was alive.

Officer Puckett asked me if I was calmed down enough to talk.

"I've got to get to the hospital," I said.

"You want to tell me what happened?"

"It was an accident." I was trying to hurry past him, so I could follow the ambulance.

He stopped me. "I'll take you to the hospital. It'll be faster."

"Thank you." I followed him across the street to his squad car. There was another cop waiting there for us.

"She just fell," I said. "She was trying to get out of the elevator and she fell."

The other officer opened the car door for me. I had to ride in the back while Puckett and his partner rode up front. I felt like I was under arrest.

We followed the ambulance as it careened down the street toward Manassas Hospital. Officer Puckett talked briefly on the radio. The car smelled of wet leather and sweat and cigarettes.

Puckett turned to me. "Is there anybody we should notify?"

"No. Her father, maybe."

"Do you have his number?"

"No. He lives in Philadelphia."

"Anything we should know about her?"

"What?"

"Is she allergic to any medicines or—"

"She's pregnant," I said.

Puckett looked at his partner, then back to me.

"She's going to have a baby. You should tell the doctors that."

He looked at his partner again, then he radioed the information to the emergency room.

I couldn't get Elizabeth's battered face out of my mind. They strapped her to a flat board, and when they picked her up and put her on the stretcher, she looked at me with a sort of pitiful expression—as though she were embarrassed for having failed to make the leap—and I felt so ashamed it nearly choked me. Then she moved her head slightly, and her eyes seemed to go blank, as if the color drained out of them.

Puckett leaned over the seat and asked me if he could see my driver's license. I took it out of my wallet and handed it to him. He studied it for a moment, then he retrieved a clipboard, which had been hanging on the dash of the car, and slipped my license under the clip. He took out a ballpoint pen and clicked it once, then he said, "Do you have a lawyer, Mr. Porter?"

"What?"

"I'd like to ask you some questions, and I wondered if you'd like me to wait until you have a lawyer here with you."

"What do I need a lawyer for?"

"Do you want a lawyer, sir?"

"No. I don't need one."

He started asking me questions. Who I was. Where I lived. What I did for a living. If I'd ever had any trouble with the police. Did I know Elizabeth. How long. He took notes, so I tried to talk more slowly than normal. His partner watched the road ahead, but I could see he was not keeping up with the ambulance.

"Can't you go any faster? We're losing them," I said.

"I know where the hospital is, sir," the driver said.

"What were you doing in the building?" said Puckett.

"I came to see Elizabeth."

He wrote something on the pad. He seemed to notice I was getting agitated. "I'm awful sorry," he said, "this is just a procedure we have to go through."

He asked me to describe my relationship with Elizabeth.

"She was my fiancée."

"Really."

"Yes."

"And you and the young woman were having some sort of difficulty?"

"No."

"Did you quarrel?"

"No. We didn't quarrel. I asked her to marry me, again."

"What happened on the elevator?"

"Nothing. She said no."

"I see."

"When I asked her before, she said she'd think about it. So I was asking her again. We weren't fighting. We were laughing."

He nodded, jotting on the pad.

"Why did you think we were having some sort of difficulty?"

"One of the young women at the scene—the victim's friend, I believe—mentioned that she was having some problems with a... with a—shall we say—persistent man."

I shook my head. "What happened in the elevator had nothing whatever to do with the 'problems' between Miss Simmons and me."

"What did happen on the elevator?"

I had nothing whatever to say to him, so I turned and stared out the window.

"Well?" he said.

"It got stuck."

"It just stopped?"

"Right."

"Just like that."

"Yes. We got stuck on it. I was trying to help her get off."

"Have you been drinking today?"

"I just had a few beers. Jesus."

"I realize you're upset," Puckett said. "But I have to ask you these questions, and now is as good a time as any."

"I just want to get to the hospital."

"I realize that."

There was a long pause, then I said, "I'm sorry."

"So. You and Miss Simmons were not having any difficulty?"

"The only difficulty we were having was the elevator got stuck."

There was a long silence. I only half realized how it might look to them. I was so worried about Elizabeth. It really was my fault. If I hadn't pried open the elevator doors, she would not have had to jump down to the first floor and she wouldn't have fallen.

Puckett said, "Let me get this straight. The elevator just stopped? For no reason?"

"Yes." I felt a sudden blast of fear.

He nodded, turned back toward the front. I didn't want to answer any more questions. It occurred to me that Elizabeth might tell somebody that I had stopped the elevator. I wasn't sure the repairman couldn't figure it out himself. Fear made me irrational. I was actually worried that they might have some sort of diagnostic computer that measured everything and the elevator could thereby claim its own innocence. That would be all I needed. Then everybody wants to know how it got stuck.

Puckett turned back to me and said, "How do you think the elevator got stuck like that?"

I was briefly speechless. Then I said, "I don't know."

Somebody called over the radio. They had this crackling conversation, only half of which I understood. They were using numbers and your basic police lingo. The two words I understood clearly were *suspect* and *victim*.

"Look," I said, "Elizabeth will tell you, this was an accident."

They had nothing to say.

It was quiet for a while, and I realized I could no longer hear the ambulance. We weren't going fast enough. I saw Puckett's eyes scanning the road in front, and then I remembered the look on Elizabeth's face when she first saw me after the fall. She was trying to lift her head, and when her eyes met mine, she seemed to soften, as though what was struggling in her found peace at the sight of me. I didn't know what it meant, but I longed to hear her voice laughing again. I wanted her to forgive me. I didn't know what I would do if she didn't ever forgive me.

Suddenly it hit me that Elizabeth might die. The thought made my heart stutter and I felt a cold wind blow right through it. *What if she was already dead?* Maybe that was why I couldn't hear the ambulance anymore. They'd turned the siren off because they were no longer in such a hurry. I felt weak and breathless because I couldn't imagine any other outcome. She was dead. She had just landed the wrong way and the fall killed her. This was nothing more than the perfect trick for the Fates to play. No matter what my thoughts were or what I hoped for, Elizabeth was already gone.

I couldn't sit still.

"Are you all right?" Puckett said.

The question momentarily disarmed me. It was so absurd, it seemed hostile.

We pulled into the driveway in front of the emergency room. The ambulance was already there, the back doors wide open, the cavity inside empty.

When Puckett opened the door, I bolted out of the car and ran to the entrance. I turned and saw him and his partner running toward me. I just wanted to get to where Elizabeth was so I could see her and know for sure how she was; so I could tell her I was sorry, and hold her and not let her go, and keep her alive.

I don't know what I was thinking, but I went through the doors of the emergency room and ran down a narrow corridor. In front of me was an empty gurney, the white sheet pulled tight around it. To the left were signs and plants and curtain-covered entrances. I didn't know where Elizabeth was or where I was going. I might have called her name. I made a right down a dark hallway. I bumped into a nurse, who told me I should wait in the lobby.

Somehow, I ended up back in the lobby of the emergency room. I paced in front of a bank of windows. I saw Puckett sitting in front of a desk talking to a nurse. I went over and stood behind him, but I really couldn't hear what he was saying. I started pacing again, then I found a chair by a thin rectangular window. I could sit there and look out at the full trees and the cars coming and going in the parking lot.

Sometime that afternoon I asked the receptionist if Elizabeth was still alive, and she smiled at me and said she would find out. She got on the phone, and after what seemed like an eternity, she gently put the phone down and said, "Ms. Simmons is in the intensive care unit. She's getting the finest care." She wanted to know if I was family, and I said no.

"Well," she said, "I need to get some insurance information for her."

"Can you find out the extent of her injuries?"

"Just a second."

I went back and sat down. People were looking at me. I don't know how much time passed. Then the nurse signaled to me and I went back over to her desk. She smiled gently and said, "She's still in ICU."

"Is she going to be all right?"

"You'll have to talk with the doctor."

She sat there looking at me through thick, dark-rimmed glasses.

"Can I go up?" I said.

"I'm afraid if you're not family you must wait."

I went back and sat down, but I couldn't just sit there anymore. I got up and walked around. Faces were a blur around me. Then I saw a pair of side doors that led out into the sunlight. The doors seemed to open on their own and swallow me. Suddenly I was outside.

I wanted to disappear somewhere in the basement of the world.

Later That Evening

I found myself sitting in a Burger King, sipping coffee. I didn't remember how I got there, or buying the coffee, but I was suddenly alert. Perhaps a police car pulling through the parking lot outside and going to the drive-up window woke me up. It hit me then, when my heart shivered at the sight of the cops, that Elizabeth might be gone. Then I looked at my hands and found the cup of coffee there. I don't even like coffee that much.

I dumped it in the trash and got myself a large Coke.

I had to figure out what I should do. I knew I had to talk to Nicole, let her know what happened. I needed to talk to Nicole before I did anything. I had this powerful urge to apologize to her—as though she could forgive me for Elizabeth.

I found a public phone in front of the men's room, so I dialed my number. Sam answered the phone, "Porter residence."

"Sam, this is Henry. Is Nicole back yet?"

"She called."

"Where is she?"

"I don't know. She said she'd be back soon. That was two hours ago."

"Something's happened," I said.

I waited for him to say something, but there was only silence. Finally I said, "There's been an accident."

"Are you all right?"

"I'm fine. I mean, I'm not hurt."

"You need me to come get you or something?"

"Have the police been there?"

"No."

"No one's called?"

"Yes, Nicole called. What's going on, Mr. Porter?"

"I need to talk to Nicole."

"What's happened?"

"My fiancée had a fall. She's..." I couldn't finish the sentence. There was a long pause, while I tried to get control of myself. I could not say the words, and the image of Elizabeth, still and cold, took my breath away.

Finally Sam said, "I'll come get you. Where are you?"

"I'm in a Burger King on Route 244, somewhere in Manassas."

"What are you doing there?"

"Jesus Christ," I said, too loud. There was another long silence, then I said, "It's a long story."

He didn't answer.

"Sam?"

"What."

"Go north. Toward Washington. Take Route 244 west. Go about ten miles or so until you're in the city and then start looking for a Burger King on the right. It's at a big intersection. You can't miss it."

"What's going on, Mr. Porter?"

"Just do this for me, will you?"

I gave him the directions one more time. "Hurry," I said.

"Am I going to be breaking any laws tonight?"

"Of course not."

"Well what's the deal with the police?"

"Just come and get me, OK?"

"I don't want to get into any trouble."

"Right," I said, and hung up the phone.

I went back to my seat and finished my Coke. It would take Sam about forty-five minutes to get there. The sun was starting to descend into a thicket of distant high-rises and apartment buildings. I thought about the thousands of human beings who inhabited the space before me, the countless little apartments, and rooms with tables and chairs, and pictures on the walls, and kitchen utensils stacked under the counters. I thought of the hours and hours of living, breathing, talking, and sleeping; the lovemaking, laughing, bickering, screaming, and crying. All the day-to-day utterances, like "hello," "good morning," "have a good one," "love you," "thank you," "see you later," and "bye-bye." I thought of the miles and miles of toilet paper and dental floss and paper towels that must be rolled up and stacked in various small rooms all over the city—in every corner of town. I thought of all the concrete, brick, steel, glass, and plastic we've manufactured in spite of the fact that every last one of us is going to be fertilizer some day.

What a human thing a city is. One city. Tons and tons of worn-out furniture, torn plastic, empty milk cartons, and used up tinfoil. A billion gallons of sewage, silt, and soapy water.

As I pondered all these things, an old man came through the door, carrying a small white bag. He had an orange baseball cap tilted back on his head, and a long dirty sleeveless shirt. He wore Levi's and high-top tennis shoes. Thick glasses roosted on the very tip of his nose. It was clear he suffered from some sort of affliction, because he was continually nodding his head up and down. Wherever he went, whatever he saw, whoever he spoke to, his answer was always a gesture that said yes. He said yes all the time, in every circumstance; and each time he did, his mouth would squinch up in a sort of half smile, half grimace, so that he appeared to proffer only grudging approval—as though he were agreeing to some inevitable thing. He looked exactly like a man who might be saying to a surgeon, "OK, go ahead; cut it off."

"Hello," he said to me.

Against my will, I nodded.

His hands were trembling. "Hot out there."

"Yes, it is."

He moved toward the counter, sliding the shoes against the floor. I thought he was going to beg me for money or rob the place. He didn't look like he'd put in a hard day's work. He looked like somebody had put in a hard day's work on him.

"Hot out there," he said, very loud, to the clerk, who was also wary of him.

"Can I help you, sir?"

"Yes. Yes, thank you very much." He reached into the bag and withdrew a small black coin purse. His hands were shaking so bad, he could scarcely get the purse open. "I should like some coffee, young man. Some coffee, if you wouldn't mind. Just a minute."

The clerk moved to get him the coffee. The old man's purse flew open and flipped out of his hands all at once. Coins scattered all over the floor. He looked at me, and I felt instantly sorry for him. He struggled to get to his knees and pick up the coins, and I got up and walked over to him. In my pocket I had sixty bucks.

"Here," I said, trying to hand him the bills. "I don't need this right now."

He stared at it, as if he didn't quite know what it was or what I had said.

"You can have it," I told him.

Now he looked at me. His eyes were bright and surprisingly alert, although they were shaded by his drooping eyelids. "What did you say?"

"You can have this." I held the money out.

"Oh, no." He shook his head. "Thank you so kindly, but you don't have to do that."

"No, I want to. Really."

He glanced at the money again. He was not easily convinced that I was serious, and he did not want to reach for it just yet. Perhaps, also, he had not completely accepted the fact that he was poverty-stricken and needed the help of strangers.

"Go ahead," I said. "I don't want it."

I saw him swallow his pride. It may have been for the very first time, because he seemed almost glad to have finally done it; and as he reached out his trembling hand, I thought of him as a father—a young father, with children; a daughter. I imagined him holding a child with those very hands, smiling and happy, years before he had to take charity from a stranger. He smiled as he folded the crackling money. "Thank you, sir. Thank you so much."

"Don't mention it." I walked over to the trash can and threw the rest of my ice, then the empty cup, into the trash and turned to leave.

"I'll remember you in my prayers," the old man said. I looked back to smile at him, and he was down on the floor, laboriously picking up every dime, every nickel he had dropped, saying yes to all of them, approving of each coin he recovered.

Outside in the heat, I walked more calmly up the street, thinking. It didn't seem likely that a man could get in the condition of my nodding friend and suffer from parsimony. He could not be a greedy man. And yet, there he was, hedging against future bad luck, insuring himself he'd have the change, even though I'd given him more money than he'd probably seen in years. And as I brooded over the old man and his bony fingers rattling the tiles to pick up every last coin, I felt once again how empty the world was, and how empty it was going to stay. I wanted so bad to go back to that morning and start the day over. I didn't know how I was going to get to a single tomorrow. I could not think of one thing I might do in the future, except talk to Nicole. I had to do that. I needed her to know, at least, that even if the whole thing was my fault, it was an accident.

I was afraid to think about Elizabeth. At some level, I think I knew what I was headed for. And unlike the old man, I had no coins to pick up.

I Was a Little Surprised

To see how ordinary the day seemed when I got outside the Burger King. People walked by me, and cars passed, tires hissing on the asphalt. I saw a bird try to light on top of a street lamp, hover around it briefly, and then fly off over the trees by the road. I strolled down the street a ways, acting normal, controlling myself. I stopped at another public phone and called the hospital.

A woman with a deep voice answered.

"I want to check on a recently admitted patient," I said.

"Name?"

"Elizabeth Simmons."

"When was she admitted?"

"This afternoon."

She put me on hold and I listened to elevator music for what seemed like a long time. Then she came back and said, "Yes, can I help you?"

"I was checking on Elizabeth Simmons."

"One moment."

The music came back. My heart was a stuttering bag by the time somebody came back on the line. This time it sounded like a little girl. "Emergency room."

"I'm calling to check on a patient."

Again she wanted the name.

"Elizabeth Simmons."

217

"Yes."

"Is she there?"

"Yes, she is."

"Can you tell me how she is?"

"One moment."

Now I had the music again. Then another woman came on the line. "May I help you?"

"I'm checking on the condition of Elizabeth Simmons."

"Are you a family member?"

"No. I'm just a friend." I wasn't sure if I was talking to a nurse or a doctor.

"I'm sorry, sir, we can give that information only to members of the patient's family."

"Can you tell me if she's all right?"

"Perhaps you should contact the patient's family, sir."

"I just want to know if she's all right; can't you at least tell me that?"

There was a pause. Then she said, "Ms. Simmons is still in ICU. She will be admitted. Her condition is stable. That's all I am allowed to tell you."

"If she was a senator or a congressman and I was a complete stranger working for the *Washington Post*, you could tell me her condition. You'd hold a goddamned press conference."

"I'm sorry, sir."

"Just tell me if anything has happened to the baby."

There was another pause. I was certain now that she wasn't a doctor. She was covering the phone with her hand and talking to someone. She came back and asked me my name.

"I'm just a friend."

"I'm sorry, sir," she said in a tone that let me know she was finished with me. "You'll have to contact a member of her family."

"Thanks," I said. "Thank you so much."

"I'm sorry, sir. I can't—"

I slammed the phone down. *what if she lost the baby* I stood there in the booth for a while, feeling numb and paralyzed. Then I walked up the street to a 7-Eleven and bought a pack of cigarettes and a bottle of beer. At the corner was a bus stop with a cement bench. I sat down and drank the beer and smoked a few of the cigarettes. The beer calmed me. When I thought it was getting to be late enough, I started back toward the Burger King.

As I walked along, I kept turning over in my mind a vision of Elizabeth's body on a stretcher with a sheet pulled up over it and a shadowy figure hovering over her, harvesting her soul. How could I have let go of her like that? I kept going over it in my mind—the way her body felt slipping through my hands. I wished I could find out how she was; I wished I could talk to her. I knew it was possible that she might actually die. That was what overwhelmed me with fear in the first place. *What if she died?* No. She couldn't do that. She just couldn't. Elizabeth wouldn't *the perfect outcome would be if she was all right. And the baby—the baby should be fine, too.*

A great dark hole seemed to open in my memory, cold air smelling of earth, the baby gone. I didn't want to have the thought. *No. The baby absolutely had to be completely healthy.* That would be perfect. *and Elizabeth only a little bruised and embarrassed no harm done. the baby has to be alive*

Maybe Elizabeth wanted to see me. Maybe she was asking for me right at that moment. I crossed the street and headed up the walk toward the Burger King. Traffic in the road next to me moved and stopped, moved and stopped. A sharp breeze kicked up dead leaves at my feet. *but what if she is paralyzed?* What if she really was badly injured, pale and cold, lying in the emergency room? She fell almost two stories to a concrete floor.

I should not have let her talk me into it. What the hell was I thinking? *the baby has to be alive in her belly, and she has to be all right* But if she was lying in a white bed, resting comfortably, in stable condition, with just a slight concussion and a few bruises, that would be such a miracle. *It would be the best thing, absolutely.* But what if she was asking for me? What if she was wondering right then where I was?

I heard myself say, "Elizabeth," out loud. It was almost a sigh, and I realized I was nearly out of breath. I'd been walking up a long hill to the intersection across the street from the restaurant. I was in a hurry now, thinking that movement somehow shackled grief.

It took Sam about an hour to find me. I saw his Wagoneer pull tentatively into the parking lot. I was standing by the signposts, outside, in the shadows. When I waved to him, he didn't see me. He pulled the car into a parking space and waited there. I had a chance to watch his scared face searching the brightly lit dining room of the Burger King, looking for me. The mixture of yellow light from the setting sun and the neon Burger King sign overhead made him look even more Oriental. His face was not just frightened, but sad, too. The delicate color of his skin made him look almost feminine in the eerie light.

I opened the door on the passenger side and got in. He let out this odd little sound.

I slammed the door. "Sorry I scared you."

"What's going on?" His eyes darted from one side of the car to the other.

"You don't have to worry," I said.

"What's going on?"

"You wouldn't believe it."

He looked in the rearview mirror, then back to the road.

"Calm down," I said, but I was shaking, too. I wanted so badly to turn the clock back—to go back to that park and offer my beer to that squirrel—and have the whole day in front of me, so I could somehow change what had happened.

After a long pause, Sam said, "Well, where are we going?"

"Back to the other side of town, to the school administration building."

He looked at me.

"My car's there. I've got to pick it up."

Clouds shrouded the sun, and now it was getting dark. We rode along in silence for a while, then he said, "Well?"

"'Well,' what?"

"You going to tell me what's going on?"

I shifted in my seat. I didn't want to put it into words. Putting it into words made it more real than I wanted it to be, but he had driven a good way to pick me up and I was going to need him in the near future, so I told him most of it. I left out the part about how the elevator got stuck. He was shocked enough that I had walked out of the hospital.

"Why didn't you stay there?"

"I don't know. I don't know what kind of trouble I might be in." I was thinking out loud now, not really talking to Sam at all. "I didn't do anything wrong or violate any law that I know. I just didn't want to wait there any longer."

"Were you worried about the police?"

"No," I said. "Hell, I don't know. They were gone when I left."

Sam said nothing. The bright lights of passing cars kept illuminating his round scared face. He would not look directly at me as he drove, but I had the feeling he was embarrassed and quite determined to get as far away from me as possible once he dropped me off.

"I'm sorry about this," I said.

He watched the lights in front of us. We didn't speak again until he pulled up next to my car in front of the administration building.

"You go on home," I said.

"Yeah. Home."

"Can you find your way from here?"

He said he wasn't sure, so I told him the way to go. Then I said, "Tell Nicole I'll call her as soon as I know something."

"Where are you going?"

"I'm going back to the hospital." I got out, and he drove off without saying anything.

That Night

I met Elizabeth's father. Like a criminal returning to the scene of his crime, I drove back to the hospital. This was not a new determination on my part to face things. It was a kind of surrender. I just couldn't stand not knowing what was happening.

I left my car in the parking lot outside the emergency room. There was an ambulance, its red and blue lights flashing almost peacefully, parked by a pair of double doors on the other side of the main entrance. The back doors on the ambulance were propped open, and its cavernous interior was empty.

I went through huge double doors next to the emergency room into what was apparently the main lobby of the hospital. I felt suddenly chilled from the air-conditioning. I searched for signs or something to tell me where to go. Admitting was to my left, but I thought it was probably too late to go there. To my right was a bank of elevators with people waiting in front of them. I walked over and read the directory on the wall. The waiting room was on the second floor, so I went there.

The entrance was a single glass door, but once inside, I realized this was a room almost as big as the lobby. At a small desk between two gray columns at the far end, across from me, was a young nurse with dark-rimmed glasses on the tip of her nose. As I approached I saw that she was writing with a black pen, and when my shadow loomed over her, she did not look up.

"Excuse me," I said.

"Yes?" She put the pen down in a distracted sort of way.

"I'm sorry to bother you, I want to check on a patient." I was still shaking from the cooler air. Or perhaps it wasn't the air at all. Maybe I was just frightened, but I couldn't get control of it.

She pointed to a long counter crowded with people on the other side of the room. "You need to see someone over there. That's patient information."

"Look," I said. "Forgive me. I really don't have that kind of time. Couldn't you help me?"

"We're awfully busy, sir."

"I know. I know. I'm sorry. My fiancée was injured today, and—" My voice broke. "I just wanted to find out if she is—if ah..." I searched for words, but my mind went blank. I was just this shuddering fool, waiting there, fighting back tears. "I should have waited this afternoon, but the truth is, I just couldn't."

I think the nurse felt sorry for me. She put her pen down and, in a softer voice, said, "What's her name?"

"Elizabeth Simmons."

"Who?"

"Elizabeth Simmons," I said again much louder.

She looked at me, considering something. "Just a second." She picked up the phone and began to dial, and as she did this I was suddenly conscious of a shadow, a presence who had gotten up out of one of the chairs and was moving toward me. I turned, and there was Elizabeth's father. He was much taller than I had imagined, and much less portly. In fact, all the pictures I had seen made him look fat. But in person he was solid, huge, barrel-chested, and apparently strong. His jaw was the sole evidence of advancing age—it sagged on either side of his face and drew two lines down from his nose so that his mouth looked a little bit like a puppet's mouth.

"I heard you say my daughter's name," he said.

"You're Mr. Simmons."

He seemed to be regarding me skeptically, as though I were trying to sell him something. "You must be Mike?" he said.

"No, I'm Henry."

"Henry."

"Elizabeth's..." I stopped. I didn't know what I should say. "How is she?"

He looked into my eyes, seemed to determine something for himself, then said, "Who are you, then?" His voice was flat, as if he were asking me the time, but his serious, tender eyes—full of grief and fear—struck me through and I couldn't look at him.

"I'm Henry."

The nurse in front of me hung up the phone slowly, as though she didn't want us to notice that she'd done so. I could see from her face that the news wasn't good.

"Is Elizabeth, is she going to be all right?" I said in a panic.

The woman looked at Mr. Simmons. "They have to run a few more tests. She's still sleeping."

Mr. Simmons put his huge hand on his forehead. His eyes were cast down, but I could see he, too, was struggling to contain his emotions.

We walked together back to a stand of soft vinyl-covered chairs. The carpet, chairs, and walls were all gray. Magazines were scattered on the tables, and people reclined in the chairs or milled about, whispering to each other.

Mr. Simmons sat down next to me. He was wearing a floral shirt, open at the neck, and gray hair rose out of his collar like escaping smoke. He was so panic-stricken, his breathing was quick and shallow, and he couldn't sit still. He kept gazing around the room, as if it was hard to believe where he was; as if he had just discovered himself in this gray place.

"She's sleeping. That's a coma, right?" he said.

"I think so. Is that what the doctor said?"

"They just keep telling me she's sleeping. That she's not awake yet."

"Are you the only one here?"

"Yes."

"Have you seen her?"

"For a little while they let me sit next to her. An hour or so."

"Did she say anything?"

He shook his head.

"What about the baby? Is there any—"

He turned to me, a look of confusion on his face. It seemed as though I had violated something in his grief—as if I had told a terrible joke or made some sort of off-color remark at the wrong time. Then he said, "We don't know about the baby yet. That was the first thing. The first thing. The hospital called me this afternoon."

I didn't know what to say.

"Elizabeth calls me on the phone and asks me to come stay with her for a while. She wanted to tell me this—about the baby, you see. I came all the way from Philadelphia." He was still gazing about the room, speaking slowly, almost automatically. "I came down the day before yesterday. All the way from Philadelphia. For a visit. And she tells me this. That she's going to have a baby. For her, it was good news."

Neither of us said anything for a long time. I stared at my hands.

Finally I gathered myself and stood up. I didn't want to be where anybody could see me, to tell you the truth. In the state I was in, I'm not even sure what I said to him, but I mumbled something and made as if to leave.

"I thought you were Mike," the old man said.

I looked at him. Something in his expression would not let me go.

"Who's Mike?" I managed to say.

"Her fiancé."

"No," I said. "I'm her fiancé."

"You?"

"Yes. She told you about me, right? Henry Porter?"

"I guess. She must have."

I stood there, afraid to leave but not wanting to sit down.

"I thought Mike said he was her fiancé."

"I don't know if she knows anybody named Mike."

"What are you saying?" he asked. He seemed offended.

"Did you say somebody named Mike was coming here?"

"I talked to him on the phone. I thought he said he was her fiancé. He wanted to see Elizabeth."

"I don't know who it could have been. It wasn't me."

"No. I guess not."

It was quiet for several awkward minutes, then Mr. Simmons said, "What is it about you people?"

"What?"

"You do it all wrong. She's going to have a baby—" He broke off. There were tears in his eyes.

I said nothing.

"She is pregnant and you say you're her fiancé." His voice was stronger, now.

I looked at my shoes.

"You do it all backwards. You don't know how to do it, really—so that it actually means something. It has no value when you do it backwards and in secret. You just sleep together and you have your fun, then when something happens, you go to a justice of the peace and sign a contract."

He sounded just like my father. Nothing he said at that moment, in that circumstance, seemed important, but I couldn't tell him that. I kept my mouth shut.

As though he had read my thoughts, he said, "You think it doesn't matter—that marriage is just filling out a document and making it all formal. It's nothing to you. You say it's nothing. You think what you mean is that it doesn't matter about marriage as long as two people love each other. That's what Elizabeth always said."

It frightened me that he was talking about her in the past tense.

"But if two people *are* in love with each other, then the only thing that really matters between them is that they are willing to tell that to God and the world, in front of everyone. And *that's* what marriage is. You don't just live together and keep everything that counts between you a secret."

"We weren't keeping it a secret," I murmured.

In a very loud voice he said, "I didn't know about it!"

Everyone in the room looked at us.

"I'm sorry," I whispered. I really was sorry. I thought he knew.

More quietly he said, "It *was* a secret, you see." Then he regarded me. His look was an appraisal, and it unnerved me. "*You* were a secret. You were." He was fighting the tears.

I must have had a pained expression on my face. "You keep talking about her as if—as if..." I didn't finish the sentence, but he understood what I meant.

"Where have you been?" He shook his head.

I had nothing to say.

Then he said, "What's your name?"

I told him again.

He looked puzzled. "I talked to somebody named Mike Puckett. I thought he said he was Liz's fiancé."

"Puckett?"

"Yes. I'm supposed to meet him here."

"Oh," I said. "No. Puckett's a cop."

"I know. He said that."

"He probably wants to talk to you about the accident."

"What about the accident?" Mr. Simmons said. "Were you there?"

"Yes."

"You were there? Where've you been all day?"

"I've been..." I didn't know what to say. He was watching my face, and I felt as though he could see the blood-filled circuitry in my eyes.

"Tell me what happened," he said. "How far did she fall?"

"We were between the first and second floor. She tried to jump down to the first floor. It wasn't really very far, but she missed and fell to the basement."

His face turned ashen. I think what I said actually robbed him of air. "My God." He stared at the carpet for a while, shaking his head. Then he sat up, looking at me with a sort of urgency and fervor, as though he needed to know all of it in a hurry. "Tell me. Tell me how it happened."

So I told him. As I talked, I watched his face, and gradually I came to see that I was not going to be able to tell him everything. I left out the part about how the elevator got stuck, and I didn't see any reason to tell him that Elizabeth had rejected me. When I was finished, although I felt as though I had offered up a kind of confession, I didn't feel absolved of anything.

After a brief silence, in which he seemed to be thinking, he muttered something under his breath.

"What?" I said.

He looked up, beyond me, and I turned to see Puckett standing there.

"Well," he said. His clean starched uniform, with its perfectly straight creases, sickened me. "Porter. I was just talking to your old man about you."

"You know my father?"

He smiled. "Everybody in the department knows Judge Porter. I know your brother Phil, too."

I sat down.

Mr. Simmons started to rise, but Puckett said, "That's all right, don't get up, sir."

"This is Elizabeth's father," I said.

Puckett introduced himself, and he and Mr. Simmons had this conversation where they cleared up all the misunderstanding about who Puckett was. "I did mention your daughter's fiancé, but I was referring to Mr. Porter, here, not myself. I'm sorry for the confusion."

Mr. Simmons wanted to know what Puckett wanted.

"I'm investigating the . . . the . . ."

"The accident," I said.

"Our thinking now is that this was an accident, yes," Puckett said.

Mr. Simmons nodded, still looking at him.

Then Puckett turned to me and said, "What happened to you this afternoon?"

"I just couldn't wait any longer."

"He was with Elizabeth," Puckett said to Mr. Simmons. "When she — when it happened. He saw the whole thing."

Mr. Simmons said, "He told me."

"Anyway," Puckett said, "I was hoping to talk to your daughter when she wakes up. We'd like to have her version of it."

"She'll tell you exactly what I told you," I said.

Puckett said, "Of course. Actually I'd wanted to talk to you again this afternoon. I thought I'd give you a ride back to your car, but I couldn't find you."

I didn't say anything. Mr. Simmons regarded me with a puzzled expression.

Puckett said, "I was hoping you could tell me what happened when the elevator stopped."

"What do you mean?"

"Did it make a sound? Were you or Miss Simmons touching anything?"

"I don't think so." I didn't know where to put my face, how to keep my eyes still and focused. The whole room seemed to be watching me now, waiting for me to say something.

"Mr. Simmons," Puckett said, "I wonder if I might have a word with you in private?"

Mr. Simmons got up without saying anything, and the two men walked to the middle of the room. Puckett leaned toward him, his hand on his back and spoke very animatedly to him. I felt like a suspect. They talked for a long time. Then Puckett handed the old man a small sheet of paper, looked at me briefly, and walked out.

Mr. Simmons came back and sat down.

"What was that all about?" I asked.

"Nothing. He says I should call him when Elizabeth wakes up. He's praying for her."

"Well, don't believe everything he says about all this. He wasn't there. It's his job to be suspicious."

"He thinks you stopped the elevator. He's not sure how, but he is sure there was no malfunction in it."

His words frightened me, but I struggled to maintain the same expression.

Mr. Simmons looked at his watch, then back at me. "Did you stop the elevator?"

"Of course not."

There was a long pause. Then I said, "Even if I did, I don't see how that's a crime."

"Yeah, well Puckett seemed to think that if it caused the accident, it was a pretty serious crime."

"What serious crime?"

"He didn't say."

"I didn't stop the elevator."

"So why didn't you wait around today?" He looked at me, waiting.

"I had to get away from this." I indicated the waiting room, everything around us. "I didn't want to face waiting like this."

He looked at me disapprovingly, so I tried to explain it to him. "I let go of her, you see." I felt my voice giving way. "I didn't catch her like I said I would. I couldn't hold her." I put my hands over my face and leaned over in the chair. I didn't want to talk anymore. At that moment, death—being dead and silent forever—seemed peaceful and comforting. It actually ran through my mind that my baby would be lucky not to be born at all.

Presently Mr. Simmons said, "I'm going to go downstairs and see about something."

I started to get up, too.

"I'm just going to the cafeteria," he said. "If you don't mind."

"No."

He waited there for a minute, as though he were trying to remember something difficult, and I realized that he wanted me to leave. He ran his hand through his hair and started to say something, but seemed to catch himself. Then he said, "I want to be alone with her if she wakes up tonight. You can understand that, can't you?"

"I do."

"Of course, I'll call you."

"Should I give you my number?" I said.

He held up his hand, shook his head. "I'm sure Elizabeth..." His hand dropped. He looked so sad, but there was nothing more for either of us to say. He turned and walked slowly toward the elevators across the room. I didn't know what Puckett had told him, but he was definitely not interested in having anything more to do with me.

I couldn't say that I blamed him.

Nicole Didn't Get Home

Until well after midnight. She slammed the door and ran upstairs before I could get from the family room to the foyer to greet her.

Sam looked at me and shrugged.

"What's that all about?" I said.

I went into the foyer and stood at the bottom of the stairs, and Sam leaned on the banister.

"Nicole?" I hollered.

She didn't answer. I waited a bit, then I told Sam to go check on her. He went up and knocked on her door. I heard him say, "It's me." She opened the door and he went in, then it was dark again in the hallway.

I went back into the family room, turned off the television, then poured myself a glass of whiskey. I was sad and tired and worried about Elizabeth. I'd been sitting with Sam all night, waiting for Nicole, listening for the telephone. Twice I called the hospital but there was no one to talk to. I didn't know where Mr. Simmons had gone. I almost called him at Elizabeth's house, but I was afraid I wouldn't know what to say to him.

I was pouring my third glass of whiskey when Sam came down the stairs, glumly, his hands in his pockets. He'd been in Nicole's room for almost an hour.

"Well?" I said.

"She'll be down in a minute."

232

I took a big gulp of my drink.

"She doesn't want you to see her."

"Why not?"

"She got her hair cut."

I had nothing to say to that.

"I don't think I masked my shock very well," Sam whispered. "She looks perfectly ridiculous."

"You didn't tell her that, did you?"

"Of course not. I told her she looked pretty."

"Well, that's the important thing." He missed the irony altogether.

"She's talking about going home. Maybe this week. It seemed like she was pretty upset about her hair before I told her about..." He didn't finish the sentence. It finally hit him that Nicole's hair was probably not as important as Elizabeth's health and survival. In a soft embarrassed tone he said, "I told her about your—about Elizabeth."

I said nothing. I took another small sip of the whiskey.

"Why'd she go and get her hair cut like that?" Sam said. He didn't seem to know what else to talk about.

"Ask her. Why don't you do that?"

"She looks so different."

"Yeah, well. There's a whole lot more going on right now that's more important than her goddamned hair."

"It's clipped so short now—it barely covers her neck. And I did ask her about it. She wouldn't say."

"I don't give a fuck about her hair, Sam."

I moved toward the stairs. I didn't have the energy to chide her for anything, so I didn't want to just leave her up there stewing about what I'd say to her when I saw her new haircut.

The whiskey taste in my mouth was very unpleasant. I leaned on the banister, put my palms over my eyes and rubbed. It felt as though I could scour everything from my mind and when I opened my eyes again I would be younger and everything that happened to me in the last few weeks would be in the undetermined and hazy future.

"You going to talk to her?" Sam asked.

"Leave me alone, Sam," I said with kindness. "OK? Just leave me alone." I stood now at the bottom of the stairs. Sam was in the hallway, between the foyer and the family room. We were both listening for her, but it was quiet up there.

Sam came closer to me. "You want me to try again?"

"Try what?"

"Get her to come down."

I heard the door upstairs open, then Nicole came out. She was wearing a white robe and white slippers. Her hair *was* short, cut evenly around her neck and over her ears.

I could see she was embarrassed about it, but she came down the stairs, not taking her eyes off me, and she reached out her hand, taking my hand in hers, and asked, "Are you all right?"

"Well, yeah. *I'm* all right," I said. "*I'm* perfectly fine."

"Have you heard anything? Is she going to be OK?"

"We don't know yet. She's still in intensive care."

"What happened?"

We went back into the family room. No one turned a lamp on, and with the television off, the room was dark except for the eerie light from the foyer. Sam sat at the opposite end of the couch, so far from the light that it was hard to discern his figure. I was on the lighted end of the couch, and Nicole sat in the lounge chair, leaning toward me. I could barely see her face and her hair, cut so short, made her look almost like a boy. I told her the story. I didn't tell her about the elevator.

"Why aren't you at the hospital?" she said.

"I couldn't stand waiting there. Nobody would tell me anything."

She didn't seem satisfied with that. "You couldn't stand waiting?"

"Her father didn't want me there," I confessed.

She was quiet. In the dim light, I couldn't tell if she was even looking at me.

"I need another drink," I said.

"That glass is almost full."

"Yeah, but it's not going to be enough. I can tell."

I found my way to the bar and poured more whiskey in my glass. Nicole remained seated, holding the robe closed in front of her. I went back to the couch and sat down.

"You haven't talked to a doctor about her yet?" she said.

"I didn't see a doctor. The whole time I was there."

She shook her head. "You want me to take you back there tonight?"

"No. There's nothing to do. I'll go back there in the morning."

It was quiet for a long time. I sipped the whiskey, not really tasting it. Finally I said, "Mr. Simmons talked to a doctor, I think."

"And she's in a coma. That's what the doctor said?"

"I don't really know," I said. "The nurse kept saying she was sleeping, that she was not ready to wake up."

"I think that's a coma," Sam said. His voice seemed to come from some holy place—as though a kind of providence had spoken through him. I got up and absently turned on every light in the room.

The Days and Weeks

Just passed one after another, and still Elizabeth would not wake up. They kept her lying on her side, with tubes in her nose and mouth, and wrist pads on her hands to keep them from folding the wrong way when the nurses turned her over. They continuously monitored the baby's heartbeat, which was weak but steady. I was told that was a good sign. I went to the hospital every day and waited in the waiting room until lunchtime, then I'd go downstairs and get a hot dog or something. In the afternoon I'd drift off to sleep, sitting in one of the gray chairs. I often dreamed of the fall and woke up wondering where I was. Elizabeth's father spent most of his time in her room. Every now and then he'd come around to let me know what was happening.

One day late in June, just before noon, Nicole showed up. She had stopped at Burger King to get me a cheeseburger. It was very sweet of her, and I told her so.

"Well, I wouldn't bring you a salad," she said.

I forced a smile. She sat down next to me. Her hair didn't look so bad after I had had time to get used to it. We hadn't talked much in the last few days, so while I ate my sandwich, I tried to make conversation.

"Where's Sam?"

"He's off somewhere. He's being a real pain in the ass about my haircut."

"Really? I think it looks nice."

"He thinks I got it cut for Chad."

I unwrapped my burger and took a bite. It seemed important to have a normal conversation with her, but I didn't know what to say. I couldn't get this impression of her out of my mind—this impression that she was an infant, fully grown, but an infant nonetheless. I kept thinking of the baby Elizabeth might lose. Poor little thing. It didn't even have a name yet.

Nicole said, "How's Elizabeth?"

"The same."

There was a long silence, then I said, "You still seeing Chad?"

She shifted in her seat. "I was never 'seeing' Chad."

"You know what I mean."

"No."

"Good."

"I haven't seen Chad since—" She broke off, seeming to decide something. Then she said, "Why 'good'?"

I shrugged. "I don't know."

She said nothing but she wasn't convinced.

"I didn't like him," I said.

"That's certainly a news flash." She seemed on edge. I thought she might want to tell me something, so I waited for a moment. But she only watched her hands fumbling with the Burger King bag in her lap.

Finally I said, "I know this visit has been a disappointment to you. I'm really sorry for that."

She didn't say anything.

"But we've a lot of time left. As soon as Elizabeth—" I stopped. "There's still plenty of summer left."

She looked at me. "Perhaps I should just go home, Dad."

I didn't know what she wanted me to say. We sat there staring at each other, then finally she said, "Do you want me to stay?"

I said, "I want you to do what you want."

"God. Please don't be enigmatic now. Tell me what you want me to do."

"That *is* what I want you to do. What *you* want."

We both fell silent. I was remembering the way her mother had left me, and what Elizabeth had said to me before the accident, and I was afraid of what I might say. What I wanted to do was tell Nicole how alone I would feel in that empty house once she was gone. I wanted to tell her but my mind would not surrender the words. It was so awkward looking into her blue eyes and waiting for something to happen. She sat there studying my face now, in silence.

"What's the matter?" I asked.

"Nothing." She seemed unhappy that I'd asked the question.

I finished my cheeseburger, staring at the floor. It seemed like the only fraction of life I could comprehend was the instant of each breath. The past and future all seemed so dreamlike and unreal, I felt like the sort of creature that lives only seconds and then passes into some raw elemental stage of entrapment—all of it driven by panic. I might as well have been a cicada, paralyzed in a mud wasp's cocoon, waiting for the egg to hatch.

It was quiet for a while, then Nicole said, "I talked to Mom."

"Good."

"I called her. I hope you don't mind."

"Not a bit."

"She was sorry to hear about Elizabeth."

I rattled the ice in my cup.

"She said to tell you she would pray for her. She really was sorry."

"What'd you tell her?"

"About the accident?"

"Did you tell her how it happened?"

"I'm not even sure I know."

"I caused it. Did you tell her that?"

"You didn't cause it."

"It was my fault, all right."

"Dad, the accident happened to Elizabeth. It's about her. It's not about you. I didn't say anything about you at all."

"Did you tell her about the baby?"

"Don't." She put her hand up as if to touch my face, then let it fall to her lap.

"I'm all right," I said. I sipped my drink, trying not to look at her. "The little guy's hanging on."

She leaned over and kissed me.

I said nothing.

She sat back and sighed. After another, much longer silence, she said, "I'm so worried about Sam."

"Why?"

She seemed to shrug.

"Where is he?"

She shook her head. She was trying to figure out how to tell me something.

"Is he in some kind of trouble?"

"No. I don't know."

"Well, what's the problem?"

Here eyes were cast down, and she was turned away slightly.

"Is there something you want to tell me?"

She shook her head, but I saw that she was denying the truth.

"Come on," I said. "Tell me what happened."

"Oh, you don't need any more trouble."

"This is trouble?"

She looked at me. "I think so."

"Well, tell me."

"It's something I can deal with. I'll just have to deal with it."

I got up and put my empty cup and the wrappers in a trash can across the room. She watched me, waiting for me to respond, but to tell the truth, if it was trouble Sam had gotten into, I didn't want to hear about it. Nicole was right, I had enough bothering me. But when I came back and sat down, she said, "When Sam left the house a little while ago he was angry. I've never seen him so angry. I think he was planning to do something awful."

"What?"

"I don't know." Now she had tears in her eyes.

"Look at us," I said. "We're sure having a fine time this summer, aren't we?"

She actually laughed. I put my arm around her. Fear and grief had completely numbed my senses, but suddenly I thought of the possibility of Elizabeth's baby, our baby, dead before air and light and sound.

I kissed Nicole's brow and brushed her hair back. "Thanks for being here, honey." My throat was burning. I wanted to tell her that I was beginning to feel closer to her again, but I couldn't do that without calling up the distance between us. Loving her again, as I did when she was small, came to me like a sudden pain in my heart, and it made me profoundly sad.

She rested her head in the crook of my shoulder, and for a brief span of time I felt once again like a good father.

Then she told me why Sam was so angry.

Nicole Said

"When I went to Baltimore with Chad something happened that I didn't tell you or Sam about. On the highway before we got to Baltimore, we saw a woman hitchhiking. She had a little girl about six or seven with her. The little girl was just standing there next to her mother, shading her eyes from the sun. I made Chad stop to pick them up. It turned out the woman was drunk. I could smell the liquor on her breath. She wasn't clean, either. She was covered with dirty sweat. She wore a dirty white blouse and cutoff jeans. Her hair was tangled, and some of it was stuck to the side of her face. Fingernails bitten right down to the cuticle. But the little girl was so cute. She was dainty and spotless, and she was trying very hard to be proper. She wore a pink dress with a white front—you know, like a small apron. The dress had a white ruffle around the hem. She had shiny black patent leather shoes on, and white socks. When the woman lifted her up and put her in the backseat, she sat very straight and patted the folds of her dress. She says out loud, not talking to anyone, really, 'It's very cool inside.'

"I said, 'It's air-conditioned.'

"The woman got in the car and slammed the door, and the little girl says, 'I'm so sorry.' The woman seemed to scowl at us, then she said she was afraid a trucker would pick her up. That she hated truckers. She spoke about being picked up by a trucker as though it wasn't something she could help. You know what I mean?

"It was clear she would have taken a ride from anybody. Anybody who picked her up. She was desperate. She started crying after we got going again. The little girl smiled bravely, her hands in her lap. She had dark hair, cut short, and a pink ribbon just above her ear. Her cheeks were flushed, and her eyes were really big, you know, the way a child's eyes can be. Gleaming and dark. She was so truly proper and well mannered, I wondered what in the world would save her. You know what I'm saying? The woman started talking about how she'd been kicked out of her house by her landlord. 'He kicked us out over fifty bucks,' she says. She was still sobbing, trying to get her breath so she could talk. 'Can you believe it?' she went on. 'Fifty bucks and he throws me and my daughter out of the house. Now we don't have any place of our own.'

"Chad wanted to know where she was going, and she says she has friends in Baltimore. She told him to take them to Route 695, the exit ramp on exit 49. She was supposed to meet a friend there.

"The little girl glanced at me, and I said, 'Are you OK, honey?'

"You should have seen her bright smile. She says, 'I'm all right. I'm not crying.' She was so proud of herself, and her voice was so soft and sad, I think I'll always remember it. I really felt sorry for her. I would have done anything to save her. And that is what she'd need. A savior. I started thinking about the money you had given me. I knew I couldn't save anybody, but I could be of some help to them — at least for a little while. If I just gave the woman fifty dollars it would probably have helped her a lot. I whispered to Chad that I wanted to help them, that I had some money I wanted to give them, and he got this mean look on his face and says, 'Are you crazy?'

"I said it would be kind, and the right thing to do.

"'Right,' he says. 'Sure. Right.'

"I asked him why he stopped to pick them up and he goes, 'Because it was so important to you,' with a real sarcastic tone, like that. And I said, 'What's wrong with you?' and he wouldn't answer me.

"The ride to Baltimore took forever, and I started wondering why he wanted me with him. He wouldn't talk. I tried to talk to the little girl, but her mother kept interrupting me and complaining about the evil of a person who would throw a little girl and her mother out of an apartment for a lousy fifty bucks.

"After a while, nobody said anything. It was real quiet, but I could see Chad was still stewing about what I'd said. He kept tightening his grip on the steering wheel, and his eyes looked fierce.

"We were going pretty good. Not speeding or anything, but still pretty fast. As we were coming into the city, he turned to me and whispered, 'I think the Lord helps those who help themselves, don't you?' I wasn't sure what he meant by that, and I was afraid he would start a scene with the woman and her little girl, so I sort of agreed with him. I mean I looked at him and nodded. Then he went into this speech. It was almost as if he'd prepared it days in advance. How the world is an evil place, full of evil people. How you've got to seek your whole life to find one honest man—as the Bible says. He kept quoting the Bible about the sins of the sodomites and the whores and the hypocrites. He said God would get even with us all. The woman seemed to agree with him. I mean about God and all.

"He didn't like that. He goes, 'You're just as bad. You're an alcoholic aren't you?'

"She couldn't believe what he was saying. She sat there with her mouth open. He asked if she'd been drinking and she says it's none of his business. Then he really got angry. He speeded up the car, and I was frightened for the little girl. I watched her. She was determined not to cry as her mother had done. She would not let on that she was afraid. I told her I was proud of her, and she smiled at me again. She was trying so hard. I felt like crying myself. I told Chad he was going too fast.

"He didn't look at me, but he says, 'Who's driving this machine? I've got a wheel in front of me, when I turn it, the car turns. When I put my foot on that pedal on the right down there on the floor, the car moves. And when I touch the pedal on the left there, it stops. You know what? I think I'm driving.' Real sarcastic, like that.

"As we approached Baltimore, he pulled off the main road and onto Route 695. He sped around a corner and down to the end of an exit ramp. The tires were screeching.

"At the stop sign Chad says, 'This is 695. Which way? Left or right?'

"The woman told him she thought exit 49 was to the left. She was crying again.

"I told him if he didn't slow down he was going to let me out.

"And he goes, 'You want out right now, little lady?'

"And I said, 'If you're going to keep speeding, right here will be fine.'

"Then the woman started complaining again about how a Christian person actually threw her out for a lousy fifty dollars, and Chad squealed the tires on the car going onto the entrance ramp of the highway.

"Now we were on 695. Chad shouted back to the woman about which exit it was.

"And she says, 'You know where 695 is?'

"Chad goes, 'We're on 695.'

"'I have to go to exit 49 on 695. I'm supposed to meet somebody there.'

"I told Chad once again to slow down. 'No one's in any hurry,' I said. By that time I was yelling at him. The woman says, 'That's right, there ain't no hurry, honey.' She was slurring her words. She goes, 'I'll jes call my fren' fum the gas station at the exit. They're espectin' me. They'll look after us, won' they honey?' She patted the little girl on the head.

"Chad says, 'Right,' but I could see he didn't believe her. Now the little girl's lower lip began to quiver, and I could see she was getting ready to cry.

"I told Chad he was scaring the little girl.

"He pulled over to the side of the road and goes, 'You want me to drop you off right here?'

"The little girl's eyes were as big as a deer's, and I could see that she was very afraid that I would leave, so I told him to forget it. He put it back in gear and started off again, this time even faster.

"I remembered that time you took me to New Jersey so you could gamble in all those casinos, and how on the way back we got stopped on the interstate because you didn't have enough money to pay at the toll booth. I remembered how afraid I was, and how angry you were at the man in the booth. I never told you this, but I was happy that the man let us go when I started crying. Remember? He pointed at me and says, 'If it weren't for the little one there, I'd run your ass in.' I can still hear his voice. I felt as though I had rescued you. So now, as I watched the little girl fighting back tears, I wanted her to start crying because I thought it might force Chad to slow down and think about what he was doing. Just as I was thinking about all that, Chad did slow down.

"We had just passed exit 38, and when he saw that the next one was 37, he pulled off at that exit and drove down a side street. He goes, 'I have to turn around.'

"Suddenly he was driving normally and he seemed to have calmed down, so I started worrying about what I was dealing with. I mean, his mood swings were beginning to make me pretty nervous. The woman had stopped crying, and now she was lighting one cigarette after another.

"I asked the little girl what her name was, and she says, 'Paula White.' Then she says, 'You have such beautiful long hair.' She was so cute, it hurt my heart to think of her life—not only what she had been through already, but what she would probably have to go through. She talked of a doll she had been forced to leave behind. She was sad. She loved the doll very much and she would miss it, but she said she was happy that at least the doll would be 'warm and safe.' She touched her cheek with a small hand, and I wondered if there was a set number of hours or days or nights that would have to pass before she'd finally ruined. I thought perhaps she was beginning to spoil as I watched her, because here she was, already forced to show all the best virtues that human beings are capable of: charity, restraint, compassion, courage, sympathy, and unselfish kindness—and she was not yet ten years old. What would be left of her when the years pushed her into womanhood? It's probably silly, but sometimes I think we are all given a limited store of the great virtues, and if we are compelled to use them as children, we have nothing left as adults. Maybe that was what happened to the little girl's mother. Maybe, in some ways, it happened to me.

"I know, I know. I'm not blaming you for anything. Not anymore. I don't even blame you for the divorce—although I was told all my life that you chose the horses over me. I know that's not true. I don't think I ever really believed it, although I think Catherine did, and it's possible she still does. But my childhood was handed to me, like something broken and finished. That's how I remember it now. You were suddenly gone. Everything in the world was broken for a while, and when it mended, it wasn't whole again. I kept waiting for a hole to fill. But it never does. It just gets larger and more empty, until what you remember about it is the space in it, nothing that ever filled it.

"Anyway, I kept looking at Paula, at her little hands smoothing down the starched pleats in her dress, and I wanted to take her away from her life, take her with me, wherever I might go. I truly believed I could save her. I even thought she might want to go with me.

"Her mother had rested her head back on the seat, and now she was smoking another cigarette, blowing the smoke up at the roof of the car. Paula leaned against her, watching my face. She forced another smile, then closed her eyes. She wanted me to think she was sleeping.

"Chad drove back onto the interstate and headed for exit 49. He told the woman he was going to let her off at the ramp but that he wasn't going to actually pull off the highway. She didn't answer him. She reached into her purse and took out a small bottle of Jack Daniels. It was almost empty. She removed the top and then put it to her lips. Tilted her head back, to drink the last of it. Then she carefully put the top back on. Paula reached up and touched her forearm. The woman opened the window and threw the bottle out on the pavement. I heard it shatter.

"Chad goes, 'What was that?'

"'Jiz a bottle,' she says.

"Again, I felt the car beginning to speed up. Chad wouldn't look at me, but he started talking again about the evil in the world, and about harm, especially harm, caused by what he called 'the dregs.' I was certain the woman in the backseat could hear him, but I didn't care. I was worried about Paula.

"'You shouldn't talk that way in front of the little girl,' I told him.

"But he went on. He goes, 'She'll grow up just like her mother.' I had just been thinking the same thing, but it made me feel bad and stupid when I heard him say it. Paula tried to smile at me, but she understood what he was talking about. She didn't know anything was wrong with her mother. All she knew was that her mother had been crying.

"When he pulled over at the exit ramp and let the woman and her daughter out, I got out too.

"He says, 'Where are you going?'

"I told him I wasn't going anywhere with him.

"The woman started walking down the ramp, right in the middle of the road, holding her daughter's hand and pulling her along. Paula was having a difficult time keeping up. I said, 'Wait a minute.'

"Chad screeched his tires pulling off, and I thought that was the last I would see of him. But he only drove a few hundred feet up the road, and then he stopped again. The woman would not wait for me. Paula turned and waved at me when they got to the bottom of the ramp. I didn't want to chase after them, but I was walking along, following in the same direction. Chad sat there for a while with his engine running, then he backed the car up and came down the ramp, very slowly. He pulled up next to me and stopped. He leaned over and rolled the window down. 'Come on,' he says. 'I'm sorry I lost my temper.'

"I told him I couldn't understand what he had been so angry about.

"He goes, 'Come on. I'll take you home if you want to go.'

"I started walking again, and he drove the car very slowly next to me. I didn't know where I was going. I kept watching Paula, the way she clung to her mother's hand as she raced along behind her, and I suddenly felt like I was her. I was Paula. The whole world had me by the hand, and it was drunk and dirty and it was dragging me off. Chad was saying something to me, and I realized I was crying. He kept telling me to calm down. 'Come on,' he says. 'Get back in the car. I'm not going to leave you here.'

"At the bottom of the exit ramp, the woman stopped and, with her arm around Paula's shoulders as if she were offering her little girl to the highway, she held out her thumb. I stopped and watched her standing there, defiant, with Paula's small hands holding to her jacket. Then a UPS van pulled over and picked them up. When Paula climbed into the cab, she turned and waved to me again. I smiled, but she was probably too far away to see it.

"Chad says, 'She was going to call her friends. Right. She probably doesn't have any friends.'

"I looked at him. It seemed a good thing to me that he appeared to know what I had been thinking. He reached over and opened the door, and I felt so alone and bewildered, I got back in. I thought we would just go ahead and go to a studio somewhere in the city, and we'd listen to music, and I would get caught up in all of it and forget about Paula and her mother and everything.

"But he drove the car to his house.

"'Come on,' he says.

"I said, 'This is the studio?'

"'Yeah,' he says.

"'I thought, I thought it was—you know, a real studio.'

"'It is a real studio. It's in the basement.'

"When I got out of the car, I was not certain I should go in there with him. Sam and I had spent a few hours there on the way back from the beach, and it was so dirty and dark in there it gave me the creeps. Also, that was where Sam had gotten so drunk, and I didn't like the things some of Chad's friends said about him. I mean he was passed out pretty much of the time, but they wanted to know how come I traveled with a little 'Jap runt,' and things like that. At the time, Chad defended him, and I liked him for it.

"But I didn't want to spend a whole day in that house.

"Chad lived there with his older brother and his father. When I got inside I asked him where the band was and he says, 'The guys will be here in a while. Relax.'

"I said, 'I thought you were going to take me home.'

"He goes, 'I will. Just chill out, OK?'

"In spite of the bright sun outside, it was just as dark in the house as I remembered it. The walls in the living room were covered with pictures of racehorses charging toward the finish line and standing regally in a crowd of people in the winner's circle. A couch with a small coffee table in the middle of the room. Several bowls full to the brim with cigarette butts, and the house smelled like an ashtray. Chad pointed to the couch and told me to sit down.

"I sat down on the outer edge of the cushions. The couch was soft and felt like it might swallow me if I actually leaned back in it. I said, 'I really wish you would just take me home.'

"He ignored me. He went into the kitchen, around the corner to my left. I heard him open the refrigerator and then the sound of someone opening a beer. A tall shadow came down the hall from the back of the house.

"It was Robbie, Chad's older brother.

"Chad came back in. 'You remember Nickie, don't you Robbie?' he says.

"Robbie smiled.

"I tried to return the smile but my heart was racing. Somehow I knew I was in trouble. I said, 'Is your father here?'

"'Nah,' Chad says. 'He works during the day.' Then he sat down across from me, in a plastic chair—the kind you see in bus stations and hospital waiting rooms—and he motioned for Robbie to take a seat next to me on the couch. Robbie was much more muscular than Chad, and taller, too. He seemed to bend himself in the middle to sit down.

"'Isn't Nicole beautiful?' Chad says.

"You have to understand, I walked up and down the boardwalk for three days with Chad in Ocean City, and we laughed with each other in the most natural way. I thought I could talk to him about anything, and he seemed so at ease with me and himself. And now, this guy sitting across from me in the plastic chair didn't even sound like the same man. His voice was deeper and more—I don't know—evil.

"Robbie tried to make conversation. It was beginning to cloud up outside, so the room got even darker. Chad kept going to the kitchen for more beer. I drank only one, when I first got there, but he kept bringing me new beers, without asking me. I left them sitting on the table in front of me, unopened. Robbie talked on the phone for a while. I asked Chad when the band was going to show up. 'I thought this was going to be a recording session.'

"'It was,' he says. He seemed very disappointed. 'I guess nobody's going to make it. If Robbie would get off the phone, maybe somebody's trying to call.'

"A little later, Robbie hung the phone up and came back in and sat down. It was quiet for a long time, and I started feeling really awkward. Robbie smiled and opened one of the beers I'd left on the table.

"Chad sighed, and shook his head.

"I asked him what was wrong. 'You seem upset about something.'

"He looked at me very strangely, and then he says, 'Do you believe in God?'

"I turned to Robbie and asked him if Chad was always so serious—you know trying to laugh it off. And then—and then Chad got up and walked around behind me and gathered my hair in his hands. He says, 'Your hair is so beautiful. Isn't it beautiful, Robbie?' I was afraid to move, still watching Robbie's face.

"'So tempting,' Chad says.

"I said, 'OK. It's just hair,' or something like that, and as I started to move my head to pull my hair away from him, he grabbed it tighter in his fist and pulled it up like that, so my head was kind of forced down, like this. I couldn't keep my head up. He kept saying, 'Look at it Robbie. Look at it.'

"'OK, I've seen it,' Robbie says. 'Let it go now.'

"I shouted, 'Let go.'

"Robbie says, 'Is he hurting you?'

"I told him, 'Yes.' I was trying to pull away.

"'Chad,' Robbie says. 'Stop it.'

"And then, I don't know where Chad got them, but he pulled out a pair of scissors and started cutting my hair.

"I must have screamed or something. Robbie jumped up from the couch and grabbed Chad's arm. Both of them were behind me, and Chad was struggling trying to cut through the sheaf of hair in his fist. I looked up and saw his face in the mirror on the far wall, and it was really scary. He had this look on his face like he was curious—like he wanted to see if I would somehow change once all the hair was gone. I can't remember clearly what happened after that. Chad finally cut through the bolt of hair he was holding, and then he pulled himself away from Robbie and waved it in my face.

"Robbie was going, 'For god's sake, Chad.'

"Chad called me a sinner and a whore and a temptress. He was crazy. I mean really crazy. He kept saying, 'I've turned you into a pillar of salt. Now you're a pillar of salt.' I felt the air on the back of my neck, and I knew my hair was gone or hanging in shreds. He'd cut through most of it. I was so shocked and afraid, I couldn't look at him. He still had the scissors. I was watching them in his hand.

"'You and your long hair and your accursed beauty,' he says.

"He moved toward me and I screamed. I think it scared him. Robbie went behind him and grabbed his arm. Then he twisted it behind his back and took the scissors out of his hand and put them down on the coffee table. He moved Chad over to the chair and sat him down. It was like he had to handle him that way a hundred times before. He put his hands on Chad's shoulders, to settle him there, then he turned to me and goes, 'Are you all right?'

"I couldn't think of what to say.

"Robbie says, 'Did he cut you?'

"I told him, 'Just my hair.'

"'You better get out of here,' he says.

"'What did I do?' I said.

"And he goes, 'My brother has a nervous condition. He's not been taking his medication lately. I'm sorry.'

"Chad says, 'Fuck you, Robbie. This has nothing to do with my medication. She's a bitch. She's a whore.' And then Chad was crying, just like a child. I mean really sobbing.

"Robbie stood up and looked at me.

"'He is crazy,' I said. 'I thought he liked me.'

"'I wouldn't blame you if you called the police,' Robbie says. 'But if you could find it in your heart...' He seemed really sad, as if he'd been taking care of Chad all his life and didn't expect to ever do anything else. He says, 'I'm really very sorry. Perhaps I can make it up to you, somehow.'

"I started to back away.

"Robbie apologized again. 'Chad's really very harmless,' he says.

"I told him he could have hurt me with those scissors.

"Robbie could see I had a point. He stood there staring at me, and then he says, 'You better go.'

"So I ran. I got out of there so fast. I made my way back to the highway, and then I found myself hitchhiking just like the drunken woman and her daughter. A young couple on the way to Washington stopped for me and gave me a ride all the way to Springfield Mall. They were very kind and wished me luck. They must have noticed my hair. I looked like one of those abandoned women in the shelter. Anyway, I walked around the mall for a long time before I decided to stop in one of those unisex shops and get somebody to finish the job on my hair. At least they trimmed it right and made it look like a normal haircut, but I still feel as though I've been raped.

"I never want to see Chad again as long as I live. I never want to go back to Baltimore, either, but I think that's where Sam went. I couldn't stop him. He was crazy mad when he left the house. I think he's gone after Chad."

The Need to Kill

Chad blossomed in my heart like a black flower as Nicole spoke. Her short hair was truly an injury, and there was a tender and frightened tone in her voice that made her seem changed in some final way. "Goddamn, honey," I said. "Why didn't you tell me about it when you first got home?"

"You remember that night. That was the night Elizabeth fell. I couldn't tell you then."

"Did you tell Sam?"

"I didn't tell anybody. But Sam didn't like my hair, and today he made some comment about how I got it cut just for Chad and it really pissed me off, so I told him."

"Well, if he's as angry as I am—"

"I've been thinking about it," she said. "About everything that's happened. About Sam's jealousy. I should have known how he'd react when I told him about this," she pointed at her hair. "I shouldn't have told him about it. I wish I hadn't. I stopped on the way home to get it properly cut so I wouldn't have to tell him or anybody. But I told him anyway. Whatever happens, the whole thing will be my fault. If anything happens to him—"

"It's not your fault."

"I shouldn't have told him about it."

There was a long silence. I felt this tremendous, almost physical sensation of having recorded the look on her face—as if I could feel the imprint of it settling on the tissues in my head. Her bright tear-washed eyes shifted from me to her hands and back to me again. I could not think of a thing except Chad and how I might find a way to hurt him.

"I'm afraid I may have wanted this," she said.

"What do you mean?"

"I was so angry when Chad did this to me. And then to have Sam accusing me of doing this to please him. I wanted—I was mad about... about everything."

"Well, I could have told you Chad was a—I knew he was an asshole the first time he opened his mouth."

She said nothing.

"He talked about how he was going to have to do something for the white people of the world, for god's sake."

Still she only sat there staring at her hands.

"Chad," I said with derision. "What kind of name is that?"

"He's sick."

"I can think of some medicine I'd like to give him."

She almost smiled.

"I mean it. We should file charges against him or something. He assaulted you."

"I don't want to file charges."

"Well, we ought to do something."

There was a long silence. I was thinking about how unfair it is that life is so unrevisable. I heard a chime ringing somewhere, a doctor being paged over the intercom.

"Listen," I said. "This wasn't all bad for Sam. A part of him had to be glad to hear it. Now he knows that you and Chad..." She seemed to draw back, and then she regarded me with wounded, serious eyes. I didn't finish the thought. "It's not your fault," I said again.

"You wouldn't say that if you had seen Sam's face when I told him."

"Yeah, well. He's a grown-up."

"I can't just sit here. But I don't know what to do. I can't go back to Baltimore. Not by myself. I wouldn't be any help to him, and he wouldn't listen to me, anyway."

"You want me to go to Baltimore with you?"

"This is something I have to deal with. I've been thinking of calling the police."

"You don't have to deal with it alone."

"I hate just waiting."

"You want me to go with you or not?"

"You've got enough trouble, Dad."

"I think I want to go. I'd like to have a little talk with Chad myself."

"For Christ's sake, I don't need you going after him, too."

"You want me to call the police?"

"No. What good would that do? We'd only get Sam in trouble. I wish I hadn't told him."

"It won't help to wish for things like that." I put my arm over her shoulder and held her for a moment, but then she pulled away.

"If anything happens to Sam—"

"Look, honey. This was not your fault. You hear me? None of it was your fault. You can't help it if Chad is a nut. And Sam is a grown-up. He can take care of himself."

"I didn't have to tell him about it."

"Just decide something. You want me to go with you?"

"To Baltimore?"

"Isn't that where you want to go?"

"Of course I do. Yes. Yes I do." Now she was crying. She looked betrayed, as if she had been forced to beg and had lost something of her pride and self-worth.

I said, "I'm sorry."

She said nothing. I could see she was really puzzled.

I wanted to say the most honest thing I could to her. "Just now, I had the feeling that I was forcing you to ask me, as though I wanted you to beg me or something."

"No. I wasn't feeling—"

"Not that I was doing that. I wasn't. I just hoped you would tell me honestly what you wanted me to do."

"Should we go to Baltimore?" She put her hands up and, very

gently running the side of each index finger under her eyes, brushed the tears away. In that gesture she was as purely beautiful as any untouchable vision or image I had ever seen. Then she said, "I'm sure I can find Chad's house."

"Well," I said, "I guess so."

"Oh." She had gathered herself, but there were still tears in her eyes. "I forgot."

"We'll go. We will. I'm sure Elizabeth's old man won't miss me."

She sniffed and I gave her my handkerchief. "Wipe your eyes," I said, getting up. "How long ago did Sam leave?"

"It was about a half hour or so before I got here."

"Well, he's not there yet, honey. He's got time to think. Maybe he'll change his mind. But come on, we'll go after him." I should have been apprehensive, but I must confess that I felt strong and good. I was going to rescue my little girl, save her. I felt like a truly good father—as though she believed in me, depended on me.

She rose next to me and I put my arm around her and we started for the door. "I wouldn't worry about Sam too much," I said. "He'd have to pound pretty hard on Chad, just to get his attention."

"No," she stopped, put her hands up to her face. "Oh no."

"What?"

"There's something else I have to tell you." She stood there, her head bowed, working up to something.

"What?" I said again.

"Sam has a gun."

The word *gun* made something leap up in my heart. "A gun. Where'd he get a gun?"

"He got it for our trip. He kept it in the dash on the Jeep."

"Goddamn, honey. You might have mentioned it sooner."

"I just now thought of it."

"What kind of gun?"

"I don't know. A pistol. It's silver."

"Jesus Christ. Did he say he was going to use it?"

"No." She waved her arm as if she wanted to stop my questions.

"He didn't mention it." Then she said, "It was just the way he said he wasn't afraid. The way he—"

"He's got bullets for it and everything?"

"Yes," she said, starting to cry again. "Now I really am afraid."

I took her in my arms, felt her trembling against my chest. "It will be all right, honey," I lied. "Everything's going to be all right."

I didn't believe it for a minute. I was absolutely terrified.

We Had No Trouble

Finding Chad's house. We had both calmed down by the time we got to Baltimore, and Nicole remembered which exit to take and what street it was on. We got there a little after one in the afternoon. The street seemed deserted. Even the driveways were empty. It was an old street lined with mature trees, and mostly well-established manicured lawns. A few houses needed fresh paint and somebody to cut the grass. Chad's place was one of these, set back farther from the road and surrounded by pigweed and dandelions.

"I don't think anyone's home," Nicole said. "I don't see Chad's car."

Sam's car was nowhere in sight, either.

I went down to the end of the street and made a right turn.

"Where're you going?"

"I'm just going to look around," I said.

At the end of the street, parked on the right-hand side, was Sam's jeep. I pulled up behind it. "I figured he might not park right in front."

I got out of the car and walked to the jeep. The door was unlocked. I opened it and then popped the glove compartment. The gun was still there. It was heavy and felt solid in my hand. Nicole was watching me, so I held it up to show her. She was so relieved her whole body seemed to shrink some, and I felt like a hero—as though I had truly saved her.

I tucked the gun in my trousers, closed the door on the jeep, then walked back to the car and got in.

Nicole regarded me with a mixture of awe and suspicion. "Is that thing loaded?"

"I don't know. It's got a clip in it."

"Why don't you put it back."

"I think I'll just keep it for now." I started the car and drove around the block. As I pulled up in front of Chad's house again, Nicole said, "Why don't we just drive around a bit. Maybe we'll spot him."

I said, "I guess we should just go up to Chad's door and knock, see if he's been there. What do you think?"

She seemed to shudder. "I'm not going up there."

"Well, I will." I got out of the car and walked up to the door. With the gun in my belt, I felt suddenly powerful and absolutely fearless. There was a small porch, but the sun was so high, only the top of the door itself was in shadow. I couldn't tell if anyone was inside looking out at me or not. Just as I was about to knock on the door, I noticed something dark on the wood surface next to the mat in front of it. I leaned down to get a closer look and was astonished to see several small shining droplets of fresh blood.

I ran back to the car.

Nicole rolled the window down and said, "What's the matter?"

I couldn't think of what to say. When I was seated next to her, she reached over and stopped me from starting the car.

"What happened?"

"We got to get to a phone." I realized this as I was saying it. "What street are we on?"

"Westmoreland. What's the matter. Did you hear something?"

I registered the numbers 3887 posted in brass numerals next to the front door.

"What's the matter," Nicole kept saying. "What happened?"

"I'm going to call the police."

I started the car, but before I could put it in drive, I saw, in the rearview mirror, a red Chevrolet Cavalier pulling up behind us.

"That's Chad's car," Nicole said.

I put my hand on the gun and waited there.

Two men got out. Chad was on the passenger side. He was wearing a tank top and black shorts. He was barefoot. The driver of the car wore a white shirt and tie, open at the collar. He looked like he was just getting home from work.

"Who's the guy in the shirt and tie?"

"Robbie," Nicole said. She made to get out and I grabbed her arm. "Sit tight."

Then everything moved as though in a dream. The gun seemed to awaken under my belt. My hand moved to it, and suddenly I wasn't thinking anymore, or aware of anything except what was happening before my eyes, which focused now on Chad and Robbie as they started toward the house. When they got to the walk in front, Chad glanced at the car and recognized Nicole. He stopped. He bent over a bit, staring into the car, and then he saw me. His face got this anxious look and he started to move fast toward the porch. I got out and held the gun over the roof of the car. "Stop right there."

He looked at me and froze in place.

"What's going on?" Robbie said.

Nicole opened the door and walked toward Robbie. "Where's Sam?"

Robbie said, "Nicole. What the hell is he doing?" He pointed at me.

I walked around the front of the car, still holding the gun in front of me. It seemed as though I was following the gun. "We're going to have a little talk."

Chad stood there, his hands at his sides, watching the gun. Robbie started toward me, and I turned it his way and he stopped.

"Dad," Nicole said, "put the gun away."

"Let's all go in the house." I swear I never felt so in control of things in my life. It was as if the gun extended from my hand to the engine of the world and whatever I wanted to happen would happen.

Nicole came over to me and whispered, "Don't. Let's just get Sam and go."

"I know what I'm doing, honey." I waved the gun toward the front door. "Inside," I said. "We're all going inside." I took Nicole by the hand and herded Robbie and Chad up onto the porch. Robbie unlocked the door.

"Wait a minute," I said. I pointed to the drops of blood. "What's that?"

"It's blood," Robbie said.

"Where's Sam?" Nicole said.

"Sam? Who's Sam?" Chad stared wide-eyed at the gun as he spoke.

"Look, mister," Robbie said, his voice shaking, "put the gun away. Nobody needs a gun here."

"Whose blood is that?" I demanded.

"It's nobody's blood," Robbie said, his voice getting stronger. "I hit a dog. We brought it inside to try and help it."

"Right."

"It's true," Chad said. "We just got back from the vet. That's where we took it. There's more blood in the car."

"Where's Sam?" I said.

"Who the fuck is Sam?" Now Robbie was loud.

"Open the door, and let's have a look inside, shall we?"

Suddenly Chad said to his brother, "Wait a minute. Wait a minute. I think I know who they're looking for." He turned to Nicole, as if he were trying to solve a complex problem for us, trying to help us. "Is Sam that little Japanese guy you had with you at the beach?"

"Yes."

"Oh, yeah. I remember him."

"You seen him?" I said.

"No."

"Where is he?"

"I don't know. I swear I don't know."

Robbie said, "If you'll put that gun away, maybe we can help you."

Now I wanted nothing more than to get inside. I realized I was standing there in plain view, holding a gleaming gun in my hand. Anyone might come along or glance out a living room window. "Let's just go on inside, OK? I'm not going to hurt anyone."

The house was dark, as Nicole had said. Chad was still talking to Nicole, asking her when she saw Sam last, what he was wearing. "He might have come by here while we were gone," he said. "Really, though. We haven't seen him."

Robbie stood in the doorway of the kitchen. Chad set himself against the wall next to him. The room was empty. Nicole disappeared down the hall toward the back of the house. "Sam?" She called.

I looked at Chad, and he turned away, watching Nicole as she walked from room to room.

"Sam?" she said, again. Then she came back into the room. "He's not here."

"Has he been here?"

"No one's been here," Robbie said.

I turned to Chad. "What'd you do to my daughter's hair, you little prick?"

He met my gaze now. The fear in his eyes almost made me feel sad for him.

"Please. Please don't hurt me," he said.

"Look, mister," Robbie started. Then he turned to Nicole. "I'm sorry about what happened, but this is... this is..." He didn't know what to do with his hands, but he wanted to do something. He was not afraid. He looked like an athlete itching to get his hands on the ball.

"I'm not going to hurt anybody," I said. "We're just going to give Chad here a little haircut."

"No," Nicole said. "I don't want to do that."

"I do."

"You can cut my hair," Chad said to Nicole. "Go ahead. I wouldn't blame you." He seemed relieved.

"Sam's car is right around the corner," she said. "If he didn't come here, where is he?"

"We haven't been here," Robbie said.

I pointed the gun at Chad. "Why don't you just sit yourself down right over here." He came toward the couch and slowly sat down in front of me. Then I turned to Robbie. "And you. Move over there on the other side of the kitchen door and stand against the wall where I can see you."

It was fun moving them around, arranging them in the room.

"Dad. Let's just go. He's not here."

"Sit back," I said to Chad. He put his head back, leaning over the back of the couch so that he was staring at the ceiling. I saw his Adam's apple move as he gulped in fear. "Relax," I said. Then I looked at Robbie, who was still staring at the gun, watching it as if he expected it to do something on its own. "I want the same pair of scissors he used on Nicky."

Nicole came over to me and took ahold of my free arm. "Please," she said, "don't do this. I mean it, now. It isn't worth it."

I don't know what was driving me. My mind was absolutely clear, but it was as if I had no true choice in anything. Power gripped my hand, pulled me along with it, just as if the gun had my mind and I was only doing its will. I was not angry, exactly, but anger seemed to pervade my intentions. I wanted to punish Chad, not just for what he had done to Nicole, but also for everything he believed and because he was so young. I touched the gun to the side of his head, and he leaned forward, bent over at the waist, hardly daring to breathe.

"I'm going to call the police," Robbie said.

"You go ahead," I told him. "Pick up that phone."

"Dad," Nicole said, "if you don't come with me, right now, I'm going to call the police." She walked over to the phone. "I mean it."

For a brief moment, I felt helpless again. "You'd do that? After all this, you'd do that to me?"

"I'd do it to stop you."

"I'm just going to cut his hair, for god's sake."

"And I just want to find Sam!" She was very loud. In a softer tone she said, "That's what we came here for."

Robbie said, "You haven't committed a crime, yet. But you touch my brother—"

"You mean like he touched Nicole? What about that crime?"

He had nothing to say to that.

"What about that crime?" I said again, louder.

"I'm sorry," Chad whimpered. He was not as brave as his brother. I saw sweat beginning to run down the side of his face.

"What about the crime she committed against Chad?" Robbie said.

"What?" Nicole and I spoke at the same time.

"The crime you committed with me," Chad whimpered. "I told Robbie about it."

"What are you talking about?" Nicole said.

"You had sex with him," Robbie said.

These words hit me in the heart. Nicole had been sleeping with Chad at the beach, before I ever heard of him. I looked at her. "You had sex?"

She glared at Robbie. "Having sex is not a crime."

"It is when you've tested positive for HIV," Chad said.

Nicole's face registered absolute shock. "What?"

Robbie said, "We know you tested positive."

I said, "Shut up. Both of you just shut up." I was waving the gun.

"Who told you I had AIDS?"

Robbie backed further against the wall, watching the gun. Chad held his head down and seemed to be praying. "Everybody just shut up," I said. "I mean it. We're done with all this bullshit."

"No," Nicole said. "Wait a minute."

"It's finished." I shouted. I realized I was caught, and in my hopeless desperation, I actually felt an odd deranged impulse to point the gun at her.

"It was your father," Chad said, still ducking down, covering his head with his hands. "Your father told me you had AIDS that day when I came to pick you up."

For a brief moment I believed I might shoot him. The room was silent for what seemed like a long time, and I was just waiting there for the gun to do whatever it was going to do. Then Nicole turned to me and made this little twisted sort of smirk, turning her head slightly, and then she walked coldly and regally out the door.

When she was gone, the gun's power seemed to withdraw itself, too. I was now only holding a piece of bright odd-shaped metal in my hands, standing in Robbie and Chad's dark, cigarette-smelling living room.

"Shit," I said. "Goddamn it."

There was a long truly awkward silence.

"Well, what's it going to be?" Robbie said.

I backed toward the door. Robbie didn't move, but Chad got up and faced me, a look of pity on his face. At the door I turned and saw Nicole walking away from the car and up the street toward the corner. I had to go after her, but what could I say to her? What could I ever say to her?

"Get out," Robbie said, in a low voice. "If you leave right now, I won't call the police."

"Go ahead and call the police," I said. "Right now I don't really give a shit one way or the other what you do."

I tucked the gun under my belt again. Robbie and Chad still did not move. "Maybe we've all learned something here," I said lamely, but I didn't believe it. Robbie seemed to nod a bit, or maybe the slight movement of his head only registered scorn. He didn't say anything.

I turned and walked out of that place. I crossed the front lawn to my car, opened the door, got in, started the engine, and drove off without ever looking back. Anyone watching me might have thought I was a man who had finished his business in there and knew where he was going.

At the End of the Road

I made a right turn. At first I didn't see Nicole anywhere, and a start of fear shot through me that she had somehow gotten away from me before I could explain everything, but then I saw her sitting in the front passenger seat of Sam's Jeep and there was Sam just opening the door on the driver's side. I pulled up next to them and rolled down my window.

Sam looked at me over the roof of the Jeep. "What the hell's going on?"

"Where've you been?"

"What are you guys doing here?"

"We came looking for you. Where were you?"

Nicole stared coldly ahead, refusing to even look my way.

"I've been right here."

Nicole turned to him. "Just let's get out of here."

"Where'd you go?" I said. "We thought something had happened to you."

"What?"

"Let's go," Nicole said.

There was a pause, then Sam said sheepishly, "I was waiting all this time over there." He pointed to a small house, back in the trees, a few driveways beyond us.

"You went to the wrong house?"

He nodded, still puzzled and still a bit sheepish.

"Here," I said, lifting the gun out of my belt and holding it out the window.

His whole face seemed to expand in shock. "Where'd you get that?"

"It's yours."

He came around the front of the Jeep and approached me without taking his eyes from mine. When he got to me, he hesitated for a minute, then he took the gun carefully from my outstretched hand.

"It hasn't been fired," I told him.

I could see he was relieved.

"I used it," I said. "But I didn't fire it."

Nicole honked the horn of the Jeep.

Sam jumped. "Jesus Christ!"

"Come on," Nicole said. "I want to get out of here." Accidentally her eyes met mine.

"Nicole," I said, "you know I didn't intend..."

She looked away.

"I'm sorry," I said.

"What's happened?" said Sam.

"Nicole," I said again, "please listen to me."

She would not bend. Her eyes were as cold and unforgiving as her mother's.

"All I can say is I'm sorry. I didn't mean any of this to happen. You must know that."

Suddenly, with a flash of anger and true hatred, she turned to me and said, "You never mean anything, do you? Nothing's ever your fault." She averted her eyes again and took up a staunch position with her arms crossed over her chest.

Sam stood there looking down at the gleaming gun in his hand.

I had nothing to say.

"Let's go," she said to Sam. "Please."

And then it hit me that I had something very specific to say. "This isn't my fault, goddamn it. Think about it."

"What's not your fault?" Sam said.

"Put that fucking gun away," I said.

He ignored me.

"Think about it, Nicole," I said. "You want to discuss this in front of Sam?"

"I don't want to discuss it ever."

"If you hadn't enjoyed a particular kind of relationship with Chad—you know what kind of relationship I'm talking about." We both looked at Sam, and he concentrated on the pavement in front of him. The gun dangled next to his thigh now, and he was just waiting there, listening. "What I said to Chad wouldn't have made any difference you know? Have you thought of that?"

"I'm going back home," she said.

"We're both at fault here."

Now she stared into my eyes.

"Would you let me explain?"

"Not now," she said. Then she shouted, "Not now, goddamnit!" Her whole head shook.

Sam leaned over toward her and said something I didn't hear.

"Let's go," she said, quietly. "Now." She was crying.

"What the fuck is going on?" Sam said to me.

"Get in the car and drive!" Nicole shouted.

He had real fear in his eyes.

"Ask Nicole what happened," I said. "She'll tell you." With that, I put the car in gear and drove off. I looked in the rearview mirror as I was pulling away, and I saw Sam moving around the front of the car in the bright sun, staring after me, the glistening gun in his hand.

I wasn't sure where I was going. I drove down a tree lined and shady street. The window was still rolled down, and I was going fairly slowly. I could have put my head back on the seat and closed my eyes. The air under the trees was cool and almost peaceful. It matched the gradual sort of helpless calm I was beginning to feel.

Somehow there's something really soothing about being finished, once and for all. There's nothing left to hope for. All you have to do is find out what's fun or what feels good and do that, and the hell with everything and everyone else.

I felt almost as if I'd dropped the great boulder and turned around and started back down the hill. The walking was easier on the way down, and I had nothing to carry. After a while, the only thing I could think about was all those benevolent summer afternoons in the grass by the paddock, waiting for jockeys and trainers to bring out fresh horses for the next race. How perfect life can be when the horses are running and the air is still and balmy. How utterly perfect the world can be when you've got only money to lose. Somewhere behind me, Nicole was telling Sam all about our day, but I didn't really care. For a brief time there, I truly believed that I didn't care about anything in the world.

Then I remembered Elizabeth, lying silent in those hospital sheets, and the weak, almost inaudible heart murmuring in her belly.

Elizabeth Started Bleeding

A few days later. There was nothing anyone could do. A cloudless, bird-less Saturday morning they wheeled her into surgery and performed an emergency abortion. The baby's heart had stopped, anyway. If Eliza-beth never woke up, she would never have to know that our baby was gone. Isn't it sometimes comforting to think of not suffering another minute of frustration or loneliness or pain or grief? Perhaps Elizabeth would prefer that.

The doctor said it was too early to tell the sex of the baby. I think he was being kind. Later I heard one of the nurses say it was a boy. I couldn't believe it. My son, dead before all time.

For days I walked around like some sort of device with gears and bat-teries. I carried myself from place to place, watching the world around me as though it were the background in a movie. Sometimes, out of the blue, I'd remember the day Catherine left me—how it felt to watch Nicole toddle down my front walk, carrying her little suitcase, her mother standing regally in the driveway; my little girl dragging a small brown-and-white teddy bear along the ground as she walked, her small, new voice saying, "Bye, Daddy." She was so brave, fighting back tears.

Now Elizabeth had lost her baby, too. It was such a terrible empty-ing out of everything important—as if a great hole had opened in the earth and swallowed up all expectations and all hope. There would be nothing left now but this mechanical movement under the clock—day after day of lengthening memory and grief.

I never thought about what happened in Baltimore anymore. At first I waited by my bedroom window, watching the street, waiting for the police to show up, but after Elizabeth lost her baby, I didn't think about it.

Nicole understood what I was going through, I think. In any case, she didn't go home right away. She hung around until Fourth of July. It was a quiet sullen existence, but she was there, nonetheless.

Whenever I could, I visited Elizabeth. I'd sit in her room with Mr. Simmons and wait for something to happen. She always looked so beautiful and peaceful lying there in the clean linen with the sun shining off her hair.

And I realized she was innocent—like a baby herself. There was so much she didn't know.

I expected Mr. Simmons, too, would be leaving soon enough, since it had to be costing him a lot of money to be away from his work like that. But he was always right there, every day. We'd sometimes watch an Orioles game in Elizabeth's room. The hospital staff got to know us fairly well. I think they liked us because we waited so faithfully for "our little girl," as they called her, to wake up. The doctors—there was a team now—continued to approve of her signs and were confident that she'd come out of it eventually. Nobody would speculate on what *eventually* meant.

Nicole seemed unable to speak to me, so we didn't talk very much about what had happened. In fact, we never discussed it until the morning she left. She interrupted her packing to sit across from me at the kitchen table and sip a glass of water.

"Don't you want orange juice?" I asked.

"No, thank you."

There was a long silence. She would not look directly at me. I thought of her mother, Catherine, of the myriad ways she refused to confront me, of the long years of advancing rancor between us because she would not tell me what was bothering her. She complained about the gambling and latched onto that, but it wasn't only that. How could it have been? No one breaks up a family over something so finally trivial as money. Perhaps Catherine herself never knew. So how could she tell me?

In a lot of ways Nicole was like her mother. I admit I was part of the amalgam, and only God knows which one of us had the worst influence on her. In my mind she could not help but be a damaged personality. She would never really forgive me for what had happened, because she could never really express the confused mixture of emotions stewing in her heart. It seemed like the only emotion she recognized and trusted was enmity. And now she recognized that in her response to me. Because enmity is more like climate than weather, she would be estranged from me for a long time.

I know it's possible she felt pity for me, too, but I didn't want to think about that.

"So, you're going then," I said.

She said nothing.

I waited awhile, then I tried to give her an opening. "I thought you were going to stay until August."

"Yeah." She still wouldn't look directly at me.

"So why do you have to go now?"

She made this short high sound in the back of her throat, but her face was absolutely impassive. She was holding herself back so far, she looked lifeless.

Sam came down the steps carrying two heavy bags. "Well, you're going to have your bed back finally."

I forced a smile.

Nicole finished her water and went back up the stairs. I didn't know if I should follow her, but I went with her all the way to the foyer. She almost ran up the stairs.

Sam looked at me, then took the bags out the door.

I leaned against the wall at the base of the stairs and stared up to the landing above me. For some reason I was afraid to go up there. Sunlight from the living-room windows made angular shadows on the wall, and there was almost no light in the hallway, so I could tell that the doors of both bedrooms were closed. She was either in her room packing or in my room picking up Sam's things. Or maybe she was up there waiting for me. I didn't see how I could let her leave when things were so incomplete between us. That prospect alone made me feel accused in a perverted sort of way—and guilty.

I looked at my hands holding the railing. I needed the evidence of my knuckles, fingernails, bones, and opposable thumbs to prove to myself that I was, in fact, human. Everything seemed senseless and fast—as though I were only an image projected on a wall—and suddenly Sam was there, behind me.

"I'm going to tell you something," he whispered, pausing briefly. Then he said, "I'm only telling you this because—well, because I love Nicole."

"Yeah," I said, "I'm sure you do."

"I want to go back to California myself," he said. "The sooner the better. And I'm taking her with me. I hope you'll forgive me for speaking plainly, but I think she needs to be away from you."

I faced him. You would not believe the bitter pity I saw in his eyes.

"Still," he said, "it wouldn't be fair to her if I didn't tell you that I think if you went upstairs and talked to her, she'd listen."

I had no response to this.

"I think she wants you to go up there." He straightened up, seemingly satisfied with himself. He was not a bad sort, and he probably disliked me for all the right reasons, but I hated him at that moment. I hated his youth and his pity and his intimacy and friendship with Nicole.

"Well what the fuck," I said. "This is really perfect."

"I just said what I think."

"You're giving me advice."

He shrugged.

A door opened upstairs and light flooded the hallway. Nicole came softly to the landing, wearing dark navy blue shorts and a white T-shirt, a towel draped over her arm. She was carrying another bag. Her eyes, even from that distance, looked cold and stolid—as if she had died from boredom and still wore the expression in death. "This is yours," she said to Sam. "I'm going to take a shower, first."

An awkward silence ensued, while all three of us stood there. Then Sam took the bag and went out. I closed the door behind him. Still facing the door I said, "You can't just leave, honey. Not like this." My voice broke, and suddenly I had this aching memory of saying the same thing to her mother all those years ago when I knew she was leaving me. "We have to talk this out," I went on, turning to face her again, struggling to gain strength in my voice. "I don't know—I just don't really know why—I need to know why..."

Another long silence. I couldn't remember anything else I wanted to say.

Finally Nicole spoke. "Why did you do it, Dad? Why?"

I found it impossible to look at her. I stood there staring at the floor, my feet, the texture of the wood on the steps. For a long time I tried to think of something good to say—anything at all—but my mind was empty. I could only remember what I should not say and why I should not say it. Finally I said, "Chad was—Chad was the one. He cut your hair off. And he was—"

"It wasn't Chad," she said. "It was you. This was your doing."

Sam opened the door behind me and came silently back in. He moved toward the stairs, looking up at Nicole, and then back to me.

"I'm going," Nicole said, her cold eyes freezing me in place.

"You don't have to go."

She said nothing.

"What else is bothering you? You can't still be angry, can you?"

"I'm sorry about the baby."

"Yeah, well."

"I'm going home. That's all. I don't want to stay here anymore."

I nodded. "Suit yourself. You can run away—"

"I'm running all right." She retreated back down the hall.

Sam stood there looking at me.

I went into the family room and poured myself a glass of whiskey and watched the *Today Show* for a while. They were doing some story about dreams coming true—nightmares as well as fantasies.

What did I care if Nicole went home? It would be the best thing for her. She would get away from me. Anyway, I was tired of being a character in her life story. She'd be telling everybody, for the rest of her life, not about Chad and how he had cut off her hair. She'd be talking about me and what I had done.

For the rest of her life.

I felt as though I were lost in some sort of terrible game where I did not know the rules and if I made the wrong move, everybody would die.

Upstairs Nicole was busy building a cathedral of faithful hatred, and I couldn't forestall it no matter what I did or said. For a time there, at least when she was little and I was flying across the country every year to see her, I wasn't a bad father. I thought I was being a good father when I drove her all the way to Baltimore that day. I loved her so long without having her there to show it, so in its own way, this too was a peculiar variety of bad luck. It was impossible to learn how to be her father at such a distance, and now she was grown.

I really didn't want to wait around for the sullen and halfhearted farewells, so I decided to get out of there. As I was leaving I told Sam to be sure to lock the door when he was ready to go. He thanked me for my hospitality.

"Say good-bye to Nicole for me," I said.

"I will."

"You guys have to come again soon."

"Sure." He didn't try to stop me.

"Next time I'll have a room all prepared for you, so you don't have to steal my bed."

He pretended to be amused. He must have thought it an odd thing that we were having this fake and friendly conversation about the next time he and Nicole would visit.

A Few Days After

Nicole left me, Elizabeth woke up. I wasn't there.

It was a gray windy Thursday afternoon marred by occasional salvos of rain. She was alone in the room, bewildered by the network of clear tubes running out of her nose and arms. She wasn't quite sure where she was or what had happened until her father came into the room with a cup of coffee in his hand and a newspaper under his arm. Then it all started coming back to her—the fall, her bones hitting the concrete slab at the bottom of the elevator shaft. She was terribly frightened and it took her father a while to calm her down. He told me he didn't know how he could tell her about the baby, but after she had stopped shaking and was more firmly awake and composed, she looked at him with a questioning gaze and he said, "No, honey."

She cried softly while he stroked her brow. He was so terribly sad for her and for all she had lost, the sense of joy in his heart that she had finally waked made him feel ashamed—as though the loss of the baby was somehow his fault.

"Goddamn," he said to me, tears in his eyes. "I was happy and unhappy at the same time."

"I've got to see her," I said. We were standing in the lobby of the hospital, where he had come down to meet me. This was his request, so I hoped it meant that Elizabeth was now ready or allowed to have visitors.

"Did you tell her I was coming?"

"I told her we'd both been sitting by her bed waiting for a miracle."

"If I could just talk to her for a minute."

He held his hand up. "She doesn't want to see anyone right now."

"Just a minute," I said. "My daughter went back to California."

He forced a kind smile. I had told him about Nicole the day she left, but he didn't know why it would matter to Elizabeth. To tell the truth, I didn't either. I just felt as though only Elizabeth would know how I felt about it, and talking to her would somehow make me feel less cornered and temporary.

"Just for a minute," I begged, moving toward the elevators.

He took ahold of my arm. "Elizabeth is very confused right now. I think it would be better if she didn't see you." He was very kind. He might have been on my side. We had gotten to be fairly good friends during the long vigil by Elizabeth's bed. I would be willing to bet a lot of money that he put in a good word for me. It was just my rotten luck that when she woke up, I wasn't the first person she saw. I would like to have had that conversation, but it just wasn't in the cards, you know what I mean? You interrupt a daily vigil to take one rainy afternoon at the track (I had another big day, if you're interested) just to relieve the tension, and you don't expect things are going to improve so dramatically.

I said, "It isn't just me she doesn't want to see, is it?"

"Well, no. She's not ready to see anyone."

"She hasn't asked for me?"

He shook his head.

"I'd like to at least tell her I'm sorry."

"Sorry?"

"About the baby and all."

"She knows you're sorry, son."

"Yeah. I guess she does."

A few days later I tried to call her and Mr. Simmons answered the phone. "I'm sorry, Henry, she's sleeping," he whispered.

"She's out again?"

"No, just resting, you know."

"I sure would like to talk to her."

"I really don't think it's a good idea to start—to pursue her just now, Henry."

"I just wanted to tell her some things. That's all. I'm not pursuing."

"Give it some time. She's had quite a trauma."

"I see. Well, I guess we all have."

"Once she's home and back into the swing of things—"

"My daughter left me."

"Yes, I know."

"Yeah, she went back to California. She's gone." I felt foolish and small. I wanted him to put Elizabeth on the phone, and I had nothing else to say to him.

He seemed incredibly awkward—as though talking to me disgraced him in some way. "She's had so many visitors, you know."

"She has?" Something cold dropped down in my soul. I was excluded by choice. She did not want to see me.

Just me.

She got out of the hospital on the following Friday. She retreated back into her quiet house, and her father returned to Pennsylvania, and that was that.

I called her house every day for almost a week and got no answer. Not even the machine. When I called her office, I was told that she was on leave. Mr. Simmons called me, though, just before he left, to wish me luck and thank me once again for all my help.

"I'm sorry about how things worked out," he said.

It was clear he knew more than I did about my future.

Since Nicole and Sam had gone, the house was quiet, empty, and mean. I couldn't stand being there. I hit the track a few times. I held my own, too. I'd lose a hundred or so one day, then win five or six hundred the next two or three days. Then I'd drop a hundred or two, and pick up three or four hundred the day after that. Somehow it didn't excite me anymore. In fact, after a while, I quit going.

Then one afternoon I woke up from a long nap and realized I was going to go over to her house. In the mirror I convinced myself that what I ought to do was just present myself and force her to reject me. Or at least broach the subject of our friendship. I know it sounds silly, but I was ready to accept that we were only going to be friends, if that was what she wanted.

Anyway, it seemed such a reasonable idea to drive by her place. Part of me probably hoped I'd see her out front cutting her grass and I'd pull over and ask her if she needed any help. But the yard was empty when I got there, and the house seemed closed up. The shades were drawn, and there was no sign of life. Even the plants on her front porch were wilted.

I still had a key and I could have gone inside, but I was afraid. If she was sleeping and I woke her, she might actually be afraid of me, and I couldn't bear that idea. So I knocked on the door. My stomach seemed to quiver and chill me through, but I waited there. I thought I heard something behind the door, so I knocked again, this time a little louder.

I had no idea what I was going to say to her.

The door had two vertical windows on either side of it, with white curtains drawn in front of them. I leaned over and tried to squint through the space between the curtain and the door frame, but I couldn't see anything. After a while, it seemed dangerous to knock again. I stepped off the porch and behind the hedges next to the staircase. Back there she had a garden hose, rolled up neatly. I turned the water on, unwound the hose, and carried it up to the front porch so I could water the plants there. I sprayed each one of them—impatiens and gladiolus and geraniums—gently, so that I did not disturb or knock off any leaves or blossoms. I liked the sound the water made, and the way it ran down off the leaves quietly, almost lovingly. When I was done, I rewound the hose and placed it back where it belonged, then I stepped back up to the door and knocked one more time. I made it loud but not too insistent. I would have felt foolish calling her name.

Still, there was no answer. I might have walked around back and knocked on the door there, but I was afraid she'd think I was stalking her. So I finally gave up. I had taken all afternoon to get the nerve to drive over there, and now I realized it was pretty much wasted. Feeling dejected and unlucky, I drove to a Howard Johnson's restaurant and had a cup of coffee.

There was no need for me to hang around anywhere. I didn't want to go to the track, and as I was leaving the restaurant, I remembered, again, that I'd be returning to an empty house. I'd have to figure out where I was going to have dinner that night, and I'd have to go there alone to have it. Three women were happily gone out of my life. Except for my mother, all the women I had ever cared for had abandoned me.

When I got back to my car I was feeling pretty shaky—almost sick with an odd sort of apprehension, as if I were about to do something truly dangerous and frightening. The truth was, I didn't know what I would do or where I might go.

I didn't want to eat dinner alone again, so I drove out onto the highway and just cruised along, not thinking. I headed for Baltimore, to see what I could see.

Oddly Enough
I Found Myself

Standing on the front porch of my father's house. I had been driving around Baltimore for several hours—right through the time when most normal people have dinner—and I realized I was getting kind of hungry. At one point earlier in the evening, I had even cruised by Chad's place. I was on the interstate near his house, and when I came to the right exit, it seemed appropriate to take it. I drove by the place very slowly, looking for any sign of life. There was no car out front, and I didn't stop. I circled the block a few times, thinking of Nicole, still with a kind of sad and apprehensive ache in my stomach. It was like I was nervous about the next minute—as if each second might extend somehow into an eternity and I'd be lost in darkness.

You know what happens to you when you fall into a great black hole that has no bottom? You fall and fall and fall until it no longer seems like falling. Then you're just in the rush of the air and the darkness, wondering what your arms and legs are for.

I wished I had shot Chad. As I drove around the block one last time and studied his front door and the steps of his porch, I wished I had at least done that. Then, maybe I wouldn't feel so much like a victim— I'd at least have the satisfaction of knowing that I was the engine of my own folly. I hated how accidental everything in my life had become.

Finally in all my wandering I came to see that I had strayed into my old neighborhood: the place where I was once a boy, the last child in a big family, and the earth was durable and sacred and my father was God. The place where it was all right to be young and wrong.

Driving down streets that I had played on as a boy made me feel so alone, it would have been impossible not to stop by—if only for a minute. Also, perhaps some part of me believed I would feel better if I simply heard my mother's voice. I knew if I wanted to talk, she would listen, and though it was irritating that she always knew what to do about almost everything, I confess I needed some evidence that it was possible for a woman—any woman—to tolerate my presence.

When I walked up to the front door, I immediately regretted it. I saw my father cross the hallway between the kitchen and the parlor. It was nearly dark outside, and the front parlor light was on. I stood there, looking through the glass of the narrow windows next to the door frame. It took a while, but finally I knocked on the glass. Unfortunately my father came to the door. I saw his dark shadow approaching the foyer, and I almost leaped off the porch and ran for the trees.

"Well, look at you," he said, when he opened the door. "What are you doing all the way over here?"

"I was at the track for the day," I lied.

The smile left his face.

"I just thought I'd drop by," I said. "Is Mom home?"

"What's the matter, son. You look awful."

I didn't know what to say to him. I knew if I tried to tell him any of it, I'd lose the wind to do it. "I'm fine," I said.

He frowned, not believing me.

"I lost a bit of money, today."

He believed that. "Come on in." He swept his arm into the room. Then he called to mother.

I sat on the couch in the den.

My mother wanted to get me something. Anything at all. She started conversations like that. "Can I get you something?"

"I don't want anything, Mom."

My father left the room. It was quiet for a time.

"What's happened?" Mother sat next to me.

I couldn't talk. I just kept saying "I . . . I . . . I . . . I," and in spite of exercising every ounce of strength and self-control I possessed, I realized I was crying. Like a true fool—a child—I could not stop it. She put her arms around me and held me, and I was absolutely terrified that my father would come into the room and see us.

"Don't," I said, struggling to pull away from her.

But she wouldn't let go. She patted the side of my face, held my head against her breast. I could smell her perfume, the faint odor of the tea she had every afternoon before she woke my father from his nap.

Finally she let go and I sat back, staring at the blurry ceiling. She handed me a Kleenex and I wiped my eyes with it.

"I'm sorry," I said, feeling hot and ashamed.

"Tell me what's happened. Is Elizabeth . . . is Elizabeth—"

"She doesn't want to see me ever again."

"Oh."

It took a long time to clean my face and get ahold of myself. She watched me.

"You wouldn't believe what's been going on with me," I said.

She put her hand on the back of my neck. "Tell me."

My father was nowhere to be seen, and her soft voice was so achingly tender, I realized I could not lie to her, but I didn't want to tell her anything.

"I've just had some bad luck," I said. My eyes burned, but I had dried the tears and all I had left was my embarrassment. I needed to get out of there, but I didn't know how to do it.

"Tell me what's going on, son."

"It's just been a rotten summer."

"Is Elizabeth all right?"

"What?" I couldn't look at her.

"She's out of the hospital?"

"Yes."

"She's not pressing charges or anything."

"No, of course not."

"Well, you never know."

"What would she press charges about?" Now I did face her. Her eyes were bright and sad.

She removed her arm from around my shoulder, then tried to overcome the awkwardness of our situation by pulling absently at a stray thread that had come out of the hem on her skirt. "Your father's been keeping track of the situation through some friends. He was worried about you."

"His friends wouldn't include a young police officer named Puckett, would they?"

"I don't know who he's been talking to—but he was concerned."

"Well, she's not pressing charges."

"I'm glad to hear that," she patted my knee. "I'm sorry about..." Now there were tears in her eyes. "Why didn't you tell me she was— that Elizabeth was..."

I waited. There was no way I was going to fill in that blank.

She sat up a bit, seemed to compose herself. "Why didn't you let us know she was pregnant?"

I looked at my hands. How could I answer her? How could I explain what it was in all the accumulated dailiness of our lives that had permanently altered any chance we would be comfortable with the truth between us; how could I explain my apprehension about Elizabeth's pregnancy, knowing what I knew about my mother's scorn for people like me?

"You know, don't you, that your father's heart was broken when he found out she had lost the baby."

"Well, I've broken his heart so many times, it must be—"

"No, you didn't break his heart. He was sorry for the loss of the child." She looked into my eyes, and she must have read my disbelief, because she went on. "He's not—your father is not always a tender man. He's a good man. A very good and basically kind man who just doesn't know how to be... warm, sometimes. But he would have loved the child. I know he would have." She was not looking at me anymore, but I believe that what she said was the most serious thing I had ever heard her say—to anyone.

"I'm sorry," I whispered.

My father came into the room, carrying a tray with a bottle and three glasses. "How about a little cognac?"

I wanted a beer, but I said yes to the brandy. Mother watched him pull the cork from the bottle and pour about an inch of brandy into each glass. The sound of the brandy trickling into the glasses was comforting and pleasant. You would have thought we were a peaceful family preparing for a quiet evening of conversation before turning in for the night. My father took his glass and sat down in the big easy chair on the other side of the room. He turned on his reading light, but he did not pick up his book or the newspaper. Holding the glass of brandy in his lap, he sat back in the chair and put his feet up on a footstool in front of him. He was watching me, so I met his gaze, and for the briefest moment he sized me up, then looked away.

"Well," he said. "You've been sharing all the news with your mother. Bring me up-to-date."

I lifted my glass and held it toward him. "Cheers."

He raised his glass about an inch, as I took a mouthful of the cognac and swallowed it. "Ahhhh," I said.

Mother sipped hers, glancing back and forth between Dad and me. I think she wanted somebody to talk, but perhaps she was content to leave things as they were. She smiled, then lifted her glass slightly toward Dad as though she were going to propose a toast. "Elizabeth's out of the hospital. She's fully recovered."

"Good." Dad did not look at her. He was swirling his cognac around in the snifter, warming it in the bottom of the glass as it rested in the palm of his hand. "We sent her some flowers."

"It was a lovely bouquet," Mother said.

I took another sip of my brandy, then I said, "Nicole's gone back to California." I was surprised at the strength of my voice.

"Oh?"

"Yeah. She's probably going to college out there."

"I'm glad to hear it."

"The wedding is off, though."

"Really."

"Elizabeth had second thoughts." I lost a bit of ground when I said that. I felt my eyes beginning to simmer again. "It's probably for the best." I took a deep breath, caught myself in time. "Yeah. She wasn't ever really sure what she wanted, so when I pressed her about it, she was forced to figure it all out."

"You don't say."

I nodded. In the steady beam of my father's eyes, I was surprised at how suddenly everything seemed to be less crucial, less painful. I gained control of my emotions, I now realize, because my father's eyes empowered me as no other tonic or nutrient could. By degrees they erased trouble and woe, and replaced them with a sense of the equity in all suffering. My father could look at me in a certain way and some-how I learned what justice was. For that brief moment I could even accept it.

"So, I guess I'm going to remain a bachelor." I smiled.

My mother put her hand on my shoulder again. I could tell she felt sorry for me, and this, too, seemed to make me stronger.

I looked at her. "I'm going to be all right."

"You just have to get hold of something and apply yourself," she said. "We've all known that."

I gulped another mouthful of brandy. My glass was nearly empty.

"Nicole called here to say good-bye," my father said.

"Good."

"She seemed upset."

"She did?"

He nodded.

There was a long silence. I took one more gulp of the cognac and finished it off, then I put the glass back on the tray. "I'm getting hungry."

My father shook his head slowly.

Mother said, "There's leftovers in the fridge."

I didn't say anything.

"If you want..." Her voice trailed off.

Dad sipped the brandy, still looking at me. I reached over the tray and poured myself some more, then I held the bottle up, offering it to him.

"I'm fine," he said.

I wondered what Nicole had told him—if she'd mentioned my lie to Chad, or how close I came to shooting him behind the ear.

I turned to my mother, still holding the bottle up as an offering, but she was getting up.

"No, thank you. Can I get you something to eat, then?" Her voice was not steady.

My father said, "So why was Nicole so upset?"

"What have you got?" I said to mother.

"Meat loaf. Leftover tuna casserole. We had grilled salmon last night; there may be some of that left."

"I'll have some of the meat loaf."

"Why was Nicole so upset?" Father asked again.

"I haven't had dinner," I said. Then I looked at my father. "What did she tell you?"

He took another sip of his brandy. Mother glanced briefly at both of us, then she left the room.

"I mean, how do you know she was upset?" I said.

"She didn't sound happy. And when I asked her what was wrong, she said I should ask you."

I studied the brandy in my snifter, the way the light seemed to crystallize in it, then swirl toward the bright edges where the wine meets the surface of the glass. I didn't know what I could tell him. For one thing, I wasn't sure any of it was his business.

"So," he said. "I'm asking you. What happened between you two?"

"It's a long story."

"We've got time."

His eyes were gray, watery, and kind—in spite of the exacting nature of his personality and the asperity in his voice, I could always tell when he was in a truly gentle frame of mind.

"The same thing that happened between you and me." I was astonished that I said that. The words came in a quiet tone that was almost a whisper—as though my body operated on its own and blurted the truth without wanting to. His face didn't change, but he heard me, and I could see that my words had registered. I could almost see him thinking.

Then he said, "And what happened between you and me?"

"You know."

"No, I don't."

"You know we don't see things the same way." I really didn't want to say any more to him. I knew it would only make things worse, and I was kicking myself for having mentioned it at all. The room seemed to get smaller, and suddenly I couldn't seem to get enough air. The walls leaned toward me, and my father's gray eyes moved down now, away from me.

"I'm going to say something to you, Henry."

I said, "We don't need to get into this. Nicole and I simply see things differently, too. She has her way, and I have mine. I don't approve of hers, she can't take it that I don't. So she left. That's all. The same thing that goes on between parents and children all over the—"

He raised his hand to stop me. The look on his face was the sort of steady thinking expression he must have presented from the bench all those years when he was a federal judge.

"I'm almost seventy," he said. "I don't have long."

He had never talked about death in his life, so he had my attention.

"I've already had one heart attack."

Those words struck me with sudden cold fear. "You've had a heart attack?"

He took another sip of the brandy.

"You never told me you had a heart attack."

"It was a mild one, last year. We didn't tell anybody."

"Phil doesn't know?"

"Your mother and I didn't see the need to worry you."

"Does Phil know?"

He didn't say anything for a moment, but it was clear that he had told Phil about it. I waited there, dazed and fearful. Finally he said, "I had to tell Phil; he's handling some legal matters for me. And we called Theresa. She recommended a good heart doctor out here. But we've told no one else, and I don't want you telling anyone, either. I mean that."

"You had a heart attack. I don't believe it." I shook my head. I didn't want to believe it.

"Listen to me. I'm fine." He blinked his eyes slowly, thinking about what he wanted to say. For a brief moment, I saw his face as it would appear from the white satin of a casket, and suddenly I felt tears coming to my eyes again.

"I'm fine," he said, "but I'm getting near the end. I'm almost seventy."

I wanted to go over and put my arms around him, but I didn't feel as though I could approach the bench, if you know what I mean. My fear of him was not his fault, I now realize. It was mine. I was the one who saw him as a judge, even when he was trying to be my father. I think I might have had some inclination of this idea then, as he spoke to me, but I couldn't bring myself to cross the room and touch him, much less embrace him.

"It's a short trip through here, son," he went on. "You have to use the time you have to make meaning out of it, you see. Your life has to have meaning, otherwise you're no different than a cicada or a clam. You understand? In the whole history of the world, billions and billions of people have come and gone, and lived their lives like bees and ants and other insects. They left no monuments or works of art or precedents at law or anything at all. They achieved—nothing. No lasting contribution to culture or knowledge or civilization. But perhaps their lives mattered after all because they gave meaning to their days. I'm telling you that if their lives had meaning, then their lives meant something—whether or not they achieved anything else. You live a hundred years, and it's only the flicker of a light beam, a flash of light, like a strobe light. That's all."

He had never spoken to me about such things. The tone of his voice was so calm and, in its own way, passionate, I thought he might be on the verge of a confession of some kind. But then he said, "Your life is meaningless until you put meaning into it."

Like a fool, I said, "I know."

"No, you don't know." Now he leaned forward, placing his glass on the footstool in front of the chair. He gazed at me with serious eyes now, as though he were going to pass sentence. "This is what our difficulty is, Henry; the trouble between you and me."

I nodded, still watching his eyes.

"I'm going to tell you a little story."

"OK."

"Just listen for a minute, don't say anything."

"Sure."

He sighed.

I shrugged, as if to say, "Go ahead."

"Do you know what people mean when they say life has meaning?" he asked.

"Sure."

"What do they mean?"

"They're talking about—well, purpose, I guess."

He shook his head. I knew I got the answer wrong, but he really put me on the spot. What would you say if your father asked you that question? How could you answer it? The truth was, I didn't want to talk about the meaning of life with him. I don't ever want to talk about the meaning of life with anyone. What I wanted to talk about at that moment was his heart attack. What it was like and whether or not his arteries were blocked, if he was on medication, and so on. I didn't give a damn about the meaning of life.

"Most people who use that phrase," he went on, "have no idea what they mean when they use it. In fact, a lot of people simply say life has no meaning, because it's easier to say life is meaningless than it is to figure out what it means. That's hard work. Nobody wants to do hard work anymore—especially the kind of work that forces you to examine your own life and everything you're up to. So instead of giving their lives meaning, people say it's meaningless. Or they talk about 'the meaning of life,' in spite of the fact that they scarcely know what the phrase means."

"I don't talk about it. I don't even think about it."

He held up his hand, smiling gently now. "Others, like you, don't even think about it, that's right."

"I don't want to think about it, Dad. I just want to live my life."

Now his face changed. The gentle cast of his eyes seemed to cloud over with his blustery brows. "You said you would just listen."

"OK."

"My father was a man who—let me tell you about my father. You know what he said to me when I went overseas for the first time, during the war?"

I said nothing. I'd been told what his father said a million times, but I wasn't about to remind him of that.

"He gripped my hand." Dad paused, remembering. His voice was a bit shaky when he went on. "He said, 'Write your mother. And do your duty.'"

"'Write your mother and do your duty,'" I repeated. "You said that to me when I joined the army."

He nodded, almost smiling. "I looked into my old man's eyes as he said those words to me, and do you know what I saw?"

I didn't say anything.

"I saw everything there was to know about him. It was as if, with that look, he gave me everything in his life that meant anything; as if the meaning in his life, became the meaning in mine, you know what I mean?"

I had no idea, but I nodded slightly, hoping he wouldn't call me on it.

"Do your duty."

There was a long silence. I took a gulp of my brandy and hoped my mother would come back or call me to supper or do something to get me out of there.

Dad said again, quietly, "Do your duty."

"Your father was a great man," I said. "And so are you." I almost choked with tears as I spoke, remembering how I had always failed him. But he looked at me gently again and raised his glass.

"Here's to your grandfather."

"Absolutely," I said, raising my glass. We each took a long sip. Then I said, "Here's to you, too."

He smiled. I finished my brandy and leaned over and put the glass down on the tray. I could hear my mother clattering dishes and pans in the kitchen.

"Is she cooking something in there?" I said, starting to get up.

"Let me finish, son," Dad said. It was the first time in our lives that his voice seemed plaintive—almost as if he were entreating me. "You promised you'd listen."

"I'm sorry," I said, settling back on the couch. "I thought the story was over."

"This is about the meaning of life. It's the best story I know to illustrate it."

"Really."

"Not what life means, but how to make life meaningful. You understand the distinction?"

I nodded. There was a brief silence, then I heard Mother close the refrigerator door. This meant she was cooking something, and I could pretty well give up hope that she might save me.

My Father Said

"I remember when I first started thinking about life seriously. I can remember the day, exactly. It was 1933, late fall. I was fourteen years old. I know it was a bright day because back then all Sundays seemed to find the sun. Enough so, that I believed the reason it was called Sunday was because most of them were sunny—even in the dead of winter. This was all I needed to conclude that the sun was God's light and a thing in which he was well pleased. He lit up his day for worship when he was well pleased. When it was a damp and drizzly Sunday, we somehow knew God was unhappy about something.

"All my young life I had loved the sound of the Latin mass. The soft, resonant, flawless mixture of sounds and words entranced me as no music or song could. The Latin phrases always seemed as if they were whispered, even when the priest said them through a microphone. And I prayed along, reading the English, as though God's language had been translated into my own.

"For some reason on this particular day that fall, instead of getting lost in quiet reverence for the individual sacred words—instead of listening to the Latin—I read what the priest was saying, and it came to me as English sentences, making English sense. The priest read a prayer from what I now know as the Fifty-first Psalm, although in my old missile it is identified as the fiftieth. It was one of the few prayers—like the Epistles and the Gospels—read aloud by the priest during the mass. I'm sure he did not read the whole psalm, but one part of it really struck me through. It said—and I remember it exactly, as I've looked it up and reread it many times—it said, 'Against thee only have I sinned, and done that which is evil in thy sight. For behold, I was brought forth in iniquity, and in sin did my mother conceive me.'

"I probably would not remember this particular reading except that, at the time, I did not know what the word *iniquity* meant, so I listened closely to what the priest said in his sermon about the psalm, hoping to find out. He did not talk long, but I'll never forget what he said about the psalmist's desire for 'moral renewal.' He said we are all like the psalmist in our wickedness and in our desire to gain redemption. Then he said we are 'by our very nature' sinful because we are 'all conceived in sin.'

"The word *sin* was absolutely clear to me.

"Now this was the beginning of trouble. You have to remember, son, I was only fourteen years old. What the priest said seemed wrong. How could we all be conceived in sin? God conceived us, originally, didn't he? The more I thought about it, the more imperiled I felt. Now, there was something very much like... like a hole in something, a chasm in what I believed was heaven's permanent dome. All my life I had been told, and I believed, that sin was evil. Love was not. I knew my parents were in love and that I was conceived from their union; a union that my parents believed was holy. How could it be sinful? And if it was sinful, what sort of union wasn't sinful?

"I came to these questions slowly, and thinking back on that time now, it seems that much of what I recall is colored by what I have lived since then. I would probably not remember that particular day if it were not for another event that happened only a few weeks later, on another sunny Sunday.

"At communion that day, instead of everybody getting up, row by row, and walking to the front to receive the Host, the priest asked that we remain seated until a young boy named Jack could receive Holy Communion. Jack was sitting in the front row, but it would take him a long time to get up to the altar. He was on crutches because one of his legs had been amputated above the knee. I found out later he had bone cancer. He insisted on going to the front by himself, although the crutches were clearly new to him. He used his arms to lift first one crutch, then the other, swinging his one leg forward in such an awkward sort of leap, other kids my age laughed at him. It was only a slight titter, but I heard it.

"Picture it, Henry. Perhaps the laughter was only a nervous reaction. But how could such a thing happen? He must have heard it, too. He had to move each crutch very quickly to keep from falling down because he kept kicking his one leg too far forward. When he tried to kneel down to receive the host, the priest took hold of his arm and gently gave him Holy Communion as he tottered there on the crutches. My mother was crying. Jack wore a suit and tie, with the one empty leg folded up and stapled to the back of the pants at the waist. There was something robotic about the way he moved. I didn't know him—his parents lived on the other side of the parish and he went to a different school—but I was truly sad and frightened for him.

"When we were all asked to offer up a prayer for Jack, I prayed fervently and sincerely—believing my soul's silent voice would be heard. I know what you're thinking, but listen. I understand now that this was truly emotional and irrational hope. A part of me might have understood it then. I have never believed, truly, that God pays very much attention to persons, as you know. But I wanted so much for Jack to heal, because he seemed so defiant and heroic to me. I thought my hope was like a gift—a thing I could proffer through God, and somehow bring about kindness and mercy. Remembering it now, after all these years, I think I may have wanted Jack to get better for my own sake more than his. Once I knew about him and bone cancer, once I saw a boy no older than I with one of his legs gone, the world seemed a much bigger and more dangerous place.

"On another sun-warmed Sunday morning later that year, we were asked to pray for the 'dearly departed,' and Jack was among them.

"He seemed such a good and courageous kid, it didn't seem possible that something so terrible could happen to him. I wanted to believe that he was somehow offensive to God, but seeing him like that and hearing those words of the psalm about how I was conceived in sin made the whole experience loom in my mind like a turning point— like something I *should* remember, even though I was way too young to understand its significance.

"Only later, as the days piled up and I grew into young manhood— later, when I went to war and saw the whole world blow up in violence and murder—only then did I come to understand what had happened to me.

"I had been saved in the only way a person can be saved. Not with a prayer or bumper stickers or television programs praising the Lord. Not even with private prayer and religious practice. I had been saved with hope and loss.

"Do you know what I remember most vividly about Jack? More so than anything about myself or my family or even what it was like living in that town back then, during the depression? I saw in Jack, and in the suffering of countless others during the war, God's power and sovereignty. You see, God would not amount to very much if he only rewarded good and punished evil. He would be a very flimsy God indeed if we could predict what he was going to do and manipulate him into doing it. Where would his majesty be if he was only at our service— providing us with guidance, helping us find pleasure and comfort? Only God, in all of his grandeur, could manufacture such horror and glory at the same time. What I remembered, and still remember, is the way Jack struggled to work those crutches. He had to conquer himself every step of the way.

"And that is what the rest of us have to do. Every day. We gain meaning in life by struggling each waking hour to conquer ourselves, Henry. That struggle is where all morality comes from, and why we have it. And it is the work of God, pure and simple. God's majesty is in each of us, because each of us is capable of engaging in that struggle. And when we can't find the courage to engage in it truly, we find a way to do it vicariously. We spend most of our leisure time entertaining ourselves with this struggle; in all literature, books, movies, stage plays, and even the imaginary world of our childhood, we pretend to be engaged in the kind of earthly misfortunes where heroism and cowardice, compassion and cruelty, generosity and avarice, must continually strive and brawl for supremacy.

"The truth is, Henry, every human being needs suffering, absolutely. Without it, life would be as plainly boring as one musical note, chiming in your ear, over and over again.

"So you see, don't you, that it was precisely because of Jack's suffering that his life had meaning, no matter how short it was. It had meaning for him and for me and for anyone who was watching him. The rest of it—what happened to him, all his days before that moment, and even those brief days afterward—that was just living.

"You understand what I'm getting at?"

Of Course I Knew

What he was getting at, but he was wrong. Maybe not about his own life and what it meant to him, but certainly he was wrong about my life. I wanted to say, "What did Jack's life mean to him, ending as it did before he was fifteen years old?"

I've never understood the reasoning behind the idea that suffering is good for us—that it redeems us somehow. If suffering and disaster produce meaning in life, then why don't we all go around with nails in our skulls? Is pain the only thing that gives suffering a bad name? Isn't it possible that suffering, not life, is meaningless, and it is only through suffering that we sometimes come to the conclusion that life is pretty meaningless, too? Was there *more* meaning in the lives of holocaust victims?

I wouldn't presume to challenge my father's vision of the world. In a way, I envied him. At least he was at peace with suffering. From his point of view, the world was perfect and the natural order was not fair but excellent. The problem was, people like my father rarely understood that an inability to accept that vision was mere disagreement and *not* depravity.

After that conversation, I brooded for days. August burned like an overheated engine, and as September approached, I started preparing for my classes with the same involuntary stupor of a mud wasp building a nest for its eggs.

When he had finished his little story that night, I didn't know what to say to him. What could I say? I felt like a weak student. I nodded my head. I tried not to make eye contact, swirling the cognac in my glass and waiting for my mother to come back in the room. I was conscious of him watching me, but I couldn't look at him. I know he told me that story because he loved me and wanted to help me, but I was afraid he was going to glare at me until I accepted it.

Finally I said, "That was a good story."

He took a small sip of his brandy, eyeing me over the glass. "But do you see what I'm getting at?"

"Of course," I whispered. "I hadn't thought of it in just that way, but it makes sense."

I couldn't tell if he believed me or not, but I found myself secretly praying very hard that he did.

There was a long silence. We were both enjoying the brandy. Outside, the sun had completely disappeared and the crickets and cicadas had commenced an early evening overture. My father was no longer looking at me, and I had a chance to regard him for a moment—the way he held his head and moved his lips as he savored the wine. His graying hair, a little thinner on top, was brushed straight back, and the deep furrows in his brow seemed to arch and dip perfectly over each eye. Briefly his eyes closed, and I had this sensation that was almost memory of having been accused and convicted; of standing before him, waiting for him to pronounce my sentence. His face was impassive, inscrutable. But then he opened his eyes again, and I could see he was remembering something dear to him—something that made his whole visage soften. He caught me looking at him. "I always got along with my dad," he said.

It was embarrassing to hear him say the word *dad*. It didn't seem possible that a man like my father was ever powerless, hoping for the best from a dad. Besides, his father never seemed like a dad to me. I don't think I'd ever heard my father call him that. What I remember about my grandfather was that he was grouchy most of the time. He smoked a pipe—all day, every day—and I don't think he liked children very much.

I drank down the rest of my brandy.

My father said, "Don't go too heavy on that stuff."

"It's all right," I said.

Mother came back in and said my meat loaf was warmed and ready.

Dad said, "In a minute."

She turned and was quickly gone.

I got up and stretched. "I really am hungry."

"You don't want to let too much time go by before you set things right with Nicole."

"I won't."

"And Elizabeth, too."

I put my hands down.

"You haven't resolved things with her, have you?"

"Sure."

"You have?"

"It's resolved."

He said nothing.

After a short pause, I said, "She won't see me, and I've given up trying."

"I had no idea."

"She blames me for the fall."

"You know that?"

"Yeah."

"She said that to you?"

I reached down and lifted my glass to take it to the kitchen with me.

"She said that to you."

"No, she didn't say it in so many words. She just refuses to see me."

"You've tried to see her?"

"I tried to see her in the hospital, after she woke up. But her father said—he just said she wasn't ready. He told me to wait, but I kept trying. Since she got out I've called her. I even stopped at her place once."

He turned the brandy glass in his hands, thinking.

"I knocked on the door and she didn't answer it."

"How do you know she was there?"

"She was there."

He slowly shook his head.

"She doesn't answer her phone."

"You mean you haven't talked to her since the accident?"

"No, I guess I haven't."

He shook his head. "It's none of my business, son, but…" He paused, thinking.

I didn't say anything.

"It's a relationship, son."

"I know."

"You don't know. You take everything so personally."

There was a silence. I felt foolish standing there in front of him, an empty brandy glass in my hand.

Then he said, "When you understand the world isn't about you— that the world is impersonal and indifferent to what you want or don't want—when you know that, you'll be a grown man, son."

"I'm not going to beg her."

"She might just be hurting because you haven't talked to her."

He simply didn't understand. You couldn't really expect him to. His generation painted pinup girls on bombers; they believed being a man was an achievement.

"Dad, she's done with me, I assure you."

He finished the brandy in his glass.

"You want some more?" I asked.

"No. That's enough."

I stood there a moment, looking at him. He sat back in the chair and picked up the newspaper on the table next to him. When he opened the paper, his hands firmly gripping the edges and snapping it open, I remembered all those days I had been in this very room, reading my books, watching him flip the pages in a newspaper. I loved him again—as I always had. If there was some way I could have put my arms around him and told him how I felt, I would have done it. But the paper was there between us, and he had finished with me. If I had tried to hug him, it would have been a kind of assault—an awkward attempt to arrest the distance between us. Suddenly he was this man reading in a chair, and I was another man getting ready to leave the room. I walked to the alcove between the parlor and the kitchen, then I turned around and said, "Thanks, Dad."

He looked at me. "What?"

"Thanks for . . . for our little talk." Even saying that was so awkward I felt as though I had been aggressively forward. I felt my face flush. To smooth things over a bit I said, "I'll try again with Elizabeth."

He went back to the paper, and I hesitated a moment, watching him, loving him. Then I went on into the kitchen.

A Few Days Later

Elizabeth called me. I had been sleeping late, after a night of too much television and too much whiskey. My classes were almost prepared and I was only waiting for the school year to begin, so I had been staying up all night watching TV and then sleeping in until well past noon.

At first I didn't recognize her voice. When I realized it was her, I was momentarily speechless.

"Did I wake you?"

My eyes were so blurred I couldn't see the clock. "No. I was just doing some work here. You know, getting ready for classes."

She said nothing.

"Actually, I was sleeping," I said. "I was sleeping."

"Are you all right?"

"Sure." I got off the bed and walked toward the window. Outside the sun was high and bare.

"I talked to my father yesterday," she said.

"You did?"

"He wanted to know how you were."

"I'm fine." I pulled the curtain all the way back and looked out on the street. It was apparently going to be another steaming hot day.

"You all ready for another year?" she said.

"I guess."

I waited, hoping she would say something important.

"I'll be glad to get back into the classroom again." Her voice was measured, careful.

"How are you? Are you OK?"

"I'm fine. I get a little drowsy now and then. Or dizzy—I can't decide which. But I'm all right."

I rubbed my face and tried to concentrate. I wasn't sure what day it was. She didn't say anything for a long time, and I realized the silence was becoming awkward.

"I'm sorry, Elizabeth," I whispered. I had no strength in my voice, and I wasn't sure she heard me.

"Henry."

"I'm here."

"It's all right."

"Forgive me," I said. "About the baby and all."

"Don't. I don't want to talk about it, now." She seemed about to cry, and I wasn't doing so well myself. I wished something I could say would cancel everything we had been through.

I got ahold of myself. "Well, it's good to hear from you."

"I just wanted to see how you were doing. We haven't talked in a long time."

"I've tried to. I've called and left messages. I've even been to your house."

"You were here?"

"I watered your plants."

She was silent for a while. Then she said, "I went to stay with my mom for a while."

"Oh."

"She's in Maryland, remember?"

"Oh, yes. How is she?"

"Fine."

It was quiet again. I heard static in the line. I said, "Are you still there?" and at the same time she said, "I was just calling to see how you're doing."

"I'm fine, I guess."

"Good."

"Nicole went home."

"Did you have a nice visit?"

What could I say? There didn't seem to be any reason to tell her what had happened. "Yeah, but she was glad to be going home."

"I'm sorry I didn't get a chance to spend more time with her. She's a lovely girl."

"Yes, she is."

Outside a green Toyota pickup slowed to avoid an orange cat. I saw a little boy bouncing a basketball up the street. The silence in the phone was excruciating. What we were not saying was bigger than the earth, and we were way out in space. I didn't know how to get back.

Finally Elizabeth said, "Still friends?"

My heart sank. I had no idea what I should say.

"Henry?"

I cleared my throat. I wanted my voice to be strong. "Still friends Absolutely. You bet."

I breathed deeply, silently, gripping the phone to steady myself, and she talked again of the coming school year. She was sure she would feel much better once she was back working with young people again. She felt as though she had abandoned her summer students and she wanted to work with each one of them to bring them "up to par."

I said I hoped she would have a wonderful year.

"And you, too," she said.

It was quiet again, for a long time. Then I said, "Well, I've still got a lot to do here." When she hung up, I fell back on the bed and closed my eyes. Everything I could see sickened me, and I wanted only to be unconscious.

I lay there a long time, and all of that summer raced around in my skull—I heard Nicole's voice saying, "You did this. You did this." I saw Elizabeth's face when they placed her on the stretcher. I heard her laughter right before the fall. And my father's voice, saying, "Do your duty."

The problem was, I didn't have any duty that I could figure out.

The next day I withdrew what I had left in the bank—about thirty-two hundred dollars. I packed a small bag with a few necessaries, turned off the air conditioner and the gas, then locked the front door of the house and walked up the sidewalk like a hobo headed for the trains. I realized I was about to be a more modern version of the rail-riding bum. I'd pay my way, but I'd spend my days riding the subway.

So I disappeared for a while. I rode the subway back and forth all over under the city. Half the time I didn't pay much attention to where I was.

I didn't think of myself as homeless, I just never went to my home. Sometimes I'd lull myself to sleep in one of the shelters, thinking about the long grass still growing, my stuffed mailbox, the high stack of newspapers on my front porch.

I actually had fun during the day. I'd get off the subway and stroll up to the street to see where I was. If there was a movie theater or a library or a museum in the neighborhood, I'd have myself a bit of culture for the day. But most of the time, I tried to spend my waking hours underground. I didn't care about anything at all. I figured if I started calculating what I'd need, I'd only be playing right into the hands of those guys with the big cigars.

Like I said at the beginning, I was not running from anything, either. What does the phrase "running from life" mean, anyway? How can you run from anything in life? You can't escape memory, after all, and in spite of my incognito existence, I still had the memory of what I had garnered from fate and luck, following me everywhere I went.

No, I wasn't running.

It had been an extraordinary summer—a memorable summer—and I admit that I was mostly responsible for the way things had turned out. I thought of myself as a man who might have become a father again, if only...

There was never any reason to finish the sentence.

After a While

I lost track of the days. I really don't know exactly how long I was underground. Through most of the rest of August and into September, the days just marched by, like horses in a parade. I did not let myself get tattered, and although I had to sleep in my clothes, I didn't look too disheveled, either. I am certain no one looked at me and felt pity for a lost soul or vagrant wanderer. In fact, no one could possibly know I was wandering. People just don't look very closely at other people. I was in the subway long enough to begin to recognize some people as they wended their way through the crowd to go to or from work. I saw a guy who wore a checked hat and carried a striped umbrella, and who walked as if the umbrella might blow up in his hand. He was unmistakable. He'd never be able to say he'd seen me before, but I got to where I saw him every morning at the Vienna stop.

As Labor Day approached, I realized that watching people made me feel a little bit like the Fates, actually—only I behaved as I thought the Fates ought to behave. I left everybody alone. I didn't fetter or hinder or complicate anybody's life. I stepped aside for everybody. I gave my seat to anyone who needed it. I never crowded an entrance or door, and if I noticed somebody drop trash on the floor, I'd pick it up. In fact, after a while, I began to concentrate on how I could help.

And yet, I still found myself worrying about my father. Sometimes I just wanted to talk to him. I wondered if he had tried to call me. I also pondered what would happen if Nicole tried to call, or Elizabeth. A part of me, I'm ashamed to admit, wanted that to be possible. It was almost gratifying to think that any one of them might actually worry about me. It fortified me to think I might actually turn up missing.

Oddly enough, it occurs to me now, in spite of my age I was still not free of what felt like a kind of judgment—as if some small tuck in my brain could produce the image of my father's hopeful and quizzical eyes. I sensed his rebuke in the memory of the look on Elizabeth's face when she said she didn't want to marry me; in the tone of Nicole's voice when she said she was "getting away" from me. Can you believe it?

Sometimes I'd sit down in an out-of-the-way place in one of the stations, stare at the walls, and imagine myself bursting into tears. I didn't actually start crying, but I always pictured myself doing it, as if daydreaming about it somehow diminished the need for it. I can't say I was feeling sorry for myself, but perhaps grief came to me that way. I wasn't happy, I know that. Most of the time, I tried not to think about how I was feeling, because that might lead to expectations and then there I'd be, back in the hands of providence again.

When school started I wasn't ready for it. I didn't want to go home yet. I came out into the sunlight and met my classes without a single book or notebook in my possession. I winged it, as my colleagues might say. When the day was over, I walked out of that place without speaking a word to anyone, took a taxi to the Alexandria substation, and resumed my sojourn underground.

Because I was working so hard to be successfully indifferent, I had no frustrations whatever. When I was tired I sat down. When I was hungry I ate. I still had plenty of money left, now I was on the payroll again.

I thought one day I might get a taxi to the house (I looked forward to seeing what the grass looked like—if the place actually looked as abandoned as I hoped), pick up my lesson plans and a few other papers. Maybe then I'd take the car and head out to the track again. Try my luck with the horses just for the hell of it.

It was a possibility I only vaguely looked forward to. Each morning when I rolled out of the sack, in whatever shelter I ended up, I'd consider it, hold it in my mind as a contingency for the day, and then go on with things, figuring I'd discover if I was going to the track or not. I knew it was not going to be a thing I planned even an hour before I'd do it. I was like a passenger inside my head, wondering where the driver might go. I didn't ever ask. I just went along for the ride. I figured eventually I'd find myself at Laurel, and if I did, I'd wager on a few races and see what happened.

After the first week of school, I finally went home and got my note-books. I carried them around in a green backpack, just like my students. I changed my hard-soled leather shoes for a thick soft pair of running sneakers. I figured they were more my style. I wore a tie to work, a sports jacket, jeans, and my running shoes. Everything I owned of any importance was in the backpack. Other teachers and administrators looked at me kind of strangely, but nobody said anything.

I was beginning to believe I could continue my vagabond life indefinitely. I actually liked the idea of being unavailable to everyone who mattered to me. Certainly I could not hurt persons with whom I had no contact. I was expected nowhere except at school. So that's where I went most of the time: nowhere and school.

The best way to get nowhere was on the subway.

There's really no weather down there. You can't get a phone call. No one will speak to you unless you speak to them. Every day's the same, rain or shine. You clean nothing. Life is one long, fairly enjoyable, train ride to the end of the line and back again. When you get to the end of the line, you look around a bit, maybe go out into the sunlight to see where you are, buy a hot dog or a greasy burger; then you get back on the train, and eventually it goes back underground and on to the central station so you can go to the end of some other line. The end of the line is always pleasant. You never mind getting there, because you can always go back.

I knew I would come back to the world someday, but I just didn't want to think about when. You might say, as my sister Pauline later said, I was under a sort of self-imposed anesthesia, feeling no pain.

And then one Sunday (I knew this because the newspapers were so fat) I was walking by a ticket office at the Vienna substation and a guy was working there in front of a television, not paying any attention to it, and I noticed a picture of my father on the screen. The voice-over was talking about him, but I couldn't hear it. Then the scene changed and a reporter was standing outside my father's house. I still could not make out much of what he was saying. I went right up to the ticket window, trying to hear it.

"Can I help you?" the ticket man asked.

"No, thank you. I just—I'm only looking at the television." I heard the words *judge* and *career*. Next, a picture of my father as a very young man—his college yearbook picture—flashed on the screen.

"What's going on?" I pointed at the screen.

"What?"

"He must have won something," I said. "Some sort of award or something."

"Who?"

"On the television," I said.

The man turned, looked at the screen, then shrugged. "Oh," he said. "No. Some bigwig died."

The Telephone

Seemed to stare back at me. For the longest time, I stood there looking at it, feeling trapped and brittle. I couldn't remember a single phone number, not even my own, and I knew what was inside the receiver on the phone: a voice, someone's voice, handing me the news. Finally I called Baltimore information, and as the operator was looking up my father's number it came back to me.

When I called, Phil answered the phone.

"Phil. It's me."

"Where the hell have you been?"

"Is it true?"

"Where've you been?"

"I just—I've been out of town. What happened?"

"Dad's gone." There was a long silence. I heard Phil breathing steadily, gathering himself. "He died last night."

The words didn't register in my mind. They dropped right into my heart, like hot metal, and I felt something palpable go out of me. It was as if my own soul rose up and slipped free. For a transitory moment, I couldn't recover any of my senses. Then I heard myself say, "How's Mom?"

"She's not good."

"I'll be there as soon as I can."

"Where are you?"

"I'm downtown, the District."

"Well, if you can, I'd get over here. I've called Theresa and Pauline and Robert." His voice broke, and I realized that in spite of his age and his fatherly approach to me all his life, he'd lost his father, too. He sounded like a small boy about to cry.

I took a cab to the Alexandria substation, then caught a commuter bus to Prince William Forest and my house. I made good time. By that evening I was in my car, headed for Baltimore.

You can see, can't you, that some providence was at work there? Without taking the time to think about it, I found myself suddenly in the world again, heading somewhere with a purpose. Whether I was paying the price for foolishly tempting the Fates, or merely reacting to the random sway of events in time, a part of me came to ruefully understand that I was not only back in the game, I was being moved readily from place to place, just like any other pawn.

I found out later that my father had walked out into his backyard to look at his nearly harvested garden. It was late in the evening, just before dark. Perhaps he wanted to watch the sun disappear behind the tall trees in his neighborhood or wander around the neat rows of green vegetables he'd planted in the brown dirt next to a small grape arbor that he tended all the summers of his life in that house. He once told me that he liked looking at his garden in the evening—it was a habit that soothed him, made him feel serene and ready for the night.

My mother found him there, lying down in the grass as though he had simply settled himself in the shade of the arbor to take a little nap. He died peacefully, the paramedics said, because his face was completely tranquil, without the usual twisted scowl of victims who die in pain or anguish.

When my mother found him, she lost track of herself for a while. She told me later that she did not remember racing back into the house to call an ambulance. She only remembered walking slowly back out to him, half believing—wanting to believe—it was all a mistake, that he would be sitting there, laughing at her ready panic and wild fear. But he was still lying there. She sat down in the moist grass and held his hand, stroking his brow until the ambulance got there. She said the tight skin of his forehead turned as cold as the grass while she waited.

At some point after the ambulance got there, she had called me. She had cried into the phone and left panicked messages on my machine.

I've played those messages over and over again—almost hoping that somehow, one time—just one time—I could actually pick up the phone and be there when she needed me. The sound of her frightened and frantic voice keeps playing over and over in my head. It's a sound I don't want to hear, and it echoes in all the chambers of my heart. She was so scared. I had never heard such terror in her voice. One of the messages ends with, "They're working on him. They're working on him." Even now these words impart a glimmer of forlorn hope. As if you could rewind life and get a different result.

I don't even remember the drive to Baltimore.

Later I read in the newspaper that one of the paramedics said Dad was dead when they first took his pulse, but they decided to go through the motions of trying to revive him because "Mrs. Porter was so upset." The doctor told the newspaper that he was pretty sure it was another heart attack.

When I pulled into the driveway of my father's house that night, Phil and Darlene were waiting for me on the front porch, almost as if this were one of our usual family gatherings. The sky was brightly lit by the moon, but the yellow porch light made everything around the house seem darker, almost sinister. Phil and Darlene were standing arm in arm, in the shadows under the light. Darlene forced a smile—one of those fond and tender smiles only women possess that make you feel cared for and loved. Phil put his arms around me and squeezed, then he slapped me on the shoulders and stepped back. Tears filled his eyes. "How you doing, Shaver?"

I had nothing to say.

"Mother's resting upstairs," he said.

I couldn't look at anybody. The house seemed larger and emptier somehow, as if the absence of my father had removed an elemental shape from each room—his carriage and appearance, the regal timbre of his voice, and the incredible range of his bright, sometimes playful eyes filled all the rooms he ever went into.

Phil kept saying, "I can't believe it. I just can't believe it."

As though I had been with her, or as if I had been sitting on the back porch watching her, I kept imagining my mother on her solitary walk to the backyard that night. I know how she must have felt when she found him in the pale glow of the new moon. How she must have spoken to him and made a desperate, hopeful attempt to awaken him, to see him move just once more and surprise her with his living; how she dreamed she'd be wrong, that he would move and she would have him there, loving her after the moon went down behind the trees again. And when she touched him, she must have known. From that moment she was compelled to become a new woman—a woman she did not ever want to be. All of her life had been a prelude to that precise moment when she knew he was gone and she was alone.

I went back into the room where my father and I had our last talk, and sat on the couch. Darlene came in and asked me if I wanted anything to drink. I tried to say something to her, but words failed me. I only looked at her and shook my head.

Phil said he would take care of everything, but he kept drinking whiskey and he could not stop crying. Darlene stood over him, rubbing the back of his head and his neck. When Pauline got there, Phil went over it all again. Mother was sedated, upstairs, grieving on her own. There was nothing for me to do, so I gathered the papers that Phil had been collecting and started looking up funeral homes in the yellow pages. I called Monarch and Kash, Daryl and Holms, Anders. At that hour in the evening, I only got answering machines and emergency numbers to call.

I was still on the phone when Phil came in and sat down in my father's chair. In the dim light of the table lamp, the way he leaned forward and put his elbows on his knees, he looked like Dad.

"I can't believe it," he said again.

I put the phone down and stood there for a moment. I hadn't gotten beyond the shock yet. What kept going through my mind was that my father had led a long and happy life. That he had been the kind of man he wanted to be and lived fully every day. And as these words came to me, I choked on them. I knew that I would never again have the chance to make him proud of me. From the first time in my life that he beamed at me and said, "Way to go, son," to the last time I saw him, I had garnered all I was ever going to have of him.

"He lived a full life," I said quietly.

Phil was fighting tears. He wanted to talk, but he was numb from all the whiskey, and he could not get ahold of himself.

"Goddamn it," he gasped finally. "Goddamn it to hell."

"I know."

He sat up and stared at the far wall. "We've got to be strong for Mom."

"She'll be OK," I said. I knew I was right about that. Everybody in the family but me underestimated her. She depended on my father so much because she loved him—not because she was helpless. Since I was the youngest and I had grown up in the house more or less alone with her while my father worked and the others were off to college and marriages and so on, I had had a chance to know my mother more completely than any of them. She was strong and willful and decisive. She would survive my father's death and be this new woman she would have to be—a widow living alone, taking care of her peerless garden and an old house, remembering her children and her husband, all of whom have in some way or another left her.

"I knew he was not well, but I had no idea," Phil said.

"We've got to make the arrangements," I told him. "We can't put Mom through that."

He nodded.

"I'll go down to Monarch and Kash in the morning."

"OK," he said, not really listening. His eyes were empty, unfocused—as though he were remembering something pleasant, long ago and far away from that room.

"You think Mom cares what cemetery?"

"Huh?" I had his attention again. "Of course. He'll want to be buried in Heaven's Gate."

"Right."

"And there will have to be a mass."

"Of course."

"What happened to you, Shaver?"

"Nothing."

"You might let people know you're going out of town. Mom was worried sick."

"I didn't know I'd be gone that long."

"Where'd you go?"

"I just took a little vacation."

He shook his head, clearly disgusted with me. "Dad had some fellows looking for you. We were all worried."

"He had people looking for me?"

"He didn't want to tell mother about it, but, yes. He did. You know he's got friends on the force. They'd do almost anything for him."

"I didn't want to worry anybody."

"Dad was more worried than any of us." His voice broke and he stopped for a moment, gathering himself. Then he said, "He even used the word *missing*, as though you'd been kidnapped or something."

There was nothing to say or do. Lamely I said, "I'm sorry, Phil."

"We all figured you were just being your usual unreliable self." He was smiling when he said this, and I saw that he was only telling me the truth. "But Dad. He was really shook up. You should have called or something."

"I've gone weeks without calling him before, and he never seemed to notice it."

"Well, he noticed it this time."

Darlene came in, wiping tears from her eyes. "Your mother is coming down."

I hadn't seen her yet. I moved to the archway between the den and the parlor and watched her descend the stairs, moving very slowly—as if she were trying to wake from a dream. She was wearing a long pink gown over her silk pajamas, with white slippers. When I looked into her eyes, everything stopped for an instant—it was as if a beam froze between her eyes and mine, and something spiritual and lasting passed between us. It was a look of tremendous loss, but love was there, too. I can't explain it. In that fraction of a second, her eyes and mine seemed to share the same soul, the same heart.

I went over and put my arms around her. She touched the back of my head with her soft hands and asked me if I was OK.

"I'm all right," I said, trying to hold back tears.

"Where were you?"

"I was out of town."

She frowned, then ran her hands lightly down my arms as she stepped back to look at me.

"I didn't mean to worry you," I whispered.

"Is Theresa here yet?"

"Her flight doesn't get in until tomorrow morning," Phil said.

"She'll take it very hard," Mother said. She squeezed my hand.

"How are *you*, Mom?"

"He didn't suffer, honey," she said.

"I know."

"He just lay down and went to sleep." She lowered her head, holding her gown closed in front. She looked at Phil and Darlene, who came up behind me.

"He didn't suffer," she said again. Then she started crying.

I put my arms around her. For the first time in my life I was comforting her, holding her. She seemed frail, and the fragrance of her hair and perfume momentarily soothed me, as if her presence was somehow a reprieve from finality and grief. I knew I would remember that moment for the rest of my life. She stopped crying almost as soon as she started. "I'm all right," she said. "We have to make the arrangements."

"I'll take care of all that," I said.

"I want you to call Father Burns. He will say the mass. Your father wanted that."

I looked at Phil. "Father Burns, right."

"I'll call him," Phil said.

"There're so many people to call," Mother said.

"We'll take care of it," said Darlene.

"That's right," I said. I realized with almost a start of fear that I ought to call Nicole, and there wasn't a way I could make myself do it. In back of that thought, lurking like some sort of predatory temptation, was the realization that I should probably call Elizabeth as well. Certainly she ought to know what had happened.

Talking to Elizabeth was the only thing I could picture in the future that wasn't soaked in grief.

My Sister Pauline

Arrived later that evening. She was alone. "I didn't want the children to see all this," she said, extending her hand toward the living room, where Phil and Darlene were comforting my mother.

I was glad to see Pauline. She was always sort of shy, but her silence gave the impression of emotional strength. People often said she had inherited my father's calm intelligence and good judgment. In fact, Pauline's reticence was her personal armor against the loud, rude world. Still, it felt as though a little bit of my father had arrived with her, to take care of everything. I knew I wouldn't end up going to the funeral home to purchase a casket and a vault, and then planning the funeral all by myself; she would see to that. She might even go with me. At any rate, I knew she would be a restrained and friendly influence on the family in the next few days.

I don't know what time it was when we all started to think about sleep. I told Phil there was no way I was going to stay in my old room, and that I was pretty used to sleeping on a couch, anyway. He and Darlene took the spare bedroom upstairs. Pauline retreated to the upstairs office, which used to be her room. My father never took her bed out of there, although it needed clean sheets and a blanket. He had been using it as a large flat surface to throw papers and books and things on. I helped her move a few boxes and folders so she'd be more comfortable. She kissed me on the cheek and said good night, and I heard a slight tremor in her voice. She would grieve, too—but not so anybody

319

could see it. Perhaps when Theresa arrived, the two of them would have their own private moments of grief—sharing what each of them remembered and treasured. They were much closer to each other than I was to Robert or Phil.

Mother came to ask if Pauline was comfortable.

"Of course I am." She smiled.

Then Mother asked me, "Where are you going to sleep?"

"On the couch downstairs."

"I can clean some things away in your old room."

"No," I said. "Don't bother."

She put her hand on my cheek and looked at Pauline. "It's kind of nice having you all together in this house again." Tears brimmed in her eyes, but she was not crying.

Pauline came over and took her hand. "Come on, Mom." She led her down the carpeted hallway to the master bedroom. I took a sheet and blanket out of the linen closet and went back down the stairs to the living room.

My old room was on the first floor. It had two doors, one that led into the hallway and out to the dining room and the rest of the house, and one that led to the garage. When I was a kid I loved that arrangement, even though as I got older and more aware of my surroundings I noticed that my room was more susceptible to spiders and daddy long-legs and other bugs that populate a garage. Still, late at night I could slip out of the house simply by opening a door and walking out. It had been such a big deal when I was a kid, getting away from the house and my parents. I'd outsmart my father, get so far from him while he slept. Now he had slipped away from me.

Before I tried to sleep that night, I went to my old room and stood in the doorway. The closet was still piled high with old toys and football equipment and broken model airplanes. The bed remained in the corner under a small window. The air smelled of naphtha and linen and vague traces of my mother's perfume. The ceiling fan my father installed for me when I was twelve years old dangled unevenly over the center of the room. All my posters were gone, but I could still see the shadows where they once adorned the walls. My mother used the room now for sewing, so the floor was strewn with strips of cloth and tangles of thread. A small table and sewing machine occupied the center of the room, and there were even some bright strips of cloth hanging neatly from one of the blades of the ceiling fan. The idea of sleeping in there—of perhaps waking up and believing, if only for a second, that my father was alive and might call out to me—momentarily shocked my heart, so that it seemed to gasp, then breathe and weep.

I walked back out into the living room, turned out the light, and collapsed on the couch. For a long time I watched the moonlit clouds outside the front window. I remembered my father the last time I saw him. He had tried to speak to me about things that mattered, and I don't think I even convinced him that I was listening. I kept hearing his voice when he said, "I always got along with my dad."

I felt the back of my throat beginning to ache, so I tried to concentrate on sleep. I looked at the moon. It was bright, as though the light emanated from there, and then I was thinking of Elizabeth and Nicole and my mother—these women in my life and all their sorrow: Nicole's childhood handed to her like a shattered doll; Elizabeth's fall, the miscarriage. And my mother, who, as a natural result of life going on as it should, lost all her children and now had to face the close of her long and happy life without her husband and friend and lover. It's no wonder that the story of Adam and Eve in the garden ends with the notion that we all ended up here on earth because of a snake.

The moon slipped behind the edge of a dense and dusky cloud, and I turned away from it, trying to keep my eyes closed, hunting sleep. I couldn't get my father's voice out of my mind—it was almost as if he was calling my name. The numberless days when I was a little boy and he called me home came back to me; the trips to the beach and Sylvan Dell. It was all a single tissue of memory, pulling at my heart, darkening it as surely as if someone had covered it with a strip of cloth. What kept going through my mind was the wordless realization that my hopes and expectations for finally knowing him—all those imagined possible days of new friendship—were gone forever. What remained was only the terrible and certain knowledge of the distance between us, of what we never really understood about each other.

Everything in the future between my father and me—all potential—was finished.

I don't know how long I lay there before the sun began to leak into the room. I must have fallen asleep at some point, but then I was wide awake and I heard people moving around upstairs.

I got up and made coffee. My mother was the first to come down, and when I handed her a cup, she said, "Would you be willing to write something about your father?"

I thought she meant his obituary for the paper.

After an awkward pause, I said, "I'll call the paper this morning, first thing."

"I don't mean that."

I just stood there looking at her.

"I mean something to read. At the funeral." She was very calm, her voice almost a whisper.

"Oh, I don't know."

Phil came down. He looked as if he'd been awake all night. His hair was tangled across his brow, and his eyes were bruised and dull looking. "I've got to pick Theresa up at the airport."

Mother told him what she'd asked me. His face brightened a bit. I thought he would be hurt, maybe a little envious of the honor, but he said, "You *should* write the eulogy. It would be the best thing for the family, and Dad would be honored."

"I don't know," I said.

"Would you think about it, son?" Mother said.

"Of course I'll think about it."

On the second day, Theresa, Pauline, and I spent the day arranging everything. We actually laughed a little, and when we had lunch together that day, the two of them spent most of the time talking about Dad. They each had different experiences and memories, and I came to see that I could come to know my father a little better if I spent more time with my sisters. They adored him. They never doubted his love or devotion. They never felt as though they failed him. I listened politely and kept my mouth shut, but it was oddly satisfying to hear about him, to see him again in life through their eyes.

Later that night, on the front porch of the Monarch and Kash funeral home, my mother asked me again if I would deliver the eulogy. We were all waiting to go in and see Dad for the first time, and she came to me with tears in her eyes, gripping her small white purse, her hair perfectly combed and styled, smelling of roses, and said, "Will you write something about your father?"

"I'll see about it."

"Please?"

"I don't know. OK? I don't have any idea what to say. And whatever I say, I just know I couldn't read it publicly."

"You can do it. I know you can."

I couldn't get away from her eyes, the way she begged me with them. How could I refuse her?

The problem was, my father was well known enough to get a lot of coverage in the press—it was even announced by ABC on the national news—and there would be many distinguished friends of his at the funeral. They would all know that I was the son who disappointed him, so it seemed much more likely that I would dishonor his memory if I spoke. I didn't know how to say that to my mother.

I told Phil I was going to be very busy getting everything ready. I still had to make arrangements with the VA about a military honors team to present the flag and fire the twenty-one-gun salute. I had searched my father's papers—with very little help from Phil—for his discharge and decorations and even his birth certificate (seeing his small baby footprint gave me a curious chill—I almost started crying again). I didn't see how I could sit still enough to think about what I might say—especially so close to the funeral.

At first I thought my reluctance to speak was going to be respected.

Pauline talked about getting one of my father's colleagues to say something, and then people started arriving for the wake and nothing more was said.

But then, the first night after the wake, when the house was still full of people and food, and even laughter, my mother came into my room where I'd retreated to read, and sat down at her sewing table. She was composed, elegant, and fragile.

"Are you comfortable in here?"

"I can't sleep in this bed. I just came in here to read, get away from some of the noise."

She smiled softly, blinked her tender eyes. I thought of what her eyes must have looked like when she was young—when she saw before her only the wide, possible future; when everything she looked upon must have seemed new and exciting and potentially hers. Now she only saw her long past, the faces of vanished children, and nothing new except a kind of emptiness she would have to get accustomed to; nothing possible except the quiet repose of loneliness turned to proper solitude.

"May we talk?" she said.

"Sure."

"I think you know that your father loved you—in his own way I think he loved you so much more than the others—"

"No." I didn't believe it. I didn't believe it because an implicit and intolerable injustice was at the center of that idea, and he would never have admitted such a thing—to anyone. Also, I didn't believe it because I had never seen any evidence of it, whatsoever.

"He did, son. You were the one he was most passionate about. He never stopped talking about you."

"Mom. He didn't even like me very much."

This had the impact of an insult. She straightened up a bit, seemed to suffer a slight pain behind her eyes. "What did you say?"

"I know he loved me. But he was always talking about how unhappy he was with me—especially since the divorce. Certainly you've been aware of it."

"How can you say such a thing?"

"It just seems true to me." I couldn't look at her.

"Your father loved you." This was a command to believe.

"I know that. I know it."

"You were his dreamy boy..." She couldn't finish. I stood up and went to her. I put my arms around her shoulders, felt her trembling slightly, like a bird gasping for chilly air. I realized I was about to fail this woman, too.

"I'm asking you to speak, to honor your father," she whispered. "I think it would be just what he would want."

"You do."

"Yes, I do. I don't understand why you won't do it."

"I didn't say I wouldn't do it."

Phil came in and stood next to her. I moved away to make room for him, and he put his hand on her shoulder, rubbed it gently, staring at me.

"Well," he said, "what's the verdict?"

There was a long silence while Mother stared into my eyes, begging me with her sadness, her grief.

"I'll do it," I said. "Of course I'll do it."

"Just tell about his life," Phil said.

"About this family," said Mother. "He was a wonderful family man."

I knew I wasn't a wonderful family man, and that she knew I wasn't, so her words made me think of the difference between my father and me. The immediate contrast must have registered with her at exactly the same moment it showed on my face.

She said, "He was a good father. And he taught you boys how to be good fathers."

"Right," I said, remembering Nicole's flight from harm's way. Remembering what happened to my unborn child—lost before the light of day because of my foolishness. My throat burned with tears, and it took all my strength to restrain myself.

"It's OK to cry, son." Mother touched my chin with the tips of her fingers. "It's OK to show your grief."

This last statement broke my heart. She just didn't know. She was so far—so incredibly far—from being right about me. The degree to which she was wrong can be calculated exactly, as though it were distance, miles and miles, if you simply examine the disparity between what she was thinking at that moment, and what I was thinking. She was still in the hot, weeping shock of her husband's death—waiting at the gate of a long, unknown, and lonely future—and here she was thinking of me and my sorrow. You know what I was thinking of? I was thinking of myself. Go ahead, measure the distance.

"I'm not thinking about Dad. I was just feeling sorry for..." I didn't finish the sentence. A confession of my failings at that moment would have been just more selfishness.

"Don't feel sorry for me," she said, taking her hand away.

"No, I don't."

"I can't complain, son. Your father and I were friends and lovers for over fifty years. I was lucky to have known him."

Phil gripped her shoulders a little harder. She looked up at him, smiling.

"I'll write something," I said.

"Just tell the truth about him," Mother said, her voice giving way a little bit.

"You know I will."

Phil reached over to shake my hand. "He'd be proud, Shaver."

"Sure," I said. "I know he would."

I Stayed in My Room

All that afternoon while the house filled with people. I stared at a blank page for what seemed like hours, listening to the noise in the rest of the house, unable to write what seemed like the single most important sentence I would ever write. The sentence that began with, "My father was..."

How could I fill in that blank? The whole world seemed diminished—as if a hemisphere had somehow vanished into space.

No doubt my father was a great man and the people around him knew it. But what does *great* mean? How could I use that word to describe him when it is used every day to describe toilet bowl cleaner and floor wax? I got up, walked around the room a bit, then sat down and wrote:

These are the qualities of a great man: Honor, courage, character, and strength—physical strength and emotional strength. "Honor" and "courage" imply a willingness to suffer for what one believes. "Physical strength" is self explanatory, but "emotional strength" suggests a powerful will at peace with itself and understanding fully what matters. Character is expressed by an unswerving ability to say no to oneself; to accept what is inevitable in the world and to regain one's innocence each day

To regain innocence. What did I mean by that? The idea stopped me. Was my father the sort of man who was born each morning? Who made no judgments about others that lasted more than the day? Could he come back to people expecting only the best from them, trusting them over and over? To regain innocence is to preserve one's ideals in the face of bitter experience, and my father was never one who squandered belief. I tore from the pad what I had written, threw it on the floor, and started over.

My father was born every morning. This is not to say he was stupid, only that he regained his innocence every day. The child in him...

I tore that page off and threw it on the floor.

My father never dismissed anyone, completely. He understood how to forgive...

If I wrote anything about his willingness to forgive, I'd only bring to mind all the times he'd been bound to forgive me. If he ever forgave me. I had to admit I never felt as though I was forgiven. Still, there was a quality in him—a way of being—that gave me and everyone who knew him strength. Not his strength, but a kind of strength nonetheless—if only the sort that was necessary to resist his implicit criticism of your way of life.

It occurred to me that just knowing him was a way of life...

I tore off another page.

He represented a way of life. He'd seen the Great Depression, a world war that tore the twentieth century in two and left a scar so wide and deep we're still, even now, fighting over how to heal it. He'd been through a lasting decline in American life.... He wouldn't use *decline.* He'd call it a total collapse. I crossed out *decline* and wrote *total collapse.*

My father saw the long crime wave of the late twentieth century: the killing in our cities, from 1960, his first year on the bench, to 1989, his last year on earth. He witnessed not only rampant and unchecked increases in crime and murder, he saw the marketing and sale of everything we cherish; the vulgar advance of the consumer society and its consumer-dominated culture. Even the word values *is an economic term. And no one knows anymore what it means. We find it every day in trivial phrases used by shabby politicians—packaged and marketed by them—so that our virtue as a nation is founded on the bedrock of popularity and consumption.*

I put the pen down, ripped another page off and threw it on the floor.

I wasn't writing about my father, although I might have been speaking *for* him. Perhaps he was trying to speak through me. Everything I'd said was probably what my father thought. I think he would agree with my assessment that his own culture disowned him. He was not a consumer of the status quo or the new pop culture, so it left him behind. Day after day he sat on the bench in his court and watched the results of a vast consumer ethics. What is right is what sells. Anything that does not sell is wrong. And *god*, how everything was for sale in his lifetime Even I knew that. Could I write in my eulogy that he knew what had happened and was powerless to stop it? What would it mean to the family if I wrote about what angered him, what made him most difficult to talk to? Sometimes I felt as though he blamed me for all of it. He talked of my generation as if it were a thing I owned.

Maybe there was good reason to blame me. Ironically, I now see, I was at least partly to blame. I bought a whole lot of what was for sale. My basement is full of junk I never needed, and I've had this culture in my eyes and ears for a long time. I buy some part of it every day. When I watch television for half an hour I've bought more of what this doomed culture has to offer than my father did in a whole lifetime.

How many of us are to blame for what has happened? For the triumph of image over substance? For the great consumer piety, which mocks and vulgarizes all things?

I wanted to write words like that in my father's eulogy, hoping he would hear them; hoping he would hear me.

I agree with you, Dad. That's what I wanted to say. *You were right, about everything.*

What would be the point of talking about this culture at his funeral? What would he say at his own parting? What would he say to me if he knew he was never going to see me again? He would not ever say anything in praise of himself. How could I write his eulogy? Every sentence I wrote seemed wrong, out of place, without merit.

The door behind me suddenly opened.

It was Pauline. "I'm sorry," she said. "I didn't mean to startle you. I just wanted to see how it was going."

Robert came in behind her. "Hey, Shaver." He came over and slapped me on the back.

There was a long and awkward silence. Then Pauline asked, "So, how's it going?"

"What, the eulogy?"

She nodded, a look of anticipation on her face.

I pointed to the paper on the floor. Robert picked up the one I had just finished and began to read. His hands were shaking, and I noticed that he hadn't shaved. He was wearing a black suit with a dark gray tie, loosened at the neck. He had been crying, I could see, and since he had put on weight, his face looked heavy and drawn. Pauline wore a blue dress with huge shoulder pads. She seemed embarrassed to be standing there in such bright colors, and when I looked at her, she said, "Robert thinks I should be wearing black."

"Of course," he said, turning to her. "That's what people in mourning traditionally wear. It shows respect."

She had nothing to say but she glanced my way.

"It's a stupid tradition," I said.

"Dad always liked me in this dress. I'm wearing it for him."

Robert went back to reading. Pauline got closer to him and read over his shoulder. "This is good," she said. "Why is it on the floor?"

"The truth is, I don't know what I'm supposed to write. I've never delivered a eulogy before, and to be writing one about Dad—"

"What's wrong with this?" Pauline asked.

"You haven't read all of it," Robert said.

"What's wrong with it?"

"It's not about Dad."

"That's what I thought," I said.

"It should be about Dad," Robert said. "This just sounds like one of your tirades. It's a lot of political crap."

"It's not crap," I told him.

"It's crap."

"Well, it's crap, but it's the truth."

"Don't you two start bickering now," Pauline said.

"It's what Dad believed." I took the paper out of Robert's hands, let it drift, like a leaf, to the floor again.

"Some of it, maybe. But he almost never talked about stuff like that, except with you."

"What's that supposed to mean?"

"Come on," Pauline said, pulling on Robert's arm. "Let's get out and let him finish what he's supposed to do."

Robert let her move him to the door, then he turned to me and, with an imploring look, said, "Don't write stuff like that about him."

"I wasn't going to. That's why it was on the floor."

He nodded, smiling for the first time.

"Just tell about him," Pauline said, suddenly fighting tears. "Tell about him."

"I wouldn't talk about what he hated," I said.

"Good." She took Robert's arm, and they went out and closed the door.

Their sudden intrusion and then absence seemed like something I dreamed while drifting into sleep, and now the room was quiet and eerie. I looked at the paper where it had fallen, and felt abandoned. I knew I should never try to say what my father would say. Maybe I could write down what he would *not* say about himself, but what we would want him to say. Or admit to? Did we ever want confessions from him? I cracked my knuckles, tried to remember the last thing he said to me. I kept hearing his voice, over and over, saying, "I always got along with my dad." It was such an unguarded thing to say; so much like a confession—as if he were revealing something he'd kept to himself all his life.

I wanted a cigarette, a glass of whiskey. The papers all around me seemed to sneer, as if everything I had written so far was an affront to the world and would reveal itself no matter what I tried to do to disguise it.

I gathered all of them off the floor, tore them up, and stuffed them into a trash can. Then I started over on the clean pad.

My father was a great man. All of us knew this. He was a war hero who did not make a fortune telling his story. He devoted his life to the law, to his family

His family. That's what the eulogy was for. Why did I care about who would be there or what they knew?

My father once said it's a short trip through here, son.

I crossed that out.

Dad once said it's a short trip through here, son.

Crossed that out, too.

Dad always said, "It's a short trip through here." We all knew what he meant. And we all knew what we had in him.

That was my beginning.

I started writing. I didn't consider style or word choice or structure or anything. I just wrote blindly, as if from memory. I was not myself, completely. It was almost as if my whole life outside my father's house had been a dream, and now, here I was, a child again under his roof— not yet aware that I will have to give up the safety and warmth of family; not yet through the numberless days clamoring with my brothers and sisters for space and words in clutter and confusion, play and work, anger and laughter and fierce competition, under the smiling, silent, inscrutable gaze of my father. And I wrote down all that I knew about him; all that I would ever know about him.

When I was finished I put the pen down, truly surprised at myself. It had taken me less than a half hour, but it would be just what the family would want. With Pauline's admonition to just "tell about him," I came to see that I did not have to speak *for* my father. I only had to speak honestly and simply *of* him.

I had no trouble at all doing that, because, you see, I really did know the man after all.

I couldn't focus on the paper anymore. Tears filled my eyes, and I was afraid someone would come in and see me sitting there like that, weeping over the paper as if profoundly moved by my own words.

I folded the paper neatly in half and put it in my coat pocket.

The Funeral

Was on a beautiful sun-spattered Wednesday afternoon. Probably three hundred people squirmed in the pews and on the benches of Holy Trinity Catholic Church. Only a cough here and there, a sneeze or a cleared throat broke the silence. Still, every sound in the church echoed. When the service started, the priest said the mass slowly, as if he were waiting for the media. But only a few reporters were there, and they waited outside to talk to people as they left the church.

My father's coffin sat at the foot of the altar, in the center aisle. The whole family was in the first row to the left, and I was on the end, right next to the coffin, because I had to read the eulogy.

The mass for the dead is a somber affair, full of references to life everlasting and the dearly departed and souls, souls, souls. And it contains the most bewildering and ironic line in the Bible: "He who loves life shall lose it, but he who hates life shall have life everlasting." I'm guessing this means precisely what it says. If you can't stand life, you can have as much of it as you want, but if you love it, you can only have a very little bit; perhaps just enough to know you love it, and then you lose it.

Even the Fates would envy such a fiendish maxim.

I knew my father didn't hate life. He just hated the way most people lived it.

When the time came for the eulogy, I was so scared my hands felt bloodless and cold. I stepped out into the aisle and walked past the coffin, gray and closed, with blue and red, yellow and white flowers, and wild sprays of green fern clustered on top of it. At the head of the coffin, I leaned down and whispered, "Help me get through this, old man." I didn't really believe he was there or that he could hear me. I wished it were true. I wanted to pretend it was true for the strength it might lend me.

I got to the altar, and the priest directed me to the pulpit. A great Bible was spread out there, a yellow ribbon marking the priest's place in the canon. I reached into my jacket and brought out what I had written.

Before me was the vast cathedral space of the church, light broken into beams through the arched windows and stained glass. In the first row my family watched: Mother with a white handkerchief touching her eyes; Pauline next to her, comforting her, looking at me as if I might simply reach out and lift all of them up, take them from this place and death. Phil and his wife sat next to Pauline, and their children sat next to them. Pauline's husband was at the far end of the pew, by himself. Theresa and Robert sat in the second row, behind Mother. Occasionally Robert would lean forward and touch Mother's shoulder to calm her, console her.

I looked at the paper in front of me, then back to the crowd. Just as I was about to start, I turned to my left, to the other side of the coffin, and there, sitting among strangers, was Nicole.

Her eyes met mine and I could not speak.

I don't know how long we stared at each other. People were starting to stir, and I realized I had to begin reading; but when I looked at the first sentence, my mind simply stopped. I stood there, my head down, not really seeing anything. At length I noticed the low, hushed murmur of the crowd.

My mother watched me with such hopeful eyes, it struck me through and I was suddenly aware of the absolute purity of grief. When it is without rage or guilt or any other human sadness, it is all by itself and as immaculate as any earthly thing.

I held up the paper to show it. "I've written something about my father."

It quieted a bit, people settled themselves. I noticed the priest, seated to my left, straighten his cassock and arrange himself.

And then I began reading, "My father would not approve of this. He would not want us to gather here and treat him like something other than he was. He didn't think he was a hero, although the record claims it. He didn't think his life was extraordinary, although that is what people are saying about him now. He did what he did. That's all. As we have to do what we do. My father would tell you now that nothing is heroic because all human beings have an obligation on their hearts to do what is necessary... to do what circumstances call on us to do. We act, in other words, not for praise, but because living calls us to it."

I glanced up from the paper in front of me. "Dad always said, 'Do your duty.' Now I know what he meant."

I looked at Nicole. She put her head down, placed her hand up over her forehead. Then she shifted in her seat, took a deep breath, and met my gaze once more. She held a small white handkerchief in her left hand, and her other hand rested on a black purse in her lap. Something in the way she turned her head, or moved herself like a lady in the seat, made me see her for the first time. I realized she was a person sitting there. A person. And I thought my heart might break.

I looked into her eyes and whispered, "I'm sorry." The sound was barely audible in the microphone, but I could see she heard me.

The people around her turned her way, but the expression on her face did not change.

I concentrated on the paper, smoothed it out in front of me on the flat surface of the pulpit. I couldn't get my voice back.

The church seemed to breathe, then someone coughed. Presently I started again. "We all know what we had in our father. So what should we say about him now?"

I paused, gathering myself. Then in a stronger voice I went on. "He knew so much and cared so much about so many things. All his life he was honest. You never had to wonder what he thought of you. Words mattered to him because he believed in saying the truth and he did not like liars." I paused briefly, my hands trembling on the paper.

"What he gave us with his honesty was his trust, and although some of us abused it over the years of growing up, we always knew we had it to come back to."

I glanced up at Nicole, but she did not see me. She was staring at the coffin.

"Should we say that he was a brave man?" My voice shook. "He led a rifle squad on night patrols and reconnaissance missions during World War II. Many of us have heard and laughed with him over the war stories. And some of us have seen the medals, the decorations he won for doing what he called his duty. Somehow he found a way to laugh again, even though he suffered in ways you and I can't imagine. You don't win three Bronze Stars and the Purple Heart by laughing your way through a campaign. He fought and bled and suffered. He was strong enough not to come home a damaged man, possessed by private demons and haunting memories. He was grateful for having survived the war, and determined to live his life fully and well."

I stopped again. It was absolutely quiet now, and I had regained the strength in my voice.

"He never once mentioned the heroism, the bravery that won him those medals. Most of us—his children—were adults before we knew he'd won a medal of any kind, and none of us knew he'd won four of them until he was appointed to the bench by President Eisenhower and the newspapers all printed his war record. The shock of knowing our father was such a hero still trembles in our hearts.

"If anyone asked him what he was proud of, he would have talked about somebody in this family. No battle ribbon could compare to Phil's law degree, or Pauline's or Theresa's medical work; Robert's success in business, or my mother's unselfish care of the family." I had not written anything about myself, and I realized the omission would be noticed—that it might be considered a comment on our relationship. I looked up at my mother and said, "I think he was proud of my work as a teacher." This last seemed to wound her. Robert patted her on the shoulder, and Pauline reached over and touched her on the hand.

With my own hands trembling I placed the first page aside on the pulpit and began reading the second. "It's not that my father was modest. He had balance. What matters most in this world, mattered most to him. He taught us all that love is a sacred responsibility, a duty. Not just a thing to feel or say."

I found Nicole's eyes again, noticed they were brimming with tears. They seemed to freeze me in place the same way my mother's gaze paralyzed me that night when I first looked into her eyes after my father died. I realized my little girl was speaking to me with a look, coming back to me, forgiving me.

"Maybe we should say my father was a good man, a truly good man. We have never known a more generous heart. He expected all of us to be, as he was, above the storms of the world. He never would have wanted his judgments to matter to us as much as they did. When there was hurt, as there inevitably is in all families, it was easier to stay away from him than to confront our frailties by facing him. We may not have realized it then, but it was his honesty and affection we couldn't face; not his anger.

"He was a truly inspiring man. He never did anything halfheartedly, and he taught all of us how to find joy in the most ordinary things. He was a great man because he was himself, and that's all he had to offer the rest of us. All of us knew that. He lived his life fully and truthfully. He was a hero not because he fought so well as a soldier but because, in the face of everything, he was truly just himself and nothing more or less. And all of us who knew and loved him, all of us who want to be, as he was, just ourselves, will truly miss him.

"We will miss his voice, his laughter, his warm smile and playful eyes. We are grieving this loss; a life force—an irresistible presence—is gone."

I glanced up again and saw that Nicole had buried her face in her hands. Someone sitting next to her—an elderly woman I did not recognize—put her arm around her shoulders. My mother held herself erect, head high, watching me, I now realize, with pride.

"Perhaps we can all be consoled by something Mom reminded me of just yesterday. She said, 'I can't complain. I knew him for fifty years and I was lucky to have known him at all.'

"We've all been that lucky, too, and more so. We've known both of them."

At this my mother smiled. Her gaze seemed to restore me.

"Now we must accept, as he would want us to accept, this loss. A powerful force at the very top of our lives is gone, and we have our duty to do. We must honor his death by living fully as he would want us to — committed to all that matters, willing to give everything the world demands, so that we might be worthy of everything it offers."

I folded the pages of my speech and put them in my breast pocket. Somebody sobbed. The priest got up and moved toward me. I nodded at him, then walked back down off the altar and sat down at the end of the pew next to my father's coffin.

From that vantage point, I could not see Nicole.

When the service ended and everybody was filing out, I walked around the coffin and waited for her at the end of the pew. She came right up to me and put her arms around my neck. I held her there, feeling the heat from her grief, the tears on her face.

"You came back," I whispered.

"No don't," she said, her face still buried against my shoulder. "Don't."

Later she told me she heard the news on the radio the day after it happened. The next day she was on a plane, back to D.C. She rented a car and drove to the house, and when I wasn't there, she drove to Alexandria and stayed in a motel. The next day she made the long drive to Baltimore, stopped at an IHOP restaurant, and looked up the obituary in the *Baltimore Sun* while she ate breakfast. Then she called the funeral home, got directions to the church, and arrived only a few minutes late for the service.

She had seen where I was sitting but she went to the other side because she was late and didn't want to force me and the whole family to move over for her. She also said she was surprised that I noticed her.

Outside the church, a few reporters waited with cameras. People seemed to cluster near the door as they came out. I noticed Officer Puckett in the crowd. He was standing with his hands folded in front of him, staring at the ground. When he saw me, he gave a start of surprise, then he approached me with his hand extended.

"It was a fine eulogy," he said.

I shook his hand.

"Your father really was a great man, you know."

"I know."

"One of the few judges I respected."

"You're very kind."

He stood there a moment, seeming to consider something, then he said, "I'm sorry for all that business about the accident and all."

Pauline came up to me and took my hand. "Henry, I thought what you said was wonderful. It was just right."

Mother was next to her, strong and no longer weeping. With a sad smile she said, "You did fine, son. He would have been proud."

"This is Mr. Puckett," I said.

"Yes, I remember you," Mother said. "Thank you for coming."

He said something I didn't hear, and then they were talking. So many people crowded around us I couldn't make out what they were saying. Then Puckett turned back to me and said, "You did your father justice."

I didn't know what to say to him. Finally he started to move away, and I said, "Thank you for . . ."

He stopped.

"I know you helped me out of what could have been some bad business," I said.

"No, not at all. The lady straightened everything out."

"Who?"

"Miss Simmons. She told me what happened."

"She did?"

"I guess it was just one of those things."

"No. It was me."

Phil stepped between Puckett and me, tears in his eyes. "It was really good, what you wrote, Shaver."

Puckett smiled, withdrew further.

"It was me," I said to Puckett. "You understand?"

He stopped, regarding me now with a slight frown.

"I forced the doors open on the elevator. That's why it got stuck. The whole thing wouldn't have happened if it weren't for me."

Puckett looked at Nicole and Robert, then back to me. "Well," he said, "it's over and done with."

"I wanted you to know."

He shrugged and moved off into the crowd.

"What was that all about, Shaver?" Robert asked.

Phil said, "Good speech, Henry."

"I just told the truth," I said to Robert. "That's all. I just told the truth."

Theresa came up and wrapped her arms around me. "You described Dad to a tee," she said. "He would have been so proud of you."

Phil took Nicole's hand and moved her toward the waiting cars. "You ride with me, honey."

"No," she pulled gently away from him. "I came in a rental car. I'll follow you."

"It was a good service," Robert said. "We're all proud of you."

"Be proud of Dad," I said. "I just did what Pauline said to do. I talked about him."

I took Nicole's hand again. When Pauline noticed her, she put her arms around her and held her tightly for a quiet moment. Then she kissed me on the cheek. I got everybody moving through the throng of people and the reporters and the cameras toward the waiting hearse and limousines. Mother walked on the grass, her head down. I moved over next to her and put my arm around her. Nicole went to her other side and took her arm.

"Such a crowd," Mother said. "So many people."

She stumbled on the root of a tree and nearly lost her balance. Under the canopy of the tree, the sun barely filtered through, and in the scattered light she looked almost holy.

I wondered what she was thinking then as we walked toward the hearse that would carry everything away—the friendship, the intimacy, and the small daily joys of her long marriage, carried off forever. The vast empty future must have been too great for her to comprehend.

We buried my father at the top of a wide, open stretch of high ground overlooking a green meadow at Heaven's Gate cemetery. It was a military funeral, but the service was relatively quick. When the twenty-one-gun salute exploded across the countryside and then taps hushed the trees, my mother wept silently into her hands. Phil could not be consoled. Darlene almost had to hold him up. I sustained myself by holding tightly to Nicole's hand. Just having her there—my grown little girl—allowed me to focus on something other than my grief.

I hated the sight of the coffin, the idea of my father's senseless body lying in there. If soul means anything, it means essence; a real presence—a spirit—was gone, and what remained was this empty vessel, wrapped and locked in a tube. The sound of the guns seemed to echo in my heart long after I couldn't hear them anymore.

At My Father's House

That evening, after most people had gone home, I went to Nicole and asked her if we could talk.

"All right."

"Come have a drink with me."

She followed me into the kitchen. Pauline was sitting at the table sipping a cup of coffee. "What a day. My feet are killing me."

"Any more of that coffee?"

She put her cup down. "I'll make some more."

"No, I don't want any," Nicole said. "Let's have a martini."

"Really?" I said.

"Sure. Why not?"

"I didn't think you liked them."

"I'm in the process of acquiring a taste."

Pauline said, "I'll see if he's got the fixings."

It was strange to hear her refer to my father that way—as if he still existed. All of us noticed it. Nicole bent her head and blinked. Pauline looked at me, then smiled weakly. "What is it again? Vodka and vermouth?"

"Yeah. Or gin if he—if there's no vodka."

"God," Pauline said, "this is so queer."

She left the room and I sat down at the table. Nicole took the seat across from me, but without the usual tense—almost defiant—posture. She seemed softer now, as if she wanted to be with me.

"I was so glad to see you today," I said. "I couldn't believe you'd come all that way."

She told me the story of her solitary journey. It hadn't been very long since I'd seen her, but her hair had started to grow out again. She looked more like herself.

I said, "You didn't have to do it, you know."

"Do what?"

"Fly all the way back here."

"I wanted to be with you. At a time like this..." She didn't finish, but she looked at me intently, and I saw the pure depth of her grief, her sadness. Perhaps she was remembering the time when she mourned me, when I had simply vanished out of her life as surely as my father had now vanished out of mine.

"Anyway..." I said, desperate to get past what had happened between us.

She also seemed eager to talk about other things. She told me Sam had enrolled at USC and was very happy. She, too, was going to school. She had enrolled in the nursing program at Santa Monica City College. "I don't know if I want to be a nurse, but it's fun working toward something again. I mean I'm glad to be back in school."

"I'm happy for you, honey," I said. "If you ever need anything..."

Pauline came back in with two martinis. "Sorry, only one olive. I cut it in half and gave each of you half."

I took the glasses from her and handed one to Nicole. "Don't you want one?" I asked Pauline.

"Honey," she said to Nicole, "I really love your hair like that."

"Thank you." Nicole glanced my way, then back to Pauline. "It was much shorter, but it's growing out now."

"Don't you want a drink, Pauline?"

"I'm going to bed." She winked at me. "You two can have your drinks in private."

When Pauline was gone, I lifted my glass in a toast. "Here's to your future."

Nicole clinked her glass against mine, then took a sip. Her face didn't register any displeasure from the taste this time.

"You are getting used to it," I said.

"Cheers."

We drank quietly for a while, listening to the house noises—the whir of the refrigerator, water running upstairs. After a while Nicole asked me to talk about my father.

"Why?"

"You seem to have loved him so much."

"All boys love their fathers, if they haven't been beaten too much. And even then, I suppose."

"And girls?"

"They love their fathers, too."

She smiled. "That's right."

"A father is the first man in a girl's life—the first man a girl loves in her life—so she has to reject him a little bit when she grows up. Some men can't take it when that happens. But the best families overcome it."

"And are we a good family?"

"Well, we're a different family."

"I'll say."

"I come from a good family, though."

She nodded, staring at me over her glass.

I drank the rest of my martini, then ate the half olive. Nicole gave me the other half and I ate that. I was afraid she'd get up and just go to bed; she had an early flight in the morning, so I stalled for time.

"You want another?"

"Sure."

I couldn't find the vermouth or the vodka. So I came back into the kitchen and poured us both a beer. "I think Pauline took the vodka and vermouth to bed with her."

"This is all right."

I sat back down.

We didn't say anything for a long time. Then when we were almost finished with our beers, she said, "You know, I didn't really go home."

"You didn't?"

"I spent the rest of the summer at Sam's."

I found myself smiling.

"It's not what you think," she said.

"No."

"I didn't want Catherine to know she was right."

"Right? About what?"

"You."

I didn't say anything.

"She said I'd be back, with a broken heart, before the summer was over. I just couldn't..." She stopped, looked directly at me. "I didn't want her to know why I came back. And then, while I was at Sam's, I got to like it. I felt comfortable and happy. But the main reason I went there was because I didn't want her to know—I didn't want her to know about us. The way it turned out and all."

Now I found it difficult to be in the light of her eyes. "I don't know what to say."

"There's nothing to say."

"I'm sorry Catherine was right," I said.

"Just as long as she doesn't know it." Nicole folded her hands around the beer can in front of her and stared at the label. The hair in the crown of her head gleamed in the overhead light. Upstairs someone was pacing the floor. The compressor in the refrigerator snicked off. She noticed me sitting there watching her, but still she said nothing.

I realized that by not going home she had been protecting me.

In spite of my sadness, I started laughing. "You poor thing."

"What?"

It wasn't funny, I know, but Nicole even laughed a little bit, too. Perhaps we were both victims of an imperfect and devastating irony, where the only thing one can do is laugh.

"I'm sorry, honey," I said.

"You don't have to keep saying that. I'm sorry, too."

"You and I are just—well, we're quite a pair."

She was wiping tears from her eyes.

345

"Goddamn," I said. "You really are something, you know that?"

"So are you," she whispered.

I had never felt so close to her—not even when she was six years old. And for that brief moment there in the kitchen, under those greasy sixty-watt bulbs and beneath the grieving members of my family, I forgot mourning and sorrow and misfortune. In spite of how my life had turned out, I saw love again in my daughter's eyes and I actually felt happy.

I put my glass down, reached across the table, and took her hand. "Do you remember the episode of the lost lock?"

"What?"

"The lost lock. You remember, when you were little—four or five—and you lost the lock to the shed?"

She frowned, trying to recall.

"Remember, I took your hand and made you walk all around the yard with me, looking for it, and then finally you panicked and lied to me about it? You've probably heard me tell the story."

"No. I don't think I have."

"Well." I wished she could remember at least some part of it. "I got mad at you, and then I held you in my arms, and you said, 'I just want to be friends, Daddy,' and I'm not kidding, it broke my heart. You don't remember that?"

"No, I really don't."

"Anyway, when you said that, about being my friend, I picked you up. I was... I was trying not to cry."

She seemed to recognize something. "I think I remember—was it a real sunny day?"

"Yes."

"Yeah, I think I remember something like that."

"I held you in my arms, and all I could say was, 'I love you.'"

She met my gaze, frowning.

"I kept saying it, over and over. I love you. You don't remember that?"

"No."

"Well, that's what I want to say to you now."

"What?"

"That I love you right now, just as much as I did then."

"It's all right, Dad," she whispered. "We're all right." She smiled, averting her eyes. I saw tears there and wished again that she was six years old and I could pick her up and hold her in my arms.

The Next Morning

Was unusually brisk, with a light frost on the grass, and I had to take Nicole to the airport. When we got in the car, the sun had heated the inside through the windows and I remembered all those frosty Sunday mornings when I was a very little boy and my family would pile into a sun-warmed car and drive to mass. My father would turn the radio on, and Frank Sinatra or Peggy Lee would sing quiet songs that seemed to accompany the wind-whipped leaves, and I'd scrunch down in my seat, feeling safe and permanent and blessed. Now the warmer air in the car only saddened me, and Nicole must have noticed it.

She cleared her throat, seemed to brace herself, then said, "How's Elizabeth?"

I started the car. "She's fine. She came out of it shortly after you and Sam left. Her father said it was just like waking from a nap."

"I knew she'd recovered."

"You did?"

"I called the hospital every few days when I got back to California. I knew when she was released. And Pauline told me a few things yesterday."

I didn't want to talk about Elizabeth, so I didn't say anything.

"And she's—is she back to normal?"

"Yeah, pretty much."

"I hated going back to California not knowing."

I didn't see how I could reply to that, since it was clear to both of us that I had driven her away. I concentrated on the road as we pulled out into traffic.

"Have you heard from her?" Nicole asked.

"She called a few weeks before... before Dad died."

"Pauline says she's working again."

"Yeah, I guess she is."

Nicole's luggage was piled on the back seat, and she reached back and opened one of her suitcases.

I said, "What are you doing?"

"Getting something."

She retrieved a white envelope. Out of the corner of my eye, I watched her open it and take out a small piece of paper. "This is from Sam."

"To me?"

"Uh-huh."

I looked at it, then back to the road.

"You want me to read it to you?"

"OK."

"He wanted to say something to you about..." She stopped. "It's just condolences, thanks and all. He wanted me to give it to you, and I almost forgot."

"Go ahead. Read it."

"'Dear Mr. Porter, I was terribly sorry to hear about your dad. I know you all loved him very much. I am proud to have met him, and I know your family is justly proud of his accomplishments. I only hope that in my life I'll be able to achieve half as much. I will never forget your help and how you made me feel welcome this past summer. I felt like your son and would be proud to call you Father. I mean that sincerely.'"

I did my best to suppress it, but the last sentence made me laugh.

"What are you laughing at?"

"Nothing. It's a nice letter."

It was quiet for a while. I watched the houses along the street—the clutter of yellow, red, and orange trees we passed by—and waited for her to continue. When she didn't, I said, "Is that all of it?"

"That's it."

"It was sweet of him to write it."

There was another period of silence, then she said, "So, what's going on with Elizabeth?"

"Nothing. She's going on with her life."

"And that's it?"

"That's it."

We passed a small pickup truck full of firewood, a field with pumpkins scattered in the white-and-brown vines and leaves. I couldn't believe my father was not going to see another season. Nicole still held Sam's letter in her lap.

At a stoplight I looked at her and she smiled. There was nothing awkward about the silence in the car. When the light changed, I drove on, watched the road in front of me, reading green signs.

She adjusted herself in the seat again. Then she folded Sam's letter, placed it carefully back in the envelope, and tossed it up on the dashboard. She mumbled something I didn't hear.

"What?"

"I just can't believe..."

"Can't believe what?"

"About Elizabeth."

I concentrated on the traffic. Presently I said, "Well, she wasn't really ready for marriage. Marriage is a big responsibility—a commitment—and she realized after a time that she just wasn't ready to do that."

I heard myself talking, and I was conscious of Nicole watching me, nodding in agreement to everything I said, as though it were the truth; as though I were pronouncing the cold, hard, unalterable facts. But then, by degrees, I became aware of her serious eyes reproaching me as surely as if she were pronouncing a sentence in a court of law. She could not possibly know the truth, but I could see that she knew this wasn't it.

I stopped talking and looked right at her. "You're not buying this, are you?"

"No."

"I didn't think so. The truth of the matter is, I hurt her so bad..."

"Oh."

Space between the cars increased, and I picked up speed.

"Pauline said she was at the funeral."

"She was?"

"Yes. She talked to her."

"I didn't see her."

"Pauline said she looked good."

I had nothing to say. I remembered that I was going to call Elizabeth—that I actually believed it would quiet my grief to talk to her—and in all the confusion, I had not even thought of her. As we approached National Airport and the traffic began to congeal again, I had this apprehension of being oddly finished, as if my life had nowhere else to go. Nicole would say good-bye and board a plane and disappear again out of my life. Time was hurrying to that moment. Very soon I'd be having dinner alone, and Nicole would be high over the Rocky Mountains, trying to sleep. Like a doubled pawn, I'd be trapped in one place, unable to move until the game was over.

Suddenly I was conscious of my whole life—not just the long past and the next few hours but all the cheerless days and long years ahead of me, right up to the moment when, like my father, I might lie down and turn cold in the moonlit grass. Something elemental had been erased from the center of all memory and belief. Whatever it was, the cavern in the empty space it left was almost palpable and it produced another sensation that is impossible to describe. It wasn't freedom or anything silly like that. (I don't think I've ever felt really free—not even when I was riding the subway all day and hiding from the world.) There was nothing in my father's absence that empowered me or made me feel any more or less a man, although I felt small. Really small—like a molecule.

There may not be a way to describe the feeling completely. I was sitting there in the traffic, just to the south of the airport. Nicole had her head turned away as she gazed out the window at the jets bellowing off over our heads, and I was overcome by the memory of my father's voice and the knowledge that it was gone out of the world forever. Authority, judgment, taste, sagacity, shrewdness, kindness, truth, humor, wit, temperament, and knowledge simply vanished from the earth, from overhead, like a murdered sky. Suddenly I awakened to myself, or I had a sensation of knowing this person I had become, as though a withered soul returned to me after a long sojourn in some other place. It really was a sort of recognition, the exact feeling you have when you see, in a crowd, the familiar face of a person you do not want to see. I was aware of myself, my corporeal and spiritual self, all alone, sitting on the seat, and I was also aware of the tiny pulsing red fist in my chest, shooting blood through a network of tubes and circuits, like some sort of device.

I must have made a sound in the back of my throat, because Nicole turned to me and said, "What?"

"Nothing."

"You said something."

"No, I didn't."

She went back to staring out the window. As we approached the crowded and interlaced roads that led into the airport, I reached over and touched her arm.

"What?" She moved closer to me.

"It's OK if you leave, but I don't want you to be gone."

"Are you all right?"

"I'll miss you." I reached for her and she moved under my arm. "Tell Sam I said hello."

She nodded, then placed her head on my shoulder. I tried to remember my little girl, but all I could think of was her plundered childhood—all those years with the two most important human beings at the top of her life more than four thousand miles apart—and I felt inexpressibly sad for her. I wished I had died before I ever let her get so far away from me.

"Tell Catherine I said hey, too," I whispered. "OK?"

She nestled closer to me, smiling, but she didn't say anything.

At the Beginning

I said I would always remember the months that Nicole was with me as "that summer." Now, the days and weeks since that summer have passed like speeding cars. Christmas approaches, and I've decided to spend it with my mother in Baltimore. I've lost myself in the routine of teaching. Dealing with one hundred and thirty-five different personalities has distracted me. I still go to the track occasionally, but now I am a lot more careful with my money, simply because I've been sending every spare dollar to Nicole, to finance a flight home for the holidays. She has promised me she will come.

If I could gamble with more money, I would. I am not, nor do I feel like, a new man. The sensation that overcame me after my father died is still with me, although it has settled into a kind of acceptable deficiency: The world is the same, but some elemental feature of my soul has disappeared; has gone into the earth and dissolved like the roots of a chopped tree. Nothing seems as important as it once did. I come home each night, to my empty house, feeling as though every action is an obligation, something I have promised: To keep going because it has been given to me to do. There doesn't seem to be anything to think about or express. In my classes I'm cruising on busy work and reliable old lesson plans. Thank god history doesn't change.

A few nights ago, I dreamed I was back in the army. I had to go through basic training all over again. The dream was so vivid I could smell my own sweat; feel the hot sand on the field where I was doing push-ups and jumping jacks.

The dream presented a series of difficult problems I had to solve or be forced out of the service. Sometimes physical obstacles had to be overcome, and at other times the barriers seemed to be more mental—although all of them exhausted me. I can't remember anything that actually happened, just the fragile feelings of luck and well-being that would momentarily enliven the dream when the threat passed as I successfully met each challenge. I was like an athlete, breathing heavy but feeling wonderful for getting it right.

Then, after what seemed like a long time, I was going home. I arrive at my father's house. Elizabeth is there, and Nicole and Pauline. I'm wearing my olive green dress uniform, with bright blue and red ribbons and gold insignia and yellow stripes. I look sharp. Dad is clearly pleased. He puts his arms around me, and I smell his Old Spice cologne, the faint odor of cognac. I feel so complete. So permanent and triumphant and strong and admirable. I don't want to let go of him. I really am home again, in my father's house.

Just like that, the dream changes. Now we are outside the house, sitting on the patio. I am wearing shorts, an oversized T-shirt, worn tennis shoes. I feel as though I don't belong there. I am just visiting and I have not worn the right clothing. My shorts are torn on the side and in the back, and I am trying to cover the holes but I can't escape the sensation of ice-cold air on my legs. I have a long flat book of photographs—a record of what I achieved in basic training, each hardship and crisis I overcame; also there are pictures of me in my dress uniform, of the way I looked in the beginning of the dream. I want to show Dad my pictures. I feel as though I need to show him.

He is talking to Elizabeth, telling her something about me that I don't want him to tell. And I realize he looks exactly as he did that day at Sylvan Dell. He's young again, and now he's in shorts, too. Phil is there, and my mother and the whole family. I try to get my father to listen to me; I want him to just look at the photographs. That will solve everything. Elizabeth will see the pictures, too. I have this apprehension that it will be an even better sense of triumph than I had in the beginning of the dream.

Finally he takes the book out of my hands and opens it. His face is expressionless. He says, "What? There's nothing here."

Elizabeth smiles.

"No," I say. He hands it to me, and when I flip the pages I realize each one is actually a small rectangular mirror. That's all. Each page is only my puzzled and curious face looking for something other than itself. And then Dad starts whispering to Elizabeth. I can't get him to turn his head and look at me or the book of mirrors.

I woke up from that dream feeling as if something cold had sliced through my soul.

Now I can't wait until Christmas. I long for laughter, a little peace, a little comfortable affection. I don't think I deserve it.

And sometimes I think of Elizabeth.

We still talk now and then. After I've seen her or talked to her on the phone, she occupies my thoughts. It's not that I can't get her out of my mind. I *want* to think about her. One day I'd like to ask her what went wrong, just to see how she would answer me. I wonder if she would say what I have imagined she'd say: That I created her, revised her in my mind, tried to keep the final draft even when she came to me and became, however briefly, a person with herself to offer. I know that is glib, and probably not fair to either of us. It makes her seem like a fool, and I don't fair very well, either.

I'd like to believe that I lost her because I was not decisive; that if I had been able to say what I wanted early enough, we would have been together. But I know that isn't true. The truth is, I lost her because I couldn't tell her the truth.

I wonder what she would say if I told her that.

When I forced those elevator doors open, I believed I could manage the world.

You'd think a man who goes to the racetrack five times a month would know better.

I sometimes call my mother in the evening after dinner and we chat. She has settled into her widowed life as well as I thought she would. Every now and then she starts talking about Dad and her voice will begin to break, or she'll be very quiet for a while and I know she is crying.

"It's all part of grief," she says.

"I know you miss him, Mom," I tell her.

She is extremely active in her community, and although Christmas this year will be really hard, she'll be busy enough to hold on until it is over.

That's what I'm trying to do. Hold on through the days until Christmas. If Nicole can make it, at least the pleasant moments between us will be a welcome diversion. Perhaps we can cheer things up a bit for Mother as well. She has always loved having family around her on the holidays.

So I'm working my way toward Christmas. The one thing I'm sure of is that, next spring, I'm going to find myself sitting in my car one day in front of Elizabeth's house.

I know I'm going to drive over there. I've imagined it a million times. It will be a bright day—perhaps morning—warm, with birds chattering in the small new leaves and budding branches. I have not thought of what I will be intending. I just know my car will seem to simply take me there.

Possibly her street will be littered with old leaves and the house will seem closed and cold when I first drive by. I'll slow at the corner and try to see if there is any sign of life—an open door or window, or perhaps music from the house—but I won't see anything. Perhaps I'll make a left and park down the street and, in the sideview mirror, I'll watch the back of her house with the sun shining through it from the other side. I won't stay there long—in fact I'll leave the engine running—but I'll wait there until I see, or think I see, her shadow cross one of the windows that lets sunlight through the house from the front. I can't be sure, because I am looking in a mirror, but the window does seem to darken and then the light breaks through again. When the children playing on the street begin to notice me, I'll put the car back in gear and drive on

down to the end of the street, turn left, and then left again, heading up
to Elizabeth's street one more time.

I know it will be morning—a lazy sun, big and cool, beginning to
lift behind the blossoming trees—and I will find myself thinking of last
summer as if it were the awful events in someone else's life. There at
the intersection on Elizabeth's street—the sun's broadening light driving darkness back into the spaces between the branches—I will almost
be able to hear once again the sounds of lawn mowers and dogs bark-
ing and birds chattering.

Maybe I'll turn left again at the corner and head down for one
more pass. At the intersection near her front walk, maybe I'll pull over
and park. I'll probably be scared. The sun will be behind me, and I'll
purposely park right by the culvert where I first saw her as she struggled
with her lawn mower so long ago.

I plan to wait there a long time, watching the house, hoping for any
sign of movement or life. I won't simply be there to spy on her, though.
If she doesn't come out, I'll get out of the car and go on up to the door
and knock. But maybe I won't have to. Perhaps I'll see something move
at the side of the house, near the back. I won't be able to tell if it was a
door that opened and closed or not.

My heart will really be pounding. Somebody will be outside, behind the house. I roll the window down, listen to the faint noise of the
children down the street, the new leaves sighing in the trees.

Then perhaps I hear an engine getting started, a small engine. It
sputters at first, then gets going. I think to start the car, feeling as if my
heart has come loose in my chest. I want to run. But I don't.

Maybe Elizabeth will emerge from the left side of the house, pushing a lawn mower. She pushes it right up the front lawn, toward where
I am parked, and like a man sitting on the tracks in front of an oncoming train, I will freeze. I can't tell if she sees me or not, but I know if I
drive off she will definitely notice me. Since I will not be spying on her,
I cannot have her thinking I am. I want so much to hear her voice.
She'll be wearing a light blue turtleneck sweater, a thin red scarf on her
head, dark jeans, and white tennis shoes. Her hair will sway next to her

face, under the flapping scarf, and she will be beautiful—the kind of beauty that by itself causes heartache.

She will approach me, pushing the mower in front of her, concentrating on the path she is making in the lawn, and I will get out of the car and walk over to her. She will pretend to notice me for the first time and leave the mower sputtering to a stop in the tall spring grass. I imagine she will turn to me, smiling, and I will know that she forgives me. Perhaps we'll sit once again on her front steps and talk about so many things: our classes, the work with students and how to get it right. We will be friends again, in the spring.

I wouldn't bet on it, but it could happen.

Reading Group Guide

1. A lot of readers feel they must "identify" with or "like" the main characters of a story, in order to enjoy a novel. Ironically, most writers strive very hard to create characters with significant, therefore interesting, flaws. The object is, of course, to create fully human characters. Henry Porter is fairly exasperating—he takes a long time to figure out the source of his troubles. Nonetheless, he is always trying to do the right thing; in other words, he is not bad, he is simply imperfect. What qualities can you point to in his character? What faults do you think the writer instilled in him to make his story worth pursuing? Discuss the source of his troubles; both what Henry thinks it is, and what you think it is.

2. Henry is a father, and he has his own father to deal with. What similarities and differences do you notice between Henry and his own father? Examine the way Henry treats Nicole, and then look at the way his father treats him. Are they different? Similar? Compare and contrast both fathers' attitude and behavior toward their children throughout the book. Are there ways in which the story of the father and daughter inform or otherwise enhance (or detract from) the story of the father and son?

3. The book is called *A Hole in the Earth,* and it opens in the "biggest hole human beings ever dig." Several passages and images in the book bring to mind both literal and figurative "holes" in the earth; examine the various kinds of "holes" in the earth the book deals with and explore the ways these images and references enhance (or detract from) the story.

4. Much is made in the study of literature of what is called the "reliable" narrator. Gulliver, in Jonathan Swift's great novel *Gulliver's Travels,* is one example of an unreliable narrator. He is not, in

other words, a truth-teller and his perceptions cannot, therefore, be trusted. Ishmael who tells the story of Captain Ahab in *Moby Dick*, Herman Melville's masterpiece *is* a reliable narrator and his perceptions and descriptions *can* be trusted. What sort of narrator is Henry Porter? Examine what he says, what his perceptions are. Is he reliable in his understanding of what is good, what is evil, what is right, and what is wrong? Is he right about Elizabeth? His father? Can he be trusted to tell the truth as he sees it? And even if he thinks he has the truth, and says what he thinks it is, *does* he have the truth?

5. The women in Henry's life include his mother, his first wife Catherine, his daughter Nicole, and his current "girl friend" Elizabeth. Examine his relationships to each of these women. What does he understand about them? What does he not understand about them?

6. Henry says his father's generation "painted pin-up girls on bombers," and that his father grew up when being "a man" was "an achievement." What does he mean by this? How has his generation changed? What does Henry think caused the change? Why does he think his generation is so ready to surrender? What does "being a man" mean to Henry's generation? What does it mean to the women in the novel?

7. Henry says gambling is really "making the right decisions" with the hope of a "little luck." Examine the "decisions" Henry makes in the novel; both the gambling ones—i.e., the ones he makes at the track—and the ones that might be "gambles" in his life. What decisions is he capable of in his life that might be considered gambles? What decisions is he incapable of making? Contrast the kind of "gambles" inherent in his life decisions, both the ones he makes without too much trouble, and the ones he can't make.